ANITA DESAI, novelist, short story writer and children's author, was born in 1937 in Mussoorie, India, to an Indian father and a German mother. She was educated in Delhi and completed her graduation in English literature from Delhi University.

Desai was first published in the 1960s and immediately praised as the finest of her generation of Indian writers in English. Her novels evoke characters, events and moods with recourse to a rich use of visual imagery and details. The origin of her stories, as she admits, is itself rooted in images: 'there are so many images that remain in the mind... stay with you....' She has received numerous awards, including most recently in 2005 the Grinzane Cavour International Prize — *Una Vita Per la Letteratura* (a Life for Literature) — one of Europe's most prestigious literary awards and often said to anticipate the Nobel Prize.

'...The style (Anita Desai) has evolved is lucid, tight, undramatic... her imagistic prose acquires an ambiguous and terrible power — the words hold down the events forcibly.'

Arts Guardian, London

GW00673818

3013

By the same author
in **Orient Paperbacks**

Cry, the Peacock
Where Shall We Go This Summer
Bye Bye, Blackbird

Voices
In The City

anita desai

Orient
Paperbacks

DELHI | MUMBAI | HYDERABAD

ISBN : 978-81-222-0053-9

Voices in the City

Subject: Fiction

© Anita Desai, 1965, 2005

Reprinted 2016

Published by
Orient Paperbacks
(A division of Vision Books Pvt. Ltd.)
5A/8 Ansari Road, New Delhi-110 002
www.orientpaperbacks.com

Printed at
Yash Printographics, Noida

Printed on Chlorine-free eco-friendly paper.

Nirode

The train began to pant, as though in preparation for a battle, sending jets of white steam violently into the night sky and on the platform people loitered in various attitudes of nervousness, impatience and regret, turning now and then to the lights at the head of the platform, waiting for them to change. No one ever betrayed reluctance for them to do so except, perhaps, the latecomers pounding along with baggage wobbling and disintegrating in the seemingly hopeless search for the right carriage.

'I'm sorry now to leave,' Arun reflected. He was one of those who never disclosed nervousness or impatience, lounged over a cigarette as though he were relaxing on a terrace at night-fall. So it seemed to the red-shirted coolies, the tea vendors and the station-master in grimy white, all stained with the sweat of haste and overwork, but Nirode, casting at him a glance made sly by envy, saw the tautness in the young man's body and saw how his eyes shone.

He threw away his cigarette and immediately lit another. 'Liar,' he said. 'You're itching to start.'

Arun laughed. He moved and from his movement one could see how right Nirode was. The man was like a bird poised on the roof's edge for flight, each feather alert and trained for it, vivid in this moment of gigantic expectation. He was alight with eagerness. Yet he laughed, stammered. 'No, it's not a moment for decisions. I can't decide *now* what I'd most like to happen...'

'I can see that,' Nirode said dryly and flung yet another cigarette down beneath the waiting wheels, immediately drew out another.

Fortunately they were of the cheapest variety and Arun did not notice. They both turned to watch the lights unashamedly, breathing with difficulty the acrid air of Howrah station and separation.

They could think of nothing else to say and feigned interest, instead, in the marriage party at the neighbouring carriage door — the groom in a white sharkskin suit, loaded with garlands of great, odorous marigolds, looking harried and damp, while the bride hid behind a fold in her sequined *sari* and decorously sniffed. Fat jovial men surrounded them, shouting obscene jokes and quaking with laughter at them. The women hung back, in a cluster, weeping heart-brokenly for the daughter.

'God, *look* at them,' muttered Nirode but Arun smiled. He was smiling, his eyes were shining. They watched the marriage party till the whistle went and the train began its preliminary lurching, as though it were unused to motion and were practising a bit before the long run. There was an uproar amidst the marriage party and the bride and groom were lifted upon one thrusting wave of obscenity and congratulation up into their carriage. Coolies threw bedding-rolls and tiffin-carriers and late-arrivals into carriages that rolled past them, the tea-vendors held out their shirts to receive the last of the copper coins. The brothers moved a step closer, but could not look each other in the eye for embarrassment and emotion. They shook hands, embraced — later neither could remember his or the other's behaviour at that blurring tearing moment of departure. Arun leant out of the window to call, 'Write to mother,' and Nirode, walking quickly along beside the moving train, scowled, thinking Arun had got it wrong. '*You* write to mother,' he shouted and Arun burst out laughing. Nirode laughed too and stood back to wave, a spurt of love rising like a flag above the crowds, but soon engulfed by them. Watching the tail-lights disappear and the crowds about him disintegrate, Nirode felt his brother's arm and shoulder still, their solidity beneath the light material of his clothing. He did not believe he would ever feel them again. Even if Arun returned, they would never touch again. For Nirode each moment rang with iron finality. He turned and began to walk away rapidly.

Those who felt him brush past them — the grimy station master, the tea-vendor, the coolie — thought nothing of a young man in haste, perhaps in despair, so many such passed them each day. The ticket-collector checked his ticket and, in an idle moment, watched him tear it up and fling the bits into an open drain, then turned away. For they all did it and the drain was choked with the sodden remnants of partings and farewells. Beating his way out of the swarming apathy of Howrah Nirode strode down the bridge, dodging the traffic that made the bridge roar and rattle beneath his feet like a tunnel of bones and steel. Trams crashed murderously past him, handcarts rolled recklessly, maniacally by. Nirode thrust them all away with arms that never moved, thrust all the thunder away thinking his thoughts in such livid, short-lived streaks of lightning as those that made the tram-lines spark and quiver — thinking how he envied Arun. How this envy was corroded with hate and how, yet, he loved him but, above all, envied oh envied him for being on the train, speeding out of this dark pandemonium into the openness and promise of the bare country, crossing the land from east to west, from the murky Bay of Bengal to the wide Arabian Sea to board ship and set sail... Nirode caressed that phrase upon his tongue, it was so sweet and even if ships bore sails no longer, he could not bear to forgo the image of that tall whiteness unfurling to accept the breeze. It might have been he, he knew that had he not as a child, an emotional and disorderly schoolboy, fallen from his horse and declared to his father, through tears, that he hated horses, sports and would never ride again. If he had not written odd twisted scraps of verse in exercise books that were confiscated and scrawled over with the obscenities of his happier colleagues in school. If Arun had not ridden like a prince, captained the cricket team and won top honours in all examinations. If his father, while dictating his will to an obese solicitor, had not weighed these distinctions before laying aside a sum of money for the education abroad of one of his two sons. If Arun had not been the favourite and Nirode a congenital failure.

Striding off the bridge into the coagulated blaze of light and sound and odour that was the city of Calcutta, Nirode cried: Unfair, life is unfair — and how faint and senseless it sounded in all that tumult of traffic and commerce about him. In the darkness of that unfairness he saw Arun's future as an undimming brightness. To have watched Arun play a game of cricket as a boy was to have been made aware of this ineffable brightness. His parents, his sisters, all had acknowledged it. Where the light came from, where was its source — each had his own theory about it. His father had thought it to be a brilliant career as a surgeon and sportsman, his mother had insisted it would be the love everyone extended to him so freely and unquestioningly. His sisters — what had they thought? What were they thinking tonight? Nirode did not know, he only saw the tedious stability of this one light amidst all the uneven glare that issued from the tea-shops, the grain shops, the stalls where the green coconuts, *pan** and cigarettes were sold. This light was crass, it stung his eyes and what he wanted was shadows, silence, stillness — and well, he told himself, that was exactly what he would always be left with. He remained in the half-dark — and each light on that street served to show up an expanse of wall, a doorway, a balcony that was darkly shadowed — and bled with longing to go; Arun had gone. Here he was still, the anonymous and shabby clerk on a newspaper, calling himself a journalist, for that is a fine, crisp and jaunty word. But the dismal truth was that all he did was cut out long strips of newspaper and paste and file them, occasionally venturing out to verify a dull fact in some airless office room. Arun would be at a college in London, amongst students, in beer-halls — Nirode fought that vision of student life abroad, that splendid vision that so dazzles those who do not know it.

Fighting it, he made his way to the silent warehouses and past them on to the Strand. Here he slowed down and wiped his face with one hand, grimacing at the dampness and grittiness there. Tired, perspiring, he stood still at the river's edge and found it to be quiet there and cool.

A soft November mist rose from the river, like steam from a cauldron but cool, frozen steam. The tide was out, the water low and

---

* The heart-shaped betel leaf which is smeared with a lime paste, sprinkled with shredded areca nut and various spices such as cardamon and aniseed, folded into a conical shape and eaten. See E. M. Forster's essay on *Pan* in *Abinger Harvest*.

a slow motion rocked the big ships, brazenly illuminated by giant lamps as cranes worked overtime at loading and unloading — coal, tea, jute, swaths of pink and white cotton, a tiger in a cage — in a kind of subdued uproar. Far below these sea-voyagers rocked the tugs and steamers, unlit and silent, except for one dark deck on which knelt a group of three Muslim boatmen with white embroidered caps on their heads. They knelt, then bowed, droning beseeching verses from the Koran. Their prayer created a minute island of stillness in the profanity of the nocturnal life of a river of commerce. Islands, too, were the small fishing boats moored to the bank, some dark with sleep, others sheltering a single oil lamp beneath a wicker cowl. On one fish-eyed prow a fisherman in a crimson *lungi* played upon his reed flute — tenderly, questingly. On the other bank the city continued to proclaim itself with neon and naptha lights, with the muttering and sudden shrieks of machinery and the low growling of men — but it had nothing to do with the river, with these islands in the river. They belonged to the night, to the design of stars lost somewhere beyond the haze of city smog, to the beating of Nirode's heart their only sounds were those of low-toned prayer and the plaintive and exquisite music of the reed flute.

On all sides the city pressed down, yet the river took one, enfolded and slid one away into the dark, silently. Nirode liked this sense of having an unlit channel flow through his veins, along which he could move in secrecy. He leant over the railing in a deep delight that this river always gave him and then felt his heart crack. One can build it so carefully, rest in it so stilly and then suddenly feel it crack open from end to end, spilling one out into torment. So it did crack that moment when he looked up to see a big Australian ship, neat as a pin in confident floodlight, its funnel freshly painted in stripes of flower — white and orange. Escape, escape, that funnel cried as Arun had escaped. As a boy Nirode had run away. Caught, run away again and captured once more — regarding it always as a temporary arrest, merely a stage in a certain journey. But at twenty-four he was already admitting, at such moments as this one, that this was no actual journey but a nightmare one in which one is unable to start. The suitcase is never packed, the tickets never purchased and the ship sails, leaving one ensnared in the net of sleep. He was not one of those born with a destination balanced like a boiled egg upon a silver spoon in his mouth. He was merely a traveller and the only reasonable thing to do was to accept the journeying as meaningful in itself.

With the wind blowing up from the river, bearing on it the gem-like notes of the flute, he could do this as he could not in the daytime. Now, with a true traveller's faith, he knew he would not always be standing by to watch his brother depart. He would not always be at the bus-stop at eight-fifteen in the morning, catching the bus to a day's work of cutting, pasting, filing and decaying. In that muddy river air, he caught a whiff of the stench of that office-going bus, the stench of hair freshly and sweetly oiled, of shoes newly blacked and then that office odour of thick white glue and soiled paper. Revulsion filled him, so huge a distaste and horror filled him that he felt empowered by it — as Arun who did not know it would never be empowered — to rise like a clumsy paper kite with a candle lit inside it that rises above the sooty chimney pots and crooked pigeon-roosts to fly, fly through an immensity of air — above Arun in his crawling train, above the painted ship on the sluggish river, intoxicatingly light and free and powerful. At that moment he was at one height with the embroidery of the Howrah bridge lights, at the next he was soaring above it airborne by exhilaration, determination and pride. Pride lapped him, so warm and wonderful that he let its candle set fire to his paper kite and suddenly finding himself without its support, he sank again, sank and sank till he was half-drowned and laughed wryly, damply, 'I haven't even begun yet.' Treading the slimy water of reason, his feet searching the clay of a scheme, a design, a purpose. Pride is not unimpeachable. Cupping a match with a curved hand, he sheltered it from the sooty wind. A tug boat hooted up the river.

Now fog-horns were blowing, full of warning and melancholy. As he listened to them, his heart quietened again inside him and he began to sketch this design, this scheme he had, sketched it with a practicality that astonished him, he had not known that he could be so cool, so calculating. Such moments only came to him briefly, just before flight. Like a sailor checking his flimsy craft, he moved carefully about it, within it, knocking against the wood, searching for inaccuracies, for loopholes that might drown him.

Then he flung his cigarette down into the river and spoke to its vanished glow. 'Three drinks,' he said, coldly and decisively, three drinks a night and a room of his own. If he could have that certain and secret, for six months, then he could accomplish it. Three drinks for inspiration — hackneyed word, not one a journalist ought to use but, hang it all, he was no journalist, had put an end to that pretence — three drinks for inspiration then and courage, but no more, for fear of courage going to his head or ruining his stomach. And a room in which to write it! Here he groaned with impatience, with agony, walked away from the river, feeling wisps of mist cling to him, brushing them away. How, how, how — he beat his hand upon his flank, as though urging on his mount, as though he longed, at last, to arrive. But how? Three drinks and a room — a princedom, too far away, how to be reached, how captured? To acquire them he must lay another plan, more complicated, involving others, involving money. He hated this calculation that smelled of glue and files, yet it had to be done. He worked on it savagely as he strode down the tree-lined avenues where houses were lit, comfortable and serene in their warm illumination, unmindful of the fog-horns and the mist swirling through their gardens and across the deserted Maidan where trees loomed like sleeping buffaloes in that white mist, and the winter night had obliterated all traces of the crowded day from its thick grass. Nirode went striding past and when he came to Chowringhee with its festoons of blue street lights, he lifted up his hand. 'I will have it,' he shouted to them, 'I will have it — you'll see how I get it!' No one heard him nor even saw him as he stood watching the traffic hurl itself by, solitary under a tree, and proud — proud and afraid, for he was aware that pride is not unimpeachable.

On the one side of the road the old cemetery slept in whitestained peace and with reassuring silence. On the other, a big house loomed, dark and as though uneasy of those who slept there, all slept badly. Here and there a window gave one a glimpse of light, but did nothing to illuminate the house which was more suggestive than the cemetery of bats, graves and bones. Entering the garden, Nirode felt damp leaves brush against him and his shoes sink in mud, then stub against a stone. It was that kind of a house. All young men swore upon entering it. Swearing, Nirode thought that Sonny alone would put up with it. The man was a pervert, he thought and threw a handful of pebbles up into a lighted window over the porch. He smiled to hear a little audible explosion of fright and the saw an elderly, whiskered face lean anxiously over the sill, ready to retreat before the next shower of pebbles flew up.

'Professor,' Nirode croaked. 'Isn't Sonny in?'

'No — no, he has gone to fetch his dinner.'

'Good, good, that suits me,' Nirode said and, quickly entering the house, tore up the curving staircase, past yellowed portraits of the landlady's late lamented ancestors, each garlanded with faded paper roses and cuckoo clocks that smelled of stuffed birds and sentimental embroidered legends that spoke in bitter reproof to the young men who stained the stair-carpet with mud and stubbed their cigarettes on the mottled tiger skins. The 'professor' had the door open for him and Sonny's dogs were barking and leaping to receive the visitor with rank licks and pawings. Boxer, spaniel, alsatian — Nirode would have none of them. 'Down!' he roared, 'down !' and slapped at them with familiarity, but also distaste. The dense odour of dogs' fur and dogs' jaws was revolting to him. 'God, how the room stinks,' he said. Dogs' bowls, chewed bones and fur-matted brushes littered the room. Nor was there space enough for these great overfed creatures and while one leapt on to the divan, the others lolled upon the bed. 'Sonny's harem!' Nirode snorted at those that lay on the bed, eyeing him reproachfully and selected for himself a straight-backed chair.

The professor giggled. Nirode in an ill temper always disarmed the little whiskered man. He twitched, plucked, giggled and appeared suddenly to have lost those belongings that normally weighed him down, gave him solidity and sense in his better moments. Now he was doomed to make the wrong answers to everything Nirode said. When Nirode complained savagely of the dust and filth of the old mausoleum Sonny lived in, he tittered, 'But it is you — Sonny's friends — who made it filthy in the first place.'

'Always on their side!' Nirode snapped in a childish outburst of bitterness. 'The landlord's side — the upper rung of the ladder from which you can push down the others with your dirty black umbrella.'

'But my friend,' cried the professor — only he was no professor and no landlord either, he merely wrote children's text books and put in the commas where he was supposed to put in the commas and used the exclamation mark with discretion. 'My friend,' he protested. 'how can you say such a thing? You know I suffer, suffer ignominiously at the hands of my own landlord. A proper demon that man is. It would not surprise me in the least if he concealed a tail in — ah, the seat of his pants.' The little eyes, slow-moving but bright as globs of honey, twinkled up at Nirode hopefully. No response. 'In fact, only today he has been to see me about repairing my courtyard at my own expense.'

'And that, I'm sure, is exactly what you will do.'

'My dear chap, I don't want to find myself out on the streets.'

'On the seat of your white and elegant *dhoti.*'

'Can you blame me?' Bose fanned out his hands, crossed his legs, rearranged the folds of his *dhoti,* all in delight at having evoked what he took to be a spark of good humour in Nirode. 'Of course you do blame me — and the landlords and the tenants and the man in the street as well. It is the righteous anger of the young and idealistic —'

'Idealistic!' Nirode exploded.

'Of course, of course,' the old man fussed. 'You will not admit it but, ah, that is only the cynicism of youth and that wears off, wears off. Which reminds me, Nirode, would you be interested in writing a piece on a young Communist who has been giving highly inflammatory speeches in my *mohalla*? With the municipal elections so close, I thought it might be newsworthy.'

Nirode got up abruptly and marched to the open window to light himself a cigarette and tossed the match out into the overpoweringly scented jasmine vines below. 'No, professor,' he said and his long yellow fingers worked at the cigarette as insects do at a chosen twig. 'It does not interest me. News, newspapers, newsworthies — all that's safely in the dustbin as far as I'm concerned. I've banged the lid on to all that. I no longer work at the stately offices of the *Patrika*. I no longer sit paring my nails while a fresh supply of glue is mixed so that I can get down to my illustrious job of pasting cut-outs into the *Patrika* scrap-books. That, my dear prof. is what I've been doing all these years. Not writing, not reporting — but sticking cut-outs into scrap-books.'

The professor gave a little involuntary start and the beautiful fall of his pleated *dhoti* became quite disordered. 'But Nirode,' he protested, 'you write the middles, you write on the editorial page, the most influential —'

'I don't, I never did. They never printed a word I wrote nor did any other paper. I've been gluing cut-outs for the last three years and I'm sick to the stomach of the smell of glue. Did you know it's made of animal refuse-'

'But Nirode,' the professor insisted, hurt and even humiliated by this treachery. 'I always read that little column, every Monday. You *told* me you wrote it and how often have I complimented you on it.'

'More fool you,' Nirode said shortly and threw a lighted stub at one of the dogs that had come slouching towards him when he moved to the window, as if hoping to be taken for a walk. Now it started away, eyeing the red stub with white rimmed distrust. Quickly the professor bounced to his feet and stamped it out with a patent leather shoe. Nirode smiled at him. 'You talk about idealists, Bose? When you are the one who is ready to trust anyone who has read your favourite books? You even trust me! What a bloody stupid thing to do, Bose. You ought to have got over that the time I talked your wife into giving me twenty rupees, telling her you owed it me. Don't you remember that?' The smile teased, despised.

'I didn't mind *that*. You needed the money.'

'Beggarly Bose, the Great Philanthropist. Well, I need some again..'

'You have not really resigned?'

'Yes, really, really, really. Oh not resigned, but I'm simply not — going there again. I've cleared out of the Y.M. too — my stuff is still there but I refuse to go and collect those blasted socks and ties I used to wear in the office. Socks and ties! Might as well have worn garters and played the *babu* game in style. But I'm not going back there, I haven't paid rent in two months. By the way, I gave them your address as my home address, when I moved in there. Now don't turn grey, I'm not going to move in with you — your wife's cooking doesn't agree with me. All that mustard oil. I think my friend Sonny, the *zamindar's* son, can put me up for a bit, till I find something cleaner. But I do need some cash.'

The professor formed a trembling cage of his fingers and over it shook his head and his sad, long whiskers. 'It is too distressing,' he murmured, 'too distressing.'

'*Too* distressing?' Nirode pounced on him. 'Too distressing for what? Too distressing to make you lend me ten chips?'

'Now, now. All in good time, Nirode, all in good time.'

'In other words, less tautological, till you've made a quick mental survey of your accounts and decided if you can spare ten chips from that little bit you set aside for tea and sweets with your cronies every afternoon.'

'That is too unfair.'

'Too, too, too,' Nirode stuttered with a savagery that alarmed the professor, made him feel that perhaps Nirode was trying to goad him, provoke him into playing something other than a whipped dog, something more commanding, more challenging. And, stroking his fat knees, he spoke in as fatherly a tone as he could compose, though he quivered still under the attack.

'Now tell me, my boy, what's the position?'

'The position of what? Of the planet Mars in relation to the planet Venus? Of Sonny's dog in relation to next door's bitch? Say what you have to say, give what you've already made up your mind to give — and then get away, get back to your snug little tea-shop, it's best not to stray too close to me again. I'll be needing money again soon.'

'I mean your financial position of course,' the professor quavered bravely. 'Have you collected your salary?'

'Naturally. Why do you think I waited till after the first before I walked out?'

'Good, good. Then you can pay the Y.M. their rent?'

'Well,' Nirode was reluctant. 'If you're so frightened of having the young Christian men at your door, clamouring for me — all right, I suppose I can do that. But I shall have nothing left over after that. And I must have a drink.' He leaned out over the sill, throwing back his head to search out the stars, dim and buried in the shroud of city smog and the professor, sitting behind him, saw how his collar-bones jutted out, how his elbows looked sharp and frail enough to crack under the slightest pressure, how bleached and unalive his skin was. He was frightened by that paleness. He thought it was wrong that it should be so. The boy was clever. In those early days of his in Calcutta, at the strident coffee house gatherings, he had easily been the brightest of the young men who argued and discoursed there. He had been aggressive then too but not rapacious, not cruel. The professor thought of the lighted stub flung at the dog and he could not understand it. The boy ought to go home — he had a home, the professor had heard of it and land in the hills. What unutterably good fortune to have such a landscape in one's background — the solidity of land, the thunderous glory of mountains. But there had been a rift and Nirode had gone astray. Adrift in the city of Calcutta: that was the grisliest part of it and seeing Nirode arched over the window-sill, angular and skeletal and unhealthily nicotine tinged, the professor was moved to compassion.

At the window, Nirode felt it upon his neck, warm and bovine and sickly sweet. Half-closing his eyes against the smoke that burnt them, he counted gravestones in the night. The founders of the British empire lay buried in the sleazy Bengal ooze where they had first founded their colonial power. Merchants, generals, vagabonds and adventurers, their brass and gold turned green amidst their clavicles and pelvises, their swords and sabres corroded by rust. Young English roses seized once by glorious ambition and then, finally, by dysentery — and so a career of balls and crinolines and harsh voyages ended. Nothing remained but Nirode's thoughts thought out in their own language and the staring bulbous monstrosity of funereal marble in towers, domes and mausoleums. Eyeless angels, odourless lilies, bloated doves with their beaks missing. Rickshaws drawn up to their flanks, coconut shells and vermilion *pan*-spittle strewn on their outskirts. The soft night weighing down, murmurous, uncalm. Nirode's unrest, his unformed designs heaving through it like some lost unhappy bat.

'You know, Bose,' and his voice was swathed in cheap smoke, almost inaudible, 'I've reached a point now — I always knew I would arrive at it one day — when it would be impossible, physically impossible to work under any man, by his orders, at a given time, at a meaningless job. I loathe those automatons at the top — I loathe their superciliousness, their arrogance, their *blindness.* How dare they be arrogant when working at such senseless jobs? Spend their lives, their entire energy and intelligence on something that *does not matter?* How can one?' He seemed to be asking the stars outside or rather, the darkness, for he was not one to question the stars and expect answers. 'Better to leap out of the window and end it all instead of smearing this endless sticky glue of senselessness over the world. Better not to live.'

'My dear Nirode,' said the professor softly, 'one must make concessions — how else can one survive?'

'I don't know. How *can* one survive? It seems hard. How do you manage, professor? Are you happy — living, writing school text-books?'

'Yes,' the old man said with an earnestness that lent him his only certainty. 'It is the only thing that I truly enjoy doing. It is a vocation. And many men have vocations, are happy, Nirode. It is only a matter of finding one, that is all.'

'Like my brother, I suppose,' and Nirode sent a lighted stub flying in the direction of the vanished train. 'A vocation — and a little, or much, luck. He lives happily. Eats, excretes, sleeps, snores — naturally, contentedly. How? I don't think I can or want to.'

'But you will, of course you will,' the professor insisted. Nirode turned to look at him, with the expression of a boy who has gone through a bad and humiliating whipping and then turns to his friends, the onlookers, to see their reaction. Then the dogs flew into the air, barking and trembling and in another minute the door opened and Sonny was there, carrying parcels of food stained with gravy.

'Sonny,' Nirode spat out his name like a shred of rank tobacco and turned to the window, his back to the young man who walked in, lithely and blithely as a fine young stag straying inadvertently into the company of a wild dog and an aged sheep. In his exquisitely tapering trousers, his magnificently polished riding boots, his elegantly aged jacket and the subdued embroidery of his scarf gleaming through a parting of it, he appeared to lack only a riding crop to swing against his thighs as he walked. Someone had once told him that he always gave the impression of just having tethered a chestnut stallion to the pillared porch below and Sonny had been flattered. Even when he was carrying stained food packages, he thought of that compliment and walked upon the pleasure it gave him. He came in laughing, sweeping a lock of hair off his forehead. When he spoke, it was with an urgency and a falter, as a highly-strung boy or a very short man speaks, ill at ease and wholly engrossed in seeming to be at ease.

'What quiet! What calm!' he shrilled, pushing the dogs away affectionately. 'The atmosphere that surrounds scholars meditating upon a new aspect of some old philosophy. What is it all about Nirode? Professor? Do tell me. Look. I've brought some Chinese grub — banjo prawns for you, Nirode!'

'I won't eat them if you let that filthy dog lick the box, look at him nosing it.'

'Nirode doesn't like dogs,' lamented Sonny gaily, as he put the parcels neatly on top of the one-burner gas stove in a corner. 'It's a sign of nerves and spleen.'

20

'Nerves, spleen and an inclination to godly cleanliness. But you've turned into a perfect specimen of spinsterhood, Sonny, I regret to note. I see you've been polishing your silver and letting the dogs chew their bones on your bed.'

'Did you look at the picture? Did you?' Sonny was rapturous and fleet-footed as an excited girl ran to pick up the silver frame and hold up to them a portrait in dull oils. 'I'm planning to take it out of this frame — vastly unsuitable, don't you think? A carved gilt one is what I have in mind.'

'Ah yes, with fat angels at the corners, each holding a paper rose.'

'Who is it. Sonny? Your father?'

'Yes, yes,' bubbled the young man, bringing it to the professor for examination. 'I don't really have room for it on my walls—' with an apologetic wave at the plastering of silver and gilt frames, calendar cut-outs, home-made indulgences, old-fashioned favourites, with no room for so much as a single varnish-loving fly amongst them '— but, I resolved, I would *make* room for it. A *vast* portrait, don't you think, though modern dress never really suited him. Yes, that's the Cambridge tie, Bose, hasn't the artist done the knot rather neatly? I wish he had posed in ceremonial dress though, with his sword in that vast scabbard that is hanging there, over my stove —'

'And a leopard reclining at his feet?'

'Now you are joking, Nirode, but as it happens, my father *did* own a leopard at one time. We had to give the poor thing to the zoo when we left Babulpur.'

'Couldn't he have taken it with him to his father-in-law's house?'

Sonny refused to hear — a sign that the malicious Bengali jibe had sunk in with sureness. Sonny had an enviable faculty of switching off his hearing apparatus as soon as he sensed someone was going to be unpleasant. He smiled down at the dusty, dapper, slightly balding man in the silver frame, his clothing a trifle too smart, his lips a trifle too full. 'I think I can just manage to squeeze it in, if I remove the Picasso.'

'The Picasso?' The two seated men started and began to search the exhibition on the walls that they normally avoided looking at when they came to visit Sonny, once they had got over the initial delight of pouncing on every small lapse of taste and every display of vulgar sentiment evident in it. There were Sonny's own water-colours of blue streams — white lines to indicate waves — running through meadows patterned with red and yellow flowers. There were greying calendar illustrations of little girls swinging their muffs and magazine photographs of the grandeur of the Swiss Alps. But Picasso? Finally Sonny had to leap nimbly against the wall, like a boy chasing a butterfly, to point out to them a little print of a sad-eyed child, pale and wistful amidst all the papery splendour.

'By all means, do away with the Picasso,' cried Nirode, waving his hand to dismiss the wraith. 'Up with Papa's portrait, down with Picasso.'

'But really, don't you think it is a *vast* portrait, Nirode?'

'My dear boy, it will convert your cubby-hole into a stately home,' Nirode assured him... 'It is most interesting to see how you keep your little self busy as a bee, without any plebian, breadwinning job to eat up eight hours of your day.'

'You have no idea how busy I am, no idea.' Sonny spun around on the heels of his riding-boots, his eyes like bits of mica. 'I hardly know whether I am standing on my head or on my heels. Our Babulpur estate-'

'Doesn't your tenant look after that?' Nirode interrupted and the professor nodded over his umbrella handle, thinking yes, he had grown cruel.

But Sonny, crying 'Oh,' crying 'Ah', slamming his fist into his palm, dancing upon his heels, then upon his toes, told them about his estate with its acres of marsh that were being converted into fisheries, of the fish that were being bred and stocked, of their being brought to the city in baskets of ice and jars of water, of the vast profits there were in the business, here in fish-hungry Bengal and of how, according to his father and his solicitor, they would soon be able to turn out the tenant from their house in Babulpur and return to it in splendour. 'And then a canning factory... export... foreign exchange... Babulpur...'

Nirode, soon bored, crossed his legs and said suavely, 'In that case, Sonny, it will be no hardship to you to put me up for a bit — till I'm on my feet again.'

He waited attentively for Sonny's response and, seeing it to be just what he expected, he smiled. Here was Sonny stammering, hesitating, pale with embarrassment and hearty in his reassurances of hospitality unbounded. Nirode smiled with contempt and satisfaction. The professor was so displeased by the scene that he ceased stroking his fat knees and got up to leave. But Nirode went one further. 'Don't you have any booze, old boy?' he called. 'Bad show.'

'I do, I do,' cried Sonny, his ears hot and his lips cold. 'Half a bottle of rum, where on earth—?' He ran behind a flowered screen and stayed away an inordinately long time, screened by a tangle of parrots and passion-flowers. Hearing the chink of glasses, the professor, with hums and haws, decided to stay on a bit and Nirode grinned across at him in a manner the old man found particularly objectionable. But Sonny, now that he was busy fetching glasses and water, pouring out drinks and passing them around, began to take this wilful intrusion of Nirode's into his stride, began to enjoy playing the expansive host. No matter if all he had was one room and a bed, he knew how an aristocratic host must disport himself — after all, his father had been one in the days before Independence. He passed around cheap cigarettes with elegant flourishes, he sipped his drink and grew more flushed and mica-eyed as he listened to Nirode talk, endlessly and compulsively talk.

For one drink following upon a day of such intensity had made Nirode transparent, revealed inside him the arterial network that now spread and grew on a plane slightly above that of Calcutta's tumultuous roofscape, but attached to it by countless wires, telegraph poles, chimneys, pigeon-roosts — one vast tangled net of the Bengali loquaciousness, the Bengali's quick emotion and fluency, his natural anarchism, his imbalance and inconsistencies, his dark and demoniac dreams that grovelled mostly in the grossness of the city, its shapeless, colourless and grim old houses and slums, then heaved up, like the radio aerials and pigeon-roosts that collected the fuzz of smog on the roofs, and now and then rose and fled like a scattering of mother-of-pearl pigeons into a forbidding sky. He spoke with conceit and malice, he disregarded his companions with fine philosophic detachment, then noisily crashed into their midst again. He boasted of his various wild experiences, declaring them unique in one of his social class, little realizing it was the city that had thrust them upon him inexorably. Then, with unconscious candour, he wondered aloud what to make of it all.

'The lack of an audience is not the problem, in this bloody country it is the choice of one. There are too many levels of education, they run into each other or they keep so distant from each other, what does one do about it? And unless one has decided upon one's chosen audience, one's readers, what sort of material can one feed them? What does one collect for them? How to put it across? How to communicate it?'

'Ah,' murmured the professor, his head lowered and his hands folded sadly on his knees, 'Nirode, do you *dare* communicate?' And speaking as though to himself — and, indeed, the warm sheen of rum had unrolled a screen about him, safe and glowing — he told them a fable from his beloved *Panchatantra*. Nirode wore a superior smile on his face but listened nevertheless, to the tale of the Lion Makers: the four Brahmins, eminent scholars each one of them, came upon the skeleton of a lion and to prove their marvellous scholarship of which they had reached the utmost heights, they decided to bring it to life. One assembled the skeleton, the second created flesh and blood and the third proceeded to put the breath of life into it. But the fourth, the only man of sense amongst them, warned them of the dangers with which a live lion would present them. They refused to be deterred and the man of sense removed himself to a safe tree-top. The lion was brought to life and promptly devoured the three scholars. The professor quoted joyfully:

'Scholarship is less than sense;
Therefore seek intelligence;
Senseless scholars in their pride
Made a lion: then they died.'

Nirode's smile in the shadow by the window was merely a crooked slit in an impassive face. 'So, I lack intelligence. Does the *Panchatantra* offer me that, Bose?' But Bose was sipping his drink and silently enjoying the wit that never failed to amuse and refresh him, gave him security in an unreliable, uneven life that he had not, perhaps chosen, but acquiesced to, accepted. He made no reply to Nirode who then began to needle Sonny with fresh loudness. 'Is an audience tuned in to you a lion come to life, Sonny? What do you think? Would you cower up in a tree and let the bag of bones remain a bag of bones? Or would you gather up all your education and ambition and ideas and breathe life into the dull thing so as to have a real, splendid lion roar at you?'

'What and be gobbled up by it!' cried Sonny, in mock horror, gobbling.

'Damn it, we're not talking of an audience physically come to life, in the sense of sitting up and scratching and going out for a cup of tea and a belch. Mentally, mentally. How to bring this scattering of disparate intellectuals together? How to bring them to life? From their separate communities, from behind the walls of their communal languages — how to bring them together and bring them to life so that they can begin to do their bit of roaring and rampaging in a country that's been asleep too long? What scope can a new journal offer them? What kind of journal must it be?' He slowed down, he answered himself, he rambled, when Sonny piped up, for the sake of something to say.

'Old boy, one must be practical, remember!'

Nirode snapped back, 'What d'you think I'm talking about?'

'Not *only* another magazine or journal or newspaper, I'd hoped but a *book,*' cried Sonny, leaping from his chair and flourishing. 'That's what we've always hoped you would do, Nirode. We knew you wouldn't remain a journalist forever and, honestly, I can't see you as an editor — editors are so *orderly*, so vastly *organizational*. But, now that you have the time, a book...'

Nirode turned aside to the window so no one saw him flush, no one saw the fury with which he struck a match. He hated being caught out by, of all people, Sonny. He resented the driving home of the professor's little point in his warning against too much contact, too close an audience. He himself knew by instinct that he was a man for whom aloneness alone was the sole natural condition, aloneness alone the treasure worth treasuring. But he had already gone too far in his confidences, he found himself incapable of retracting. 'That isn't at all what one was talking about,' he growled. 'That's a luxury for decadent hypocrites like you, with no work to do other than rake in other people's earnings. I mean harder work than *that*. I mean something more sustained and powerful. This is no time for retreating to crumbling old palaces and sit scribbling with a quill among the cobwebs.'

'Oh come,' said Sonny, foolish and emboldened by rum, 'you know I know you can very well do that if you like. Why,' with an uncertain giggle, 'you can do that more easily than I. All you need to do is swallow your pride and go home. Your mother would provide you—'

'You pimply little idiot,' Nirode threw the words at him with scorn. 'You snotty public school prig. You haven't the courage to throw away those bloody riding boots ten years after you lost the last of your horses and you speak to *me* of swallowing my pride? You direct *my* choice of a life? You, your people haven't had an original thought since the time that one ancestor of yours went into the bogus property and inheritance business. Tell me, has anyone of you ever thought a *thought*, Sonny, in all your petty, simpering, useless little lives? And you set about teaching me what to accept and what to reject — after I've thrown off every stinking undergarment of family fortune and family—' he stopped, very abruptly, and groaned to think of himself letting go and saying things for which surely the rum and his exhaustion alone were to be blamed.

'Oh, oh,' lamented Sonny. 'Oh-hic. When I get the hiccups, they simply-hic-never stop.'

'A proper fate for you, you mongoose,' snorted Nirode. 'Since you can't drink, why don't you go and heat up those prawns. If I don't eat in the next five minutes, I shall die horribly of starvation. And a Brahmin requires a wealthy funeral.'

'I am leaving now,' piped up the professor from the depths of a peacock cushion, then struggled to rise out of it and assemble himself before he quietly trotted home to his wife and her *hilsa* fish cooked in strong mustard oil, thereafter to read a little of the *Panchatantra,* nodding and smiling in a partly alcoholic and partly habitual daze.

He left the two younger men behind in a state of amicable domesticity, heating the prawns and rice and eating off the bed, spread carefully with newspaper. Having eaten all but two of the prawns, which he left for Sonny, Nirode became friendlier, less intense and Sonny, pleased, did not know what to think: whether Nirode was stricken by conscience and trying to make up for his insulting behaviour or whether he was done with a show put up purely to baffle and anger the old professor who had once been his mentor or whether — and this was the most probable — he had simply forgotten all that he had said in this last hour and was completely pre-occupied in the next.

Leaning over the balcony rail together for a last smoke, Sonny was flattered to hear Nirode's plans for starting a magazine and to be asked his opinion on who should be approached for financial aid, and who for articles and poems. Below them the tombstones of the old cemetery slept, as white as sacred bulls in the black mire.

Into Nirode's sleep the bright birds of the past came serenely winging and the wide gestures of their wings ushered into his sleep the gemmed loveliness of a holiday home of his childhood. The birds cast their shadows on an uncertain violet dream and the shadows turned to light, to colours, vivid as gems, as paints... the red and blue and yellow prayer flags whipped by a breeze into a flutter against a sky so blue, hills so purple, snows so white that it was like an illustration of a fairy tale, animated by the sweetly melancholy tune of cow bells drifting up and down the hillsides. A nicotine-tinged hand rose to shield the dreamer from the wild, white wind that swept across from Tibet and, with mock-obedience, the gesture was copied by his mother who sat on the wind-wild veranda, working on her embroidery. He could see it so clearly, the worked span of the embroidery ring, that his shellblue eyelids moved faintly, with an oyster life. Red and green threads striped the young girls' aprons, vermilion silks spread sheen upon the curving monastery roof and white and lilac silks went to make the small stars of the bamboo dahlias. In reality it would have made an enchanting scene. On the rough cloth stretched tautly across the ring, it acquired a tasteless vulgarity and the exquisite fingers that worked on it seemed as detached as those of a god who creates a cretin. He touched her water-cool palm, he looked again at the rings loaded upon one finger of her right hand — the diamonds that he hated for their undimming, electric glitter and the large oblong of a sea-deep emerald that he had always loved. One short white scar at the joint of her thumb, one she had never explained to him. 'Mother,' he said — and his voice was not a child's voice but issued from his man's throat — 'do you really think that worth doing, that hideous mass of squeezed out paint tubes in your lap?' Her rich, large mouth curved with sarcasm — a sarcasm she had rarely directed at him, but then pitilessly. 'My son,' she said, and her voice was like the thick fur of a winter beast, 'my son, you would have made an excellent Jesuit.'

Anger and impotence tore at the light sheet of his sleep, tore holes into it that admitted a new, harsh and uncoloured light upon the dream scene. Something about all this prettiness and brightness turned macabre and horrifying and he soon saw why he himself was not an inhabitant of it. He stood some distance away from it and between him and his mother's brilliant territory was erected a barbed wire fence, all glittering and vicious. To his astonishment, he found at his side, also on the wrong side of this cruel division, his father, lying slovenly in the prickled shadow of the barbs, asleep, his mouth half-open, the buttons of his silk coat undone. He looked back at his mother to ask her to explain this unsightly apparition of the dead man, but she looked not at him but at his father and in the curve of her mouth and the sullen lowering of her brows there was so much contempt and resentment that she seemed to forget herself in this passion. Then something distracted her, footsteps, a voice and she turned to greet with a ravishing smile her neighbour, that retired major or brigadier who, with his bestial jaws and small eyes and hairy hands repelled Nirode, made him shrink away. He watched the large, bumbling creature grope at the garden gate, walk past the clump of bamboo dahlias, then the pear tree, the row of azaleas, to where his mother sat on the veranda, smiling a slow, sensual smile. Hideous to see in his mother, hideous to see in the heroine who had led his crusade. He turned over, away from her and in his sleep groaned, for with Nirode sleep was no deeper than the thin sheet that covered him and it was riddled with holes spanned by ineffectual darning.

Sonny awoke to hear him say, 'No, mother, you can't,' and sat up in astonishment he would not have felt had Nirode merely said, 'No, mother, I won't.'

All that winter Nirode worked in a fashion so fox or weasel-like, no one could tell whether he was at work and serious or idle and at play. Sonny, who optimistically held the former theory, cooked for him on his one-ring gas stove and when Nirode declared his meat-balls and *pulaos* were fit for the dogs alone, he trotted out and fetched noodles from Peiping and *tandoori* chicken from Friends' Home. (Could he afford it? Sonny paid another visit to his father's solicitor. Khan picked his teeth with a match-stick and said it would be a long time before the fisheries began to yield profit and that Sonny had overdrawn again...). Nirode soon gave up eating in the flat that oppressed him and sickened him with its canine odours and abominable picture exhibition. He visited friends and visited them till they wondered what was on his mind. He even called on an elderly aunt in Ballygunge for tea and asked her if she wished to make amends, in her old age, for a long life of philistinism, by contributing to the foundation of a magazine that would electrify the eastern world. Startled, she signed a cheque. He took to spending his days at the coffee house, became a permanent fixture of it, so that the young men going in and out of the swing doors in perpetual ebb and flow, thought him to be a part of the establishment, like the sticky flies or the slowly ticking fans overhead. His friends, wanting to inform him about an artist who had agreed to do the cover of the first issue in return for an appreciation of his work in the same paper, or about a wealthy industrialist's ambitious wife who had turned, in dissatisfaction, from social work to Indian culture and therefore might prove easy prey, knew they would find him always at the coffee house, the stable nucleus of a constantly expanding and contracting circle at a table in the centre. All these friends had more time and hobbies than they knew what to do with and if Nirode accepted their proposals, they were gratified; if he did not but only spat out a contemptuous insult, they merely turned the talk to their own office-gossip or Bengali politics or left in a herd for the cinema. As long as one had coffee and the cinema to fall back on, what need to take anything seriously? Did Nirode? No one could tell, he never confided.

To many he seemed merely to be showing off and prancing in his new-found, if uncertain, freedom before his old colleagues and employers. Elbows on the greasy table top, he snatched at every opportunity to rail against them. 'Literature?' he cried. 'No, no, they have no such pretensions. No such word exists in a newspaper office. Don't you know, there is a vast incinerator at the bottom of the stairs in every newspaper office, where all undesirable words are thrown and destroyed. As you walk in at eight in the morning, still stinking of last night's adulterated booze, yet boiling over with the great reviews, the magnificent articles you are going to start spinning the minute you get to your desk, you find a quiet man in khaki uniform, standing there at the door, waiting. A red label on his jacket says Incinerator Attendant. Oh yes, he's on the pay-roll and you've just got to stop and submit to his inspection. He goes through your pockets, your boot-toes, your ears and finger-nails and every now and then he gives one loud snort and digs out an Undesirable Word that he has found in some dirty, dark little corner that it would only be civilized to keep private and over it goes, into the incinerator. No arguments, please. Literature, my dear David, is one of those words. At the most, at the *very* most, an old-timer in the Sunday section, with forty years of meaningless meandering behind him might, just might as a great favour,be allowed to use it. There are other more dangerous words: lies, hypocrisy, retract, communal, religion...'

David laughed. 'What made you go into such a profession, Nirode? I know you have simply stacks of undesirable words to your credit.'

'I might have gone in, but I've come out. I felt sick, I vomited and now I wallow in undesirable words to my pig-heart's content.'

David winced. He was a man who revered cleanliness and fine feelings though one might not have thought it from looking at his ragged *dhoti* and sandals and the black tatters of a cloth bag he wore over his shoulder with all his designs in it. 'More coffee?' he asked and continued to ask as friends and acquaintances came jauntily in through the swing-doors, searched the humming crowds that were glued, like flies, to the sugar-sprinkled, coffee-stained woodwork and then dragged their chairs up to Nirode's table — for as long as Nirode talked, it was his table, it did not matter if David paid the bill.

'Do you know why they wear those green eye shades over their eyes, David? Do you, Jit? I'll tell you — it's because they have no eyes. Editors are born without eyes, without pupils or corneas or irises. They have two sets of shutters instead — just like they have in cameras. And these little built-in cameras are at work, clicking, clicking and putting down on a long sticky black film everything they've clicked. And do you know why journalists never keep their hands still long enough for you to see them? Why they're always tapping on typewriters, crumpling up waste-paper, doodling and scribbling? It's because they don't want you to know they actually have no hands — they are born with iron claws, the kind they make for men who lose their hands in the war or get them rotted away with leprosy. Clack, clack, the claws pick other people's brains, as butchers do with sheep.'

'I didn't know you were so full of self-contempt, Nirode.' That came from Jit Nair, the dark and suave Jit, hiding always behind guileful dark glasses and a great pipe. Jit who had been the brilliant prodigy of a Southern university and had come to Bengal to assert himself amongst the renowned artists and litterateures there, only to be lured, with astonishing lubricity, into a large, prosperous and benign British tea firm that so pampered and indulged him that he had to escape, every now and then, to the more bracing climate of the coffee house, notorious gathering-place of the displaced and dangerous literates of Bengal. And Jit's words issued as a serpent's forked tongue, flickering, quick and false for, of course, the poison was not there but in the secret fangs.

Nirode, with quick anger, turned to remind Jit of all these things — the early University honours, the hasty downfall, the beer and Scotch fed prosperity that glittered darkly amidst the shabby off-white that was the rule in the coffee house. But David, furiously wiping up spilt coffee, cried, 'Have some potato chips?' and then softly to Jit, 'He's given up working for the *Patrika*, didn't you know?'

'Given it up?' Jit's romantic eyes could be felt to widen behind the shield of his dark glasses. 'Well, who would have thought that our budding editor-in-chief of the illustrious *Patrika*, circulation —'

'Don't be an ass. You know I've always — loathed it and I'll be damned if I work another day for any other man.'

'What have we here?' cried Jit, throwing up his hands in mock horror. 'A communist?'

Communist. The word ran around like a flame that is passed from cigarette to cigarette. Flickering, flaming, it made certain young men sigh in boredom, others muse and blow thoughtful spumes of cheap cigarette smoke. Dipping the remains of the potato chips into a chipped saucer of ketchup, clinking cups against saucer rims, scratching their heads and then violently throwing themselves backwards into their chairs, or forwards on to their folded arms, the young men thrashed it out. One amongst those who had sighed now stirred and said, 'One must draw a distinction, of course, between Russian communism and Chinese communism and you'll see it's the latter we'll have to deal with.' Another cried, 'The fountainhead whether you go on a pilgrimage or a crusade, you must go to the fountainhead.' And the fountainhead was then set up on the table, in the centre, so that they could talk around it and roar approvingly when one of the cynics spoke up and said, 'Russia has been aspiring towards the American way of life only since 1953. America has had it for the last two hundred years and surely the original is to be preferred?' But the headscratchers, the blowers of blue smoke, they discounted such levity and 'No,' they said. 'The Congress will not do' or 'Compare India with Italy, with France, with the England of fifty years ago and see where they are now. But we, we are still poor, poor, poor.' Through all the opposing strands wound the quiet and insistent refrain of 'Better Red than...'

But neither Nirode nor Jit took part in this. Still seated at the table, they seemed to have stepped backwards to emanate a shadow about them that made their faces suddenly alike in inscrutability — the one who had just triumphantly taken up what the other had long ago deserted, now admitting, unwillingly, this unwanted bond, this continuity.

Without malice, Jit said 'But for a writer there can surely be worse professions, Nirode?'

Nirode did not care to disclose at this moment what his true occupation at the *Patrika* had been and he shook his head slowly. 'No. The newspaper carries the writer further and further into the impersonal, it only follows the You. The You is everything in news. There is never an I. It is the I that interests me now.'

Jit reared back, out of the conspiratorial shadow, like a cobra rising out of its basket when the pipe begins to play. He was smiling his horribly fixed and knowing smile for all to see.

'And have you made quite sure,' he smiled, 'that when you meet the I, you will find it what you want it to be?'

But Nirode did not rise to the defence. He drank his coffee slowly. 'That is exactly what someone else asked me the other day. But he made his attack from a different point — intelligence. I think, though that was not quite the word he meant,'

'What difference does it make? One is vulnerable at many points but all that it means is that one is vulnerable.'

Nirode pushed back his chair. 'Come, let's get out,' he said and Jit rose and followed. David, watching, was hurt, for David enjoyed nothing so much as discussing with Nirode the Westernization of the Educated Indian, the cult of Tagore worship in Bengal, the system of education in Indian universities... rather, he enjoyed listening to Nirode expound, while he wandered about the city with him. Calcutta assumed new dimensions of meaning as he listened to Nirode repeat and contradict himself, theorize and laugh and muse all in one breath. He had even, he thought plaintively, paid for the coffee. Then he turned to Fernandez who was a member of the Magnolia dance-band and of the Communist party as well. 'But would you abandon your religion, Fernandez? The last clinging superstitions? I don't believe it,' and a great shout went up as fresh coffee arrived.

Out on the streets, walking — for Nirode refused to let Jit hail a taxi — the city slid past them in alternating cubes of white and black and its din was as omnipresent as the smog of smoke and dust and the odours of diesel oil and damp rot. Each man on these streets was hurried and intent and even the obvious loiterers loitered to an obvious, if unspoken, end. Yet some amongst them must have noticed the almost painful expression of concentration on the thinner man's face, some must have heard him declare, 'Three drinks a night and a room of my own, that's all I ask...' But no one stopped to question or even to wonder and in the endlessly feeble and dispirited way of its black wisdom, the city fell away, allowed the two to proceed to and enter Jit's home. This was large and Victorian, marble-pillared, green-shuttered and inlaid with the shadows and remembrances of East India Company days of more than a century ago.

Leading him up to his wife who lay on the divan, a voluptuous porpoise of ebony flesh encased in green silk, Jit introduced Nirode to her, saying in a manner suddenly turned stagy and unsound, 'Here is a young man, Sarla, who declares that all he needs to become the greatest Indian writer is the promise of three drinks a night and a room to himself. What do you say to that?'

'No, how romantic,' she drawled and to Nirode she seemed to belong to the same century as her house, to that class of courtesans who had clung like bracelets, or vampires, to its wealth and leisure and decadence. She eyed him too, seeming to make even more mocking observations on him. 'We can start on the drinks straight away,' she said and so ordered Jit away to his little bamboo bar at one end of the room while she continued to scrutinize him. 'But it is foolishness to want a room to yourself. Why?' She laughed and stretched against the cushions. Evidently she had been drinking before their arrival.

Jit had not been deaf while stirring the drinks at the other end of the cavernous room and he came to them to hand them their glasses, saying, 'Ah yes, Nirode, a room to yourself would be something we cannot offer in our house. There are too many of my wife's admirers lurking about, you'll soon see them — white ones mainly and a few that she calls honey-complexioned...'

Nirode had nothing to say. He sat through their ferocious snarling and sniping in absolute silence, like a man in a dark room watching a film, a film very polished in execution but describing something intrinsically uninteresting. He drank so fast that his throat burnt and then he decided that even the drink was not worth enduring this exhibition and left to hear Sarla direct her only other observation on him to his departing back. 'He's dumb,' she complained petulantly: her voice as much warm-flesh and cool-silk as her body. Out on the pillared porch, Nirode spat into an oleander, for he felt as though he had swallowed a mouthful of Sarla's sweet perfume. Marriage, bodies, touch and torture... he shuddered and, walking swiftly, was almost afraid of the dark of Calcutta, its warmth that clung to one with a moist, perspiring embrace, rich with the odours of open gutters and tuberose garlands. All that was Jit's and Sarla's, he decided and indeed all that had to do with marriage was destructive, negative, decadent. He would waste no time on it and for once he did not linger in the city's palm-edged squares and on the arresting street corners, but strode on not wasting time.

As if to underline and emphasize the insidiousness of such love, such antagonism, a letter from his mother lay waiting for him on Sonny's divan. Feeling exhausted and resentful, he considered tearing it up, but of course that was impossible and he stood at the window reading it grudgingly. She had written in Bengali which was unusual. Bengali had been the childhood tongue in their house, the tongue in which she had sung songs to them and they had begged for kites and whistles. They had outgrown it and brothers, sisters and mother now conversed and corresponded almost exclusively in English. It touched him — he did not want it to — but the softly rounded, chirping sounds of his childhood language touched him. And she wrote in a quick, minute, frightened hand, betraying reserves and uncertainties of which a son could never know

'My son Nirode,' she wrote. 'It is hopeless, quite hopeless I know, to expect a letter from you, my busy, far-travelling son. But, sitting out on the veranda which is washed by a thin honey sun and the scent of my spring orchids which are all flowering in long sprays from their moss-baskets, I caught myself waiting to hear the postman's steps and the creak of the gate which Sharab will not oil. The postman did come — patience rewarded or was it prayer? — and brought me letters, though not from you. Monisha wrote and seemed happy, at least with their weekend in the jungle. The Deputy Commissioner took them on a shoot but shot nothing, they only saw a leopardess with two cubs by a stream. There was a letter from Amla, a short one, for she is preparing for her examinations with too much ambition, I feel. And, of course, from Arun, who writes every Tuesday. Can you not see him making a point of remembering to do so, every Tuesday? And very little in it except enthusiasm for his work and the professors and doctors — no red-knuckled nurse so far, thank God! — and a thousand questions about me and all of you. What shall I tell him of you? May I tell him that you will come and spend a holiday with me in Kalimpong this summer? May I tell him that you were given leave at last and would get away from your newspaper and come here for a rest? There, that is all, I won't go on and on please, mother.

'There is such a profusion of spring in our garden, though I have sent baskets of it to everyone I know, even to unfortunate Frau

Gunther who still sits painting the Kanchenjunga so very badly. There are still masses of rhododendrons, azaleas and magnolias and I am leaving them to the bees. What honey I shall have in autumn. Under the mulberry tree Rinchin and Pem Pem (they are Sharab's little girls, do you remember?) in their striped aprons, are trying to decide whether the mulberries are ripe enough to eat. Of course they are not, they still look like tiny white caterpillars.

'This morning I walked down the hill to the valley and came upon a gypsy camp (it made me think of my gypsy son). Delightfully poky little huts made of sticks and leaves with blue smoke coming out of every crack. A filthy old cobbler hammering at a wooden saddle, his plaits stiff with brown dirt and festooned with red ribbons. All the other gypsies were out with their mules and I soon ran into their midst and felt myself to be in the heart of a temple, so many bells were ringing dolefully. One skittish young horse came romping into their midst and they scattered in panic across the stream. How angry the tall Red Indian-faced woman in charge of them was, how she pelted that horse with stones and called heu-heu to her mules! I laughed and laughed.

'My dear mother, how bucolic you sound. Indeed, there is little company for me besides the gay figures of the embroidery you scorn, my books and my letters. Frau Gunther comes for coffee once a week. Rinchin and Pem Pem play in the garden all day. And Major Chadha is kind enough to come and see if I need anything. He is the soul of helpfulness.

'This is not confirmed yet, but Monisha writes that it might, might just be possible for Jiban to manage a transfer to Calcutta. Would you not like that? And to think of two of my children together I would be twenty times happier than I am now. My golden son, I remember you. Otima.'

That was the letter. Like a warm, enveloping succubus in the shape of a bright-winged butterfly. He read the letter and it was like sinking his teeth through a sweet mulberry to bite into a caterpillar's entrails. He began to undress for bed busily, thinking of Major Chadha — how unashamedly she wrote that hideous name, so like a cooking pot full of yellow food or a rag of dirty underwear. How helpful was this Chadha, providing her with male company and admiration. How solidly he planted himself on her little square chair, gay with Tibetan tapestries, how he cleared his throat before he paid her a pompous compliment, with what confident patience — or prayer she waited for him to finish before she began to chatter with ravishing gaiety and youthfulness. And then the gifts: a plate of rich carrot *halwa* covered with fine silver foil, made by his own daughter, with which a good Punjabi makes his advances; a pot with a dreadful insect orchid, all speckled and rubbery and ready to spring. Invitations to a walk around the garden, perhaps up the hill...

That little tapestried chair in which she liked to place large men, to embarrass them and amuse herself. He saw the soft, pendulous flesh of his father over-flowing from it, like a mass of runny dough that she had moulded into a funny shape, a helpless one.

But you have lost, he told her quietly. You have no right any longer to laugh at the thighs too fat to squeeze between those merry little wooden arms. No longer any right to despise and scorn. You do not laugh at Chadha while he squirms on the toy seat, you invite him, watch him, encourage him. You have lost the game.

And he washed his feet with that fastidious care for which Sonny laughed at him, determining to go next morning to the Catholic Orphan Press and finalize matters with them.

With the first heat of summer blowing up dust from the earth and spring blossoms down from trees, the pace, the pulse of life seemed abruptly to slow down. Blood warmed and thickened and ran slower. There was a heavy listlessness in the air that defied the sharp breezes from the sea beyond the marshes and lay groaning like a caged lion. Walking at the lake's edge, Nirode felt his head aching, his limbs sluggish and leaden with it. They walked past the stalls of soda water and green coconuts, past the young men who lay on the grass singing of fountains and romance and the large families that, like avid crows, sat about icecreams and paper cones filled with puffed rice. The farthest of the lakes was quieter, here the water lay unlit, of unknown depth and treachery. Three ancient cannon reared out of earth and grass under an immense rain tree. Three men were having a late dip in the lake, with quiet infrequent splashes and low recitations of Sanskrit hymns. Nirode and David walked away, up the lake where only lovers went and then rarely: there were not many lovers in Calcutta. A little suburban train went shrilling by, hoot-toot-tooting a long and melancholy whistle that made Nirode arch his neck and raise his arms above his head and cry, 'God, that makes me want to get away! Pack up and clear out as far as I can get from here! There's nothing but good-bye, good-bye in that sound.'

David smiled shyly, hugging his tattered cloth bag to him with one arm, as though it were a pet goose. 'Isn't there invitation as well? I enjoy that sound, when I hear it at night. It makes me think of the many places I still have to visit — Badrinath and Kedarnath in the north and in the south Mahabalipurum, Mamallapurum, Mysore...'

'And are they always as wonderful in reality as in anticipation?'

'Always.'

'Simple, simple David. If I ever meet your mother, out in the streets of Galway, calling for her Davy-boy, I'll tell her not to worry: you might travel round the whole world thrice and take a different way each time and yet remain simple, simple David.'

Again a soft, self-conscious laugh, gentle and self-effacing. 'And you, Nirode? If you travelled round the world thrice, what would happen to you? Would you remain Nirode?'

Nirode groaned. 'I'd never go, David, I never shall. I pack my bags, I arrive at the station and when I have one foot in the train, I hesitate. That's my undoing — this lack of faith and this questioning. I just stand and watch the train rush off, leaving me behind like a ghost in a bloody nightmare.'

'I find the ticket alone answers all my questions, reassures me completely.'

'Ah, do you? For me, all tickets are marked with question marks. That is all I ever find on them.'

They wandered back and sat down to rest on the cannon, finding the metal cooled by night and dew. The bathers had gone, the rain tree whispered aloud its private dreams, in the wind from the south. Nirode's lit his cigarettes one with the other so that the pinpoint of light glowed without stop, like a light at a level crossing in a desert. David was moved by its smallness, its insistence. Hesitantly, he said 'You are not sure of the magazine then? Whether you will start it or not?'

'Ah, the magazine,' Nirode spat in disgust. 'What has the magazine to do with my journey? It has only to do with my days — it occupies me, it gratifies my friends. It feeds me meals and drinks at their expense. I've collected a few patrons, enough companies have promised me advertisements — that's Jit's doing — and it will soon start rolling. But at night — what answer or reassurance does the bloody thing give me then? How can it? It is only a collection of little pieces — little poems, little reviews, written by little men. Perhaps the best available, perhaps even a means of contacting, kindred souls, my long-sought brothers with whom I shall found an Ithaca for which I shall write the constitution. But at night can I, can anyone, believe this?'

'But Nirode, then it will never succeed. If that is all you feel for it, all you want it to be, it is damned from the start. It's a failure already.'

'Of course it is. I want it to fail — quickly. Then I want to see if I have the spirit to start moving again towards my next failure. I want to move from failure to failure to failure, step by step to rock bottom. I want to explore that depth. When you climb a ladder, all you find at the top is space, all you can do is leap off — fall to the bottom. I want to get there without that meaningless climbing. I want to descend, quickly.'

'That is more than defeatism — Nirode, it is absolute negation.'

Nirode sat upon the cannon like a statue of gun metal, with a profile as severe as a battleworn soldier's and the pinpoint of light burning. burning. How the young can believe in their attitudes till the attitude becomes the self. He was aware of this, but lightly and in patches. 'I have been reading Camus, you know. He says, "In default of inexhaustible happiness, eternal suffering at least would give us a destiny. But we do not have even that consolation and our worst agonies come to an end one day." He paused and ran the words over his tongue again in silence. It was as if this had become a habit with him. 'Happiness, suffering — I want to be done with them, disregard them, see beyond them to the very end.'

David shook his head. 'I could not live if I began by emptying out my heart like that.'

'No, you couldn't, but I feel as if I was born with my heart emptied out.'

'Then I would fill it! '

'With what — ceramic designs?' Nirode laughed.

David was hurt. The trembling eagerness on his white face retreated like the leaves of a sensitive plant — but some Irish obduracy remained. 'No, of course not. They do not fill mine. But come, travel with me Nirode. I think you are like me. There is something in travelling that fulfils people like you and me.'

'And where shall we go to start with?' Nirode still laughed.

'I'm leaving for Shantiniketan tomorrow. Why not come?'

'What, in the time of the mango blossom?'

'Oh all right, in the time of the mango blossom.' David seemed irritated by Nirode's frivolity following upon a few moments of such engulfing sadness.

'Mind, the girls will pelt you with flowers till you fall.'

'Oh Nirode,' David sighed, rising from the cannon, but Nirode would not leave him alone now and accompanied him laughing, 'There you and I *are* alike, Davy. We're both terrified, aren't we. Do you know, Jit once tried to make me visit a painted lady...' and he became garrulous and coarse again, delighting in silliness, till David thought that perhaps it was because he had confided in him his secret worries that he now felt so lighthearted — just as his old nanny would say 'making a clean breast of it' would make him feel, after he had been to the larder for forbidden cake. Trustfully, like the little boy in the white nightshirt, he believed this and laughed whenever he thought Nirode expected him to laugh.

They wandered away together, leaving the lake to suck in small waves at the clay bank beneath the rain tree. But even the lakes formed no pocket of solitude and balm and here came the train, rocking and wailing and warning away all travellers that were fearful. On all sides the city pressed down, alight, aglow and stirring with its own marsh-bred, monster life that, like an ogre, kept one eye open through sleep and waking. Calcutta, Calcutta-like the rattle of the reckless train; Calcutta, Calcutta — the very pulsebeat in its people's veined wrists. The streets where slaughtered sheep hung beside bright tinsel tassels to adorn oiled black braids and a syphilitic beggar and his entire syphilitic family came rolling down on barrows, like the survivors of an atomic blast, then paused to let a procession of beautifully laundered Bengalis in white carry their marigold-decked Durga — or Lakshmi or Saraswati, or Kali — on their shoulders down to the Ganges, amidst drums and fevered chanting. In one shadowy doorway an old crone lit a fire, mumbling. Beneath a brief canvas roof a skeletal old gnome with electric white hair served *kebabs,* still sizzling on their red-hot spikes, first to an urchin who had his day's earnings knotted at his crotch and next to a party that waited in a long American car drawn up to the pavement. From the balconies above the streets long *saris* hung limply down and voices murmured, reciting prayers or lessons. Down below funerals passed by, the bearers of the white, flower-laden stretchers vacant-eyed and smooth-browed as they chanted 'Hari om, Hari om.' 'Sweet lily, sweet Li-ly,' cried the flower vendor who carried garlands of jasmine and tuberose strung upon a bamboo frame. Wedding marquees shivered in stripes of red and white bunting and blue neon tubing and; within them the *shehnai* wailed of the folly of man in endeavouring to perpetuate his name. Trams and barrows rolled by, klaxon horns honked. Odours of naphtha, gasoline and rotting mangoes, cinders and frangipani, open gutters and temple marigold mingled together. Calcutta, Calcutta, prayed its victims and Calcutta stirred as though in answer, as though it were a living spirit. Calcutta was not merely the bazars ringed by cinemas, slaughter-houses and *pan* booths, but also the history of those old Georgian houses that still lined gas lit streets, their sweeping marble staircases and deep pillared verandas, their shuttered windows that seemed to enclose and hide their memories of the balls and crinolines and horse-drawn carriages of a hundred / two hundred years ago. The city was as much atmosphere as odour, as much a haunting ghost of the past as a frenzied passage towards early death.

Walking past a neon-lit wedding marquee with its gay bunting and perfumed riot of garlands, pausing to let a blind beggar go by with a yellowed skull in his hand extended for alms, Nirode and David came at last to the cemetery where white gravestones loomed like sacred bulls transfixed in immortality — a city immortality that would soon sink, like Calcutta, into the waiting marshes and vanish.

'Are you not afraid?' David asked timidly, but feeling he had to know.'

'Yes,' Nirode agreed with studied carelessness. 'But I think I should be more afraid if I were climbing up the ladder knowing I would be thrown off the top.' He flung his cigarette at a famous gravestone that still lamented in the dusty moonlight:

'Ah, what avails the sceptres race!
Ah, what the face divine!
What every virtue, every grace!
Rose Aylmer, all were thine.'

He sang Landor's lines in a quavering falsetto, then broke raucously into the schoolboy battlecry of, 'Hit him on the boko, hit him on the boko, *Jericho!'*

David stood laughing as the shouting died away in the night stillness.

David Gunney, closing his book — but keeping a finger in to mark the place — leant his head back against the wooden seat and was filled with that extraordinary elation that came to him only in

43

trains, in moving trains, for the moment they came to a standstill, he became uneasy. It was as though only in flux and in passage could this balding, myopic waif from Galway find the security necessary to joy. It was not in the adventure of his runaway life, his travels, his hand-to-mouth existence or his ceramics that David found the greatest joy, but in this — the rattling apart of the bones of his skull by the grand galloping of the train, the feel of the wheels turning and turning and reducing his bones to crumbs, to nothing and the sights and scenes flowing past like a bright river stained with colour — and the knowledge that in another minute he would be elsewhere and, in another hour, far, far beyond. He looked out on the Bengal countryside with the smile of a child to whom the strange and unknown had quickly and inexplicably become known and beloved. The meandering canals, the ponds covered with a powdery mauve mist of water hyacinths, the ducks waddling out of the thatch-roofed village in an orderly line, the moist, juicy verdure of the land — he loved them with a Bengali's ardour. And the man driving out his team of oxen, waving a long whip over their haunches, the kingfisher poised upon a tingling telegraph wire the instant before it plummeted down upon its prey, the small naked boy in the ploughed field who jumped up to shout an ecstatic greeting to the passing train — seeing these somehow familiar figures, these symbols of a wanderer's world, David was filled with a passionate wish that the whip may remain forever poised above the angular haunches of the oxen, never upon their hides, that the bright bird may remain always in the air, taut and rippling with static speed and desire in the moment before its downward flight and that the small boy remain always in mid-air, in the ecstasy of his jump, never to land on his feet, in the mud.

The train was slowing. Soon it would be at Shantiniketan. David returned to his book, the Gitanjali, which he was reading proudly in the original. Before he began, however, he said a silent prayer to the small boy. Jump, he urged him voicelessly, jump higher and higher! Oh boy, never come down.

The child spinning a top on the edge of the wooden seat, the woman opening out a giant tiffin-carrier in order to feed her brood

44

on her bread and pickles, the old man nodding over a black umbrella — all looked up and saw the white man smiling.

Like all others who knew Dharma — so he signed his pictures, Dharma, that was all — Nirode, on opening the narrow door that led from the dusty, chicken-feathered lane into the long, low white house, felt as though he were opening a door on to that secret courtyard where, in the still shadows and secretive shrubs, he would find — something unique, astonishing, valuable. He did not know what: love, wisdom... His heart expanded and he entered with a fearful eagerness as one might enter a ruined, long-forgotten shrine which might have, who knows, in wiser times, contained a prized truth. He walked through the long room, empty except for squares of canvas and twilight, to the veranda where he knew he would find Dharma, eating *pan* out of a silver box at his knee and watching the evening invade his hidden garden and drown in the deep green pond over which a single palm arched longingly, its grey leaves spattered with the white droppings of water birds. Dharma's geese chattered to their master from the hibiscus bushes and his wife's holy *tulsi* plant. The sky was streaked orange and ash over this rural scene that was separated so completely from the raucous street by the low white house.

The geese immediately set up an offended hissing and honking and Dharma chuckled at them before he turned to greet Nirode. 'My young friend Nirode,' he said in his slow, dramatic tone and the geese fell silent and walked peevishly away to their pond. 'My young friend Nirode, with yet another ten pounds missing from his frame. Have you given up eating altogether?'

'Not quite.' Nirode dropped to the mat beside the painter and wiped the perspiration from his face with a dirty hand. 'I should like a *pan* too.'

'Excellent nourishment, excellent,' drawled Dharma with heavy sarcasm but he held out the silver spider with its many dangling silver chains. Attached to these chains were the folded, prepared *pan* leaves, skewered by silver pins. Nirode drew one off and packed it into his mouth.

45

'It was hot and filthy in the bus.'

Dharma raised his voice and called, 'Gita Devi, a glass of sherbet.'

'No,' called Nirode. 'Plain water.'

'Must one be an ascetic to edit a magazine? It might be an exciting and enthralling profession, Nirode, but I assure you it is not a holy one.'

'Here, I brought you the first issue. Look at it. Tell me what you think.' Nirode handed it over with an exhausted, bloodless gesture and leaned back against a wooden pillar, half-closing his eyes to the livid sky and the blinding white of the geese now paddling through the green. When Dharma's wife, large and placid and bovine in her red-bordered *sari* and *kum-kum* marked hair, placed a tumbler of water beside him, he smiled, barely noticing — no one, not even Dharma, ever did — for all her bulk, she was the least obtrusive of women. When she left, Nirode turned to watch Dharma.

Dharma had his head bowed low over the magazine so that his copious white hair was like a plume of white smoke against the flagrant sunset sky. Nothing else about his attitude could be called theatrical — his dark face seemed shrouded in the worn old leather of historic tombs, his gently closed mouth and the heavy lids that always remained, at least partly, over his searching, troubling eyes, all denoted withdrawal, composure, reserve. One looked at his paintings which seemed studies of the finer secrets of nature — the mauve, sealed lip of a sea-wet shell, the moist underside of a flake of peeled bark, a silent growth of anthill and fungi, half in shadow, half in light — and when one looked up into the face that observed, apprehended and shrouded these wonderful facts in its private and somehow tragic mystery, one was left strangely uneasy, melancholic. Dharma's house was as quiet as his face. He rarely, if at all, came out of that narrow front door into the lane. His days and nights were spent in his two large, open studios and this secret garden with its deep pond. His past had been very different and he had lived elsewhere, his work had once been less confined and recondite. One wondered where his veiled eyes wandered to, to what his heart reached, as his hands worked amongst twigs and pebbles, paints and rags, and he turned out, in surrealistically magnified form, these seldom seen aspects of leaf and earth to an audience that seemed, at the very most, to amuse him.

Now he turned the pages of the limp little magazine with long fingers and ran their tips along the lines of a short poem, as though he were reading Braille. These lines immediately became excruciatingly painful to Nirode and he was relieved when Dharma turned to the line drawings that illustrated the article on the painter who had done the cover design and lettering of the title: *Voice*. He studied them without expression, then ran his fingertips over them delicately, nervously. Having done so, he turned rapidly to the next page. He seemed to devour each word, each asterisk but entirely without hunger and without satisfaction. In his paintings there was nothing but evidence of his senses at work, yet in the man they seemed completely absent.

When he came to the blank back cover, pale grey and white, he ran the whole lined palm of his hand over it and turned to Nirode. 'What do you think of it?' he asked him gently and sweetly. 'Are you pleased with it, my friend?'

Nirode ran his fingers through his hair, streaked grey with dust as with age and harassment. 'Don't ask me, Dharma. It's fresh from the press — I had to come and show it to you, immediately, almost before I looked at it myself. I can't tell yet. All I know is, I feel immeasurably more involved and responsible than I had thought I would. It *pains* me.' He ripped out the unhappy word unwillingly.

'I will tell you what I think,' said Dharma and taking Nirode's arm led him down to the garden where they walked around the pond in the crowding twilight. He made his observations in brief, precise sentences, dealing with the magazine page by page, each imprinted, it seemed, upon a phenomenal memory. Those veiled eyes of his, shadowy and saurian, seemed to be fitted with magnifying contact lenses: when he painted, he focussed them on minute portions of vegetable and animal matter, seeing each pore as a minor volcano. This same acute gaze he now applied to Nirode's *Voice*, Nirode listened intently and found himself agreeing with all that was said. (Dharma was the only man whose criticism and advice Nirode took seriously and then his seriousness was wholehearted and unflawed). Sifting through all the material, Nirode found that Dharma approved of a very austere and quiet lyric of David's, an appreciation of Tagore's paintings by a young journalist who had unexpectedly come up with it to Nirode in the coffee house, some book reviews that Nirode had done and little else. He disapproved of the paper, the print, the colours employed, questioned Nirode about the finances of it and immediately picked out all the loop-holes.

'The foundation is so shaky, the structure will have to double its strength. How will you do that? Firstly, do not shun crude attraction value. Alter the size, indulge in better paper and enlarge the print — who is so keen on reading an unknown poet's work as to ruin his eyes over it? Also, you are not doing honour to the poet if you reduce the print every time you come to his work. That will cost money, I know. Here is where you can cut down costs — cut out these illustrations. You cannot, in any case, afford the best of them, so why put up with the third rate? And talking of drawings, I admit I do not care for my old friend Ranen Sen's cover design. He has marked *Voice* with a tombstone and it will be hard for you to break that reputation and place it on another shelf when your next issue appears. This same idea dealt with a little more freely...' and with a twig he quickly made a drawing in the dust under the temple tree. Appropriately, a flower, just browning at the edges, dropped into its centre as though bestowing approval. Nirode nodded and they paced on, padding through the heavy, listless warmth of a summer night. A white moth blundered into their faces, then sped away over those vines and bushes, white-flowered and sweet-scented, so beloved of the Bengali. In the house Gita Devi was performing her *puja* — they heard her little brass bell tinkling, her large, hoarse conch shell honking ominously and saw the lights of her *diyas* flicker before an array of brass and flower, vermilion and saffron. The air was loaded with her odorous piety as with summer.

'How much time have you before the next issue appears?'

'Two months.'

'Splendid, that is quite sufficient for you to redo the entire design. If you follow my plan, you can cut down on the number of pages, enlarge their size...' Nirode felt a pang of protest within him arising out of a wan tenderness for the day-old magazine, so pale and barely breathing and at the same time, anger with himself for having betrayed to Dharma, at having invited collaboration when he had determined that aloneness was to be the very foundation of this venture. He thought of Professor Bose's wry query as to whether an audience was what he wanted — association, response — and he replied now: No, of course not, but can I? Why did I? Oh, if I had to, then Dharma was the best man for it — but did I have to? The memory of his unhappy confession to Dharma of his involvement now made him catch his breath as he suppressed a groan and he interrupted Dharma's measured cogitation with a completely irrelevant remark.

In an effort to overcome this early, regrettable betrayal of privacy, Nirode accepted an invitation to dinner and was determined to alter the entire tone of the evening during the course of it. They sat on mats at one end of the kitchen while Gita Devi served them in heavy-breathing silence, talking to each other only, acknowledging her second helpings of fish and rice with mute nods, only occasionally glancing up at the alcove at the other end of the room where bright plaster images of her chosen deities sported amidst marigolds and oil lamps. Dharma demanded news of the big city, Nirode supplied it and it was to remain always unknown whether Gita Devi cared to listen in or not.

'Jit is considering leaving his firm — though he has not told me so in so many words — and joining up. He is waiting to see if *Voice* will be a success. Of course I tell him it will *never* be a success, it can't be, it was not planned as one. Simply because there are too few people who would want to read it. He won't believe me, though he says he does. He feels one can educate people and make them read it. But education's all rot and the instinct is missing. Jit's wrong, Jit's fatal, if he touches my *Voice,* he will kill it. Have you noticed this black magic touch of Jit's? I think he is possessed by black spirits.'

'Yes and his wife also.'

'Have you met her?' Nirode was astonished. He regarded Dharma as eternally solitary and inaccessible, certainly never in conjunction with women such as Sarla and thought momentarily of the dark flesh in the gaps of her green attire. Gita Devi came in with a dish of sweets, enormous and sunken in thick syrup, and immediately withdrew, slow and dignified as a great duck.

'He brought her to see me once — they wanted to buy a picture. She asked to see one in brown and gold. I asked her why and she replied that those were the colours of her drawing room. I said nothing and went back to my studio. I believe they waited a while, then left. There was nothing but vacancy where that episode had been, where they had stood. That is their fatality.'

Nirode spoke of Sonny, laughing. 'He is in a bad way, I haven't seen him so dejected since they left their Babulpur estate. I told you of the fishery, didn't I? And Sonny believed fish were multiplying and fattening in his marshes and that in no time at all the canning factory would be coming up, and an export licence be issued, and we should sit down to dinner every night and feast on Sonny's fat shrimps. But then he paid a visit to that oily solicitor of his — Khan, I think his name is. He wears rings on his fingers, huge coloured stones set in bright gold — and picks his teeth with a matchstick. Sonny went bouncing in, expecting the first bulging wad of cash to be handed over and was told instead that the whole enterprise had had a great set-back. It seems the industry is scourged by the most terrible bandits in history since the thugs.'

'Bandits?'

'Yes, armed and escorted bandits, black villains every one. One night they cut the dam that surrounds Sonny's fishery and flooded three-quarters of his stock into their own marshes. When Sonny's men went out to fish next morning, all they found was mud and slush — no water, no fish.'

'It would happen to poor Sonny. He has taken it to court?'

'Impossible. Khan says they are the most wily bandits in the business, it's impossible to pin anything on them. They heard of

50

Sonny's accusations and they invited him and Khan to a sumptuous breakfast out in their own fishery. They served them with curried lobsters and pastries from Firpo. They discussed the problem of thieving in fisheries and came to the conclusion that nothing could be done about it.'

'Then it has failed? Sonny has given it up?'

'No, no, not Sonny, he's our most indomitable optimist. He's borrowed a vast sum of money and put it into another stock of stinking fish. He says it is only a temporary set-back. But he is morose — and so am I. I had hoped to see something of the profits myself.'

'It is better not to. Sonny might have expected you to put in one of his pictures as a mark of appreciation.'

'Little lambs frisking in flowery fields? Never.'

After the meal Dharma showed Nirode his latest canvases. It took a great deal of painstaking study to reduce these overpoweringly magnified details of minute slivers of bark, or masses of dead and etiolated leaves, to their proper proportions. Nirode felt himself a wandering caterpillar as he roved up and down the fine and rough, the grained and silken textures that spanned the huge canvases and always he foundered. It seemed to him that, like the blunt head of a caterpillar, he was nosing about the paradox of Dharma — Dharma who had made that dramatic exit from the city to come to the still remoteness of this walled garden and the massed green life within it, but had never cut the fine and golden relationships that still strung him to the life of the city and so often felt his way to them, held on to and questioned them. All these delicately stirring and proliferating roots, the gigantic patterns of leaf and flower into which they erupted, these seemed to envelop and protect him, on the one hand burying and obliterating him and, on the other, offering him a new and secret existence in a mythical underworld of his own creation. At the same time, there was a resemblance between those tautly drawn tendrils and roots to the multi-seriate telegraph wires and telephone lines that not only led out of but also into the city. It did not appear to Nirode that

Dharma was creating a new sphere of animated nature to which to escape, but that he was illustrating a myth that bore a constant relationship to a reality he had, for some reason, rejected and for no reason loved.

It would not do to question Dharma, so all friends of Dharma had long ago discovered and Nirode could only draw his little finger down the pale velvet of a blue-green leaf saying, 'There was a plant with leaves just like this in Kalimpong. I used to like stroking and fondling them, quite lasciviously,' and his questions were restricted to 'Ink mixed up with paint here, Dharma?' and 'Doesn't this sand crumble away after a bit?' Dharma made brief replies. He had picked up a cat's hair brush and begun to work in lines so minute that Nirode could see little point in bothering about them at all. Were they the veins of a transparent leaf or of a bee's wing drawn taut as a screen against a nocturnal sun? Nirode watched till his eyes tired of the effort required to draw Dharma's lines into correct focus, and then he sat in the open doorway, watching bats streak away through the dense violet air, low-hanging and heavy with the intoxicating odour of night flowers.

'Dharma,' he said suddenly, 'is it for the sake of painting mushrooms and wings that you came here?'

Dharma had his back turned to the open doorway, but somehow his big, bent shoulders conveyed a faint and inscrutable smile on his lips, a half-lifting of those heavy eye-lids. 'Yes,' he said, 'partly. Not quite. If it were only that, I should have gone much further away, shouldn't I? As far as your home, Kalimpong, who knows?'

'Then —'

But Nirode and his friends had started upon far too many such discussions with Dharma and they had never led through a mystery, that Dharma seemed quite to enjoy, to an acceptable explanation. Perhaps one day the painter would put down his brush, wipe his hands on a rag, turn to them and speak. But tonight he smiled his familiar smile, teasing and yet remote and asked, 'Are you going to hold a brief for Calcutta, your adopted city? All right then, I am listening. Persuade me.'

'That it is worth your return? That it is alive, challenging, satisfying, constantly in the throes of destruction and rebirth?'

'Persuade me . To me it is dead and I do not return to visit a tomb. I see the lights going out one by one, all those faint, ineffectual blue gas flares that line the streets. I see it sinking inch by inch into the marsh. The river is silting up: ships will not come up it much longer. The old mansions and all those eyeless marble nymphs are crumbling away. One day they will burn the last tram, hurl the last brick and then even the mob will fall away. Business will dwindle. Artists will grow old. The refugees will begin to drift away from their filthy haven and die before they get away from it. And then, my friend, where will Calcutta be? Buried and gone and no archaeologist will ever bother to excavate the Victoria Memorial. It will be lost irretrievably and to me it is lost already.'

'Ah, Dharma, you have been reading the newspapers: I should never have believed it of you. Why not come and visit one of the younger artists' studios? Why not go to an all-night music conference, just for the spectacle of us emotional Bengalis getting thoroughly tiddly on music? Or go to a tea auction! I defy you to hear funeral drums anywhere.'

'That is because there are none in your own heart, young Nirode. I heard them long ago and obediently lay down and died — as far as Calcutta was concerned. I don't think she noticed me creep away to live on elsewhere. As far as she is concerned I am dead and I return the compliment to her.'

'Then you are being purely subjective about it after all!' Dharma washed his brush carefully in a jar of turpentine, then turned to Nirode. His lids were drawn low over his eyes, but he was chuckling. 'Nirode,' he said, 'I think you will make a good editor. I think *Voice* is good for you. It seems to have started up a dynamo inside you. When I heard it, I mistook it for my own pulse.' He picked up a palette and began to work again with cloistered concentration.

Rumbling and quaking, the little shack leant this way and that, the tin roof lifted up at the edges, then at the centre — a tin roof that cracked like gun shot in the storm — and so loud was the thunder that Nirode roared back at it, 'Shut up, shut up, will you, won't let me hear myself swear? You shut up!' But the storm heaved and blew and howled and the little room cowered beneath it, grovelled and complained. It had no window so finally Nirode had to tear open the door and go out on to the roof for air. A tumult of air met him in wild, joyful greeting and immediately he was gladdened, lightened, cooled. Out on the roof there was no hideous noise of war and bullying but only the rain streaming down, washing over him evenly, lushly. He lifted his head, drank gulletfuls of it, spouted out a mouthful, whooped and shivered and leant over the parapet to feel it flow over him and down into the city below which now floated, now sank into the floodwater like a monster ark. Watching the sodden walls of unlit houses peel away in the wet, film posters dissolve and fade, seeing motor cars and trams stranded hub-high in water, noticing how the crowds had melted away and only a solitary rickshaw — heroically mobile amidst all the waterlogged vehicles — churned and splashed nobly through, it was easy to believe in Dharma's prophecy, to see in the annual monsoon the shape and design of the final dissolution.

Dissolution — glorious thought. Newsprint and manuscript, proofs and printing errors had so suffused his brain, stuffed his eyes and choked his mouth that gladly would he have offered the whole heap of paper and livelihood and honour up to the monsoon, offering them like a fleet of paper boats to drift away on the flood. Now he lowered his head and felt the rain stream through his long hair and pour across his face and down his neck and at least some of that squalid, frustrating existence was washed away, as small-pox and cholera were washed away by the lavish annual monsoon. Now a barrow loaded with mangoes was dragged through the water, the fruit cleansed and brilliant green, streaked with pink and gold. A light was lit, its tail darted across the waterway. Though the rain lightened, the sky darkened and in the night the sodden sagging city regained some pride, some brilliance and Nirode hung over it, a dripping gargoyle — grotesque, offensive, comic emblem of the black and powerful magical rites of the city, one of its many...

When the rain softened to an even drumming on the tin roof, he returned to its shelter, tore off his clothes and lay naked on the mat, picked up some proofs and began mechanically to correct them while one half of him lay already lulled and asleep. He was exhausted — quarrels with the press, interminable discussions with uncooperative artists and touchy writers, the humiliating and tedious search for advertisements, for funds, these marked his hours and days with harsh urgency and he was sick of it all. By the time a new issue of *Voice* appeared and he set about peddling it from bookshop to bookstall, there was little pleasure left in the sight of the increasingly slender volumes that he shaped and formed... So sordid was the struggle for survival that, like the deluged city, it hardly looked worth the hard work of making it survive. Better for it to drown, for it all to drown, city and paper boat, man, thought and disease.

When day flared out of the damp mass of clouds and dully lit the puddles on the concrete roof on which he lived and quickly settled about the corrugated iron shed, he wondered why he toiled at it still. Only in defiance of the subscribers who were already suspiciously and angrily demanding why they hadn't had their promised money's worth? The monotony of the work appalled him and he was not altogether indifferent to the miseries imposed on him by living in this small tin shed to which he had moved from Sonny's more spacious and fantastic dwelling because he could no longer bear, he said, the odour of dogs kept indoors. Sonny was hurt but came to visit him and cried out in horror at the cockroaches that waggled their whiskers out of every crack in the walls, and at the filth of the little food stall on the pavement below where he ate his meals.

'But Nirode, must you?'

'What a boob you are, Sonny. You know just how much the magazine makes. Nil. I'm still in the red.'

'But only Jit knows that and he'll forget it the minute you ask him to. Now, now,' he stuttered, backing towards the door. 'I know you're proud, I respect your pride —'

'Pride. How does pride get involved in this?' And Nirode brought his foot down on a large and arrogant cockroach There was a gritty scrunch and they looked at the yellow miasm on the floor with blank disbelief.

'There must be,' Sonny persisted bravely. 'If there weren't you could so simply go and stay with your mother, while you wrote or edited.'

'Look, do me a favour. Don't keep bringing my family in, Sonny boy. I know you have no existence without that painted backdrop of Babulpur behind you. Remove those portraits of turbanned ancestors, remove those tatty leopard skins and silver polo trophies and you would vanish yourself, like a bloody moth when the cupboard is aired . I neither inherited nor do I now borrow a single damn thing from *my* family. May they rot, may they flourish — as long as they leave me alone and I'll hand this to them — they more or less do.'

'Now, now.'

'You're getting as tautological as that booby Bose. He's become a pest with that fat manuscript of his he keeps trying to ram down my throat — his own interpretation of the *Panchatantra,* as though the *Panchatantra* needed any interpretation. I told him if he did one of the *Kama Sutra,* I might consider it. That got rid of him. God, this blasted rain. Like one hundred latrines flushing all around you. I could do with a bottle of rum. But your fisheries are still floundering, aren't they, Sonny?'

'Ah, I'm afraid so. All I can afford these days is coffee.'

'Coffee'll do.'

It did well and the coffee house reeked, during the monsoon of drenched umbrellas and muddy shoes. The damp and the soft, corrupt growth of mildew filled the brash hall with their own pluvial aura. Yet the crowds grew denser and young men came in from the rain and flooded streets, more than ever in the spirit of adventure and of camaraderie, for a cup of coffee while they waited for the rains to subside and the trams to start moving again, towards cinemas and cheap bars. When Nirode entered he was always faintly astonished to find how many young men besides himself were unemployed or, at any rate, unoccupied at unusual hours for long stretches of time.

Here he met friends and foes and he had many of both. One taut and angry young poet who had waited for him all the week at the coffee house, grew furious when Nirode carelessly told him. 'Sorry, I don't have your MS with me, you'll have to collect it from my place if you want it back,' and began to complain and argue, whereupon Nirode sat down at his table and told him, in succint terms, his opinion of that MS. Silenced, the poet scuffled off in shaking rage, but Nirode called him back. 'You'd better pay for your coffee, I won't. I'm not that kind of an editor.' While he paid, Nirode muttered some lines from his poetry with a scorn that soon dissolved in huge laughter.

'Ever since last autumn,
I have loved you from my heart's bottom—

'Poor woman that, to be loved from such an angle,' he roared and he recited other outrageous howlers that he had collected in his few months of editorship, to a table that quaked and rippled in appreciation. 'Dharma suggests I collect them and make up a nonsense issue.'

'Oh, have you seen him? What's he up to, the shady old devil?' For once he had intrigued them. Once he had only to stalk into the coffee house, leonine, inscrutable, aloof, to make heads turn and young men call out greetings filled with respect and mystification. And yet, when he had ceased to come, few had missed him, though they had taken to analysing all possible motives for his sudden and abrupt departure. With the rains wafting old ghosts about in the uncertain lamplight, old doubts and puzzles regained their attraction.

'It was his last exhibition that did it,' was Bose's theory. 'He sold one painting to a relation of his wife's who had made up his mind to make money on it *somehow,* even if he sold it at one rupee profit. And he was approached by one American tourist who asked him if he would decorate her new pig-skin travelling kit with those "dreadfully erotic, tendrilly things you're so marvellous at." So then he moved out to Barrackpore and never held another exhibition.'

'But then he might have retreated all the way out to a desert or up a mountain and never met anyone at all.'

'Ah, how can he? He was born in Calcutta. His house is one of the oldest in Bow Bazaar, it is next to the most fabulous sweet shop in Bengal. He will never be able to tear up his roots and transplant them. He needs the Calcutta earth, the Calcutta air.'

'But he says these are the very things that poisoned him, nearly killed him.'

Jit who had, as usual, been reluctant to go home after work, removed his pipe from his mouth to say, 'I'm surprised none of you recalls the event that really led to his retirement. He had a daughter who died of cholera during one summer epidemic. She must have meant much to him because his wife thought he would lose his mind if he lived on in the same house where she had died and so they moved.'

In the brief silence that followed, the rains seemed to soften and even the close and warm conviviality of that evening coffee session was gravely undermined. Then Bose cleared his throat and called to the waiter, 'One double-egg omelette here and two plates of chips — in double-quick time too!' and Sonny clapped his hands for more coffee crying, 'Oh, aren't the rains jolly when one is safely out of them!' But Nirode left and Jit followed him.

'You're not walking home in this weather. And the trams aren't moving yet,' Jit said and, taking Nirode's arm, led him into his waiting car. It had begun to rain hard again. Nirode sat back against the upholstered seat and watched the wash of rain upon the window turn silkily from night to wine to neon to night again. He laughed.

'I haven't felt so like a filthy fat plutocrat since — I can't remember when.'

'A fine plutocrat you make by selling five hundred copies of your magazine once in three months.'

'We're down to a more realistic three hundred now.'

'Realistic!' Jit sneered through his thick smoke screen. 'Do you really believe you are being realistic when you try to earn your living by editing that absurd little paper of yours that only a handful of insignificant writers and artists ever read?'

'There are livings and livings, Jit,' Nirode said in a friendly way, for he was enjoying the sheen of streaming water and the dramatic city glowing through it with its own brilliant eccentricity. He talked with greater pleasantness than he usually showed Jit. 'I live in a room for which I pay a rent of fifteen rupees — because it isn't a room, only a corrugated iron shack someone erected on his rooftop to house his pigeons: they all died.' He laughed. turning towards Jit. 'I'm sure you didn't even know rooms with such rents were available — for you they come in the one thousand rupee bracket, don't they? Well, it wouldn't house your Rajasthani miniatures or your bronze collection, but it houses me. For meals — I scrounge off friends. It's amazing how many willing victims we parasites find ourselves. Society must have some kind of guilt complex about us after all. As for clothes, I haven't needed any for a long time now. When I do — tell me. what *shall* I do?' Inevitably the two of them walked together up an alley into a dead end of mutual malice and contempt. 'Perhaps you could tell your wife to think of me next time she weeds out the old stuff from amongst your London suits.'

'My wife. It might even occur to her to do that. She asked me the other day whether my seedy friend had managed to get a room and three drinks a night and whether he was writing, painting or composing his masterpiece. Which reminds me, we're having some people over for cocktails tonight and I'm late. Will you let the driver take me home before he drops you?'

But in the porch, while the car muttered a respectful reminder of the cocktail party; Jit lingered. and was obviously disinclined to go up the sweeping staircase to his spacious and discreetly ornate flat or to his large, voluptuous wife. He put his face in at the window and spoke hurriedly, as though he were afraid of being overheard, 'I would like better to come to your place, Nirode. I should prefer to come with you and have a long talk.'

'Would you? Well, I haven't invited you nor will I. What's more, you'd be a bloody idiot to desert your miniatures and your bronzes and, most important of all, that bar full of bottles and bottles of booze.' And, he silently added, your rich, rutting wife and the hearty clap on your shoulder from your beefy British boss as he tells you you're a good sort, down for a big promotion soon, Charley. But he only said, 'For so many bottles of booze, I don't know if I wouldn't sell my own stinking soul, if I got the offer,' and he got out of the car and left the puzzled driver and a nervous Jit to appeal to his back as he strolled away through the rain, between the dripping oleanders, towards the nearest bar and a more convivial group of friends.

'My golden son,' his mother wrote in her impulsive hand. 'There is reason for me to forget you entirely. I have almost forgotten how many months it is since you wrote last. It is over a year, I know. It is very melancholy now in the rains, I have not left the house for days. I look out on one vast waterfall. Occasionally the rain thins and the mist lifts and I see the outlines of the bamboo grove, or one white flower, but never the gay prayerflags or my red-cheeked Pem Pem. The azaleas have been brought into the veranda for shelter, they are very sodden and sad, the flowers chilled. I would like to sit by the fire but it is so shrouded with damp, steaming laundry, I keep far away. This is the sort of weather when we would all sit on the old Tibetan rug and play Ludo and Monopoly, snap and mah-jong. I was so crazy as to persuade Major Chadha to play a game of Monopoly with me last night and in no time we were reduced to a pair of squabbling children and I spent the night with my many gay memories of my children when they were small, scarcely bigger than my Tibetan terriers and so much sillier.'

Nirode considered tearing it up and scattering the fragments in the river below, but it would have been a melodramatic thing to do and, grimacing, he pocketed the letter. He knew, also that he would be drawn to read it again, if only for the sake of resurrecting the feel of the chilled white azaleas brought in wet from the rain. He grasped the iron rail and found it slippery still with large rain-drops. There had been a break in the rains that afternoon and the sky was mobile with torn shreds of white cloud racing on the grey surface of the stationary ones, and pools of sky and light between them, pale and apocalyptic. Steamers and tugs wore a washed and chastened look, they were shining black blobs on the cloud-and-light reflecting river. People held their umbrellas furled, their shoes were polished with rain. A vendor walked by with a great basket of roasted gram and monkeynuts on his head, a little pot of fire in the centre of it and the clean evening air was spiced with the odour of hot, roasted nuts.

Nirode drew away from them, close to the running water. It was the first time in three weeks that he had left his room except for necessary visits to the tea-stall below and he felt like a man who has spent three years in jail and emerges to find he is afraid of the plangent and populated world. He folded his arms closely about himself and wished he had a bell to ring. I am a leper, he wanted to ring and call, leave me, do not come near. I am a leper, diseased with the loneliest disease of all.

It had to do with *Voice,* but only partly. He had not paid the press and they refused to release the next issue till he did. He had not paid a single contributor so far. Both the quantity and quality of the material sent in was diminishing at an appalling rate, for even those who had rejoiced to discover a magazine with certain aesthetic standards to which they also adhered, were now discouraged. Many people would have helped, financially, had he only approached them — his mother the first, who would have let loose a monsoon of money to fall at his feet. Was he a fool, childish and stubborn, not to reply to her letters, not to do what she so powerfully willed him to do — request her for love and assistance, admit that he needed them in order to live? But the habit of withdrawal had become too strong, the history behind it grown too illustrious to discard. Jit, too, was there, waiting, willing to do more than merely collect advertisements and supply the basic funds, if only Nirode made this vital admission. There were others as well, relations — the elderly aunt in Ballygunge with her dusty legacy, for instance. But Nirode grew more and more wary of contact with them or with anyone. The intricacies of relationship — approach, recompense, obligation

61

— these aroused in him violent distaste and kept him hovering on the fringe of the world that invited and spurned by turns, and for which he daily cared less. He had grown chary even of artists and writers in whom he had, for many years, quixotically believed. Dharma's advice and interest had proven hollow, stillborn and had never been pursued. Once he had received a grudging kind of recognition in the form of an invitation to a poetry reading by a circle of eminent Bengali poets, known and lauded by an intimate group of admirers, all conscious of this exclusive eminence of theirs, of the holiness of their profession and their nobility in pursuing it. In their beautifully mannered way, they had been kind and had offered help in the form of translations. They had made his hair stand on end. Recoiling from the polished elegance of their terribly refined little society, from their lilting verses that rang with spiritual melancholy, meandering conventional images and flatly sentimental sweetness, he had behaved with ferocious gaucherie. He knew, when he left, that they were shaking their heads over his crassness and enquiring how so ill-bred, so arrogant a youth could aspire to the stature of a literary editor. A man had to have silver locks for that, drape himself in immaculate white and keep apart from the coffee house crowd, upon an Olympian hilltop. Spitting his cigarette into the gutter, Nirode had raucously sung on the streets a Tagore ditty, somehow contriving to make it sound ludicrous and obscene and making a parked rickshaw coolie guffaw. Now he could think of no one to whom he cared to talk or listen. *Voice* was a farce. He respected no single contributor, his letters of acceptance and rejection were usually formal and uninspiring. He had formed no glorious bridge of contact between them and himself nor between them and their dwindling number of readers. He wondered if contact had ever been the intent of this venture.

The glowing embers and ashes of the sunset sky were now beginning to dim, the molten gold of the river turning to murk and he leant over the railing, wondering if this was the climax of the failure he himself had willed. He had failed obviously but where was the will to get up, select another ladder and begin the journey of absurdity all over again? He had talked to David of the pursuit of failure with grandiose and adolescent authority. Now he was — not dismayed, no, he had never believed in the magazine so much as to be depressed by its sorry condition — but left flat, inert, reluctant to rise to his feet again, to start the weary business of constructing a new and still more hopeless adventure. The book he had meant to write, once he had created the proper conditions for the writing of it, seemed no more urgent now than it had one misty autumn night long ago when he had first thought of this plan. Nothing existed but this void in which all things appeared equally insignificant, equally worthless. Would he one day, he wondered, walk to the temple at the edge of this void, lay himself down on the flagstones smoothed and oiled by the passage of so many worshippers, bow his head at the feet of an inscrutably smiling idol and, inhaling the dense smog of incense, give himself up to the tolling of bells and a silent, shapeless God? The question had no substance, for Nirode knew he would never approach a God housed in a temple bustling with libidinous priests, vendors of garlands and plaster images and women perspiring with piety. That odour of hair-oil, joss sticks and decaying flowers, the odour of worship, made his stomach heave.

He was wearied by his own unsureness in which he swept back and forth like a long weed undulating under water, a weed that could live only in aqueous gloom, would never rise and sprout into clear daylight. He was proud to the point of being a fanatic, he was intense enough to be capable of whole-hearted dedication — yet he drifted, a shadowy cipher and his life consisted of one rejection following another. He loathed the world that could offer him no crusade, no pilgrimage and he loathed himself for not having the true, unwavering spirit of either within him. There was only this endless waiting, hollowed out by an intrinsic knowledge that there was nothing to wait for.

Now the tumult of monsoon clouds rose to bury the flagrant sun, black silhouettes were ripped apart and toppled, roses and ashes rioted, mocking the black squalor of the grimed city beneath — unlit, exhausted, waiting for the kinder night. Was it true, what Dharma said, that this was a poisoned city and he who breathed its air was doomed? Would there be escape then in leaving it and returning to — but no, return was as pointless as proceeding on the journey and, standing stock still, he saw nothing progress, nothing advance, but everything turn slowly about him and fall in a shower of ashes and rain.

He knew now that vocations and employment need be no more stable than human relationships, that one could tire of editing poetry as one could tire of an old love. That one merely touched devotion to an art, to a creed, as one touched, so slightly, the heart or hand of another human being — and as soon as the touch ended, the sensation was forgotten and one turned to other business, other men, women. To think that all through his life he had despised his father and adored his mother, only to turn, after his father's death, to pity for him and loathing of that same, unchanged mother — this moved him now. He felt that his belief in *Voice,* whatever of it had existed, was passing away and, with instinctive pessimism, he feared the strain of another occupation, another dream beginning as, the world told him, it must.

He hung upon the railing, watching. the fishing boats bob up and down on a river that ran purple and black, in the slumped attitude of a lifeless creature just let down from the gallows. Then David, walking up with the cloth bag over his shoulder, looking a little more ragged and dirty than before, touched his shoulder and Nirode leapt. When he faced David he was panting. He had expected the priest with the lighted faggot come to set fire to the wooden pyre of one dead dream and to light the fire of another.

'David!' he exclaimed and to calm his confusion he jerked a cigarette out of a crumpled packet. 'Do you know, I was hanging around here, waiting to see a leper so putrid as to make me want to go to Mother Teresa's hospital and begin to nurse the poor boobs. Or to meet a sailor who would offer me a job on his ship. D'you think it's significant that I looked around and saw you instead?'

David chuckled his shy, self-effacing chuckle and grew pink as a rabbit's nose with pleasure at finding a responsive and communicative Nirode .

'Everyone told me they hadn't seen you for weeks, so I came down to the Strand. I thought you might be here.'

The Strand was no place for chance encounters. In summer it was too crowded with families that spilled out of the stifling city for a breath of south breeze and an ice-cream and for the rest of the year it was deserted. The two regarded each other with matched delight and curiosity, then began to stroll across the Strand, past the low hillocks of Fort William, across the sodden Maidan where flocks of sheep roamed bleating under the great trees and around the bullet-grey statues of past Governors of Bengal. They were dirty and spotted with rose and saffron and were being driven to the slaughter-houses. Swallows darted and flocked about the pale bulbous dome of Victoria Memorial. Light-haired children in stately English prams were being wheeled out of the Cathedral park. But on Chowringhee and in the rolling tram, the atmosphere was different and they drew closer together defensively, uncomfortable on seats that had half their foam rubber filling ripped out of them, resenting the close odour of perspiration and hair oil mingling upon dirty necks. They sat watching the flash and flare of neon and naphtha spotlighting rapacious women in the markets, swooping upon gay *saris,* gold ornaments and sacks of grain and sugar.

'What did you do in Shantiniketan, Davy? I thought you were going for just a week.'

'Ah yes, but I stayed to study the *veena.'*

'Really, Davy, you are going all the way, aren't you, becoming that familiar Occidental eccentric who goes astray in the Orient, takes to wearing rags and open sandals, drinks unboiled water, eats native food and the rest of it. So far your ceramics at least were all your own, you never painted parrots or elephants — or did you? But now it's the *veena* and Indian music is fatal. Once you sit crosslegged on the ground and give yourself up to Indian music, Davy, the game is lost, there's no hope left for you.'

David smiled. The tram slowed . A brass band trumpeted past on its way to a wedding. The tram ground on.

'In the end you'll turn Hindu. You'll discover a *guru* fasting on some grisly mountaintop and become his disciple, draped in Mission orange. But I must admit I can't see you wandering about with a begging bowl. Perhaps you'll be a *yogi* who never needs to eat.'

David smiled, blinked. There were many things he wanted to ask Nirode, about himself and his magazine, but he could not get a word in, for Nirode was off on a compulsive talking spree, never pausing to allow David to answer or comment. David was uncertain whether this was because Nirode was truly so interested in his affairs or was only covering up the tumult of a deep unease, or whether he was mocking, praising or envying David. He reached up to buy the tickets with a rabbity pride, immediately hiding them away in his bag.

When Nirode paused to glare at a man who had knocked his head with a stout umbrella handle, David said shyly, 'It will be some time before I can set off in search of my *guru*. I have a lot of work to do before I can take that holiday.'

'The *veena,* you mean?'

'No — ceramics. I've deserted them for so long. I must get back to clay again.'

'And have you taken a room at that robbing house again where they called you a P.G. and fed you on left-overs from their plates?

'Oh Nirode, they never did that, I'm sure. Only the leftovers in the cooking-pots.'

'Uagh — I remember that mess of cooked green bananas you once made me eat there.'

David laughed. 'You gave a very realistic imitation of being sick on the stairs when you left but I don't have that room any longer. I couldn't afford to keep it on while I was at Shantiniketan. I'm looking about again. Last night I slept at the Ramakrishna Mission. They'll have me till I find a place suitable for setting up my things.'

'There, I told you, you were turning crazy in the very best tradition of eccentric Western theosophists,' Nirode declared with satisfaction.

Satisfaction, too, was the key-note of a meal of tepid tea and potato fritters eaten out on the roof, above the city and while they sat smoking, Nirode decided that if there was one person whose presence, even at this stage, did not revolt him, it was David, who was too like a familiar, cheerful little budgerigar, or a tough little potted plant, to be objectionable as other men were to him. When David went to stuff the greasy newspaper and earthenware tumblers into a rubbish bin at the head of the stairs, he even smiled ironically, thinking that now he had acquired the power of a true anarchist, the power to attract a disciple. He knew he could make David stay if he wanted, fetch him his tea and cigarettes, run errands to the press and post office and various patrons and subscribers, console and hearten him with his guileless trust. Was he so weak now as truly to need a whipping-boy? One might as well marry, he thought briefly, with a twisted smile. Yet, when David returned, he lay back against the parapet and said, 'This roof would be an ideal place for you to spread out your clay and paints and things, wouldn't it? Once the rains are over, that is, and then of course the room is an oven.'

At night the rains broke again, washing out the lights and sounds of the city below, drowning all traffic and bustle and life, isolating them in their crackling, thundering shelter and imbuing their conversation with an adventurousness that appealed powerfully to the schoolboy in both of them. As they sat smoking and talking, the pinpoint beams of their cigarettes the only illumination since the storm had blown out the electricity, they knew they were too comfortable to alter the arrangement, at least for the time being. They lay down on the mat to sleep, unusually at peace.

The corrugated iron shelter was soon crowded to bursting point with the tools of David's art. Jars and bowls and pots of clay littered the roof. In time a miniature kiln appeared, a gift from a philanthropic American who was interested in promoting Indian handicrafts and, in his search for a suitable Indian craftsman to promote, had confusedly picked David. With the kiln came other potters and ceramists and their litter, waiting to be fired or emerging from the fire. Amongst them was an impeccably well-dressed young woman whose pots always drooped, melted or collapsed, but she went on potting, blithely undeterred, till one day very early in the morning she came upon Nirode lying asleep and naked on his mat, and fled, to David's vast relief. David worked like an ant, hunched about his work as if he were ashamed of it or wished to protect it from sight. However, he did not mind Nirode strolling across to watch and since Nirode was often busy with proofs, or off at the post office or press, they did not get on each other's nerves at all. Often they took the bus down to the coffee house. Occasionally David sold a batch of ashtrays and they celebrated at Olympia or Isiah's with rum. Sonny, envying them this conspiracy of friendship that could exist in so pure a form only between two waifs, two travellers, came often, bringing with him a packet of noodles from Peiping or a melon, scraps of gossip and news of the progress or setbacks of his fishery which had become a standing joke in all his company.

Nirode began to look less gaunt and 'criminal' as Sonny had once described him, nervously laughing. Infected by some of David's dedication and industry, he was heaving and pulling at the sinking magazine again, making it move once more without asking himself why he bothered. The work involved continued to sicken him and often he returned from a long wait in the queue at the post office to work off his frustration on David, mock and taunt him, watching carefully to see when and how much he hurt. But David's simplicity was unimpeachable and hurt to the quick by some crude taunt, he would silently turn to his work and in a little while would turn back to Nirode with perfect confidence in his resilience. Subjected to a spell of vicious leg-pulling his face would retreat, close up its pale leaves. But, inevitably, the leaves would open again slowly and with a dull glimmer as of a sensitive plant, to receive another touch. There were always the wildly gay evenings to make up for these occasions when Nirode was relaxed . David was grateful and they shared a high spirited drinking bout with a group of sailors at Isiah's or wolfed an enormous meal at some filthy Chinese soup kitchen where the food was cheap.

Only Dharma was oddly ironic. Picking up a twig and wrapping a rag around it to form a particular sort of brush he needed he asked, 'And is divorce permitted in this society? Or was the possibility of it banned from the marriage contract?'

Nirode, the perpetual baiter, could take no baiting himself. It was hot and humid and the long ride to Barrackpore in the roaring bus had exhausted him. He had come solely to show Dharma, with some pride, the new issue of *Voice* that had at last appeared after enormous obstacles being surmounted, purely on account of the publication of three short poems by a famous English poet with socialist leanings, who was on a lecture tour of India and had met Nirode and promised them to him, of which word was spread rapidly to all subscribers. Nirode was rather shamefacedly proud of these poems, none of which was very good or original but which automatically gave *Voice* a prestige it had so far lacked. Their appearance in this issue was bound to double the number of subscribers and he looked forward, with more eagerness than he cared to admit, to this new lease on life suddenly presented to the little gasping thing. Dharma had read the poems with his fingertips and said nothing, merely making some comment on the English poet's brand of socialism which involved unlimited charity to the underdeveloped East. Disappointed, Nirode turned the subject to David's forthcoming exhibition of ceramics and the living arrangement the two of them had struck up.

'What do you mean?' he asked now, hot and scowling and thoroughly annoyed.

'Merely that neither you nor David Gunney ever struck me as being made for domesticity. That little phrase about husbanding fires or candles — what is it? I always imagined you two young rebels ran away from just that and actually preferred the cold outside.'

'I'm not sure what you are talking about. Is this something that exists here in your house? Ought I to recognize it?'

He was being vicious and he would have liked to think that he had aimed well and wounded deeply, yet Dharma merely glanced in

69

his direction, a flash of very clear black and white appearing under the heavy purple lids, then sinking quickly. The painter began, slowly and with obvious delight, to coat a new canvas with a sort of rough whitewash. This he wiped off with a rag and began to prepare another, thicker wash. He said nothing more and presently Gita Devi entered with two tumblers of tepid water. Each accepted a tumbler wordlessly, as was the custom of the house, and drank. Nirode gathered up his papers and left with a curt farewell.

The lane outside was a streak of glare, white dust and sun, strident with cycle rickshaws and vendors calling their wares — earthen jugs shaped like birds, live chickens, shining steel cooking pots to be exchanged for old rags and cheap toys made of bamboo splinters, feathers and paint. The bus came lumbering down the main road that crossed the lane and Nirode began to run. His sandals slapped the thick dust, cycle rickshaws clamoured and clanged and got in his way. The bus left without him. In a vile temper by now, he leant against a rusted lamp-post, waiting for the next one. At a little distance from him, a man had set up an aerated water stall, built of flattened kerosene tins that blinked separately in the sun. Now a man in a tired *dhoti* would wander across, slap down a coin and demand a 'double-gas soda', listen with rather sheepish relish to the extra-loud pop and drink it off with many enormous, satisfied burps. A yellow bitch with long, slack teats swinging from her belly slouched about, nosing the litter of empty cigarette packets and bottle tops. People came lounging up to the bus stop, complaining about the transport service with resigned bitterness. One of them carried a big basket of dirty laundry and this he placed on the roadside and sat down in its small shade for a nap.

Nirode, at the head of the queue, had the lamp post to lean against while he smoked. He was choking with resentment against Dharma, but realized that at the heart of his anger lay a grain of insecurity. It seemed to him his friends were forcing upon him a crusade, a career, a way of life and a set of ideals that sat upon his shoulders like an iron custodian, grasping and restraining. The freedom of impulse was taken from him by these people who forced on him an idealism to which they themselves lacked the courage or opportunity to conform. Be true, they pleaded, be alone. Starve, but do not resign. Succeed — somehow, in some way — succeed in persevering, in surviving. But do not fail, do not fail us. Something — the passive force of an inborn but unconfessed religion or the memory of harder and finer times lived by other generations — prodded them into prodding him. He spat out a cigarette into the open gutter. He longed to remind them of the two rights Baudelaire had added to the rights of man — 'the right to contradict oneself and the right to leave.' He wanted to feel able to fling *Voice* to the winds, turn monkish, open a bookshop, go away, come back, as and when the instinct moved him. But he was ringed around by these many friends and enemies. Bose warned him with ironic verses from the *Panchatantra*. Dharma's encouragement was soured by his sarcasm, Sonny applauded like a trained baboon, David cleaved to him and Jit waited, sardonic and envious. He longed to tear them up like so many scraps of paper, toss them down into the gutter that ran at his feet. He stared across the road at the white, cell-like suburban houses with their barred windows and the jungle of cannas and plantains at their gates. Behind them stood factories, their busy black chimneys bayoneting the hot sky where kites wheeled with effete, listless grace.

He swung away from the lamp post and approached the aerated water stall. Bottles of virulent rose and orange soda water stared back at him, glassily insulting. He ordered one, flung out the straw and drank from the small mouth of the bottle, swilling the flat liquid about his mouth with disgust. So the magazine tasted now to him — artificial and a waste. The fact that his friends so believed in it, so encouraged it, made him despise them all the more. Yet he was responsible for it. He hated this being responsible for anything at all. How did one get rid of it? How did one avoid it? And could one, for long? Dharma and David tried to, yet they were only like marsh birds who could not fly long, but hopped along the ground, about the water, in the rushes. To be a marsh bird was not enough, their voices were broken and plaintive, their movements harried. One must be a king kite wheeling so far away in the blazing empty sky as to be merely a dot, almost invisible to the urchins who stood below, stones in their fists, ready to be aimed and flung.

71

The bus came toiling up the road. He ran to it, along with the others from the queue, feeling queasy with the awful drink swelling and fizzing inside him. He had to fight for standing room. The washerman was turned away by the conductor, but managed to leap on once the bus started up and even to haul up his laundry basket with him. The bus reeked of stale, sour laundry. Nirode felt lurching inside him an increasing burden of dissatisfaction and irresolution.

He strode across the roof, scowling bitterly at the ardent ceramists that littered it daily, thanks to the philanthropist's kiln and entering his room, found David alone inside, sitting on the floor and building a curious structure of bamboo splinters and brown paper, using no tools but his thin, nimble white fingers.

Nirode flung himself down on the shredded mat. The room was like an incinerator, its tin roof having burnt to white heat in the sun. He wiped the perspiration off his face with one sleeve. 'What the bloody hell are you up to?' he asked thickly. 'Got yourself a pet bird or something?'

'It's a lampshade,' David said with timid joy. 'I thought it would be nice to have a shade over that bulb. I had some paper to spare and pulled out some splinters from that bamboo curtain at the door.'

'How terribly clever of you,' Nirode lay down abruptly and stared up at the long cracks in the ceiling. 'So now it's bloody lampshades. What's wrong with the bulb? Perhaps you also feel the place needs little cushions and trailing plants?'

'But Nirode,' David tried to laugh him out of it but too nervously. 'You've often complained of the glare of that uncovered bulb yourself.'

'Have I? Well, I never suggested you go making little shades for it. It's there to glare, what else. Why d'you waste your time?' he added savagely. 'Why don't you clear that fairy rabble off the roof and let me have some peace again?'

David said nothing and sat still for a while, then began slowly working on the shade again. Nirode watched him, then rolled over on to his side, turned his face to the wall and fell asleep.

'I say, I say, would you like to drive down to Firpo's in the family Rolls?'

'Naughty boy, you've been drinking.'

'I swear I haven't. Get up and take a look for yourself. But do hurry: Papa is waiting and he's vastly eager to meet you.'

Nirode and David, once more amicable and buoyant hurried to the parapet and leaned far out in order to look over all the ornate balconies with their loads of grey and brown washing, down into the street. A Rolls it was and though neither Nirode nor David knew anything of such matters, it was evidently of some vintage year; an immense black hearse with ominous headlamps and navy blue curtains at the windows. Vociferous admirers thronged about it — urchins, of course, leaping up and down in excitement and making quick, adventurous darts at it and also shopkeepers who stepped out of their cigarette and green coconut booths, hitched up their slack *dhotis* and came close, chattering knowledgeably. A mad beggar who walked the street stark naked except for a battered carnival hat with a green paper plume bobbing above it, hurried up, gibbering and hopping with bent knees, putting on a dramatic performance of incredulity, awe, fear and hilarity. Glorious source of entertainment as he normally was, the urchins had no eyes for him today. In the car the chauffeur and the sole passenger in the back seat stared straight ahead of them, their lips compressed with disapproval and affronted dignity.

'Do hurry boys. Papa is so impatient to meet you,' cried Sonny. In his excitement and shrillness he somewhat resembled the madman below who had just poked an exploring finger at the rear lamp and now bounded back with his knees up in the air, hooting loudly, as the urchins stood about applauding.

Papa was indeed impatient and when the three young men clambered up into the car, he said, 'If you had taken any longer. I should have had to summon the police to clear this rabble,' and he tapped his walking stick on the window pane as a signal to the chauffeur to start. 'Firpo's,' he said.

Nirode and David, reeling like a pair of schoolboys unexpectedly being taken to the circus by a not quite real benefactor, did not

73

know whether to focus their eager attention upon him or on the unaccustomed sense of unreality and aloofness that they felt in breasting the lowly Chowringhee traffic in this ponderous hearse from another age and world, a gasping mammoth of prehistoric times.

'It's my uncle's really,' Sonny babbled, 'and he never lends it to me-oh no, Papa, I've never really asked — but when Papa comes, he very kindly puts it at our disposal.'

Papa nodded slowly. 'I am not of an age when I can undertake to start learning the exacting art of hailing taxis in Calcutta. Having just come up from the country — tea country you know — I can hardly bear to face the city, even when enclosed in this ..

'A *fortress!*' cried Sonny. 'Isn't it like a vast fortress?'

'Yes,' said Nirode. 'Keeps the rabble in its place. Outside.'

When they arrived at Firpo's, the old man shrank a little, saying, 'Now I am not sure if this is still the place to visit for tea, but in my time, in my time, I assure you, it was the most, the most...' and he trembled a little as Sonny helped him out. He preceded them up the red-carpeted staircase, Nirode and David looking distinctly beggarly as they trooped after him, beggarly in their shabbiness and in their insouciance. The waiters looked uncertain at the appearance of this strange company and seemed undecided whether to receive them or not. But Sonny's Papa led the way, as though he were sleepwalking, straight to a table by the railing of the long veranda. He sighed 'Ah', touching the table, the railing, recognizing them from a past more substantial than this papery, clownish present. He himself was ensconced in the shabby elegance of another generation. His pale vanilla silk *achkan* sat too large upon his frame and from his pocket peeped a silk handkerchief that had been dipped in cologne so old that it had soured. About his neck and jaws hung folds of loose, yellowed skin, left by a prosperity that had faded too fast, giving him a deflated appearance. On one finger he wore a ruby of alarming size and cut, but the nails were stained and broken. His face? It barely existed, was merely a semi-transparent paper mask over which flitted an indistinct shadow play of long years and changing fortunes, of bewilderment and regret.

But once the tea had been drunk and the little pastries with their pink icing and the chicken patties and sausage rolls devoured, he seemed to change, subtly but surely and an unexpected creature began to emerge from the paper cocoon of his wrinkled face. His eyes grew brighter and a smile tinted his lips as he summoned a waiter and, before his astonished guests, ordered 'Whisky and soda!' He did not immediately offer it to the boys who were still tucking into pastries and fritters, Nirode with rare voraciousness and even David aroused to unprecedented buffoonery. Papa sipped his drink merrily, growing younger and gayer by the minute, while Sonny's buoyancy subsided. He crouched on the edge of his chair and eyed his father with pleading anxiety. Now and then he tried to chatter, trying hard to distract his friends from too intently observing the old man, but they were fascinated and stared openly, beaming with joyous anticipation as the second and the third drink were ordered and consumed and the old man began to hum and eye the ladies at the neighbouring tables, began to cock his eyebrows at them and comment on contemporary fashions. He paused to take note of his thirsty guests and expansively ordered drinks for all. Nirode and David accepted the best foreign whisky they were offered, but Sonny bit his nails and refused not only liquor but even a fresh pot of tea. Behind his worried head a pink sunset flared over the blue, yellow and black traffic mingling chaotically on Chowringhee.

'Now in my time, even when we played tennis the ladies wore their skirts down to their ankles. I remember one intrepid Mrs Das Gupta, a very emancipated young woman from Oxford she was then, who played a superb game of tennis dressed in her *sari* — a white one of course. We used often to make up a foursome with Sir Timothy and Lady Birdswood at the Calcutta Club...'

'Ah, then you did come up to the city occasionally, sir?' Nirode asked sweetly. 'You did not like being buried at Babulpur all the year round?'

'Babulpur?' A loud guffaw rang out from behind a ruby-starred hand. 'Babulpur was there for my wife and for the occasional visit to reassure the tenants, so to speak. We had some gay parties there too, of course. Sonny is too young to remember the really splendid ones when we had musicians and dancers up from Calcutta. Perhaps you

75

young men haven't even heard of Mumtaz Begum, but when she came to sing at Babulpur, she had the reputation of being the greatest ghazal singer of her time. What a voice, what a voice that woman had. I'd give a fortune to hear a voice like that again, why yes I would.' The old man turned to the pink cloud that hung over the darkening street and his son gazed into an empty tea-cup.

'You don't keep up with the musical world any more, sir?' asked Nirode.

'Papa, Nirode is the editor of a vastly artistic little periodical. Nirode, won't you let Papa —'

'What good would that be?' cried the old man. 'These new artistes, they are not like the ones who used to come to entertain us at our parties. All they are interested in is going on a foreign tour. In my time, a singer knew where he would find his most appreciative audience and it is that what mattered most to them. Not agents, not contracts, not the money they made. Oh yes, they would be rewarded with gold armlets and with pearls, but at times the only reward they would accept was a jasmine, a rose, a little applause. I've had Mumtaz Begum sing at our house from ten in the evening till four o'clock in the morning and when she left us, we were in such a state of intoxication, we didn't think of payment nor did she remind us. Those were the days...'

'Oh Papa, that must have been very long ago, certainly not within my memory.'

'Not so long,' the old man said sharply. 'I believe my old idol Jahanara Begum is still living in Calcutta. I even hear she occasionally dances — perhaps only for very intimate friends, she couldn't perform on a stage any more, I agree. It is my misfortune that I have had to break with my past, I have lost touch with my friends,' and he wavered a bit, turning to Nirode with appealing eyes for it was a long time since he had had anyone willing to listen to his reminiscences. At his wife's family home they had long ago grown tired of that reedy voice gloating over the tinsel glories of his not untainted past, and his son went so far as to discourage him. Now he said wistfully, 'If I could contact her...'

'Surely it would not be too difficult. David, couldn't you ask that great chum of yours, that fellow who plays the *sitar?* He should know — they always do.'

Sonny looked at Nirode, appalled, and his father cried, 'Is that true? Is that possible?' But David was deeply embarrassed and said, 'No, no, he's not in Calcutta at the moment.'

'But he's bound to come this winter and then you could let Mr Ghosh know. Do you think you could come up to Calcutta again, Mr Ghosh?'

'Naturally, naturally, I am not in exile.'

'No, but the journey is very strenuous, Papa. Your doctor forbade it.'

'The doctor.' The old man gave a sly snigger, knowingly tapping the side of his nose. 'The doctor even forbade drinks. Long, long ago he forbade drinks. Yet I maintain it is my life saver. "Ram *babu,*" I tell my secretary, "Ram *babu,* my life saver," and he knows what it is. He brings me my drink, not the doctor's little pills.' He laughed but eyed his son with some anxiety. 'It does me no harm and very, very much good, you know.'

'Of course,' said Nirode, 'we can all see that, sir. Besides if you are used to a way of life, it is difficult to give it up altogether.'

Sonny took his chin out of the tea-cup with a determined movement implying that he wished to forgive, forget and start again. 'Yes, those were the gracious days, I'm always telling Nirode. Now Papa is here to persuade you of it. Nirode, since you never believe anything I say.'

Nirode twinkled across at the old man. 'But, basically sir, the ways of graciousness haven't changed all that much, you know. There are still artistes who will perform for exclusive audiences merely for the appreciation that goes with it, the very special kind of appreciation that has nothing to do with money or contracts or things.' The old man, who had been on the point of draining the glass of liquor that so revived and warmed him, slapped down the glass and gave an exceptionally loud and uncouth laugh, a snorting bray that shook the papery wrinkles of his face like an explosion.

'I'm glad to hear that,' he said. 'Well, what do young men go to see when they go to a dance performance? What are young men for, I always say — perhaps they can't give rubies any more, but they have better things to give, haven't they? Ha ha. Well said, young man, well said!' It was as though the grey and silver skeins of the aged cocoon had finally been shed and what emerged now was the true possessor of the shell — a vulgar, bumptious old thing with raw, red skin, bulging moist eyes and many pairs of tickling, hurrying feet, an altogether unattractive, lecherous little beast that made straight for its meal and avidly began to crunch it.

Sonny ran his fingers through his hair, stood up, sat down, crying 'It's time we left, we must return the car to uncle,' but Papa did not look at him, Papa was still ogling Nirode and saying , 'That is the way we used to be in my time. Gold and rubies are all very well, but the true reward comes later, in private. Ha ha. When I think of the excitement that grew while we watched a great and beautiful dancer perform, knowing she was doing it purely for our enjoyment — ah, then I think that was the best part of my life. Yes, you are all young men here, I can speak out and tell you what it is that matters in life. The sweet drink in my glass, it is only an appetizer, isn't it? And I will tell you something — there were never any people who understood life like the artistes of my youth did, Mumtaz and Jahanara Begum...'

'Very great beauties they were, too, I believe, besides their artistry of course,' Nirode said, because the old man had turned to the sunset again, lost in a vision that knew no fading but grew steadily more resplendent.

'Beauties? My friend, you don't know what beauty is unless you can claim to have seen Jahanara in her prime. In her prime,' he rolled the word upon his tongue like a purple grape. 'Her huge, brilliant eyes and hair that came down to the backs of her knees. What a sight it was, that cloud of black hair swaying about her body...

David grew uneasy but it was quite unnoticeable besides Sonny's agitation. Nirode watched him with a broad grin then turned to egg on the old man with another encouraging conspiratorial twinkle.

'And the perfume they used at that time — none of these pale French waters that your modern young women dab behind their ears. Jahanara bathed, so it seemed to us, in Attar of Roses and Ashes of Violets. When she entered the house, you knew she had come from her perfume, from the music of her anklets. How she dressed! None of these heavy South Indian silks in which women swathe themselves today, but *saris* of transparent silver and gold gauze, so that you missed no movement of her body. You could lie back on your cushions and watch her every part moving to the music: He shook his head. The veranda was shadowy now, the lights had not yet gone up and it was hard to say if his eyes were bright with the visions they saw or with the tears of senility. He turned to the silent, unhappy David. 'If you ever hear the name of Jahanara spoken,' he said softly, 'if you ever hear the name —'

'Oh, he will let you know, won't you. David?' urged Nirode. The old man raised a hand in Nirode's direction and continued to speak in a faltering undertone. 'If you hear the name of Jahanara — then bow, then bow low, place your head in the dust because you will have heard the name of the most beautiful woman in the world, my friend — '

There was a small silence. Traffic seemed to pause in that brief second and the sun hung pendant from the ashen cloud. but did not drop. It lingered, softened and melted out of shape, a quivering mass of bygone light. There was a secret alteration in the expressions of all those who sat about the table loaded with empty glasses and tea-cups. It was too dark for anyone to read their faces, to discover pity, compassion, scorn or disgust.

Then Nirode swept himself off his chair with a furious jerk. 'I must go,' he said roughly. 'I'll take a tram. Coming, David?'

'Sonny? What does it matter what he felt?' Nirode asked angrily. 'Sonny's nothing, nobody — just a reflection of all that tawdry tinsel and glimmer-glamour of his father's wealth. Oh! the father must have been real enough at one time — *very* real in all that raw vulgarity. God, how I hate the physicalness of the loves of that kind of man — heavy bags of gold coins, moist pink flesh and smothering perfume. My father too shared it, he was brought up to it, but at least he had my mother to keep him in hand. At that time she was terribly keen on being a lady and an intellectual. She's changed now and is as vulgar as the rest — as father was. But Sonny's Mamma — have you ever heard him speak of her? I can imagine what she's like — one of those vast, soft, masses of rice Bengali women with a bunch of keys at her waist and nothing in her head but a reckoning of the stores in her pantry and nothing in her heart but a stupid sense of injury and affront. Their generation's full of those types of ignorance. They did wake up a bit during the Independence movement, that seemed to bring out something rather fine in some of them, but they're back to their old beauty sleep of neglect and delay and corruption. I suppose it's a result of so many centuries of slavery to foreign rule — we've always been a conquered race and I can't see us getting on our own, not with the Ghosh family around. I sometimes feel we are just letting things go deliberately, waiting for the next conquering race to sweep in and put things right for us. In the meantime, bright sparks of our generation compose poems like, "Ever since last autumn / I have loved you from my heart's bottom" and others — like Jit — rake in all the money they can hoard in a tin trunk under their beds and some — like Sonny — go on idolizing the decadent old lechers who had more time and money than us for music and dance and fat old tarts. Don't you think that that's what Sonny really wants from life? Not independence, not challenge, not change or progress, but a return to the drugged slavery his father lived in, as happily as a pig. Do you think anything will ever shake Sonny into wakefulness? I don't. If he's shaken, he will get a fatal heart attack on the spot. He couldn't bear to see things as they really are. How many can? How many people do you know who can open their eyes and then have the courage to keep them open? I could count them on the fingers of my left hand.'

But Sonny, either because he chose to ignore Nirode's contempt or because he had, after all, sufficient courage to try and make him change his mind, invited him and David to visit his country estate before the fisheries swamped it completely. 'We're expanding in a big way — some European countries have shown a great interest in our cheap tinned fish. Would you believe it? Soon there'll be no paddy left and no mahogany and then it won't be Babulpur any longer. You must come and see it before that happens.'

'Will it? If it does, it will be thanks to that Khan fellow's greed not your own enterprise,' Nirode grumbled.

They went then — all three of them crammed into a small suburban train along with the fishermen carrying their wares in leaking baskets and harried clerks going home to their sad brown villages. At one of them Sonny ordered them to get off, straight into the fray of the weekly market. Turnips, live chickens and glass bangles spilled out of their barrows and the three men pushed their way past handcarts and buffaloes, to the village shoddy with its windowless mud walls, its greasy cycle repair shops and grain stores, where Sonny tried to hail a tonga.

'No, no, let's walk,' Nirode said, impatient of the suspicious curiosity of the shopkeepers and the small boys torturing a yellow pup in the gutter. 'If we come to the country, we must behave like the buffaloes, I suppose.'

'You Calcutta-*wallah*s, spoilt urbanites all of you,' scolded Sonny. 'Ah well, it might be a good idea — if we walk we can go past my old fishing pond. Can you imagine, five years ago it was the only place in Babulpur where you could get fish?' He babbled on senselessly, quite unnerved by the squalor of the village Babulpur of which his father and his ancestors had been the patrons. Out in the fields, amongst waterways mauve with hyacinths, the lean white cows ambling over close-cropped grass and the date palm groves, he gained a little of the family assurance and strode on in his riding boots, one dark lock falling over his brow, the very picture of the young lord of the estate.

The fish pond was at the bottom of a flight of stone stairs, concealed by a grove of trees that swarmed down to the edge the pool with quiet passion — the wide-spread mango trees that drew all shade, all stillness, all the repose of deep summer into their hearts and the extrovert palms that leant out over the pool, shadeless and thirsty. Here was silence, broken only by the small peeping of a wakeful insect. Here Sonny paused, hands on hips, graceful, as though he had just sprung off his chestnut pony, tethered it to a tree and come to visit that of which he was master. Not any longer though — for here was a poacher, too, a West Bengal peasant, so dark that his skin assumed a polish and a sheen, wrapped in a *lungi* of maroon and crimson checks. Even he recognized that bright lordliness in Sonny — those hands placed on slim hips, the tilt of the long chin, that casual garb — and his eyes flashed, glistening bits of white porcelain in that dark face. Nirode and David watched, with a growing tenseness, watched and breathed (If he dares, if he dares bully that man...) and Sonny, sensing this hostility, was surprised. He was the master after all, there was no need for a scene. He gave the poacher a brief and perfunctory scolding in the local dialect, then took the rod from his hands and, waving to his companions, called, 'Come and try your luck. This pond is *choked* with vast fish.' Nirode and David came slowly down and the poacher gave a relieved smile of gratitude, helped place the bait on the hook, then withdrew to squat on the steps and watch the frolics of the ruling class.

Sonny's delight and pride began to bubble like a playful guppy in water. 'Come here or you'll get stuck in the mud,' he shouted, waving his arms, jumping. 'Not like that, David throw it out, out! Swing your arm, like this!' He pranced on the steps, finally took the rod himself and flung out the line with a gesture that swept over all his holidays from public school, the afternoons beside the pond, with his sisters, Lila thrashing the water with impatience and Rina sitting upon a log and singing. (Lila had married for a title and lived now in squalid penury, in a crumbling house in which she took in paying guests who drank or wrote her insulting letters. Rina had married for money, during their father's greatest despair, and it was her husband who drank and wrote scandalous notes to other women.) But of this no shadow fell on Sonny, he thought of them in their English lace dresses shining like fallen flowers amidst that damp foliage. And he laughed to see the red float bobbing, laughed when the fish got away. The poacher watched inscrutably. When

Sonny held out the rod to him he ran up to take it and disappeared. One moment he was there, ravishing in maroon and scarlet, the next he was not.

'Is your house haunted?' asked David, turning to see where he might be. All was green and still. He shrugged.

'Oh, not by *poachers'* ghosts, David, how can you imagine such a thing? Sonny's ancestral ghosts are all attired in white and gold Benares brocade and have swords at their sides and come sweeping up in a carriage and pair.'

'Oh I can almost see one sweeping up this drive,' David said immediately with his quick generosity. 'It is beautiful, Sonny.'

It was long and lined with soft-needled casuarinas that waved their plumes in a murmur of breeze and at the end of it stood the house, pillared, green-shuttered, deep-verandahed and rapt in the consciousness of the passing of a hundred years of time. Compared with other country houses, colonially regal in lines and design, that they had seen from the train window, standing isolated in fields along the railway line, festooned with refugees' rags and caked with cow-dung pats, this one was indeed impressive. As they drew closer, however, it became only too obvious that this was no stately home but a busy district government office. A hive of clerks and peons bustled about in the great rooms of the ground floor, rattling their typewriters, shuffling through files and emptying cups of sweet tea. They paused (their inclination to pause grew with the afternoon till, at five o'clock, they rose in a buzzing cloud and disappeared) to see the strangers come up the drive, murmured and speculated, for some recognized the former master of the house and all recognized the out-of-place sophistication that had to do with the city, not their district. As the visitors went around to the back stairs and from there to the Sub-divisional Officer's private quarters on the first floor, their bee-like hum rose to a crescendo of surprise and curiosity, then dropped, with sighs, into dusty paper files.

Nirode and David exchanged looks on seeing Sonny's shoulders sag as he led them up the dark back stairs that creaked and shook alarmingly. They emerged in an unexpected flood of light, pollen yellow and warm, streaming through the skylights on the landing where great doors stood open on the reception hall. A servant, small and lost but undismayed, a ragged urchin astray in the stripped splendour of the hall, came up to inform them (cheekily, thought Sonny, who remembered the fine manners of his own servants and their long beards) that the Sahib was out, unveiling, he said, a portrait of a local saint at the new school. He led them through several rooms where there was nowhere to sit, for they were bare and spartan, so sadly so as to make Sonny's eyes glaze at the remembrance of the Persian carpets and the chandeliers they had once held. The new Sahib had evidently not felt up to tackling the furnishing or been discouraged by the immense proportions of the rooms that seemed even larger now that they stood open to the light and the flat countryside around them. One room held a camp-cot, small and sagging, in the centre of the floor (why the centre?) No electric fan hung there nor chandelier and at the end of the room a dressing table with a stained mirror, bottles of hair oil lined up on it and draped about it several white and khaki bush-shirts and a tinsel garland, remnant of some official function. Against the opposite wall a desk stood burdened by several heavy, well-thumbed law books and a small brass vase crammed full of short-stalked common pink roses. Piled up beneath it were stacks of files.

David was moved to say, 'But why not sit out on the veranda? I should like to see the view,' and to lead the drooping Sonny out, for Sonny was as subdued as a beaten dog and looked at David with pleading gratitude.

One more hall had to be traversed before they came to the veranda with the view and here the dirty urchin's striped bedding-roll stared out of the shadows, his pictures of a sportive Krishna and photographs of film actresses were lined up above a green tin trunk. Here, too, was the master's dining table, laid with a white cloth and two yellow plastic salt cellars. David, losing his nerve, began to murmur, 'Never mind, never mind,' which made Nirode burst out laughing as he preceded them on to the veranda which ran about the entire first floor, deep and cool and green-shuttered.

They leant on the rails, breathing in the honey scent of sunburnt grass, the milky smell of pastureland and looked out on to the grassy plain where cattle grazed and an occasional jackal darted out of the jungle upon the fringe, then quickly flashed out of sight. Aged trees loomed out of the grass, gnarled and wide-spreading. To his distress, Nirode felt creep over him something of Sonny's own despondency and nostalgia. Lazily he told himself it was the warm, indolent open air to which he was not accustomed but he found himself thinking of his mother on her veranda, looking out at her view and wondered if she still expected him to come or even write.

'See, see,' cried Sonny, making a sudden, bouncing recovery. 'See that old mahogany tree? It seems to have been struck by lightning. I didn't see it last time I was here — it must have happened during one of those April nor'westers. Half of it's already dry,' and they all looked out to see that it was nearly split in two, one half upright and flourishing with green resiliency, while the other lay upon the ground, dead and brown. 'Good ripe mahogany, it'll fetch thousands, I'll have the auctioneer down at once,' Sonny shrilled excitedly. 'My tenant didn't even tell me. Isn't it just like them, they can't manage an estate and expect to manage a country...'

He grew progressively buoyant, and began to point out old landmarks — the old elephant stables which now, typically, housed fallen women turned into seamstresses and the red Civil Court building and the new club-house.

'It didn't exist when we lived here and one of our few connections with the world was through a tunnel, a *secret* tunnel but it was always so dark and hideous I never dared explore it.'

'That must be where your grandpapa whipped his slaves and left them to die,' Nirode said, fighting with his own lethargic surrender to a sense of property, ancestry — things that imbued this house, that he imagined he had forgotten and now rose fresh and sweet as the smells of grass and field. It was not a sensation strong enough to incite to action, but an insidious one that caused a fading, an etiolation of what had so far been new and young and strong inside him. Somewhere in it there was a tinge of — regret? doubt? Nirode loathed to regret or doubt and he went and threw himself violently into a long, old-fashioned armchair, with its arms extending into grotesque leg-rests and groaned at the lack of comfort.

'These things were built for two-hundred-pounders taking a rest after a twelve-course banquet, not for me.' He insisted on staying there, however, while David and Sonny went to take a look at the fisheries. 'I'm not interested in ponds full of stinking fish,' he told them. 'Couldn't you fetch me a bottle of Napoleon brandy from your cellar, Sonny?' and David made haste to lead Sonny away. Nirode tried so hard to concentrate upon the trials of his magazine and upon a book that had slowly begun to form in his mind, that he tired of the effort and fell asleep.

When they returned from the fisheries, they brought with them the tenant, the Subdivisional Officer, an earnest and energetic young man from the south, very much a component of the present, the busy organization that hummed below stairs and the spartan functionariness of the quarters above stairs. A tireless worker for 'national integration' and 'unity in diversity' — the pet themes of his many speeches — he was working to rid his newly learnt Bengali of the hard, clicking Tamil tones that the peasants in his district found uncongenial. His greatest concern was for the rehabilitation of refugees who poured across the border from Pakistan (now Bangladesh) and the keeping in check of the Communist element in his unruly and trouble-ridden district.

He arranged for coffee to be sent out and settled down to an earnest conversation with Sonny, while David and Nirode sat back, gazing on to the pasture where cows grazed and shepherd boys flew kites and up into the milk-blue sky stitched by the meticulous flight of white cranes, but listened all the while with thinly disguised curiosity.

'Undoubtedly there has been a mistake,' said Raghavan, tapping his foot and blowing lustily on his coffee. 'A grave misunderstanding. I suggest you refer the matter to your agent.'

'My solicitor?'

'Yes, yes. You will see that it was not only the toddy palms that were sold to us, but every tree on the grounds — mango, palm, mahogany, even those useless, dying-looking things along the drive.'

'Those casuarinas were planted two hundred years ago, by Lord —'

'Yes, well, these details may have escaped your attention at the time the contract was signed. Understandable, quite understandable. As a matter of fact, the auctioneer has already been informed and is expected to arrive on Wednesday morning. They will deal with the sale on our behalf. We have very little time for running the estate, naturally, but the sale will be a great help to us. You know yourself the high cost of maintaining such a house. I am put to an incredibly high expense just to maintain a standard of decency in my own quarters.'

'I thought you preferred to forgo such expenses altogether,' said Sonny, imitating Raghavan's speech unconsciously. So did he feel, so great was his distaste for this chattering upstart, the government he stood for, its progress and philistinism, his shoulders stooped and his lips and words were unnaturally severe.

Raghavan's good humour seemed unimpeachable. He sighed. 'It is so noticeable. Is it?' he exclaimed and filled up his cheap pottery cup again. 'You know, merely to paint these gigantic doors and windows would cost me nearly a month's salary. Of course the government maintains the ground floor as well as the house for displaced women.'

'Displaced women?' asked Nirode.

Raghavan blew at his coffee. 'Yes, yes, these refugee women from Pakistan, also a few women from the city, unemployed women,' he said. assuming the authoritarian and careless manner of an older man — a worshipped District Commissioner perhaps or a Minister who had paid him a visit and left a permanent impression on the ambitious young man. 'We have supplied each woman with an Usha sewing machine so that she may earn her living by honest — by new means. Rehabilitation of refugees is not possible on a large scale here in my district, due to the unbelievably high rate at which they are still crossing the border and the lack of employment in an area that has so far been purely agricultural despite the fact that it is not blessed with the most productive of soils...' Now thoroughly in his element he rattled and clicked over a seemingly endless track of duties and responsibilities, challenges and opportunities. He jigged his knee up and down with greater and still greater vigour and the bachelor's buttonhole in the lapel of his faded blue bush-shirt twinkled with a like energy. 'Refugees,' he said, 'troublemakers, riots, doles, Communism, processions, demands, rice, rice, rice...' Then he stopped jigging. sat up in his long chair and smacked Sonny on the knee. 'Together with you, we are all looking forward to the success of the fisheries. As I have shown you this afternoon, my friend, it is not in a promising position. It cannot be run in this fashion, by the swindlers to whom you have entrusted it. However, I have already outlined my plans and I suggest you refer the matter to the Department of —'

'Yes, yes,' Sonny snapped irritably and sat back, glaring at the empty sky.

'The fisheries keep you busy too, Mr Raghavan?' Nirode enquired politely.

'Busy, busy, I am always busy,' cried Raghavan in a tone of enchantment. 'That is how it should be in young India, where we are all marching forward. We must keep up the pace, keep up the pace.'

'Of course, the pace,' Nirode chimed in enthusiastically. 'You are at the very helm of our great procession, Mr Raghavan. You are the one who waves the banner over our heads and urges us to charge. How exhilarating it must be! Is it also a little exhausting?'

'Ha ha, so it would be, my friend, so it would be, but I believe in reserving certain hours of the day for complete recreation that I may emerge from them, refreshed and filled with new vigour. Three evenings a week I play bridge at the club with the magistrate, the health officer and the medical officer. Quite an interesting foursome it is. There are more progressive-minded and educated people in the districts than you Calcutta-*wallah*s believe. The place has greater possibilities than have ever been looked into before — but we are setting that right now. Yes, we shall do so in time.' Then, taking them completely by surprise, he suddenly jumped to his feet and apologized, 'I'm afraid I must leave now. I have an appointment at Writer's Building at six o'clock and it is a long drive. If you are yourselves returning to Calcutta now, may I offer you a lift in my humble jeep or have you any other mode of transport in mind?'

'The humble jeep, by all means,' Nirode said, jumping up. He was too impatient with himself to spare Sonny anything.

The room was unrecognizable. The two men stood in the doorway, gazing on space they had not imagined existed inside those corrugated iron walls.

'Well, that's that,' David whispered. 'It's all gone.'

'Every saucer, every ash tray. Have they paid you?'

'No, they said they would once it was sold . I don't mind.'

'Ass, you should have taken it in advance. You really are a fool David.'

'Oh! I'll get it. They're all society ladies in that committee that buys up stuff for the Cottage Industries showplace — very energetic and very thorough they are. I'll get it.'

'What makes you go and trust society ladies? My mother used to be one in her Calcutta days and I wouldn't trust her further than I can spit.'

'Oh no, Nirode,' David stammered and they wandered out on to the roof, also cleared of his tools and art, even of the kiln which he had sold and of the ceramist clan that the kiln had attracted.

'I don't know what to do next,' he said, gaping at the flat, empty roof-top, looking as lost as a white rabbit in a desert. Nirode perched himself on the parapet. 'Aren't you starting another batch? This one's been such a smashing success.' 'N-no, I don't feel like it at all, somehow.'

'You could take up the *veena* again.'

'Y-yes.' David always stammered when uncertain, as though language were one of the props that had been taken away from under him.

'You don't sound convincing. Does that mean you're off on your travels again?'

David smoothed his thin ginger hair with slow fingers, considering.

'Don't feel you'll be letting me down by going,' Nirode said quickly. 'Everything is temporary for people like us. If we had thought it was going to be permanent, neither you nor I would have agreed to this kind of a relationship, you know that. You and I will always be travellers, David and we'll always travel alone.'

They glanced at each other briefly, then leant over to watch the traffic below. Then David said, 'I've a little money left from the kiln sale. Shall we have a proper dinner tonight?'

'A Chinese one.'

'At Ta Fa Shun.'

They started off on the long tram ride to China Town in buoyant spirits. The tram rattled briskly, they passed pink and green cinema houses, neon lit *sari* shops, marriage processions and brass bands. Then came streets with dark, gap-toothed houses where the half-dead and the half-alive lived and the tram grew so packed and airless, they got off at Esplanade and walked. But the second-hand bookstalls where they had hoped to spend a pleasant half-hour leafing through torn, yellow-paged volumes and lift them to their noses to breathe in the odour of age and rice that good paper has, were in the process of shutting down. The shopkeepers were impatient with them. They spent fifteen minutes of incredulous delight, standing outside Girichand Ray and Grandsons Sweetmeat Store, watching a young man in a *dhoti* seat himself at a marble-topped, spindle-legged table and order an earthen pot filled with sweet curds, then a second, third and even a fourth, before he came out smoothing a moustache with icicles of pink curd trembling upon it. They wandered into a cinema house and vaguely studied the posters, for the film had already started and the hall was empty except for some bored loiterers. The pavements were slick with mango peels and coconut shells. Beggars were stretching out on their rags. China Town, with its narrow lanes that the pale gas lamps did little to illuminate, was thick with violet shadows and redolent of lard, uncured leather and open urinals, at its most pungent under the 'Commit No Nuisance' signs. A bald Chinese grandfather sat on the doorstep of a grimy house, smoking and shuffling his gnarled yellow feet in their wooden sandals. A little old woman in blue trousers spooned noodles into bowls held out by two small, moon-faced children, patient and inscrutable upon a bench. Outside a large restaurant a young man stood twanging a guitar, singing cowboy songs and love ballads and contriving to make each sound exactly like the other. Around the corner from it a group of prostitutes waited, ribbons in their hair and spangles on their frocks and *saris*. The lane to Ta Fa Shun was flooded by a burst drain-pipe and David and Nirode picked their way through the puddles, past a tiny shop that sold jasmine tea, chopsticks and Chinese magazines to the restaurant. By the time a tall, lean waiter had found them a cubicle, airless and echoing with party noises that filtered over the tops of other open cubicles and smelling of greasy rice and lard, they were both limp with depression and all sense of celebration was gone from their party.

Dipping bits of spring chicken into a saucer of spiced lemon juice, Nirode asked, in that tone of aggression that his friends dreaded, 'Tell me, David, what did you think of that last issue of *Voice?*'

'We're all wondering why you've stopped there and haven't brought out another. That one was so successful, your subscriptions nearly doubled, you told me. Jit says people are offering advertisements all on their own at last.'

'But what do you think of it?'

'Well, it was the closest it ever came to being successful, Nirode.'

'Do you think that a matter for congratulation?'

'Why not, Nirode?'

'Because I refuse to be caught by its success. Damn it all, that blasted newspaper I worked for had been successful for years, everything moved smoothly, it employed people to work for it like a lot of dumb clogs in an oily machine. I don't want mine to become like *that,* for God's sake. It's getting to be bad enough with Jit breathing down my neck and panting, "Why don't you hurry the next issue? Hurry, hurry, this is your chance to break even at last." I have Sonny jumping up and down like a monkey on a stick and squealing, "We'll make a respectable man of you, Nirode, we'll see you happily married to your profession one day." And bloody Bose wheezing, "Ah, Nirode is turned communicative after all." Why? Because I got a popular English poet to contribute three bloody awful poems to it. That's how the magazine got a reputation and became popular. Urghh — reputation, that's like a white collar about your neck, stifling you. It's suffocating me.' And he raised the flaps of his worn bush shirt and waved them up and down in the air in that small cubicle where the air grew steadily more stale and steamy as the cadaverous waiter brought in more and more dishes of food for them. 'And don't look at me so disbelievingly, you know exactly what I'm talking about. If you didn't, you'd be busy making another batch of charming ash trays for the ladies of the Cottage Arty Crafty Society. But you know it's only one of their nets, this thing called success or reputation and when you hear it singing about your ears, the only thing to do is to drop everything and run — run to the Ramakrishna Mission or to a bleak old mountain top, just run. I think what I hate most about this magazine of mine is the people it has attracted to it and, therefore, to me. Not one of them I'd like to see anywhere except at their funerals. I hate them breathing down my neck as though they have the right to do that. I don't know why I ever got involved in anything that brought me into contact with them. I want to lash out on my own now and whether I sink or swim, I'll do it. David, you are the one who knows how to keep them at their distance and if they get too close, you run.'

David sniffed first at one small teapot on the table, then at another, detected the soy sauce in one of them and sprinkled it lavishly over his rice. 'I don't know — I don't think things out in — in words, as you do, Nirode. All I know is when it is good to rest and when it is time to go. I like to travel, that is all. It is very simple.'

'Everything that concerns you is simple, David — to yourself.'

'Oh, I am quite happy,' David said vaguely.

'Happy? Then you are done for, you fool. What worse death than at the hands of happiness? Anyone who feels happy deserves to die. If we were all to become — happy,' he used the word with unfamiliarity, 'the world would come to a stand still and no one would move another step. How would you like your trains to stop dead once they've arrived at some lunatic happy station? Wouldn't that be death to you?'

'We've different ideas of movement and progress, Nirode. A yogi sits for years under the same tree, getting up only to wash himself in the same stream — but his mind still travels, doesn't it?

'There you are!' Nirode's voice rang with bitter triumph as he tossed down a shrimp's pink tail. 'You'll end as a barmy theosophist in some shady, orange-toned mission house. And what's more, you'll be happy.'

'There is a point in happiness, I think.'

'I don't believe in points. I believe only in the lines that radiate from them and the longer and vaguer and crookeder, the better.'

'How long can you go on dragging yourself along them? Can you do that to the point of giving up your magazine just when you've finally established it?'

'We'll see,' Nirode said, 'we'll see.' Over the faint feminine odour of jasmine tea, they talked more amiably and only of friends and adventures in this city that seemed to offer, they agreed, endless opportunity to the eccentric, 'and none' Nirode complained as they stepped out into the flooded, putrid lane, 'for pleasure.' Talking of happiness and pleasure and the disparity between the two, they wandered past the empty food stalls, the prostitutes who still stood at the corners, now and then crying out in the harsh, arresting tones of night jars, into the wide streets where vendors and beggars lay sleeping, wrapped in white sheets, against empty barrows and on doorsteps. From some concealed nightclubs came the frenzied sounds of drums and castanets and the wistful passion of a violin. At a traffic signal an urchin stood trying to peddle his last bunch of roses, their petals already veined with the dark purple of asphyxia. Under a mauve gaslight several watchmen had gathered to play cards and, in the intense silence, their dice rattled like small skulls. Before they had come to the end of that road, an argument broke out among the gamblers and quickly developed into a small riot. David and Nirode walked faster, hearing the screams and blows. Brooke-Bond Tea... Brooke-Bond — Tea... stuttered a red neon sign, like a desperate semaphore sent out by this black city floundering about in the marshes, slowly sinking into it.

'Another fifty years, that's all I give it,' Nirode said. 'Then it'll be gone — beastly, blood-thirsty Calcutta.'

In the coffee house Nirode and Jit met for what Jit called with a little sardonic contempt smearing his lips into a smile their monthly business meeting.

'It has arrived at last, Nirode, your *Voice*. It's broken even, you know.'

'Poetic words for nothing at all. You can pay off my debts for me. Will there be enough left to pay yourself?'

'Oh, not to worry, I haven't gone into that yet.'

'Naturally, naturally,' Nirode felt disgust beginning to foul his tongue.

Jit laughed and poured out more coffee. 'Aren't you at all pleased? Or are you just trying to keep me from seeing it?'

Nirode said sharply, 'Look here, Jit, I'm not one of your kind. When I'm pleased, I laugh. When I'm fed up, I roar. I don't sit swaying my head and hissing in a monotone while I wait for a victim to come along. If I'm bored and impatient right now it's because it means very little to me whether we've broken even or not, have arrived or got left miles behind.'

'But what do you mean to do with it now?'

Nirode laughed straight into Jit's disbelieving face. 'I might tell you. It will cost you three drinks to find out.'

'Three drinks to inspire you for your night's work? Right I don't mind,' Jit said. 'Come across sevenish then.'

'To your house? You know I bloody well won't. We'll go to Isiah's.'

'Please, let's not be juvenile about this. It isn't so often my wife gives me the evening off.'

'Scheherazade then. That's slumming for you box-*wallahs*, isn't it? Nothing worse than the occasional gutter rat popping its head out of a bottle to leer at you,' Nirode snarled and that was where they met that evening.

'Do you know what those gutter rats are called?' Jit asked him as one large specimen slithered through the shrubs behind their table, disappearing where the kitchen smells emerged powerfully. A cageful of frantic budgerigars twittered and twizzled and fought the wire-netting with ancient claws. An empty dance floor was being swept. Presently a wistful Goan in a dinner-jacket came out, sat down at the piano and began tenderly to tinkle. The palms drooped as listlessly as dish rags in the stale air enclosed by the walls of the hotel around them. Drain-pipes, backstairs and unlit windows provided the backdrop for the nightclub and about its edges slithered these gutter rats, like apparitions seen in delirium tremens.

'Bandicoots,' said Nirode, rapidly eating all the monkey nuts in a saucer on the table.

'Good name, isn't it? Expresses everything there is to know about a rat.'

'Trying to tell me something?'

'Just passing on observations of nature, old boy, for what they are worth. Not to worry.'

'I never worry about anything you *say*. That's not the dangerous part about you.'

Jit laughed, settling back with a glass of beer, smoothing out into relaxation as with warm oil. He wagged his finger at Nirode who was still wolfing down the monkey-nuts while his beer whispered fizzily in front of him. 'Now you've given yourself away, Nirode — you're frightened of me really, aren't you?'

'Of course I'm frightened of you — I have an aversion to cold-blooded animals. I prefer a bandicoot to a reptile any day.'

'No, it isn't quite that. It isn't I you fear but my position.'

'Hah?' Nirode's hand halted in the act of tossing a monkey-nut into his open mouth. 'Your position, you say? Do you mean your family estate, your wife's dowry, your bank account?'

'No, no, just the fact that I represent the box-*wallah* class you profess to loathe so much. You rant against us precisely because you realize our danger — we entice you. We hover in the foreground like an oasis — and once you've done your little stint of adventuring in the desert, you'll get very thirsty. So thirsty you will drink anything — anything that resembles the patriarchal security and comfort and the matriarchal indulgence that you broke away from, so boldly and recklessly. You're sowing your bright little wild oats, having your lop-sided little adventures, but always with a sense of that comforting background to which you could always return when things got too hot. You know you'll go tumbling right back into it, don't you, Nirode? You'll be able to fall into its warm lap, exhausted, but satisfied that you did not let it smother you, that inspite of it you managed to live, fully and dangerously. You even *deserve* a return to that easy land after so much hardship bravely endured. Even if you do take on the despised box-*wallah*'s job and salary in the end, none of us can blame you because you've worked for it, you deserve it. I shall reserve my pat on the back for you till you arrive at that beautifully logical end to your adventures.'

Nirode quietly ate the monkey-nuts one by one while Jit delivered his speech. When speech and monkey-nuts were finished he dusted his hands together, picked up his glass of beer and drank in great gulps. 'So,' he said, putting the glass down half empty. 'So that's what you expect of me, Jit. I do believe my mother expects something very like it. My father certainly never entertained such hopes. Sonny, I think, likes to see me at the head of a vast international arty magazine which he will patronize in much the same fashion his old man patronized painted women. David? He never says. It is all very, very boring.' He was watching people enter and order drinks, the men smiling soporifically into mugs of beer and the women with eyes drawn out by kohl and wrists weighed down by white flower garlands. He turned from the spectacle to smile at Jit in a friendly way. 'It is very boring to find you've been going at a blank wall with hammer and tongs, knocking at it with tooth and nail and every bit of guts in you and yet all there is to see for it is — that same blank wall. I do believe I shall get so bored one day I will just give up, simply not go on.'

'And become the hard-drinking, golf-playing bourgeois box-*wallah* at last, just as I said.'

'But I didn't say. What of my little *Voice,* Jit?'

'You just said you've lost interest in it.'

'Well I have — it's just a part of that bloody blank wall. Whatever have I published in it that's worthwhile? Nothing so merry as obscene limericks on any public lavatory wall. Nothing so touching as the anonymous initials scratched on the walls of old monuments. Just a lot of trivia, worthless scribbling no one bothers to read, apart from the writers themselves. And, prominently, three very mediocre poems by a famous foreign poet. What do I do with this very stupid and uninspiring wall, Jit? Do I give it a coat of whitewash, ask Dharma for a new design and layout, change to better and bigger paper and print, hound out new contributors and begin all over again? Or do I merely kick it down and leave you all sneezing in the dust?' He drank his beer and smiled over the brim of his glass while his eyes remained absolutely dark. No one could tell whether he asked this question in order to elicit an answer or merely to be politely, tepidly conversational with the man who was paying for his drink.

Jit seemed, from the smile on his face, to feel himself at the edge of an enigma and determined to uncover the secret tonight, this warm night that fell in folds from the dark windows and the listless palm trees. He said loudly, 'Whatever it is you mean to do, I don't for a minute flatter myself by thinking you will take my advice before doing it. Besides, it is all a matter of passing the time. I have already prophesied your future.'

'But not my little magazine's.'

Jit shrugged, his eyelids flickered briefly, then became bits of turgid rubber again.

'I am not being unkind but, after all, you know as well as I do how many ambitious and indiscriminating young men give birth to how many little magazines every year, in our country as in every other. No one exactly likes to count the funerals — a morbid thing to do — but funerals there are, as many as births, I should say.'

The waiter came to bring them another bottle and a bill that Jit slid under the ash tray and the band began to trickle onstage and to tune up, so that little tinkles and cascades of unharmonious sound invaded the nightclub like harmless mosquitoes, subtly emphasizing the lassitude, the faint tension and sad expectation in the atmosphere.

After several long gulps, Nirode said, 'So you think I might as well wrap it up for the funeral?'

Here was the cue for Jit to smooth down his silk scarf and with his familiar cynical smile, to say, 'But of course, my dear chap, what else?' Here was Nirode's cue for winding up the unsavoury evening, finishing his beer and leaving in familiar disgust. But here the atmosphere changed, the dissipation and desultoriness suddenly drew up their several long strands into a tight cord that whipped a new, sharp-edged awareness into the air, an awareness of vulnerability, candour and pain that had not existed before.

'No,' said Jit, bowing his head and placing his fingertips upon the table, delicately, tentatively. 'No, Nirode, don't do that.'

Alive to the turn in the current, but uncertain of its direction, Nirode asked, 'Why?' with genuine surprise.

Jit began to fret the top of a cigarette packet with dark, nervous fingers and spoke hurriedly, not looking at anyone. 'If you do, then I am lost. I need you — and your *Voice* before me. Oh, I do not ever read it — it is very boring in an academic fashion and I have lost any talent for coping with that. What I need is the knowledge of you up in your fifteen rupees-a-month shack, with its cockroaches and its corrugated iron roof baking in the sun. I need to think of you in order to humiliate myself and each time a new issue of *Voice* arrives on my desk, to surprise me and make me say to myself, "Well, he's done it again inspite of everything, he's managed to do it again." I am humiliated.'

'But why? What is humiliation for? Remove it, Jit, throw it out.'

Jit looked up at him, smiling a taut smile no one had ever seen before on that suave face. 'It is the only meaning my existence has. Strange meanings we ascribe to our meaningless lives, don't we? Perhaps liberty is yours or rebellion, I don't know. Humiliation is mine. I am humiliated by my life as a box-*wallah*, by my Sunday afternoon golf for which I spend the entire week trying to get someone senior and influential to partner me. By the cocktail parties I give, at which I watch my wife asking the boss's wife to a bridge party the next morning.' He smiled again, compulsively, as if something amused him or hurt him in stabs. 'All very trite, isn't it? It's a silly sort of humiliation to complain about, rather a baseless one when there are so many compensations — "perks" we call them — comfortable, even luxurious ones, which I enjoy very much. The miniature collection that I owe to it, the bronzes, the good food and travel. But, you see,' and he crumbled a soft little piece of the cigarette packet between his fingers, 'it is all so different from my parents' lives, from what I wanted my own to be.'

Nirode dragged at his cigarette, gulped beer and twisted about during Jit's speech, distressed because he felt it was calculated to make him feel smug and complacent, sensations that he dreaded now that he saw them fluttering about the squawking budgerigars and trickling from the sad little fountain. He could not adjust himself to thinking of Jit as the tragic hero and he did not like him so lachrymose, and yet he felt that if Jit confessed so much, with so much pain, he owed the man some sympathy. He found himself talking too loudly and using Jit's own unreal speech.

'That's the way it is with all of us, old man,' he cried, refilling Jit's glass and his own. 'I certainly didn't expect to grow up and live amongst cockroaches and edit a stinking, useless magazine. Should I,' and he made a bid to stem Jit's self pity with reckless kindness, 'should I tell you what I expected to find myself doing at twenty-five? I was always certain I would be a stowaway, a traveller and live in London or Paris, be a poor and brilliant student there, spend my time drinking absinthe and talking dazzlingly of Hindu philosophy and the *Kama Sutra*. I rather fancied myself leaning over poetic bridges and contemplating suicide in limpid rivers, then being halted by a sudden inspiration too marvellous not to be immediately translated on to paper or canvas. Well,' he said, waving his hands, more than a little drunk by now, ' it hasn't turned out at all like that, has it. I feel humiliated too every time that wretched magazine appears and I know I haven't got it in me to do anything about it. Then it seems such a farce — this wandering about in foul streets, wasting time with useless creatures like Sonny and Bose and dramatically tearing up my mother's letters into tiny little bits. I'm quite sure there is something to what you suggest, Jit — why don't I give it all up and go back to her? She'd put me on my feet again and I'd probably find it a relief to be on them again instead of lurching about on my knees and tipping over on to my head every so often.'

'No, no,' Jit insisted, with a dark mournfulness that had settled about his shoulders like a dark cloak, becoming the one garment in which he could be known, could be himself. 'Stand on your head, Nirode, stand on your head — that's the only way to get a correct view of this stupid, senseless world, this stupid, senseless country that one horde of invaders after the other has taken over and shaken about and destroyed till we've lost all sense, all proportion. I think my parents retained theirs, but they have been shaken clean out of my head. All the things that ought to have been sound and stable and dignified are ugly broken bits and all the small, shapeless bits of nonsense that ought not to mean anything to an intelligent human being, they're the ones that have been set up permanently, kept fresh and polished and sparkling all over.' He shook his head slowly between the palms of his hands, a primaeval gesture that monkeys are seen to perform. 'What would my father think of me if he came to visit me in Calcutta? Do you know,' he said, in the small voice of a disgraced child, 'I have never invited him or my mother to visit me. It is their right, as my honoured parents, to live with their son, but I have never invited them and they have never come. I cannot, you see, I *cannot.*'

'I've never asked *my* mother to visit me,' Nirode said beckoning to the waiter for another bottle of beer. 'I never will. I won't honour that old she-cannibal and I wouldn't have her in my house if I had one.'

'Please don't,' Jit begged, in a pained whisper. 'It isn't fair, it isn't seemly, Nirode. It is our duty to honour—'

'Don't get worked up, old boy. I never will have a house of my own, so the question never will arise, as our eminent Professor Bose is wont to say.'

Nirode was terrified of regrets and tearful confessions, he did his best to be loud and breezy and distracting, but Jit was not to be diverted. He clasped his glass and smiled at it dreamily, tenderly. 'I like to think of my father, it consoles me to think of him sitting in the garden in the evening. There are coconut trees there, tall curving ones and one pomegranate tree. That is my father's favourite tree and he has had a little concrete *pyal* built beneath and around it. In the evening he sits there and his friends join him: all his neighbours are his friends. They talk — as a young boy, I used to lie on my bed on the veranda and listen to them talk — of the weather, of their health, then politics and, inevitably, as though they are mounting a great staircase that leads up, up, up, they ascend to philosophy, then poetry and from there to music. Someone will go and fetch a harmonium and the singing begins. None of your classical northern stuff, all harsh and geometrical that, but our own southern religious *bhajans,* on and on, half through the night...'

In tune with his line of memory, the band at the other end of the dance floor now congealed, cohered together and began to spread through the darkened nightclub its thick, cloying honey of sound. Drums and castanets, trumpets and a piano began to play and a blonde in violet silk to sing. Dancers with fatuous smiles upon their faces surrendered to the senseless, elemental rhythm of this music, but the waiters continued to hurry up and down with their trays, checking over bills and tips with brief flickers of their eyelids, and Jit continued to mourn the lost world that he seemed to have rediscovered at the bottom of his glass of beer, for he caressed it and spoke to it with a tenderness that alarmed Nirode and then bored him.

'Under that pomegranate tree,' he crooned. 'What fruit that tree gave us. My father would split one open with his hand and show us the globules laid side by side in a perfect design inside the rind and we would eat them with pepper and salt. My mother collected the flowers — blood red, Nirode, blood red — and offer them in her prayers. How much time she found for her prayers,' he said as though in surprise and took a gulp of beer. By this gross act he seemed to have muddied the clarity of that lost vision, defiled it and now he grimaced and spoke, not of it but of his wife. 'Sarla, she would laugh if I suggested she make herself a prayer room. My parents have never seen Sarla. We were married in Sarla's home in Bombay. She is not of our community, you see. I did suggest we travel south to visit my parents but she won't go. She says she is not interested in coconuts and buffaloes and holy oils; can you understand that? I can't. I want to return, Nirode.'

'Do then, Jit, why don't you?'

'I can't now, how can I?' Jit wailed, opening out his hands as if Nirode would see the answer written across his palms.

Nirode grew impatient. 'You haven't exactly sold your soul to the devil, have you? You've only left your pretty backwoods and taken to the big city. You've only given up a bloody frustrating job as a village schoolmaster and become a prosperous, successful young box-*wallah* on his way to becoming director of a reputable business concern.' He took a cigarette stub out of his mouth and flung it with violence at the incessantly wakeful budgerigars.

'A *reputable* business firm?' Jit cried. 'My dear chap, you're too innocent, you just don't know what you are talking about, what really goes on there. I am an accomplice, do you hear, an accomplice to their crime. These British are not here to pay us big salaries and help us live comfortably like Sahibs. They are here to make money, money, money,' and he tossed one imaginary coin after the other on to the table-top with fingers that snapped with the disgrace of iniquity. 'By any means whatsoever. Money to take home with them, money out of our own land, so that they prosper while our country starves. And that is what I help them to do. Should I tell you how they rob our Government, our people?'

'There is nothing, Jit, there is nothing that interests me less,' Nirode groaned but]it told him. In great detail, with a lurid sense of injury and dishonour, every now and then trailing off into an incomprehensible litany of fatalism, to be drowned in the sweet flood of inconsequential music from the band.

Couples danced past — Anglo-Indians as thin, sharp and quick as knives, the girls in short, flowered dresses and the boys in close-fitting black trousers and pointed shoes and Punjabi couples more self-conscious, clumsy in pastel pinks and pearls — and now and then the tempo would rise to a climax that made Nirode faintly expectant, whether of a mass tumbling into the berserk or a quiet crumbling into sleep, he did not know but always it ended merely as an interval of perspiration and ill temper when the growls of the drunkards would become more audible and the dark backstairs and back windows of the Grand Hotel that hung over them would become more sinister.

In one such interval, Nirode managed to persuade Jit to leave but his progress down the red-carpeted vestibule was so uncertain, Nirode wondered how far they would advance, for Jit insisted on leaning against the show-windows, studying the mangy tiger skins, the Kashmiri walnut book-ends and shawls with his red eyes and asking, 'Tell me, Nirode, are these beautiful? Have they form? Design? If so, let me stay here with them, old man — I need form, I need something to repair me, Nirode, old man.'

Fitting him into a taxi, Nirode studied him with eyes cleared by the fresh night air sweeping across Chowringhee from the deserted Maidan. The metamorphosis of Jit's features which had been blurred by the overwhelming atmosphere, sleazy and overworked, of the nightclub, now seemed to be shockingly obvious to Nirode. He sobered down instantly, and as they rattled sedately down the streets made more crepuscular and menacing by faint gas flares, he realized that he could do with Jit what he pleased now and that he might, after all, turn the progress of his lachrymose humiliation into an adventure, an amusing one. Leaning forward, he tapped the driver on his shoulder and directed him to another bar. By the time they arrived there, he was alert, high-spirited and gloriously in control of the situation again.

Here many rounds of rum were downed, here there was no music but the carefree brawling of a purely masculine gathering, uninhibited by the slightest touch of the feminine. Sailors abounded, fresh off their ships. Nirode they knew and drew into their circle and Jit hung on to its fringe for he still needed to hold to him. The jokes were crude, the drinks many and Nirode laughed loudly at their stories of the captain who had been flung into the sea for not paying the sailors their wages and congratulated the young Chinese, his mild face as bland as a bowl of curds, who had actually thrown him overboard. 'And why aren't you in jug?' he asked, delighted that Lee was not and smiling serenely the sailors replied, 'No, no, not necessary. Tomorrow we sail for Panama. They will not hold us up, I think.' While Nirode dipped privately and briefly into that old vision of sails cutting through clear sky, Jit broke in heavily. 'Of course not,' he said, with a remnant of his old cynical smile fluttering across his face like a ragged flag. 'Business first, boys. Bananas, cloves, spices — whatever it is you carry — that is what is important, not a captain's bad habits nor his disgrace. Business first,' and he launched into an anecdote of such length, regarding people so boring, that no one listened to him but told, instead, bawdy stories of Hamburg and Hong Kong and in these Nirode, for once, revelled. Jit's tearful confessions, the suspended *Voice,* impatient subscribers and complaining contributors all retired to some mean wasteland. Something of the grandeur and unmindful liberty of these sailor friends combined to confuse and dazzle him and, after several more drinks made him turn bitter and behave more sharply and devilishly with Jit than he had intended. When they emerged from the bar to stand on the steps over which a neon sign blazed with urgency: REPENT AND BE SAVED — JESUS CALLS, he decided it was time to topple Jit's shapeless figure into whatever it deserved. 'Should I tell you what you can do to get away from it all, Jit?' he asked slyly. 'I can help you, you know.'

'Yes, help, Nirode. Help.'

'Now wait a minute,' Nirode ordered, and made Jit wait while he had a *pan* made for himself at a little stall, bought a fresh supply of cigarettes, before he continued with him down a sleeping Free School Street to the next bar. As he chewed the *pan,* relishing the sharp, styptic flavours of lime and *pan* leaf and cardamom, his head grew clearer and clearer and he felt himself master of the situation. 'I'll tell you my plan, old boy and if you're the man your Scotty boss thinks you to be, you'll jump at it. Here we have this little magazine of mine. I'm bored with it and it isn't getting anywhere with me as editor. Bring here I have lost interest in it and there is something else I want to do much more urgently. And here we have you, Jit, sick of your job and all its perks and the intrigues and the corruption it takes to keep it. Right?'

'Right, old man, more right than —'

'All right, all right, so what is the simple solution to a triangular problem? I give up *Voice* and you take it on,' and having said it, he came to a halt at the brazenly lit door of the bar which shook, rumbled, growled and rioted in the sleepless night. He turned to see the effect his proposal had had on Jit and made a dreadful face at what he saw.

Jit stood there with his mouth fallen open, his eyes bleared with alcohol and tears, his habitually smooth hair and silk scarf rumpled. The suave Westernized gentleman in him had disintegrated into a dark unwholesome heap and Nirode instantly knew this would never shape into anything at all, for there was no despair on that face, no agony of doubt and will, but merely an uncontrolled vacuum, a blank. He stammered, 'B-but how can I?'

'Why not?' Nirode snapped, all patience gone, all pleasure in having goaded this too-tame beast. He wanted only to be done with him and on his own again. 'Why not? I thought that's what you've been blubbering about all evening, how you wanted to give up your rich, corrupt life and lead one noble and academic and creative.'

'But, Nirode, you-you know it hardly supports *you,* in the manner *you* live. And I-I and Sarla —'

'Well, you've got some money to last you a year or two haven't you? And by that time you might get the paper going in a profitable way. Don't you want to take the risk?'

'Risk? But how can I?'

'To hell with you then.'

Nirode ran in and was immediately engulfed by dancers, drunkards, sailors and prostitutes, all raucous, all disreputable, all joined in some wild celebration, while some of the best dancers and the sleepiest drunks seemed still, even to be in prayer. The air was dense with perspiration, fumes of rum and cheap perfume. Here quarrels raged, knives flashed, prostitutes were insulted, they screamed, noise subsided, music broke out ... Nirode, backed up against the bar, began to feel a known claustrophobia press in upon him. For a while he held it at bay with a glass of rum but when he saw Jit approach him again, heard him mumble about, 'My position, my status Sarla, you see — ah, you travel light, you — for me, too late...' then Nirode fled. This was not, after all, the free land of adventure for which he longed and out on the street he vomited.

It was towards dawn when he found himself in Sonny's room, eyeing a letter addressed to him, lying on the divan. It was not in his mother's hand, so much he could judge despite the pain that cracked his skull from ear to ear. He opened it and made out, through a ferocious sleepiness, that his sister Monisha had arrived in Calcutta and wished to see him. Monisha, her presence impressed his throbbing head only faintly. Then slowly the message filtered in, Monisha in Calcutta and over the still cemetery a pale dawn breeze wandered silently in through the window.

Monisha
HER DIARY

The Bow Bazar house. Central, an idol in the shape of an umbrella stand. Hung with folded black umbrellas like the offerings of pilgrims and worshippers. On either side of it, the reception arranged by the heads of this many-headed family. In the small of my back, I feel a surreptitious push from Jiban and am propelled forward into the embrace of his mother who is all in white and smells of clean rice and who, while placing her hand on my head in blessing, also pushes a little harder than I think necessary and still harder till I realize what it means and go down on my knees to touch her feet. They are rimmed red with *alta*. Another pair of feet appears to receive my touch, then another. How they all honour their own feet! More — I lose count — but many more. Feet before faces here, but the jumble of sounds is soft, tolerant.

Into the courtyard we go in a procession and the tiered balconies — four tiers of them — rise all around us, shutting out light and enclosing shadows like stagnant well water. The balconies have metal railings, intricately criss-crossed: one could not thrust one's head through them but one could climb over. Upstairs to our room. Here the idol splits into two: a black, four-postered bed in the centre and a gigantic black wardrobe against the wall. But it is not they that intimidate me — after only one night I already feel familiar with them, their smells, their silence — but the bars at the windows. Through the thick iron bars I look out on other walls, other windows — other bars. When we are left to ourselves in this room and the vision of many red-soled feet ebbs away, sound breaks in with coherence. A black, bitter, terrifying sound that repeats and repeats itself like the motif of a nightmare.

'What's that?'

'What's what?'

'That sound.'

'What sound?'

'It seems to come from that house, that window there.' 'Oh. Probably one of the children there preparing for a test, an exam.'

What kind of an examination could it be that exacts from a child this mindless, meaningless monotony of empty sound, hour upon hour, for it seems to have no end? I long to thrust my head out of the window — and cannot, the bars are closely set — and scream: 'Stop!' When I have achieved silence, I will shout, 'You are not preparing for an exam. You are preparing for the devil — a black, dead devil!' Will that secure silence for me and make it permanent? Or will this continue — this low, hurried, fevered recitation — through all my days here? I expect there to be many of them. Everything in this house is impressive in size and duration.

The last time I saw Nirode was at my wedding. He was dressed respectably in white muslin and sat somewhere on the fringe of the family, while I sat beside Jiban, in front of the fire and the priest and when I caught his eye, he smiled at me mockingly and winked with sympathy. So when I see him now, amidst my large new family, each one of them so solid, so rounded with a prosperity that has entirely to do with rice and rich sweetmeats and the security of Government posts and pensions, I look about and wonder where that Nirode is gone. There is nothing left of him but this small, shrunken shell — no, shell is the *wrong* word because it is the shell that is gone, the protective covering that one could touch, stroke or knock without fear, it is gone and what is left is this snail inside, transparent, fragile, something so bare and irreducible that I start back, I cannot possibly touch anything so exposed, it might bruise. Later on, I think how surprised they must all have been, my large, secure, round keepers, to see us meet in that hall, under the sacred umbrella stand and immediately, without touching, spring apart. I see his great black eyes alone reach out towards me, with something of the old mockery, the old sympathy and a curiosity that alarms me for it seems to sense in my condition something that he understands instinctively and profoundly and I do not know what it can be for, if he is all interior, I am all exterior and where can we possibly meet? What to say? What to say? Oh where to go and how to say it, this unsayable greeting?

Eventually, the hospitalities over — the tea, the questioning, the perplexity — we are left alone. Oh yes, Jiban remains sitting with us, but Jiban is never with us at all. Then I find my voice flying out of me — grown light and high and sharp after its long invalid confinement — and I cry, 'Tell me, Nirode... Nirode, tell me,' and he smiles for he knows exactly what I am asking him and gives me his most honest reply. 'I'm done with most things,' he says, his speech as urgent as mine. 'Most things I'm done with. Very little is left now. It suits me.'

'No, it makes you *ill!*' This high invalid voice of mine cries and I see Jiban give me a curious glance.

'No, not illness, not really,' says Nirode, but his fingers tremble as he strikes a match, lights a cigarette. 'It is only that the little that is left is the most exacting of all. I thought it would be easy now, easier than when I had to force and strain myself against my disposition. But, without strain and force, it is even more unbearable.'

'Tell me, tell me, tell me.' But that is all there is to tell. The family returns, hospitality and cross-examination — oh the questions the uncles ask him, about his post, salary, accommodation, prospects. . . He has none of these things, don't you see? He cannot reply. He disappears. I run to the window and watch this unshelled snail slip away, down the street, growing smaller and smaller, contracting himself to avoid the touch of passers-by. What is this little that he has left to him? It is so little, it will evaporate, blow clean away.

And that would be the most blessed thing that could happen. Look at me, my equipment, my appurtenances. My black wardrobe, my family, my duties of serving fresh *chapatis* to the uncles as they eat, of listening to my mother-in-law as she tells me the remarkably many ways of cooking fish, of being Jiban's wife. If all this were to blow away, what would be left would be very small too, transparent and vulnerable. Yet it would be lighter to bear. Nirode is lighter now.

Kafka, a scene for you.

All these days and nights I have heard the recitation that filters through the barred windows from the neighbouring house. I am still unable to decipher any meaning in this long, dull warbling rolled out quite flat into such monotony as only the insane could tolerate. All day it accompanies my thoughts and actions in this room seems to have overpowered me and taken my mind in its grip, yet it remains subdued enough to keep me from screaming out loud.

Then, this morning, as I come quickly walking down the passage that runs right round the third floor, my floor, I hear this voice, this recitation quite close, shockingly close. Not in the next house at all but here, here, here where I live. I fling aside the curtain at the door through which I hear this sound coming and I find sitting on the mat with a heap of greasy school-books, no madman, no yogi in meditation but Nikhil, my beautiful little cousin-in-law, reciting his lessons. When this terrible tumbling of my heart stills, I ask him, 'What is it you are reciting, Nikhil?' He smiles, so relieved at this interruption and holds up a book. In Sanskrit. 'I am learning my slokas,' he says. And his mother, whose teeth are black and who wears a gold armlet on her right arm up near the armpit, calls from the room next door, 'Why have you stopped, Nikhil? If you don't finish your work, boy, your father will whip you.' Nikhil's wide fresh smile contracts and wilts into a harassed, pinched grimace. He picks up his book again and begins to recite, trying to imitate his teacher's sonorous reading with his own inadequate broken piping. I leave him to it. I know the source now, of this haunting burbling that I had thought had been contrived solely to drive me mad...

As I walk away down to my own room, mine and Jiban's, I hear the sound die away and oh ! the relief is like rain, like night, like a splinter drawn from under my skin. I open my door planning to rest and sleep at last and am struck in the face, brutally, savagely, by a new uprush of this manic recitation, once more loud, once more deadly. It has crept around the walls and is once again pouring in through the barred windows. There is no escape from it. It surrounds this entire house, imbues it and drowns it. I lie on my bed and resign myself to it. I find my lips moving in keeping with it. It has become my own language...

'No, no, the doctor has said it is not the womb. It is these tubes, what d'you call them, Fallopian or Pallopian, what is it — they are blocked.'

'Is it? I heard once of a woman whose ovaries —'

'An operation?'

'The womb may be in the wrong position, then also an operation is required.'

'But it is the tubes, they are blocked.'

Like a burst of wild feathers, released full in my face, comes the realization that they are talking of me, my organs, the reasons I cannot have a child. I can't leave these vegetables I am cutting up for them — that would create a disturbance — but I stop listening and regard my insides: my ovaries, my tubes, all my recesses moist with blood, washed in blood, laid open, laid bare to their scrutiny"

Nirode. He has come again, after all, to see me. Down the street he comes, creaking and crackling in the largest and oldest horse carriage I have ever seen — huge wheels, high seats and the rich, rumbustious odour of horse. In the house, all lips compress with disapproval as I actually climb up into the carriage, beside Nirode, my *sari* lifting high enough for the whole street to see my leg right up to the knee I'm sure and they watch silently from the window as we go rolling off. Had Jiban been here, I can hear them say, he would not have allowed her to go. But Nirode was clever, he came when he knew Jiban was away at the office and so it is only the two of us who are locked up in this remarkable box of black leather and lumpy stuffing and violent, steaming smells. Rumble, rumble, creak jolt and tumble. Down the street and down the street we go. Where to, sir? Leave us at the Maidan

Leave us here under a young green tree where we may sit on a bench with our feet in the grass and the babies with their *ayahs* and the vendors of hot gram and ice cream are at a distance, in the sun, we in the shadow. The escape seems complete, absolute. Now I can ask Nirode, again, those vital questions.

He sags against the bench, like a doll from which most of the stuffing has leaked out. He wears a shirt that would better fit Jiban — only Jiban would not wear one that had only two buttons left to it and has had its collar torn off, leaving the neckline frayed. He wears, not trousers, but loose pyjamas that are stained at the rims above his sandalled feet. Nirode, you are so thin. If mother saw you her heart would — this I cannot tell him. 'Why?' is all I ask.

'The other things I did away with,' he explains to me as he smokes his cheap cigarettes. 'So that I could have time, at last, to write.'

'What? Poetry? Philosophy? Tell, Nirode.'

'Only a play,' he tells me and his eyes reach out to gather my reaction, dark and tentative.

'Only a *play*. *Only* a play, you say. To write just two coherent, lucid lines would be so much, Nirode. A whole play!'

'It is nearly done. That is why I came to see you. I thought I could relax a bit now. When I go back, I'll write the last words, I have them in my head. Your face is so clear, Monisha. I wanted to look at it first.' He smiles.

'And will you read it all through then? Will you give it to anyone else to read?'

'That seems inevitable, doesn't it? I've avoided so much lately, but I don't suppose I could avoid that, I don't know how to. But I should like to.'

'Of course, I know — keep it all to yourself, a secret, quite private, all your own, to keep and *gloat* over. It will hurt so much to show.'

He looks at me with a shrewdness that has to do with this new acuteness, this brevity of his. He says, 'Yes, *you* know how much it will hurt. But I think, I think that since I have written a play, my concern — subconsciously, at least — must have been to communicate, first with these characters I invented — there are just two of them and only one's alive and then to make these characters communicate, on my behalf, with an audience, this tiresome, bloody audience that one cannot get away from. I've just got to nerve myself to do this, Monisha — present my argument, my thesis to the world, have them boo and spit at it or do whatever they will. It's the most violent and dangerous bid for communication that there is.'

'The artist's? Is it more so than the non-artist's? Yes, yes, of course, Nirode, I see. How does an artist survive that, I wonder?'

'Do I look as though I will?' He snorts as he says this, gives a great honking laugh, showing his stained teeth and his face is too thin to bear this laugh. It seems cut in two and I feel certain there will be blood.

An urchin comes by with garlands for sale over his arm. Nirode says, 'I cannot buy you one,' and though their perfume is already in my nostrils, a pale green, chaste perfume, I say, 'I can't buy one either.' But when another urchin comes by, this one with a basket of hot gram, I buy a large bag of it and watch the hunger with which Nirode eats it all, never dropping a grain into the grass. When the bag is empty, he takes me quietly home. I am thinking of him in his private room, working at his play.

I am glad they give me so much work to do. I am glad to be occupied in cutting vegetables, serving food, brushing small children's hair. Only I wish I were given some tasks I could do alone, in privacy, away from the aunts and uncles, the cousins and nieces and nephews. Alone, I could work better and I should feel more whole. But less and less there is privacy. Even my own room, which they regarded at first as still bridal, now no longer is so. (The tubes are blocked, it is no good) and sisters-in-law lie across the fourposter, discussing my ovaries and theirs. Kalyani *di* throws open my wardrobe in order to inspect my *saris*. 'How many did you get at your wedding?' she asks. 'How many?' and sees my books. The whole wardrobe full of books. To my perplexity, she laughs. She says, 'I got a hundred and eleven,' and I am no longer perplexed: I see that of course she cannot know that there is nothing to laugh at in Kafka or Hopkins or Dostoyevsky or my Russian or French or Sanskrit dictionaries. But I wish they would leave me alone, sometimes, to read. Or that Nirode would come again and take me away to sit under a tree with him. He has not come.

Almost as often as I catch myself thinking about Kalimpong, I find myself thinking about Jiban's last posting, out in a district, away from the city and the family. The solitude of the jungles there, the aqueous shadows of the bamboo groves and the earth laid with great fallen leaves. The bell-like dignity of the elephant on whom we rode through the jungles. Jiban away on tour, I alone with myself, no visitors at all. Our house which we had to ourselves, its rooms almost bare of furniture, its squares of empty space and silence — friends to me and I've had to leave them behind.

From all sides their moist palms press down on me, their putrid breaths and harsh voices. There is no diving underground in so overpopulated a burrow, even the sewers and gutters are choked, they are so full. Of what? Of grime, darkness, poverty, disease? Is that what I mean — or the meretriciousness, the rapacity, the uneasy lassitude of conscience? Has this city a conscience at all, this Calcutta that holds its head between its knees and grins toothlessly up at me from beneath a bottom black with the dirt that it sits on?

The uncles take me to see the sights. I see the great Belur Math, the Jain temple, the Kali temple and then the newest biggest and most popular one of all — New Market that was once known, more appropriately, as Hogg Market. It is fairly early in the morning when we visit it, the merchants are yawning and rubbing slime out of their eyes and the itch out of their noses as they light joss sticks in their stores of jewellery and silk, confectionery and fish, hardware and fruit. I watch them pay obeisance to their favourite celestial pair,

Ganesha and Lakshmi, God of Fortune, Goddess of Wealth. These two I meet everywhere in this bright temple of commerce. Behind vast businessmen who sit picking their teeth and speculatively waggling their feet, up on the enormous iron safe that looks as though it is about to emit a great rumbling belch, there they sit, our celestial benefactors — sickly white plaster figures painted orange and pink, crude and garish amidst the paper flowers and joss sticks, but so powerful, so awesomely powerful. Here they dwell, in these houses of cut-throat, eye-for-eye rapacity, of money greed and money ruthlessness, to bless those who fatten upon it, to bless them and not to forgive. There are no ethics in these houses of trade anymore than there is anything aesthetic in the little plaster idols. Ethics are shunned, all is shunned except the swelling and fattening of the iron safe and of mortal, male flesh.

Quick, quick, out of here, out on to the street — straight into the thick quilt of pungent blue smoke that rises from the countless fires that are lit on the city's pavements. Once the smoke clears, slowly, I see another face of this devil city, a face that broods over the smouldering fire — a dull, vacant, hopeless face. The rickshaw coolie, the street sweeper, the tanner, the beggar child with his limbs cut off at the joints, the refugee who litters the platforms of Sealdah Station with his excrement and offspring — they share one face, one expression of tiredness, such overwhelming tiredness that even bitterness is merely passive and hopelessness makes the hand extend only feebly, then drop back without disappointment. Two faces — one rapacious, one weary — gaze at me from every direction. How to reply — with loathing or with compassion? Loathing's a fine fertilizer — the more putrid the manure, the more flourishing the crop of hatefulness. And compassion — would that answer this beggar whose arms have been chopped off by his kidnapper, trainer, mutilator and master? Too inadequate, too terribly inadequate. Forget compassion then, leave it to the dead.

No, there is no diving underground. There is not even the possibility of turning one's back, for fear they would spring on me, claw the flesh off my back and devour it. There is no escape from them. What am I talking about? Them — what them? The masses, as senior uncle calls them with a sigh? These dreadful ghost faces behind the smoke? No. Only this lack of solitude, this lack of conscience, that is all I mean.

I am so tired of it, this crowd. In Calcutta, it is everywhere. Deceptively, it is a quiet crowd — passive, but distressed. Till there is reason for anger and then a sullen yellow flame of bitterness and sarcasm starts up and it is vicious, mordant. Not the anger that brings up two fistfuls of defiance or makes the curved dagger flourish, but an anger that broods and festers like a pus-filled boil. This boil erupts, every now and then, now that the weather is so hot, the heart so parched. Ink bottles are hurled in the West Bengal Assembly, oaths and insults at meetings of the Calcutta Corporation, examination students overturn their desks, tear up their question papers and go on strike. Trams are burnt, the bonfire given a strong meaty savour by a roasting tram conductor or two and an old crone who, like me, stands watching, leans over and vomits.

'Be a little friendly to them,' Jiban begs. 'That is all they ask of you — a little friendliness.' 'Still depressed?' smiles the black-toothed aunt who kneads dough all day. 'A little more cheerful, is she?' sniffs Jiban's mother when she hears me singing to Kalyani *di's* baby in its cradle that hangs from the rafters.

Cheerful, cheerful Calcutta — these young girls with their soft bread faces and luxuriant hair falling pitch-black to their waists, who lean over the balconies with tender smiles directed at imaginary lovers beneath, as they drape yards of wet *saris* over the railings to dry; the busy passage of uncles who work in Writers' Building and come home to discourse heatedly and verbosely, on Bengal's rampant Communism and the high price of fish; the street outside the house with its jolly madmen, magicians, marriage processions, coconut vendors and pink and green and faded walls bleeding with virulent film posters and bristling with such felicitous signboards as 'Needlefight: Tailoring and Suiting'; such touching ones as 'Vigil: India's Most Sensitive Weekly;' such sound and satisfying ones as 'Girishankar Dey and Grandsons: Sweetmeat'. An occasional visit to the roof-top where Nikhil and his friends and cousins fly kites and pigeons and I watch a sunset that is all ashes and roses, poetry and flame. But it is swamped by smog and the stars that follow it are pale with tuberculosis. And where is Nirode?

'May I take Bun Bun and Annu to the zoo?'

'And why not my Tuk Tuk?' snarls Kalyani *di* who has begun to think me dangerous, an infidel who ought never to have been allowed into this stronghold of soundless practicality and chatter. I am too silent for them, I know. They all distrust silence.

So Tuk Tuk comes too. Hand in hand we go, dressed in our satin best. And for a while I think there is, after all, some place in Calcutta where there is rest, a relief from claustrophobia. Here the *jaruls* are in bloom, they extend many wicked candles of lilac flame to the smokeless sky and all the milk-white peacocks dance on tip-toe, strumming their fanned feathers like many-stringed harps. A kangaroo lies on its back to sun the soft honey fur on its belly, but its pouch, alas, is empty. Right across the lake wild ducks are scattered as thick as dry leaves and like leaves they crackle and stir in the wind — why don't they fly out of the city into the open, I wonder? Fat white geese give up chasing the skittering water beetles of these meandering green canals and paddle up to the shore to stare inquisitively at us, as we do at them, cocking their heads to one side and exclaiming with guttural quacks of astonishment at the world of human beings... The Anglo-Indian girls, hand in hand like a child's paper cutting, in flowered frocks made by the little tailors of Entally; the smooth-faced Bengali grandfather in a spotless white *dhoti* and grandmother in a cloud of starched white respectability and their numerous grandchildren, all picnicking out of an enormous tiffin-carrier on the lawn; all the vast families that emerge full strength from their ancestral homes deep in the city to bring the children to the zoo on a Sunday morning; the lover boys of Sham Bazar in navy blue and black bush-shirts, curling their little glistening moustaches and singing of *'Zindagi O zindagi...'**

I see many women, always Bengali women, who follow five paces behind their men. They wear *saris* of the dullest colours, beige and fawn and off-white, like the female birds in the cages and there is something infinitely gentle, infinitely patient about their long eyes, the curve of their shoulders, their manner of walking, which arouses not aggressiveness in one as the women of the north do, but a protective feeling. They make me a little ashamed of myself — of my defiance towards Kalyani and Jiban's mother — and I think of generations of Bengali women hidden behind the barred windows of half-dark rooms, spending centuries in washing clothes, kneading dough and murmuring aloud verses from the *Bhagvad-Gita* and the *Ramayana* in the dim light of sooty lamps. Lives spent in waiting for nothing, waiting on men self-centred and indifferent and hungry and demanding and critical, waiting for death and dying misunderstood, always behind bars, those terrifying black bars that shut us in, in the old houses in the old city.

The tiger paces up and down. Now and then he groans and his eyes are like the glass eyes of a stuffed trophy on the wall, for he is dead already. The eyes of these silent Bengali women are not dead, but they anticipate death as they do everything, with resignation. There is no dignity in their death as in the death of that proud and glorious beast, but only a little melancholy as in the settling of a puff of dust upon the earth...

What does it all mean? Why are lives such as these lived? At their conclusion, what solution, what truth falls into the waiting palm of one's hand, the still pit of one's heart?

Here is the answer — here, here, here. 'Look,' I will scream. I cannot believe — but here it is. Look through these bars, into this cage of doves — look, look at the terrible answer. Doves like balls of rain cloud, but in each soft breast a great open wound, bleeding, scarlet seeping over tiny feathers in a blot of fresh blood. Wounded

---

* 'Life O life...'

and bleeding, but scurrying about their cages, pecking grain, while over them fly blithe budgerigars like animated splinters of rainbow. These stay on the ground, restless, in flux and bleeding. The dove's stigmata — what does it mean? How can it be possible? How can they live, eat, work, sing, bleeding through life?

'They are called Bleeding Heart Doves. See, you can read it on the board up there,' says Tuk Tuk, who shares her mother's disdain of me. 'What is the matter?' asks Bun Bun, leaning against me in fear and on my other side Annu presses her hand over my wrist and says, 'It is only the colour of their feathers, aunt, it is only the red feathers that look like blood.'

'It is the answer,' I tell them but what the answer means, I cannot explain. Fresh blood gushing from their breasts, unstaunched, the doves murmur and croon. I wonder, I think that Nirode could explain.

To pretend to have forgotten, to pretend to believe in these trivialities, these pettinesses of our mean existence — is that right? To sort the husk from the rice, to wash and iron and to talk and sleep, when this is not what one believes in at all? What force of will does it require to shed, as I believe my brother has, at least to an extent, shed, the unnecessary, the diverting and live the clean, husked, irreducible life? If I had religious faith. I could easily enough renounce all this. But I have no faith, no alternative to my confused despair, there is nothing I can give myself to and so I must stay. The family here and their surroundings tell me such a life cannot be lived — a life dedicated to nothing — that this husk is a protection from death. Ah yes, yes, then it is a choice between death and mean existence and that, surely, is not a difficult choice.

Our South Indian neighbours have given senior aunt tickets to a music conference that they have helped arrange and, since no one else intends to waste his time at a concert of music, I am offered it. I and the old poor relation on the roof top, who is asked to escort me.

How simply laughable! We have never spoken to each other. I and the old roof-top dweller, whose lack of teeth completely disintegrates the stability of his face, are sent out together in the black hearse, like two black sheep, with the family standing in the doorway, shaking their heads, glad to have such troublesome *betes noires* away for an evening but uncertain of what might come of it — nothing good. I can hear them murmur, nothing sound. Music — vaguely they regard it as dangerous when not confined to the assets of young marriageable girls.

How right they are. It is extremely dangerous. It brings me to the edge again and again, catches me up and draws me to the edge and I am plunged down into something too intense to be borne. Or caught back and rebuffed at the last and most urgent moment. Utter humiliation and desolation.

At first it seems to be merely the surroundings that waylay me and confuse me. I long for the great *shamiana* to be cleared of its audience. I am sickened by the moist, odorous, swelling, vibrating welter of their reactions — the greased black heads swaying to the music, the hands beating out the rhythm on fat thighs. The going to and fro of vendors of *pan* and fizzy drinks. The babies waking up in sudden alarm when they should have been asleep in cool, white beds. The crowded garlands of jasmine and tuberose that smother blue-black hair and the sweet, stifling *attar.*

I am impatient, too, of most of the performers — that squat, sober woman singer who constructs a *raga* of such intellectual intricacy, then draws it to shreds with a dispassionate curiosity in dissection and ends it upon so flat a note, simultaneously pushing a pin down into her untidy bun of hair and rising and disappearing with her ragged *entourage* of elderly tutors and young, dazed pupils. How dare you? I swear at her. How dare you present me with so beguiling a problem and leave me quite helpless to find a solution? The dancer, too, young and zestful and gorgeous as a piece of sculpture from Konarak come to vivid, painted life, she sketches for me this entrancing mystery, with her exquisite fingers, performing gestures with them that contain the essence of it all in their stark evocation, their stylized perfection. Then, in reply to enthusiastic applause, she stretches out those agile arms and performs a snake dance, a peacock dance, I don't know what, only that it is vulgar, stupid, meaningless and I am betrayed again into confusion.

Then the *sitar* player comes out to play. By the way the sleepers are roused, babies stilled and attention conjured up out of the dissolution of a too long evening of too varied a programme, I know he is famed and respected. Yet I trust him — something withdrawn and brooding in his sculptured face tells me I can trust him to be himself, not to compromise, to remain singularly thoughtful and genuine. As a blessing upon my trust, he pours his music down upon me. Not wildly, not indiscriminately, but evolved with purity, with lucidity and presented with a tender undertone of deep melancholy and solitary sorrow. To each note my every vein and artery responds like a taut, sweet *sitar* string, plucked by my own emotions that match his faultlessly. I wander in this labyrinth at will and, blessedly, we never touch, merely remain in mystic communion with each other. I am willing to follow till I die.

But the *tabalchi* is waiting for an opportunity to enter — the duel or the duet — what? It is both, it is neither. With a little tap and run of his fingertips, he breaks into the *sitar* player's so carefully constructed *raga* and I hear the young intellectual clerks beside me say, in disgust, 'There now, the *alap* is over and the *gat* begins. From here on it is only showing off.' And so it appears, in the beginning, when it is merely an exercise in Benares courtesy, a somewhat flamboyant display of mutual admiration and rivalry. Exquisitely and elegantly they play to each other and for each other and I am proved right in my patience, my trust, because it is obvious that they are purists and play, not for an audience waiting to be titillated, but to each other, to their combined muse. And now begins that discussion, that philosophical argument that causes the *sitar* player to trace a dangerously complicated pattern, thoughtfully and wonderingly and the *tabalchi* to follow it, ironically, unconvincedly, both arriving at the answer with a simultaneous flourish. The more intricate the pattern, the more dazzling their performance in unravelling it and arriving at the sweet, lucid solution. More and more intense, violent and brooding grows the *sitar* in its quest. But the *tabla* is not to be shaken off, it always has a reply — ironic, reasonable and pertinent. Then the *sitar* flies into a passage that is surely climactic, tangled in that ultimate question that no human being may answer without first having glimpsed the face of death. Yet the *tabla* follows with nobility and heroically accomplishes an answer. There seems nothing left to say — not for human beings, city beings, body beings such as these, such as myself. But the musicians still have a supreme and most devastating trick of all to play. The *sitar* player, bowing low over his instrument, plays a bar that has divested itself of all the passion of argument and discourse, is magically subdued, gentle, imbued mothlightly with a human but inexplicable sorrow — my own sorrow, my own death. And softly the *tabla* replies to it, handing back the little bar with total compassion. It is over. Who has won? Who is defeated? What was the question? What the reply? Is this what life is then, my life? Only a conundrum that I shall brood over forever with passion and pain, never to arrive at a solution? Only a conundrum — then is that life?

Aunt Lila has not seen Nirode either. She sniffs and snorts like an old black mare at the mention of his name. She is offended, he has not been to see her for months. Where is he then? It is a large city to search. Aunt's car drives me home very slowly, down streets so different from the ones I see from my house, my windows, where past and present merge to form an unchanging sameness of trade, the joint family, disease and poverty — they have always been that way and are thus still. But here history lingers like a long twilight and the streets and squares belong to another period that will never live again. The houses here have aged with grace and are faintly lit by low gas lamps glowing a pale blue in the foliage. The darkness that subdues these roads is warm, clinging, womanish. Large Victorian houses are screened by royal palms; the shuttered windows and lacy balconies make them look like houses in a once-fashionable resort somewhere in Europe, grown very old and deserted long ago to the vicissitudes of soot-black rain and plaster-peeling sun. They suggest strange happenings behind their shutters, in spacious pillared halls

— parties, perhaps not ordinary parties, but parties to which ladies in crinolines are driven up in grand carriages by drivers wearing turbans; ladies who waltz and polka and flutter fans of lace and sandalwood; parties of people who lived long ago and died long ago, leaving behind only a few brass gongs and ivory elephants to descendants on grey British farms.

Here a period in history is preserved and somewhere on this cloying night its essence lingers. But it does not speak to me. It is only a passage of time from one date to another. Why did it happen? Why did it involve these strange, forgotten people, plunge them into exotic lost events? To what purpose? Why history? Why time?

Nirode is like this broken bird I saw in the aviary. Lying on a mat in his tin-shed room, so solitary on a roof-top splattered with pigeon-droppings and a million cigarette stubs that speak of nights of insomnia and despair. Too high a fever to be able to say anything or even to see. His lips cracked and peeling. It takes so long to do the necessary things — and it is Jiban who does them, mostly — and during all that time he lies on the mat and I, beside him, wish him a quick passage. Much fluid, the doctor commands and fluid we pour down his throat. Much of it is spilt because he does not swallow. He opens his eyes and looks in my direction but his eyes remain deep down in their sockets, they do not reach towards me and he does not swallow.

At the hospital, so much more efficiency. The tubes taped down upon his face, nourishing him. The glass jars of fluid gurgling. The grim tautness of darned sheets on an iron bed behind a faded blue screen. The odours and sounds and sighs of the diseased. With friends of his I cower in a corner, avoiding the nurse's eye because I cannot bear the cheerful strength in them. Let me be weak and Nirode also.

He is still lying broken on that spare yet adequate hospital bed, and we have to watch keenly to see his breath stir at all. The fever has stupefied him, it seems to have taken the place of blood in him. I

125

wish him the strength to be weak and submit to it, lie still and allow it to hold him or lower him, as it will.

The stupor gone, the fever still high, he raves and raves. Compulsively, gaspingly, he talks to the darkness, not to me or to his friends and the doctor says, 'Normal, quite normal.'

Jiban tells me the doctor's simple diagnosis is 'starvation combined with heat exhaustion'. Sonny, this flighty, nervous, light-headed young man who brought me to Nirode's tin-shed that afternoon, having found my address in the letter I at last wrote to Nirode, ' This is unlikely,' Sonny says. It is overwork and neglect and malnutrition that has been gathering for years. The dark, sinuous, underground creature called Nair, who seems too slick a man to be a friend at all, he says it is 'disappointment — and the heat of course.' All these have combined, they say, to make Nirode what he is now — an unshelled snail, a flightless bird on the iron bed, so uncharacteristically at the mercy of the syringe, the tubes, cylinders and the deadly cheerfulness of the nurses.

And what has Nirode to say about it? So much. I cannot cope with it all, sort it out and impose coherence upon it. Sometimes it seems to be a dialogue he is repeating very slowly as though striving to make precise something that has become blurred in his memory. Trying to follow the alternating lines, I think it is an argument in which he is pleading, eloquently but over-dramatically, for something he has done or made and in which he has a faith of which I had not thought him capable, which I had thought him too slight and too cynical to bear. The answers to these pleas for understanding and recognition are ironic in their excess of politeness and their total negativeness. Then the voices drip and drop and become inaudible. He seems to have fallen asleep. Then, in this restless sleep, he murmurs into his stubbly beard and flat pillow what seems to be a recitation, with the cadence of uneven poetry, again over-dramatic. Possibly he is quoting from the play he told me about under the tree, but I can understand no single word of it. Then he laughs, a thin, splintered laugh that goes on too long, breaks off shrilly and turns into a gulp, then sobs — at which point I cover my ears with my hands and the young men beside me excuse themselves and go out for a smoke on the veranda.

While they are still outside, he turns on one side — the tubes and tapes try to hold him back, but he manages somehow and his face seems a little more relaxed. His eyes are open but focussed upon a point a little to one side of me, so I know he does not really see. He begins to chat, softly and pleasantly, about mother — not of mother in the years when he so inexplicably turned against her, just after father's death, when we thought he would grow closer and dearer to her than ever before — but of mother when we were all very small and she would play Chinese checkers with us on the bright mats, and put us to sleep with stories from the *Mahabharata*. He becomes incoherent, uttering phrases that are too personal and unrelated for me to follow and I turn my mind away, leaving him astride a pear tree bough, and wish the nurse would bring him something to make him sleep and rest. Forgetfully, my hand reaches out to touch his, give him an assurance of rest and he catches it by the wrist and weakly flings it off. Flings me off. Lightly, not with distaste, but as if to say, "It is not you I need.' What does he need, this grounded, broken brotherbird? Merely his mother? Or a justification of his birth? Whom does he converse with so fiercely, as if he were involved in a dialogue with death itself? Not merciful physical death, but with Oblivion, Meaninglessness. Again and again he tries to explain, to plead, to convey something which no one understands or approves or accepts. Always he is beaten down, spurned, turned away into an anonymous solitude he seems unable to accept. Accept, I plead with him, accept defeat, accept insignificance, accept solitude, a truer gift than any communication, any art, any faith or delusion in the world can offer you. If he accepts, he will survive.

I read in my book:

'Arjuna said: "O Keshava, what are the signs of a man of steady wisdom, one who has attained God-consciousness? How does the man of steady wisdom speak? How does he sit? How does he walk?"

'The Blessed Lord said: "O Partha, when a man is satisfied in the Self by the Self alone and has completely cast out all desires from the mind, then he is said to be of steady wisdom.

"He whose mind is not agitated in calamities and who has no longing for pleasure, is free from attachment, fear and anger, he is said to be a saint of steady wisdom.

" He who is free from all attachment and neither rejoices on receiving good nor is vexed on receiving evil, his wisdom is well established.

"O son of Kunti, dangerous are the senses, they even carry away forcibly the mind of a discriminative man who is striving for perfection.

"The man of steady wisdom, having subdued them all becomes fixed in Me, the Supreme. His wisdom is well-established whose senses are under control.

"Thinking of sense objects, man becomes attached thereto. From attachment arises longing and from longing anger is born. From anger arises delusion; from delusion loss of memory is caused. From loss of memory, the discriminative faculty is ruined and from the ruin of discrimination, he perishes.

"But the self-subjugated attains peace and moves among objects with the senses under control, free from any longing or aversion.

"In peace there is an end to all misery and the peaceful mind soon becomes well-established in wisdom.

"There is no wisdom for the unsteady and there is no meditation for the unsteady and for the unmeditative, there is no peace. How can there be any happiness for the peaceless?

"For the mind that yields to the uncontrolled and wandering senses, carries away his wisdom just as a boat on water is carried away by wind..."

"As the ocean remains calm and unaltered though the waters flow into it, similarly a self-controlled saint remains unmoved when desires enter into him; such a saint alone attains peace..."

Knowing Nirode as he was in these years after he ran away from college and floundered about in such torment, I would have thought him capable of precisely that action without regard for the fruit of action which the *Gita* tells us is the finest wisdom of all. So was his action when he worked on that grim newspaper, so was his action even when he edited his own magazine. But this play has trapped him at last. And he is more involved with mother and the past than I had suspected. 'Cast away involvement,' I plead with him silently, 'cast it away and be totally empty, totally alone.'

In pleading with him, exactly to what extent am I trying to persuade myself? I suffer his fever so deeply because it is mine also. My silence, I find, has powers upon others, if not on me. It has made its impression on Nirode at last. I see it diluting the irises of his eyes, down at the shadowed pit of those dark sockets. Today he lies still and regards me with recognition. He tells me, in a flat, toneless voice, 'What a waste it has all been. What a complete waste,' and he tries to laugh at himself but performs only a creaking grimace. After a while he says, 'The Ajanta murals, the temples at Konarak and Khajuraho — not one of them bears a single signature, does it?' He asks it like a question of potent interest. So I reply, 'No,' and this makes him smile, the white skin on his lips cracking as he does so. 'But writers,' he says, 'writers were always a vain bunch from Kalidasa downwards. Blasted fools, the lot of 'em. It's only a waste.' His throat is dry from so many days of uninterrupted talk and he croaks and falls silent, regarding his toes that appear from under the bottom of the sheet which the nurse keeps so scrupulously smooth across him, as if she thought him a corpse.

'I'm done with everything now, Monisha,' he says, without even an attempt at a smile and I am content to have his face free of grimaces. 'Even that grinning, smirking, disastrous old witch — art. All art is communication, that's the popular cry of the day, isn't it? Well, if so, all art is —' he uses a rough word, casting it off his tongue like the thick coating of fever. 'I never did listen to anyone, did I, Monisha? Well, I've given up talking and telling now as well.

129

I've sealed up my ears and my mouth, only my eyes are open — but just a slit. It's blessedly peaceful.'

I nod with slow and heavy emphasis. I have never felt so at one with this rough, unaffectionate, undemanding brother. We are completely in accord at last — for a moment, a second, before I feel the familiar pain of tearing apart into separateness again.

'You'd better go and tell my landlady she can have her pigeon-roost back, Sonny,' he tells this butterfly friend of his who still hovers. I had forgotten him. 'I don't pretend I can keep it on any longer. Independence is too damned expensive.'

'Let me take your things back to my flat, Nirode.'

Nirode makes a gesture with his skeletal, iodine-yellow hand. It is barely a gesture, only a thin flow of blood in those veins made visible for a second, that is all. But it is his gesture of acquiescence and I don't know whether to feel relieved or enraged, whether to say 'Good, now rest, now sleep,' or whether to cry 'Don't, Nirode. you mustn't.' I realize simultaneously that whereas I started by praying for him and teaching him — in silence, of course, silence *my* sleep sister — he has progressed beyond me. Here is a combination of acquiescence and renunciation I have not yet made. Here it is, in this plant gesture, this wind gesture of a weak invalid hand. Back he goes into the captivity of friendship, concern, criticism and the world. Yet he will never again be a part of it as he once was with such passion and anxiety — this gesture has removed it all to a safe distance from his self. This time he will be wary, he will walk alone in the dark and he will not stop to talk to strangers.

When Sonny leaves the room, Nirode looks at me as if he has sensed *my* thoughts. This one-dimensional existence, how acute it has made him. I return his look and see the beginning of a shell growing very silently across the body of this snail. Soon he will be covered. I shall be left tapping.

'If you'd like to read the play, you can get Sonny to give you the MS. Then throw it away — or keep it, just as you like. It's the most absurd incidence of *my* life, the most futile thing I ever did. When these sickening Theatre Group amateurs turned it down — "Not

130

quite in our line, old boy," they minced, "afraid we're not quite up to stuff like that" — and then that publisher, that fat, well-greased Bengali who said, "It has no sentiment, my friend, it is sentiment the public wants", I thought *they* were absurd and inferior. But I've been going through it, word for word, while lying here in bed and really it seems too ridiculous to have made this painful attempt to convey — oh, anything. I made myself inferior to all these frauds by making an attempt to make them read anything I'd written. Anything that is of any value to oneself should be kept A Great Secret.' He closes his mouth and utters these three words in a low hiss and his eyes have a glow-worm of a smile in them. Hoarsely he whispers, 'Secretive Monisha, you understand perfectly what I mean, don't you?' I nod, but do not try to tell him of the pain of bearing secrets, the frequent miscarriages and stillbirths. He'll know them for the rest of his life now. 'Never tell them your secrets,' he continues in that graveside whisper. 'They'll only laugh and ram them back down your throat. You see, it means nothing to them, nothing.' He is staring at me with eyes that seem to sink further and further back into those shadowy recesses. We are still, motionless.

Then the nurse enters and briskly she begins to fold up the faded blue screen. She carries it away, thus proclaiming Nirode's return to the world. We find ourselves in the centre of the general ward, only one narrow iron bed amongst dozens of others, each with its ghostly occupant, each ringed by fly-like visitors. The sounds and odours that the old cloth screen could not possibly have kept from us and yet did, now assail us with triumphant violence. Bed-pans, rags, disinfectants, soiled bedclothes, sores, whimpers and complaints, they crowd the ward like shadow invalids, ghost and shadow invalids.

After staring mutely at them for long minutes, Nirode stretches his neck, throws his head backwards and groans, 'Tell your secrets, don't tell 'em, do you think it makes the least bloody difference?' And he places his hands over his eyes and I know one of his headaches has begun and there is nothing to do but leave.

Nirode's play. Carelessly, I forget it on the bed when I have been through it, paid it my visit of condolence and Jiban seizes it. Seeing

Nirode's name on it. he leafs through it and begins to question me till I realize, with a start, what has happened, snatch it away in fury. This violence of action — where has it sprung from? I thought I had subdued everything inside me, laid it in a dark and quiet place to sleep. Yet it has leapt out, this violence that has made me snatch the manuscript out of Jiban's astonished hands. We stare at each other in equal confusion. 'It's nothing, just scribblings,' I excuse my brother and put it away. The humiliation of touch and communication — I'll save Nirode as much of it as I can, as I save my own self from it.

And Nirode's secret could not really hold any value for anyone else. This play, this dialogue, it is difficult to say why he wrote it, at such cost, leaving me, at the end of many thousand words, in petulant dissatisfaction — not despair, not disappointment, merely this dissatisfaction. Here we have a blithe young box-*wallah* who has had too much to drink at a night club, reeling down a dark street. He stumbles and falls into an open manhole. Emerging from it, greatly altered in looks and spirit, he is confronted by a passer-by, an Englishman, dressed impeccably in a ruffled silk skirt, plum-red waistcoat etc., who, in introducing himself, reveals himself to be a tradesman belonging to the East India Company. They continue their walk home together, all the while discoursing on the city of two hundred years ago and the city of today. They then enter the same house and who is to tell who is the present occupant and who is the ghost of whom? So much I gather. But why Nirode wrote it and wrote it with such wild incoherence, such formlessness, such lack of subtlety, grace or vision, I do not know. Perhaps they are all there and I cannot see them. But I pay it my condolences and I promise to keep it a secret.

The problems mother presents to us all with her wide-flung and seemingly ageless love! She wants to open a bank account in Nirode's name. 'Tell him all he needs to do is go down to the bank, fill in papers and sign. I shall keep it filled with a monthly cheque. If I send it to him by post, he will not bother to open the envelope, but if I do it like this, with the greatest discretion I have been able to plot, then he might use it and eat and dress as I wish my son to do.' I imagined Nirode would turn down this suggestion as he has done all others — with bored impatience. But he grows fierce. Raising himself on an elbow which shakes and trembles with the pressure of his shrunken body, he speaks with ferocity. 'Tell her to go shove it up that old major of hers, all her stinking cheques. Tell her I want no share of it, no share of banks or finance or insurance and all the rest of her bleeding equipment. Tell her she'll never get me to sign my name or fill in a form. I'll not put my name to anything again, to be gloated over by her or smirked at by those Theatre Group goats. I'm done with signing my name, believing my name, or *having* a name. Tell her that. I'm nameless. Tell her that.' The trembling spreads from his elbow to the rest of his body and he abruptly lies down, stonily regarding the world to which he will never lend his name again.

He looks like a skeleton dressed in these clothes given to him by that dark friend of his who so enjoys giving Nirode things, for reasons I cannot quite grasp though I sense they are ugly. I stand him on a sheet of newspaper in the centre of this brightly paranoiac room of Sonny's and cut his hair. It is long since I have felt such sensuous delight in anything as in cutting through Nirode's thick uneven hair with a pair of blunt scissors. It lies about our feet in tufts and wads and the dogs bark at it. I think this is one of the most memorable things I have done as a member of a family, a human being. I have cut my brother's hair.

He swings around and catches me smiling. He says quickly and roughly, 'You're not going back to that house tonight, are you?'

'Yes, I must. The car is waiting for me.'

'Why must you? Why the hell must you? Can't you stop going back? Can't you just turn and go in another direction, by yourself? Leave the whole fat mess of them to wallow in their kitchens and bedrooms without dragging you in as well?'

He glares at me with such contempt, my joy falters and dies. I kneel and sweep the fallen hair into the sheet of newspaper and carefully fold it up, like a wrapped, prepared gift. I address his feet gently. 'You said yourself these things do not matter. To leave and destroy, to stay and concur — what difference is there?'

His feet move towards the window, harshly scraping. I wedge my gift behind the chair leg, against a wall, where the draught will not dislodge it and leave.

I rarely see anyone outside this family now that Nirode has recovered and I am no longer granted the privilege of having the car and driving out to see him. But today he comes again, more uncertain on his feet than ever, more pale, more strained, but with the black stubble of his beard removed and with him a strange friend, David. This friend's glance I do not mind, as I do the others' looks. His smile is so timid, so self-effacing, that I smile back and wonder how he manages to efface himself with such discreet success. He and Nirode address each other in an affectionate, bantering tone that always stops short on the right side of respect, never falls into familiarity that could offend two such intuitive hermits.

As we stoop over cups of black, bitter tea in a wooden stall, I discover in this unattached, drifting bird-creature that vital element that is missing from Nirode and myself — the element of love. And I discover that it is the absence of it that makes us, brother and sister, such abject rebels, such craven tragedians. In place of this love that suffuses the white face of this mystic waif, we possess a darker, fiercer element — fear. I see now that both Nirode and I shy from love, fear it as attachment, for 'from attachment arises longing...' If only love existed that is not binding, that is free of rules, obligations, complicity and all stirrings of mind or conscience, then — but there is no such love. It is not there in my relationship with Jiban, which is filled only by loneliness and a desperate urge to succeed and once plunged me into the most calamitous pleasures and pains, fears and regrets and never again will it possess me. Nor is it there in my relationship with mother which is filled with an inbred and invalid sense of duty, of honour, of concern. Besides, she is too whole and complete in herself to need our little offerings — actually need them, not merely their symbols and exercises, which she demands and collects with such touching ardour. But I do not mean these physical passions and congenital connections at all — I mean by

134

love only an awake condition of the conscience. I fear this and avoid it and so we step backwards from love and allow our hands to drop from her too warm flanks, unable to respond because we are frozen with distrust. Nirode's conscience sleeps, it has been so battered and bruised that it sleeps from sheer exhaustion. Mine has withered and died away. Never, never wake to draw us into the dreadful ring again. Allow us just this — to stand back, apart in the shadows and watch the fire and the flames, the sacrifices that are flung into it, the celebration, the mourning and permit us not to take part.

'Who was he, Nirode, that funny Irishman?'

'Oh, more than funny, I assure you. He is many things I know of — ceramist, linguist, *veena*-player, true friend and guide. And something else that has only now come into being — a seeker after God. He is going up into the mountains now. I told him to be careful and not run into mother by mistake — to find a monastery where he can meditate and find the true God.'

'Yes, I thought so.' I turn around to see the waif disappear down the street and bid him farewell with admiration — but without envy. I do not envy any man who is walking into the ring of love, faith and betrayal.

I am accused of theft.

These pettiest of people, they regard me as meaner than them. They think me a thief. To be regarded so low by men and women themselves so low, it is to be laid on a level lower than the common earth. I find that I am alone here. I find on this level that solitude that becomes me most naturally. I am willing to accept this status then and to live here, a little beyond and below everyone else, in exile.

It was the money I knew Jiban had left in a biscuit tin in the wardrobe, just behind my *Idiot*. He had already left for the office when I remembered Nirode's hospital bill and went and took this money and paid it to the hospital — which looks as if it really needs to have its bills paid. And spent a very congenial afternoon in Sonny's crazy room, drinking tea and listening to Nirode tell, lightly and cynically, of his encounter with the Theatre Group amateurs and then Sonny had amusing tales to tell of his interviews with various company directors and managers, and I laughed and had many cups of tea.

Coming home, I found the big house shrunken, drawn together like a boil about to burst — so dense was their suspicion, their fear. All the men and women who, by leading such scattered, disunited lives, had managed to give the closed, barred household a certain spaciousness, a false reflection of the big, free world, were one in their distrust of me and I saw the same expression on every silent face I passed on my way up to my room. They did not allow me to enter it. Just as I was about to open the door I have been ordered to keep always shut, Jiban's mother called out. 'Money has been stolen, you know, Jiban's money.' I turned to look at Jiban standing disconsolately down in the courtyard below and he did not look at me. From the other end of the balcony, his mother shouted the details across to me. 'He left it in the cupboard when he went to the office: my son is always careful of his things. Only you were in the room at that time. When you left, you shut the door and none of the servants could have gone in. Of course the servants will be dismissed, all of them. I will not have a thief in my house, I say, I will not have a thief in my house. Who is to tell who this thief is? After all, you were the only person who was in the room all day.'

I could no longer meet her eyes. It was too late to say anything now. I opened the door and went quickly in and on my back felt their white-hot brands sink in and burn through my skin: Thief.

When Jiban came in — much later, the room was dark and hours of my guilt had gone by to consolidate it — I told him quickly. He did not say, 'Why did you not tell them at once?'

He said, 'Why didn't you tell me before you took it?'

A secret: that hour when at last the house is asleep, even the servant boy in the kitchen, even the old crone at the water tap. Then I creep up the top-most flight of stairs, on to the roof. Ah! splendour — splendour of stars and solitude! At last the kite fliers and the pigeon trainers are gone, the young girls who love to lean over the parapet and the old poor relation who has at last been found room below. All gone, fallen through the trap-door into that dense well, all sighing and stirring and groaning there as in a mass grave. I above them in splendour. The splendour of the city outspread below me, like a mantle that invites me to step on it. But, queenly, I refuse this singular privilege. I prefer to be at so great a distance from it as to only see its lights, not to hear a single sound from it. Do you hear me, city of Calcutta? City of Kali, goddess of Death? Not one word from you, I said, not a sound. No shriek, no groan, no cry. I come here for silence, my few moments of night silence, so cease your moaning and wailing a while — that never really frightened me, you know, you melodramatic old witch. I'll have only those tiny lights from you, in a looped skein across Howrah Bridge, ember-like on top of radio aerials, lowly glow-worms in the murky streets. Thank you. Now leave me, leave me to the sky. Leave me to gather the stars, frosty and distant and cool. Leave me to gather — and then to reject them. Queenlike. I'll have only the darkness. Only the dark spaces between the stars, for they are the only things on earth that can comfort me, rub a balm into my wounds, into my throbbing head and bring me this coolness, this stillness, this interval of peace. Even sleep has not this sweet, swaying stillness as these immensities of night sky to which I tip my face, allowing them to fall into my eyes and fall. Sleep has nightmares. This, this empty darkness, has not so much as a dream. It is one unlit waste, a desert to which my heart truly belongs. I think that what separates me from this family heaving and rolling beneath me in its dreams of account books, pensions, examination results, store rooms, births, marriages, ovaries, wombs, dowries, locks, keys, property, litigation, wills, bequests, orphans, adoptions, relations, marriages, births and property — I think that what separates me from this family is the fact that not one of them ever sleeps out under the stars at night. They have indoor minds, starless and dark. Mine is all dark now. The blessing it is.

For two hours my exile is lifted from me and I am summoned to massage her legs, for the aunts are all worn out. I go and massage them. It is not difficult at all. My heart stays perfectly quiet, enclosed in a sheath of such darkness as none of them would ever dare to touch. And as I massage, I do not tell myself, ' She is Jiban's mother, her legs give her pain, I am helping to relieve it because she is Jiban's mother and old.' I tell myself, ' She thinks I am touching her. She thinks I am touching her feet. But I am not. I do not touch her nor does she touch me — there is this darkness in between. They will never reach through it to me.'

I am still allowed letters. Here's Amla's. She is coming to Calcutta, to work. Amla in Calcutta. I wonder what she is like now, my little sister. Oh not little now — with all her talents, her career, her confidence, her gaiety, she's very large indeed, much larger than I. I grow smaller every day, shrink and lose more and more of my weight, my appurtenances, the symbols of my existence that used to establish me in the eyes of this world. I am already too small to be regarded much by anyone. I will be invisible yet.

Sometimes I wonder, would mother take back this shrunken, etiolated, wasted thing into her house if I begged her to? She did, when I failed again and again at school and crept home to her. But I know I will never ask her again. I do not fear her disapproval, no. Her disapproval I could adapt myself to, but it is her disgrace in which I will not involve myself. I will involve myself in nothing anymore. Try, even, to avoid — and that is not so easy as the rest — despair. Think only of the ultimate wisdom. I am turned into a woman who keeps a diary. I do not like a woman who keeps a diary. Traceless, meaningless, uninvolved — does this not amount to non-existence, please?

Amla

'Is there another *sandesh?* Is there one left?' Amla asked and, leaning over, she jumbled about in the tin she had brought with her, a faded picture of a flowery English inn on its lid and lettering in mustard yellow and neon blue that said: Puja Sweetmeat Store. Haricharan Das and Nephew.

'Amla!' her aunt reproved her in a broken twang of a voice. 'Your mother sent that tin for Monisha.'

'But Monisha doesn't like sweets,' Amla said contentedly and leant back to nibble at yet another *sandesh.* 'Besides, I didn't eat on the train.'

'Only because you couldn't get anything sweet, I'm sure,' her aunt grumbled, but Monisha only smiled and her eyes seemed to look beyond her newly-arrived sister to a vision of the railway tracks that had brought her here, spanning jungle, parched earth, a great swift river.

'Mother really made them herself?' she asked, in a heavy, remembering tone that Amla must have heard before, but never had it disturbed her so inexplicably. 'Even though she loathes cooking?'

'Yes, she does, but you know what a fetish she makes of motherhood.'

'Yes, yes, her capacity — she has a great capacity,' Aunt Lila muttered, not approvingly, and put her spectacles on her nose as she searched in her sewing box for something. 'If I were you, Monisha,' she said, suddenly, decisively, 'I'd go to her. Now Amla's left and she's alone. Not for her good so much as for yours. Is she not pale, Amla?'

141

The sisters glanced at each other, but something made them drop their eyes and look away — these three years had separated the changes and growth in them. The truth was that Amla was deeply shocked and confused by some change in Monisha that was not exactly blatant — that is, it was not so much a change on the surface of her face and body — yet seemed to have seized the girl and turned her inside out, giving her an eery unreality. Something, Amla saw, had laid its hands upon her, scarred and altered her till she bore only the faintest resemblance to the quiet and subtly uncaring elder sister Amla had remembered. Monisha seemed to suffer some shock, too, in thus regarding her sister — shock at feeling such a crepuscular passion of remembrance and longing at the fresh sight of Amla. Both sipped the cold dregs of tea in their cups and were silent. The cold, dusty room visibly darkened with their reservations. Aunt Lila's huge sigh raised a flurry of dust, each particle of which was a past hope that had come to nothing.

'It is this city,' she sighed. 'Of course I'm glad you've come, Amla, it was inevitable and perhaps you will not let it oppress you but will enjoy your new job and independence.'

'Of course I will!' Amla insisted with laughing relief. 'And Calcutta doesn't oppress me in the least — you can't imagine how exciting it is to arrive, to drive through Dalhousie Square with all its red gingerbread houses, their domes and cupolas and pigeons. When I drove into Ballygunge and saw its weatherbeaten old mansions and palm trees, I kept thinking of John Company and Sir Thomas Roe at Jehangir's court. It *excites* me, aunt.'

Aunt Lila immediately threw down her sewing as though it were a petty thing compared with the excitement Amla felt at her arrival in the city and the advent of her career in an advertising firm. 'Good,' she called in a ringing tone that rattled the garlands of faded paper flowers draped about the yellowed portraits of her late husband's ancestors. 'That's the spirit in which to start your career, my girl. That's what I like to see in young people — spirit. There's not too much of it around,' she added darkly.

'Do you mean Nirode?' Monisha asked with a sudden twinkle in her still eyes, as improbable as a star reflected in a bog.

Aunt Lila seemed not to like that question. She did not like men. 'Nirode,' she said with a snort. 'He's a dark horse — I don't know anything about him. Why, has *he* spirit?' she asked Monisha, dilating her nostrils with distaste, disbelief. Even her spine had stiffened, exactly as it had done in the days when her husband was alive and she had looked across at him, obese and self-satisfied in that black box chair in which Monisha now perched so timidly. 'Well, that's another matter,' she said suddenly, shrugging her thin, angular shoulders. 'It doesn't cost *men* much to show spirit. It's when I see it in a woman that I'm pleased. My daughter, she has it and it's done her good, no matter what your mother might say about it. A girl must have spirit and a profession, I always say, and no one can take up a profession from which she gets no pleasure. Am I right, Amla?'

'Of course, aunt. Only I don't know yet whether there'll be *much* pleasure in drawing ladies wearing pretty slippers or gentlemen relaxing with prominent cigarettes.' She laughed, to herself, at an inward joke, and Monisha's eyes widened with a fleeting curiosity and astonishment at this naive levity. 'Of course, I'm going to try.'

'My dear,' said her aunt hoarsely, 'even if you don't, take pride in your *independence,* in this wonderful liberty you have of choosing and undertaking a career, any career. Our country belongs to its men,' she twisted her lips bitterly at this. 'But it won't always be so, not when there are girls like you and my Rita...' here she began to mutter. The recollection of her daughter often brought on this confused, shadowy relapse into the eccentricities of old age and loneliness.

To smooth over this tiresome embarrassment, the girls began to chat at last, with a forced intimacy and tentative laughter, Monisha doing the questioning and Amla telling her of her years in an art school in Bombay. Slowly some confidence, some verve lifted out of their unease and they did not notice their aunt abruptly heave herself out of her private pit of shadows and sit there on the edge of the slippery sofa, watching them and listening to them with open-mouthed hunger. She was so moved by their youth, so dismayed by her age. Soon she struggled out of that and, seeing them so slender and singular as they sat eating sweets, the doorway framing them and the veranda and the sunlit garden behind them, like a sentimental portrait of youth's vulnerability, she began to feel that what they were in need of was not, after all, her encouragement — youth gave them that and illusions — but her protection, the protection of her bitterness and experience. She spread out her long, thin fingers as though to seize the rays of afternoon sunlight that slanted in from the lightflooded veranda through the great arched doors, as though she longed to drape it about their shoulders, twine it into their hair, give it to them in strands to hold. And hold tightly, tightly, she pleaded and her huge eyes flashed, so that the girls grew aware of her once again, though they overlooked her passion and wondered only why she had chopped her hair short in that absurd bob, what she had gained by so futile a gesture of emancipation. Nor was she aware of their chatter, their smiles, but only of the elusive light that now hovered about them, now retreated to the veranda and from there to the lawn which it brushed with its bright lacquer, in quickly dissolving strokes. Hold, hold, her clumsy hands implored, *this* is of value, *this* is important. Don't you see? Not that gay party, not the silliness of young men in a bus — but this light that is within your reach, here now, but there already. Her severe little cap of white hair stood out stiffly, her eyes started out of her head and at last she spoke out aloud.

'My dear, how marvellous to see you like this, Amla, absolutely free and in the centre of such an exciting world. You *do* have fun and how right you are to make the most of it — not all of us had that pleasure in our young days. But Amla dear, don't let all your spirit spend itself on that, don't let it dribble away, don't let it all empty out, because that isn't worth very much in itself.' She did not see their embarrassment, the surprise on Amla's face or the wry cynicism on Monisha's soft lips, the brief glints of grudging admiration in their eyes. She saw only the glow of their faces, the unused fineness of their skins, like stretched golden petals in the twilight. She saw something — the future, the possibilities, the endless traps — that troubled her and she talked on in her large, intense way, drawing all the fire to her, to give away as a precious gift. 'You belong to such a uniquely free generation — and that is something very new in our country. At last we have won our freedom and you can do as you choose. How much you *can* do — how many careers and vocations and all the spirit and intelligence to do it with. My dears,' she said and her lips were trembling, 'my golden ones,' she said, because she was so afraid for them, yet believed in them and wanted so much for them, 'I hope you will not think it enough merely to be young, to be able to read any book you choose to read, to ride on a bus amongst silly young men, to go to a concert at night. With such opportunities at hand, you must surely want something greater than pleasure alone or the security of marriage alone — something more *rare,* more responsible...' Her fire crackled incoherently now, while outside the sky melted into smudges of pale orange and lemon and mauve, faded into the smog and smoke of the city twilight and birds were left crying in the trees. Poised on the edge of the sofa, she urged and coaxed them, praised and encouraged them, fanning the dancing sparks she saw in them and they sat toying with their teaspoons. Amla had tired of her speech, Monisha had sunk into sullen immobility. So she paused, sank back for breath and her purple eyelids slipped half over her staring eyes. The twilight mood of the garden, the girls silent in white, Monisha's growing and intensifying defensiveness, these overcame her at last. 'You are very different from my generation,' sighed Lila Chatterjee who had once started to be a doctor, turned nurse, married and become a social worker who watched, anxiously and wistfully, the travels and adventures of her daughter Rita who had lost her faith in men, after a spectacularly short-lived marriage, and was seeking something 'more *rare,* more responsible' in the Physics laboratories in Paris. 'When we were young, we believed, we stood on the rooftop and shouted to the world that we would come and conquer it! But the young don't do that any more. How sad to be so realistic, so cynical, so without dreams...'

'It isn't that,' Amla stirred in a little frowning surge of resentment. 'Perhaps it is just that we believe we should do things first, then shout about it.'

'Yes, yes, of course you are right, you young — you young...' nodded Lila Chatterjee and searched about the sofa for a handkerchief with which to dab her forehead and eyes, found only the untidy

145

muddle of her sewing and used that instead. 'Perhaps we didn't achieve so much after all,' she said, hurt to the quick, then suddenly flashed. 'But we did win freedom, remember that! We gave your generation your freedom and it is your heritage to do with as you please. I envy you,' she permitted herself to say, with a rough growl in her voice to eradicate all self-pity from it, for she now quickly surveyed the ruins of her many careers and admitted that it was not *all* of it Mr Chatterjee's fault, no, not all. And the last sunlight had slipped away from the garden, the sunset was wreathed in grey.

For a few moments they sat there like shadows merged with the vast dark furniture and the dust and deadness of the big hall, overcome by the atmosphere of that old house — its exhaustion, its disillusionment, the dry and unlovely remains of glories that in themselves had been tarnished and false. So silently that no one even heard her, Monisha had risen and was collecting her belongings. She began to leave without saying anything. Amla jerked into wakefulness, overwhelmed by a new fear of this sister who had turned sleepwalker, ghost, some unknown and dread entity. This unnatural silence and unobstrusiveness of hers, it seemed to emphasize the distance she had travelled from reality into a realm of still colourlessness.

'Monisha,' she cried, her voice quite weak with unidentifiable fear and since Monisha did not pause, she ran in a rustle of starched *sari* and anxiety, and her aunt, too, rose gaunt and stiff to join her in this chase after someone, something who had already escaped from them, making their chase futile.

It was not their voices that halted Monisha in her passage, but she did halt and when Amla caught up with her, she was standing and regarding a bronze statue that stood in a corner, almost obscured by a lush green plant. She was looking at it with a smile — not the aloof, superior smile of one who has side-stepped sanity, but a childlike, mischievous smile that made Amla gulp and blink when she saw it, so unexpected was it in that withdrawn and joyless face.

'Aunt,' Monisha's voice rang out in the passage crowded with overgrown plants, many-armed umbrella stands, yellowed portraits and metal and marble sculpture. 'Where did you pick up this strange thing?'

Aunt Lila eyed it and then nervously looked away. She stood cracking her finger joints with horrible brittle cracks. 'That — that Nirode of yours,' she said in a rush. 'What he is up to, I never do know. One day he comes and plonks it down at my feet, looking as though he hasn't eaten for a month, so what am I to do but write him a cheque for it? Who knows what he's up to. Do you, Monisha? Someone should tell your mother,' she added darkly, pressing her hands together. 'Oh, the telephone,' she cried and left them with haste that betrayed her relief, leaving the girls to study the unusual bronze: Shiva and Parvati locked together in an upright embrace that pulsed with so grand a desire, so rich a satisfaction that soon the girls, too, looked away from that inscrutable smile on Shiva's face and the taut buttocks of Parvati who had turned her back on the world as she pressed upon her consort her purpose and her delight, inexplicable to both the girls.

They went down the stairs together to the drive where Monisha's car stood waiting, and Amla began to laugh, but more uncertainly than Monisha who was cat-eyed with conspiracy in this piece of Nirode's mischief. 'What *does* she mean?' Amla asked. 'Nirode sold it to her?'

'Yes, he did — for an astronomical sum, the sort museums pay. And it was made by some dubious friend of his in his own backyard and buried underground for three weeks to give it the appearance of three centuries of age. Nirode himself got it for, I think, twenty rupees.' She settled into the car and closed the door, leaving Amla outside, stripped of her merriment and stiff with dismay.

'But, Monisha, why did he do that?' she cried as the motor began to vibrate.

Monisha's eyes blurred and went dark as if the sense of it all had guttered and gone out. She pressed her lips together and looked old, harsh, eager to get away and be alone. 'Nirode has spirit,' she said through her teeth and the car moved smoothly down the drive and disappeared behind the untidy hedge of over-coloured crotons and flowerless oleanders. Somewhere in the compound, a servant woman began to beat clothes under a water tap, with a cacophony of whacks, hisses and splashes that aroused Amla and made her trail up the stairs, through the house and towards the still back garden.

She sat down abruptly on the marble stairs that led to it — a flight of them, cracked and held together only by its lining of damp moss. On two posts that flanked the steps stood blind, dispirited marble goddesses — the Greek ideal copied and recopied till the last drop of immaculate blood had been sucked out of it — holding what looked like ugly metal cages for Birds of Paradise long flown from them. Actually they were meant to shelter lamps that lit the stairs on gala evenings, but Amla could not remember and nor, for that matter, could her aunt, when last such an evening had enlivened this dank, unbreathing garden where the unmown grass housed singing swarms of mosquitoes and spider webs alone multiplied and reproduced amidst the leaves of plantains and mango trees that had years ago surrendered the desire to propagate and fructify. Only a few grotesquely crooked temple trees were starred with bridal flowers and, at the edges of the grass, a row of tuberoses closed thick white petals about their secret scent. The halfhearted lights of neighbouring houses looked down upon this pocket of decrepitude and dankness and were not bright enough to illumine it. Better so, thought Amla, moodily lowering her chin on to her knees and hugging them with her arms. The journey had tired her, she now realized and the day had proved too long by several hours. All the tingle and the thrill of entering the big city, of beginning a new career, all that now curled up inside her tired head and went to sleep. She was aware only of this giant exhaustion growing and swelling inside her, of a feeling of sick apprehension and despair. Monisha... Monisha had always confused her, often mystified her, but never to such a degree as to more than exasperate her. Now she stirred with foreboding — this sister had wandered away, into some unholy garden of her own, stood there now like one of these lifeless statues, on the brink of a stone fountain, and seemed not to realize that the fountain was dry and what confronted her was no ripple and tickle of cool water but only dry, hard flagstones.

No, no, she was only allowing the sad spirit of this garden, this house, to lead her into such fear. She stood up and waded through the tickling grass to the temple trees. But if she left Monisha behind on the broken marble stairs, it was only to meet a phantom Nirode under the crooked, resilient branches of the low trees. She had known Nirode was not 'working,' that he accepted no money from his mother and therefore, he must be, financially in a very precarious state. But she could not visualize poverty so great as to invade a young man's soul. She was no prude and far more a prankster than either her sister or brother, but what Monisha had told her, too briefly, horrified her. Perhaps it was only her tiredness, this enervating humidity of a Bengal autumn. She scraped with a finger nail at the barkless flesh of the tree in childish absorption and remembered her aunt's warning against the city. It had seemed to have no concern whatsoever with the bright streets through which she had driven this morning, its busy river traffic hooting and bobbing on a spacious waterway or with the flocks of bleating sheep on the Maidan and its benign raintrees, or with the historic houses of business and their gingerbread gaiety, or the urgency of traffic that poured in its wayward and madly individualistic fashion up and down the long-named streets. Aunt Lila's house had been oppressive enough, even at noon, but the spirit of this garden, shadowed as it was by the brooding city, was more than merely oppressive. It was a dampness and a darkness that swarmed with uneasy, dissatisfied spirits, all sighing, complaining and warning, warning the young and living of the city's gory history, of slow mortality, of the swamps that flank it, the corruption that rose from it in hissing odours and seeped first into the business houses, then into the rich houses that were founded upon these businesses, and the rag-and-thatch huts that huddled beneath the high walls, finally invading the tired and listless mind, then laying waste all that was fine and moral.

That mortality seemed to creep into her bones like the damp itself and she heard it sing in her ears like a mosquito. Quickly she bent and picked the fallen flowers, waxen white and golden-hearted and put them in her hair like so many badges proclaiming her youth, her aliveness, her courage. She was unaware that, at the very earliest falter of dawn light, urchins crept over the garden walls to collect these very flowers in their baskets, that at every street corner these flowers were hawked in garlands, that every woman wore them in her hair in the evening, each one aware that by next morning the perfume would have turned rotten, the pristine whiteness would yellow and the whole garland hang limp and repulsive as a dead serpent. They would be thrown into the rubbish bins with mango peels, fish scales and stained newspaper.

Nirode would not come to see her at her aunt's house and this made her disturbance grow for it confirmed what she had that first evening already perceived — that this monster city that lived no normal, healthy, red-blooded life but one that was subterranean, underlit, stealthy and odorous of mortality, had captured and enchanted — or disenchanted — both her sister and brother. Nirode said, in his note, that he would give her tea at a riverside cafe where tea was cheap and though he gave her some directions, he seemed not to realise the difficulty a young girl might have in finding her way to it.

It was an afternoon of streaming winter rain and when the street lights came on at four o'clock and the streets were slick and aglitter with their unquiet reflections, Amla could sense her apprehension altering to excitement. The taxi went wailing across the Maidan where trees loomed out of the swaying grey rain to shelter some sodden sheep, and one happy boy fished in a pond for fish that leapt to receive the raindrops. On the Strand, she got out of the taxi into the rain and grew hesitant once more. Customs and Port officials taking shelter in dark warehouses eyed her with mixed approval and censure. After stopping to ask the way of a clerk under a leaky umbrella, she gingerly made her way across a swaying gangplank that spanned a dirty strip of river, to Nirode's floating cafe. A Chinese cook and an African sailor, both in aertex vests, were listlessly playing billiards on a ragged, moth-eaten green table. She went through the room to the open balcony where Nirode waited for her.

They spoke each other's names and embraced surreptitiously. Nirode tipped over a tin folding chair to let the rain run off in trickles, then pulled it up to the table for her. They sat across from each other, arms squarely on the table, each openly studying the changes and the samenesses of the other. Having done so for a few moments, Nirode smiled at her with straight lips through a haze of cigarette smoke, thick in that damp air, he seemed to have found exactly what he expected, neither more nor less. She smiled back from her eyes, only the tightening of her fingers about her handbag betraying her agitation and behind him she saw how the sky above the river was smudged with sooty rain, how the tug boats shot streams of black smoke into the air as they churned busily up and down, how the big ships rocked like old women lulling themselves to sleep, how the waves slapped the sides of the cafe, making it tilt and rock, how strange were the names of the barges and tugs.

"Kamala" and *"Kola"* she read, finding it an excuse to turn away — whether from Nirode's lightless eyes or from the pungent, cheap smoke of his cigarettes, she herself could not tell. *"Kola"*, would that be an Australian boat? And *"Klootie"* and *"Vowchopie"* — what could *they* be?'

'You make this sound like a shady tryst.'

'You made it sound that way in your note,' she retorted and her voice at last opened and expanded. The old easy rapport that had existed between them long ago, now lifted itself off the dirty river in a cold, refreshing gust. 'Why this mystery?' she teased.

'What mystery? That's your romantic, gossiping schoolgirl mind. I like this place — don't you?'

'Nirode,' she said, opening and shutting her eyes quickly. 'What have you done to your shirt?'

'Ah, you're mama's daughter alright,' he snorted, making an ugly face and spitting out half a cigarette in order to immediately light another.

'No, but tell — those aren't buttons, what *are* they?'

'Staples,' he grinned. 'I lifted a stapling machine off a friend's desk when I went to see him in his office. It's so much quicker to staple your shirts than to sew on buttons.'

Again she shut and opened her eyes swiftly, like a butterfly fanning its wings, brilliant black ones. 'How do you get out of it? Or don't you?'

'Should I show you?' Placing the cigarette between his lips, he prepared to tear open the ragged blue shirt.

'Don't be foolish,' she said quickly.

'You do sound like mother, Amla.'

'I do not. You have no idea what she sounds like now.'

'What, has she changed, that old statue of consistency?'

'Of course she has, everybody does. It's years since you've been home.'

Nirode got up so abruptly that he left his concealing mask of yellow smoke below him, at the level of his waist and, alarmed by it, Amla looked up to see his face narrow and compress into that of an animal contemptuous of its captors and observers. Behind him the menacing network of a ship's crane loomed cage-like.

'Has she sent you down here to remind me of that?' he asked quietly.

'Don't be silly,' she exploded then, standing up to be his equal in antagonism — and how she loathed antagonism, mistrust, suspicion, violence! 'Didn't you read my letter at all? I've come because I've got a job here, in an advertising firm, as a commercial artist. I start work next week. I thought it was going to be exciting and wonderful but — ' she waved her hand at the clumsy, formless traffic on the curdy river, 'this city, this city of yours, it conspires against all who wish to enjoy it, doesn't it?'

He seemed to relax and drooped over the railing beside her. He was smiling. 'You're a bright one. You've only been here a few days and you've found that out already.'

'Oh not *found* it out, just felt it,' she said in exasperation because she was feeling sick, physically sick. Could I be seasick? she wondered and turned away from the sight of the grey-lipped waves sucking and sucking at the sides of the boat. 'Aren't we having tea?'

Tea arrived, a great white pot of it, dark as the river below them and filled their cups with bitter leaves. The yellow cake was several days old and crumbled like dust in her mouth. But the tea was hot and the rain had softened to a mild drizzle, its spray blown in by a cold, rough breeze that rippled and fluted it so that the dark riverway, seen through its undulations, was softened into something melancholy and gentle. She began to get over the shock of seeing Nirode less than half the size he had been at their last meeting, four years ago, at the nervous and ceaseless movements of his skeletal hands, burnt at the finger tips to an iodine tinge by nicotine, at the unkempt and unclean mass of his long hair, his clothes, too big for him and worn thin, hanging loosely as shrouds upon his bony frame.

After they had chatted a bit more amicably, mostly about Arun who struck them both as being exquisitely neutral ground, she asked, 'What do you do when all your stapling and tearing apart of shirts finishes them off? It must do so very quickly.'

'Oh I get a new set of old rags from a friend who is approximately my size — a lot more prosperous that's all.'

'Have you many friends, Nirode? Is it difficult to make friends in Calcutta?' she asked, stirring the leaves in her cup.

'You'll make dozens,' he smiled at her, a mocking and disquieting smile. 'Young men will take you dancing at the "300" and the Golden Slipper. You'll learn to drink small gimlets and sherries. Young girls in your office will envy you your years in fashionable Bombay, old ladies will ask you to tea...'

She made such a face that he broke off with a laugh, but there was little affection in that laugh, mainly a bored mockery. 'I've come here to work,' she said, made defensive by that laughter. 'I've played enough in Bombay. And I've heaps of ideas — I wonder if I'll get the chance to use them, as a commercial artist.'

'Commercial artist. Sounds too bloody awful for words. Poor old Amla, do you really expect anything from a career stamped commercial?'

'Ah, I heard you had lost your faith in commercial writing,' her hurt pride gave her the nerve to say. 'That much mother gathered from Monisha's letters, but she was very reticent and never said what you *were* doing — not even when I met her. Perhaps she didn't want to, in front of aunt. Aunt doesn't much believe in you, you know.'

'She believes in the goods I peddle,' he said, cocking both eyebrows and laughing in a way Amla could not help feeling was slightly, vaguely hyenaish. 'If one is to go by the sum she paid for it.'

'I heard about that,' Amla said. 'She's hidden the statue behind her bushiest potted plant.'

'What did you think of it, the bronze?'

'I thought nothing.' She hesitated, lifting a spoonful of soaked tea leaves. 'It's awfully earthy, isn't it?'

'You're earnest about the wrong things, Amla,' he snorted. 'Perhaps you ought to marry after all, like Monisha. Nisha laughed. She thought it was hilarious.'

Amla's extreme distress made her face blur as she looked out on the river where *Klootie* and *Vowchopie* bobbed up and down in unison like a pair of sooty twins. It hurt her to find Nirode allying himself with Monisha, not with her who had been his pet sister once. But, though in pain, she could not break this fouled and knotted thread of conversation and drop it disgustedly into the river before she asked, 'And you really bought it for just twenty rupees?'

'Thirty, thirty, my dear girl, metal isn't cheap any more, not even the shoddiest kind.' He spat out a cigarette and opened a fresh packet with such a crooked grin upon a face too thin and fine to take it that Amla began to feel sick again. The cold spray of rain blew in, her hair was damp with it and the metal tabletop was beaded with moisture.

'I got a lot more than I expected, I'll say that for the old bag. She was so anxious to get rid of me and dump my amorous Shiva behind the shrubs before any of the servants saw it, that her hand shook while she was writing out the cheque. Much to my advantage, that. The first good turn an odious philistine ever did me. I needed that money,' he said and struck a match with a short, harsh scratch.

154

'To buy a new set of shirts? Or a box of staples?' Amla tried to make light of it. Nirode had always been her favourite in the family.

'More than that. A book shop.'

'A book shop!' Her voice rose and quivered like a band of bright evening light in all that mass of raincloud and twilight, and Nirode seemed to be watching her face freshen and flower. 'What *fun*, Nirode. You never told — oh, may I come and see it?'

'Certainly not,' he said but he was smiling. 'It's not a picturesque little bookstall for browsers. You'd never even find the street if I gave you the address. It's close to the University, that's what I wanted but all I could get was one foul store room at the back of a big, gloomy house. One has to go through the kitchen and past a row of latrines to get to it. Not very conducive to brisk sales, I admit.'

'Nirode, you're not selling *dirty* books in there?'

They laughed together. They remembered past conspiracies ending in similar gaieties. Both leaned on the table, closer to each other, relief at this all-round approval lifting the very rainclouds above their heads.

'It does sound as if I am, doesn't it? And now you've given me the idea, I don't see why I shouldn't branch out into that lucrative field. But later, I'm still stocking up on musty, scholarly text books and dictionaries and first editions and only editions and things. It's at its worst stage now, the one of haggling and bargaining and snooping around.'

'But,' cried Amla, made careless by the headiness of this gay understanding between them, 'why on earth don't you tell mother about it? She's got pots of money that she's just waiting to give you, Nirode, the minute you ask for it and she'd be thrilled to finance a book shop, especially if you tell her its arty.'

He grimaced so ferociously that she stopped. 'Mother,' he said. 'When do little girls get over their mother complexes? That's the worst of having a family — see just one of 'em, even the nicest and in no time she's signalling to the rest of the clan to come and catch him, catch him and brand him with the family name, family money,

155

family honour. I've given up using a family name, Amla, and I want no more of family life.' He began to pay off the waiter and prepare to depart. It was darkening now and the rain had ceased. A yellow light came on in the billiard room, falling upon Amla as well and he glanced at her as if he wondered if she was actually the same freckled child who had played in the sun with him in Kalimpong, the geranium-scented sun that chequered the blue hills and whitened the wild daisies that grew in every green groove and cranny of the mountainside. He seemed to wonder and not to recognize. 'She's written to me often enough, offering those pots of money,' he continued. 'But she insisted it be safely put in a bank. Well, if I were to run an account, I'd have to start signing all sorts of papers and sign I will not. That's what everybody wants — my signature. Then they have me, you see. But I don't sign and I won't have a bank account.' Swinging across the gangplank he felt himself free of her again and spoke more casually. 'I'll tell you my ambition, Amla — or rather what all my ambitions have come down to: to earn only as much as I need immediately, never so much as to spill into a bank,' and striding down the Strand, he burst out singing:

'Ghosh Mosh Chunder Bose my name,
    In Radha Bazar I keep my shop.
O I'm a veree good Bengalee babu.
    In Radha Bazar I keep my shop.'

She thought he meant her to smile and she smiled dutifully, a small and pallid smile. On the river a tug gave a long-drawn hoot-hooot-hooot of comic alarm and the short hairs on her arms stood on end with fear. Now it was dark, ships were conglomerations of light, brilliant after their bath in the rain and jaunty since it had ceased. She could still hear the slap and suck of the little, dull, persistent waves and she drew down the corners of her mouth as she reflected that the years of sweet sun on daisies had come to an end and that in the vicinity of her strange brother and ghostly sister there was no sun at all, only the darkness of a rainy winter evening and the indifference of an ancient river.

As she got into the taxi he hailed for her on the Strand and waved good-bye to him from behind a misty pane, she realized that she had quite forgotten the main thing she had planned to do — find out from him about Monisha. But then, she thought, rolling down the pane to let in the night air, what point was there in asking one stranger about another?

Despite all the stimulation of new experiences, new occupations, new acquaintances and the mild sweet winter air this sense of hollowness and futility persisted. Daily it pursued her to the office, hid quietly under the black mouthpiece of her telephone, shook — ever so slightly — the tip of her pencil as she traced the severe lines of a well-draped *sari,* then engulfed her in the evenings when she attended parties at which she still knew no one well and at night when she tried to compose her unsteady thoughts for sleep.

The most defined and concrete form her uneasiness took was in her concern for Monisha for, like Nirode, Monisha made no attempt to contact her younger sister again or arrange another meeting. In dismay, Amla realized that neither admitted the slightest need of her. Strangely enough, when one considered that Nirode was the one in the family to whom she had always been the closest, she did not worry so much over his neglect of her; she was able to persuade herself that he was engrossed in his new enterprise and she had seen that he had grown tough, invulnerable, could well protect himself. Obviously he had pulled himself through a crisis, both mental and physical, and it had clothed him with this prickly, unsightly, but very safe armour. If she worried about him it was because of his wasted appearance and his alienation from their yearning mother. But Monisha...

With an eruption of energy, Amla finally invaded the house in Bow Bazar. She felt curiously as though she had been there once before, she knew it so well from Monisha's detailed, ironic, gently amusing letters. The monstrous umbrella stand with the furled black umbrellas hanging from its many tortured antlers, the tap in the courtyard that leaked, the tiered balconies that rose on all four sides of it and the women hanging long *dhotis* and *saris* to dry on the wooden rails, the voice of the child monotonously reciting his lessons... all these she knew and recognised from Monisha's letters, yet she had not, not quite, expected to find Monisha actually living in its midst.

They spoke not more than two sentences to each other on that fatally lost afternoon for Amla was shown straight up to Jiban's mother's private balcony and Monisha brought there to meet her. The afternoon that Amla had impetuously prepared, in its wrapping of honeyed winter air to hand over to Monisha as a token, a gift, a bribe was taken over by the old woman who opened it with her capable and practical fingers and extracted a silver *pan* box with which she busied herself for the next half hour, spreading and rolling one exquisite *pan* leaf after the other. While Monisha sat silently on the divan beside her sister, the mother chattered and chirruped avidly as a sparrow at a social gathering. She had so many questions to ask of Amla, concerning her career and her education in Bombay. 'Is it true that the Parsis there throw their dead to the vultures? They do — ah, so I had heard... Is it true that young girls there wear frocks?... Were there any men students in your college with you?... Do you draw these pictures we see in the newspapers? They are getting more and more improper. There is one of a girl coming out of her bath, it is an advertisement for hair oil — do you know who drew it?... How do you go to work every day? Will you not marry? Has your mother spoken to you of marriage?' Her small quick eyes devoured every detail of Amla's dress and behaviour, and her mouth curled in tolerant amusement at them. Finally, accepting the fact that she would not be given any time alone with her sister, Amla rose to leave.

She was asked if she had a car waiting for her. No, she replied, she had come straight from work, by bus. And how, then, did she expect to go home? By yet another bus. Impossible! At this hour of the day? A young woman travel alone by public transport? No, no, not in our house, such things are not done. Quickly messengers were sent — who was free to escort Amla safely home? None of the uncles were back yet, but a young cousin was found on the roof, flying kites and made to put on a clean bush shirt, comb his hair and fetch a taxi. A few minutes later the old crone who washed pots and pans in the courtyard below, called to say that the taxi had arrived. Voices called back from all tiers of the balconies, 'Coming, she is coming!' Monisha was permitted to accompany Amla down the many flights of stairs and on each landing women with faces like freshly baked bread looked out, drawing their *saris* like vermilion-edged cowls about their heads and children watched silently, so that Amla went tiptoeing down, aghast at the damp pressure of critical attention impossible to avoid in any corner of this house.

The cousin, now that he was not being watched by his relations, cast aside his sullenness and smiled a white coconut smile, eager and excited by this unexpected little adventure that had come his way: he had never been entrusted with an errand so important and so charming. He began to laugh and chatter. Amla followed him out on to the street with a sigh.

Monisha, standing in the doorway, suddenly called out her first independent sentence of the evening. 'Amla,' she cried in the sudden, harsh tone of a night jar, a wild bird flushed from some unexplored depth of jungle, 'Amla, always go in the opposite direction!' When Amla turned with a puzzled air to ask her what she meant, she caught only a glimpse of the colourless face, narrow with intensity, before Monisha turned and ran away up the stairs at a speed that made Amla fear she would slip and fall. She got into the taxi and settled back against the embroidered upholstery and then saw *why* Monisha had been in such a hurry for now she was leaning out of a window on the first floor, waving and smiling and nodding, in an optimistic and encouraging manner, at her stupefied sister. Her head, protruding from the dark window, was like that of a stuffed rag doll with a very white face nodding insecurely on its neck, its eyebrows and mouth painted unnaturally dark.

The taxi did not wait for Amla to deal with this situation that Monisha had turned, by her smiles and nods, into something uncannily disturbing and oppressive and she sat back, pressing her hands to her temples, then firmly and slowly smoothing back her hair. The boy at her side was chatting, calling her 'Amla *di*' with a familiarity and an affection that somehow touched her despite her preoccupation with a tragedy she could not understand, but sensed.

'I am myself thinking of working in advertising firm. I cannot be artist like you — Monisha *di's* family is so artistic — but perhaps I can be copy writer. What do you think? My father thinks I must join Government service, but *everybody* is in Government service, I do not like to join also, it is so dull. I would like to work with commercial artists like you, in some advertising firm. What do you think, Amla *di?* Perhaps you will like to see some of my writings first. I can lend you.'

'Nikhil,' she said, remembering his name with stuttering difficulty, 'tell me — Monisha herself will not tell — has she been ill?'

The boy was disappointed. His vivid face seemed to step back a pace and he bit his lip, rather dramatically. 'She is very thin, isn't she? She was thin when she came from Jalpaiguri with Dada, now she is also thin.'

'Yes, yes, but has she been ill, here in Calcutta?'

He squirmed, not liking these too direct questions that seemed to hammer down from a schoolteacher's taut lips, not the soft mouth of an artistic and exotic young woman whom he had immediately begun to idolize. 'I don't know,' he grumbled, 'how can I know? Women are always locking themselves into their rooms. I do not know if she is ill when she locks herself in her room or not. How can I know? Next year, I have my finals and I am working very hard, my teacher says I must get first class to be admitted to a good college like St Xavier's.'

She turned around to face him and her face was not demanding, only pleading. 'Please tell me,' she said. 'I had not seen my sister for a long time. Now I find her very — changed. Do you see much of her? Do you talk to her ever, Nikhil?'

'I *like* to talk to her,' he said in sweet confidence. 'In the beginning I showed her my writings and borrowed her books and we talked very nicely.'

'In the beginning? And now?'

The boy faltered, but so briefly that Amla could not tell whether it was because he suddenly recalled a dire warning from his father,

160

uncle or grandmother or because he had again lost interest. 'Now she is much in her own room and I am studying for my finals. I have completed one revision and will revise two times more, then my teacher says I will be well prepared for my exams.'

Amla persisted. 'Does she sometimes see her friends?'

'Friends?' he was amazed. 'Yes, many friends come, also relations. Many relations.'

'Your cousins, not hers.'

The boy began to regret the whole confusing episode, it was not at all what he had bargained for. He became quite agitated and spoke rapidly in short sentences, sounding remarkably adult in his harassment. 'I don't know. I don't know. So many uncles in this house, so many aunts and cousins. Everyone having guests and visitors, all coming and going. If I want to speak to them, my father says, " Go to your room and do your lessons." If I go to my room and study, my mother comes and says, " Why don't you come and pay your respects to them?" I know nothing, then they complain I know nothing. It is a bad system, this joint family, it makes it very hard for me to study and pass exams. It is not easy to prepare for final exams. Last year twenty-seven boys of our school failed.'

Amla sighed. She straightened her handbag on her lap and said, 'So you plan to join St Xaviers. What subject will you take?' She was rewarded by a smile that bounced to his lips like a new tennis ball and a flood of soggy confidences punctuated by affectionate, even adoring cries of 'Amla *di*' that lasted all the way home.

Feeling aged by at least ten dreary years, Amla escaped from the young man in a patterned waistcoat by slipping aside to put down an empty glass. This only brought her too close to two women on the divan, one very large and damp with perspiration, dressed in pink georgette and pearls and the other very tall and angular and bespectacled.

'But is it quite safe, this sealing of tubes?' asked the plump one in an avid undertone.

The sharp one spoke loudly. 'Nature,' she said, 'is a wonderful thing, Kunti. If Nature wants something to happen, it will happen no matter what scientists and doctors do. But send her to me and I will do my best. Just after delivery is the best time.' Brood sow and veterinarian, Amla tacitly named them and edged past on to the balcony which, though not empty, was cooler than Mrs Basu's drawing room. This was a party thrown by the accounts executives of her advertising firm for their clients — an annual affair to which the staff looked forward on account of the lavish entertaining for which the Basus were well known. It served her right for having come inspite of knowing all this. Amla gloomed over the railings at some dry palms that stood rattling their fans in the dark garden below. She had gone to parties alone in Bombay, but here she was overcome by a stifling fear and she wished she could have Nirode or Monisha with her and knew it was hopeless to ask either of them to accompany her into society, a word Nirode used with scorn and Monisha with disbelief. She made a sour face at these dry, sparse palms and listened to the evening being noisily shredded into trivialities till they floated as thick and dry as confetti — not coloured confetti, but newspaper, brown paper confetti.

On the other side of a flowerless potted plant two youthful voices discussed matters of vital importance.

'It's the perks that add up,' insisted a nasal voice wrapped in a silk scarf. 'I agree the basic is much lower than yours, but there are these perks.'

'Ah but then you miss out on the expense allowance,' bellowed a voice inflated with whisky. 'And you can count on that going up, together with the taxes.'

'But my dear chap, there's the house, the furnishings, the entertainment allowance, the tour allowance,' chanted the silken voice belonging to one who was known, in his office lunch room to be 'slow on the uptake.'

'My boys,' interrupted a voice like a sack of concrete crashing into a cosmetics store. 'My boys,' it roared, 'do not speak of taxes. Taxes! Taxes! Taxes!' and with arms still flung up in protest, the vast and stolid Mr Basu who looked as though he and he alone stocked the entire Calcutta stock market, rounded the potted plant and drew himself up before Amla. He lowered his arms stiffly and made a little gesture with a glass of whisky and soda. 'I beg your pardon — we have not met.'

'Amla Ray.'

'Miss Ray, Miss Ray — ah-ha, the brilliant new-comer to my wife's little playpen. Now, now, no offence meant — I wasn't making fun of your company. I was only making fun and only a little — of my wife, of this whim of hers of having a career. Ah well, I say, women must have what they want, gold bracelet or advertising firm...' and laughter rumbled inside the big belly and rippled the white nylon shirt that covered it, and his sly little eyes beamed at the young girl who reminded him, unfortunately for her, of the daughter he would have liked to have. So he stayed talking while she ached to get away.

Amla tried to avoid looking at him as she unwillingly conversed and wondered if these were the sort of parties her mother had had to give for her father's business friends and if, indeed, her father had not, in his youth, been very unlike this crater of commerce placed so irrevocably in front of her. She began to feel uncomfortably warm in her silk blouse, and her replies grew so vague and prim that Mr Basu at last began to flicker his little eyes about till they caught those of some accomplices. With a commanding arm he drew them up to be introduced, a ginger-haired and somewhat shakily gay Scotsman and a younger and more severe South Indian. The ginger-haired gentleman slapped Mr Basu on the back with hefty affability that made Mr Basu guffaw as though this were a joke in itself and Jit Nair, with a pipe obstructing the true line of his mouth, was left to talk to the young woman on the balcony.

They discussed the financial wizardry of both Mr and Mrs Basu, various young people littered about the room in the attitudes of public speakers and street-corner cadgers, copywriting as a form of literature and theft. At last he removed the pipe from his mouth and confessed, 'The resemblance is so striking, I simply must ask you — are you by any chance related to Nirode Ray?'

163

For the rest of the evening, as they sat eating chicken curry and *pulao* on the divan, drinking their coffee on the balcony or turning away those who interrupted with coldly dismissing looks, they attracted the glances and comments of all, every one of them running in the same well-worn groove. 'That Jit,' guffawed Mr Basu, light-heartedly punching his ginger-haired friend in the midriff, 'he has quite a way with the females, doesn't he?' and received an answer that made both of them double over and giggle in silent senility. 'The youngest girl at the party,' sighed the young man in the patterned waistcoat, 'what do you think they see in that black, old lecher, Sonny?' The women were uneasy and it was not just the old gossip about Jit that made them so ruminant and suspicious, it was something about the young Amla which they could not, with any fairness, describe in their own jargon as 'standoffishness,' but which distinctly and emphatically set her apart from them. The older ones, quite deafened by their diamond-studded ear-rings, wondered if it was this singular fashion of hers of not wearing any jewellery, of dressing so simply, while the younger ones who sipped small gimlets with little nostril-pinching shudders, felt it was something she had probably acquired in Bombay — 'it is a very cosmopolitan city,' they said — and defined it, inadequately and inaccurately, as the social poise which they lacked. They did not see that Amla, in talking to Jit, displayed no confidence and no poise, any more than the envious young men noticed that she barely looked at him as he talked and leant forward to light her cigarette for her.

'I used to think that myself,' he was saying as he watched her suck in the smoke till her cheekbones stood out in all their sharp-edged gravity. 'But I can assure you there is no need to worry on that score. With another young man brought up, as he was, on comfort and security, you might worry if he were deprived of them so completely. Not with your brother, Miss Ray, not with your brother. And,' he took the pipe out of his mouth and waved it for emphasis, 'I think you insult him if you feel he is so inadequate that he cannot get on without all those props that lesser men like me need.' He bit his pipe stem and his eyes seemed to engulf her in their lonely misery. 'I place my full faith in him. I always did. Did you know what a success he made of that magazine — absolutely singlehandedly? '

'But Monisha — my sister — said that it failed,' Amla said with blank surprise and began to take a little more notice of him, his discrepancies, the shifting shadows and the slight beetling tic at the corner of one eye. She wondered what it was in him that was lacking — some essential that gave man reason and security and which he seemed to have mislaid or mishandled. 'I thought it folded up, it was such a complete flop.'

'No,' he grimaced to show her that he was the one she ought to consult, he was the one who knew the inside story, though he was too modest to say so. 'That last issue was a tremendous success — oh, literary, financial, every kind of success — and he could have carried it on to the winning post, made it the best literary paper in Asia. But Nirode wouldn't do that. It is hard for cynics to believe it, but Nirode quite honestly didn't want success. He refused to get entangled in it, he wanted to be alone to write.'

'Oh yes, that play Monisha told me he was writing. But I don't think he actually did, Mr Nair,' and Amla stubbed out the cigarette in an ashtray of heavy silver. 'He seems to have given up that too and he is happy enough about it."

'He's given it up?' Jit was evidently disconcerted by this piece of knowledge that he had not foreseen, but the thick oil on which his many complicated wheels turned, soon flowed and smoothed away the little corroding suspicion that Nirode was, after all, neither idealist nor hero nor even artist. 'Is that what he told you?' he smiled past his pipe. 'Oh, don't let that amusing little shop of his fool you — it's only a front, you know. Perhaps he's taken it up for the sake of some ready cash. He has quite a good collection of books already and it might fetch him some lolly — he never pretends to sneeze at that. But it doesn't wholly preoccupy him, Miss Ray, not that deep, strange, hidden mind of his, that's still involved with the play and when one day it appears on stage, it will take the world by storm.'

Behind them, the sleek record player beneath an artful bower of tuberoses exploded into a glorious sunburst of *sitar* music. Someone rushed up to lower the volume and the sweet notes of the *raga* Bhairavi scattered amongst the party guests like so many flakes of broken light. A dark young woman and a lively colleague of Amla's began to discuss Ravi Shankar's artistry with great animation, frequently shutting their eyes to express extreme reverence and appreciation. On russet raw silk cushions a gaggle of matrons discussed the enormous dinner they had just devoured and the problems of digesting it.

The atmosphere of underlit reality, of incomplete life, began to overtake Amla again. She cradled her small purse in her arms and said, 'You take Nirode very seriously, Mr Nair,' and was certain she heard, amidst all the loud tittering and soul-searching music and emphatic chattering, Nirode's deep growl of disgust and this made her smile. 'What if the play never gets written? Or staged?' She turned to Jit, refreshed by mischief and did not notice when he gave a start of recognition at the family resemblance that lifted itself out of the welter of individualities and stood there, bright and insouciant. 'Will you still continue to take him so seriously?'

Jit drew the silver ashtray to him and began to perform an elaborate ritual of which only pipe smokers are initiates. Amla sensed that his pipe meant a great deal more to him than a rich smoke; it was more like a protective mask that the man treasured with dark passion. He nodded sagely. 'Evidently you don't know Calcutta very well yet, Miss Ray. Just take a look around this room. Look at Mr Basu there, groping around the record cabinet like an elephant, trying to paw out "something livelier for the young ones". Tomorrow morning he'll go and sit on one of his innumerable Boards — coal, jute, tea, what have you — and sit on every other member there as well. Oh, I'm not running down my host — an excellent man, shrewd and hospitable and a good friend to his friends, an excellent fellow — like the rest of them. There's McNab whom you'll find at the bar in Spence's every day from eleven in the morning till three in the afternoon when he gets carried back to his office his nose a trifler purpler than it was in the morning. A fine chap, McNab, he can stand his drink. Not very bright, never had much education — just grammar school and the Army — but a hard drinker. Hard drinkers are very much admired in Calcutta, Miss Ray. And those two young boys with him, laughing at his jokes, they are Bunty Dutt and Jimmy Chawla. Their real names are Biren and Jawahăr, but the Englishmen in their office find such outlandish names hard to pronounce, so they've been given good, honest British pet names which they have accepted with alacrity. It's considered an informal kind of promotion, this baptism. They are both very promising golfers too. They've taken the game very seriously, practise four times a week and that's the main thing: dedication. Now look at that shy, handsome young chap sitting at Mrs Basu's feet and holding her coffee cup for her while she lights a cigarette: that's Sonny Ghosh. He's a newcomer to my firm — I'm in tea, you know — and he's a nice boy, comes of an excellent family that's come down in the world lately so that he's obliged to work for a living now, but he's young and adaptable and he's taken it in his stride. Bunty's giving him golf lessons and he's doing very well. I see Mrs Basu is giving him lessons in party behaviour, so he'll soon shine, he's just a bit nervous still. He went through a bad time when his bid for an independent living failed — it was a big fishery, but he was swindled out of it and his Papa was ruined. He's only just getting over it and his artistic pretensions too. He used to paint bilious landscapes and write dreadful poems, but fortunately he no longer has time for that. Golf and cocktail parties take up all his time after office hours. I'm not complaining about my firm, they certainly don't slave drive you, we're just a little busy during the tea auctions, but people like Sonny and myself have the easiest time of it. There's always time for a quick one at Spence's before lunch. On Fridays we have the expense account luncheon at Firpo. You haven't heard of the Friday-lunch tradition, Miss Ray? Oh, an amusing legacy of East India Company days when the mail boat used to leave with the week's labour on Thursday afternoon, leaving the box-*wallahs* free to celebrate a day of well-earned relaxation on Friday. The point, Miss Ray,' and here he struck a light to his well-fuelled pipe, 'the point is this — can you see Nirode anywhere amongst us? At Spence's, laughing at McNab's alcoholic humour? At Firpo, in the expense account luncheon crowd? No, no, he's unique in this city of commerce. He's unique in this city of compromise and relative values. If I didn't have faith in him, in the consistency of his values, the courage of his beliefs, I do not think,' and he cradled his pipe and looked at it sadly as at a loved deaf-and-dumb child, 'I do not think I could survive it all. I need to watch him, admire him.'

In the course of that evening Amla found out a great deal more about this distressing need of Jit's. The party drove on to the Golden Slipper — 'It's Saturday night, we can sleep late tomorrow,' Mr Basu consoled his yawning wife, but Bunty wailed, 'It'll ruin my golf' — and Amla danced with Jit, very carefully keeping her distance from the acrid odour of smoked tobacco and the morbid yellow glint in his eyes. It was very dark and they could scarcely make out anyone from the crowd that pressed upon them, and once when, in that overpopulated murk, a shabby yellow slipper floated into sight, encased in a dry and dusty aquarium, Amla caught her breath with fear at the great pressure and pull of the current of Calcutta's night life. While she tried to tug her mind away from it and hold it out above the waterline, Jit talked to her compulsively and with every drink seemed to melt and disintegrate a little more till Amla feared he would be reduced to a glaucous, sprawling jellyfish at her feet, at the bottom of this stagnant aquarium. Why, she wondered, clutching a brocade purse and a wristlet of jasmine in one hand while Jit clutched the other, why is pleasure the most rotten sensation of all in this city? When, where is it to be found clear, fresh, unadulterated? Not here, not now when Jit laughed his slithering laugh and said, 'Now I'm running down my colleagues again — a pet hobby of the Calcutta box-*wallah*, Amla. How we love to pretend that though the rest are brainless, snobbish opportunists, one is apart from them. Actually, I am dedicated to the clan. Let me confess, I *belong* to it. They pay me so well, how can I help it? It permits me to indulge in expensive hobbies — expensive for this country, at any rate. I owe my imported stereo set to it and my collection of Rajasthani and Moghul miniatures. Ah, that reminds me, I must show it to you one day, particularly one painting of a young Rajput princess standing on a balcony, waiting for her lover. She has a red rose in her hand and beneath the balcony there is a garden of red tulips in which white birds are performing a dance. You remind me of her when you look so faraway and thoughtful. All you need is a rose in your hand, then you would be my princess. Yet, when you laugh, you look exactly like Nirode in his wickedest mood...'

At last he took her to the bar for another drink and there she managed to slip away from him, from the tottering pyramid of drunkards and the bright pink nudes of the mural and found herself dancing with the young man in the patterned waistcoat who pranced about with an energy that suggested that dancing was an athletic exercise to him rather than a social grace, and so they swung into the other couples and nearly romped into a table as he panted, 'Has Jit been telling you what a lonely and misunderstood soul he is?'

Amla smiled. 'No, only asked me to come up and see his miniatures.'

Bunty, lifting up his knees and thumping his feet on the floor with vigour, laughed. 'Yes that usually happens between two and three in the morning, I'm told. Poor chap, I really feel sorry for the blighter: his wife ran away with another chap from our office, an Englishman. He never suspected a thing and it came as quite a blow to him. They're living in Malaya now — his wife and Haddely-Smith — I mean. He never even resigned, the bounder, just fiddled a transfer to another division. They get away with murder in the colonies, but,' and he whirled her around with powerful golfer's arms, 'I'm sure you've had enough shop talk from Jit,' and he took her to meet Sonny Ghosh, meekly guarding ladies' handbags at a table in the corner, who apologized for not knowing how to dance. The three of them went down to the street below to a *kebab* stall that was still brightly lit and in a hubbub of business for, three o'clock in the morning was when the night-club crowd descended upon it for hot *kebabs,* Bunty told her.

'Sup-pecial or pull-lain?' asked a harried looking urchin who came out of the mirrored and tinselled stall to their car for their order.

'Suppecial, of course. Do *you* have to ask *me?*' Bunty was very offended at not being recognized, and Amla smiled with relief at having got away from Jit into the company of these two disarming and refreshing young men. The *kebabs* arrived hot and greasy and

Amla gamely ate her way through one while they drove up and down the deserted Strand before taking her home.

She did go and see Jit's miniatures and found that Nirode had been invited as well and was already walking up and down in front of the bamboo bar Jit had had constructed at one end of the gracious hall with rounded pillars and immense doorways, looking as out of place as a wooden crate in a princely reception hall. This did not seem to worry Nirode who was swiftly draining his first drink in order to get the second which Jit, behind the bar, was waiting to pour out. His eyebrows flew up and scattered like feathers at the sight of Amla in an elaborate brocade-edged sari that she had worn under a perverse impulse to appear something like the Rajput princess she was to be shown.

'Is this a party?' Nirode asked suspiciously.

'No, no,' Jit reassured him. 'I only wanted to see brother and sister together. You know I wouldn't invite any of my friends to meet you, Nirode.'

'No, bloody sensible of you, too — I'd get their ears red and their noses purple and their teeth chattering in no time. All your Firpo birds and smart Park Street riff-raff. You two met at a party of that kind, didn't you?' and he looked distastefully at his sister who stood before him, feeling the sensation of unreality swamping her inkily.

'Yes and we sat together and formed a little island of sense and sensibility in the centre of that murky bog — didn't we Amla? We talked about you and we decided — what did we decide Amla?'

'Amla knows better than to make any decisions about me. She nearly did, before she heard of one of my financial peccadilloes. Then she decided not to. Have you started drinking gimlets yet, Amla?'

'I've something better for her here,' Jit said and poured out some sherry with exaggerated pride and courtesy. She sat uncomfortably on a high stool beside Nirode and wondered which of the two men she resented and despised more this evening.

'Anyway Jit,' Nirode continued, unaware of her cold stiffening beside him, 'it's interesting to know you are aware of living in a murky bog. Can't give you full marks for that little bit of perception, but half, yes, all right. The next logical step would be to get out of it, wouldn't it?'

Amla, her face taut with anger at herself for having dressed herself into this ridiculous brocaded doll, at Nirode for his selfishness and at Jit for so meekly filling and refilling the glass that Nirode mockingly pushed across to him, snapped, 'Others could say the same of you, couldn't they?'

'What?' Nirode's eyebrows rose again and he struck a match as harshly and gratingly as he could. 'That I'm living in a bog? Yes, I dare say they could. That sounds to me like a sentiment straight from mother's lips. Did she tell you I was a pig wallowing in my own filth?'

'You've completely forgotten mother if you think she could use such an expression.'

'Mother's never forgiven me for not allowing her to be my benefactress. Jit. Isn't it strange how many benefactors I attract? You all seem to actually encourage me to stay contentedly in my smelly little pigpen. I wonder why. Did Jit tell you why, Amla?'

'He did and I think he's an —' she stopped short, in agony at the ugliness and formlessness of an evening that should not have been. 'I think he's too gullible where you're concerned. I don't know why you should have supported Nirode in writing a book — a play — when the chances are ten to one it's pornographic. Do you support his bookshop as well?'

'According to my sister, that's pornographic too. Aren't we the living examples of what high caste and a good home does to one, Jit?'

'My dear chap, speak for yourself,' said Jit, refilling his glass and Amla's and as she gazed into the secretly glimmering rich liquid in her crystal glass, she could have cried at the perversity and antagonisms of this world into which she had strayed and the men

171

who peopled it. Hold still, she wanted to plead with them, hold still, hold your thoughts still, don't think at all, allow yourselves only to feel. But feeling could soon dull and when she was at last shown the miniatures, they seemed flat and vapid to her and she could never later remember a single one of them.

Soon the rot crept into her working hours and even the security and the good humour she had at first enjoyed in her office, as an extension of college days that had kindly followed her into this harsh city, now deserted her and left her an outsider in the group of colleagues that gathered about a trayful of coffee cups, wreathing the blue smoke of one cigarette with the white smoke of another. When she had joined them, it had been with an eager, adolescent enthusiasm that arose out of a certainty that they shared memories similar to hers, and looked forward to fortunes and fates not too wildly discrepant from what her own might be. When she learned of the love affair of Jaya Chaudhury, whose father was a Minister, and Abhay Mukherjee, whose father never seemed to have existed, she supported them with puckish romanticism, encouraged Jaya, rallied Abhay and grew thoroughly involved in all the complexities of arranging their meetings and escapades. Then there was the oldest copy writer amongst them, the melancholy Mr Biswas whom they all called Dada, and to whose expounding of the Communist doctrine Amla listened with just that right mixture of solemnity and flippancy that stimulated and aroused him. She ignored and eventually managed, with as much kindness as she could distractedly summon, to discourage the adoration of Adil Aibara who could never be more to her than ten trembling fingers that smudged the carbon paper across her art paper and spilt her coffee into the saucer, and an adam's apple choked voice that at times touched her with its hesitations, and then maddened her with impatience. There was an attractiveness about them all and they welcomed her with a warmth that was only partly a tribute to her talent and her impetuousness, but a great deal more than that. Jaya and Abhay offered her their confidences as a gift to an already established friendship. Dada droned at her with his ceremonious, avuncular air that, she pointed out to him, was more in keeping with the character of a genteel Chekhovian landlord than with that of a revolutionary. Adil gazed secretly at her, his eyes glazed with calf love. The small studio where they worked was the loudest and the gayest in the building, it crackled with their practical jokes and repartee as with the brisk, whipping sounds of pennants in a smart breeze.

Then the rot set in — overnight, without warning. Amla was melancholy. 'Another late night?' they asked her and she could not bring herself to reply. The thread of communication was broken, she saw how friable it had been. Lassitude overcame her like a fever, weighing against her temples, making her rest her elbows on the table and her head droop over unfinished work. It seemed to her that the coffee always came to her cold. It seemed to her that her colleagues smoked too many of their ostentatiously cheap cigarettes, that Jaya and Abhay made too much of their 'star-crossed lovers' attitude and that, in reality, they relished it, that Dada was merely a garrulous daydreamer who had carried his daydreams too far, too close to the region of nightmares; that Adil was spineless and despicable. It seemed to her that Mrs Basu was a queen of unscrupulous commerce, that her clients were sharks and liars, that the round babies she drew got no benefit whatsoever from the gripe water she was advertising, that she was involved in a shady and unconscientious organization, business and art. She thought her drawings were awful. She thought the summer was never going to end.

It draped and enclosed the city in its loose, damp hold. The trams ground slowly round the square and the little scraps of shade thrown by an equestrian statue here, a shrivelled tree there were peopled with sleeping beggars and vendors. Lakes of perspiration oozed slowly over the backs of every shirt and blouse in the sun. The pavements were thick with coconut chips as vendors chopped off their tops and handed them to thirsty customers to tip back and drain. Tempers were easily frayed, feelings injured, quarrels flared up and there was a general atmosphere of disintegration. At night mosquitoes rose humming from the surrounding swamps and made sleep fitful, puncturing it with reminders that there was no peace in sleep. Amla sighed.

Jit, turning his head away in a brief and unexpected gesture of despair, said, 'I don't understand it — this terrible destructiveness in all of you. You seem to worship it, shelter it inside yourself as though it were essential to you. Nothing will persuade you to forgo it — not you, not your brother nor that strange sister of yours.'

Amla, who had been infinitely bored by a long drawn out dinner at Mocambo, said in surprise, 'But what do we destroy?'

'You destroy — you destroy yourselves and you destroy that part of others that gets so fatally involved in you. There is this — this dreadful attractiveness in your dark ways of thinking and feeling through life towards death.' He wiped his face and looked at her incredulously. 'I think I am drunk or mad or just fatigued by this horrible weather. I can't imagine why I am saying all this to you — perhaps I imagined I was talking to Nirode.'

'No. but tell me — this interests me much more than your golf score or that stupid film we saw. Do you really think we are masochists, Nirode and Monisha and I? How strange. We all of us feel we have nothing in common at all.'

Jit, who had not liked her remark about his golf score or the film to which he had just treated her, said shortly, 'I think you all involve yourselves in tragedies of your own making. I think you all drive yourselves deliberately into that dead end where you imagine you will find some divine solution. But there is none, not in a lifetime, all of us discover that and we force ourselves to turn and take another road. I know,' he added thickly, for he had drunk heavily that afternoon at Spence's. 'I know, because I visited that dead end myself when my wife left me. But I made myself turn away and go on, and now I can honestly say...'

'Yes, yes,' Amla said hastily, dreading the maudlin tail end of his drunken spells. 'I heard about that, someone told me, I forget who...'

With the quiet return of his habit of bitterness, Jit said, 'I'm sorry. I forgot that a man's private tragedies cannot be used to entertain a young lady,' and ostentatiously he opened the menu and asked her to choose a sweet, then began to talk of the holiday he planned in Kashmir. Feeling guilty about it but only in a vague, slack way that she connected with the vapid atmosphere of the summer city — she did not pursue his sorrowful remark but chatted, instead, about the glaciers of Kashmir, the strawberries and the lakes she had never seen. And Jit did not, after all, go. He continued to take her to cocktail parties, to dinners and dances and after the first drink always began to whine and sigh again with self-contempt and pity, then attempted to straighten out the unsightly mess with a slickness and urbanity he mistook for sophistication. This sluggish endeavour to get the most out of many worlds by the least possible effort dragged Amla through the long summer, bleaching it with its own morbidity and leading her one claustrophobic evening when a nor'wester had promised to bring the city relief and then disappeared wantonly into a sallow sunset, to kick the hunchbacked temple tree in the back garden and exclaim, 'Why ever did I come to Calcutta? Why didn't I stay away in Bombay or go home to Kalimpong?' and to look ferocious when her aunt, at a silent dinner too hot and spiced for an evening like this, recommended fruit salts.

When she had ceased to hope for them, the rains broke. For a brief moment drawn taut and glistening with primaeval joy, Amla, who was cutting pinched, half-wild roses from a tangle of thorny bushes, raised her face to feel the cool, unstinting rain lave it and the red rose leaves about her. There was a royal lushness, a religious ceremoniousness about the first monsoon shower and, having surrendered to it, it took her some time to realize that she was soaked through and the stalks in her hand stripped of their flowers. She moved towards the cracked marble stairs, now turned into a frantically uneven waterfall, and as she did so, frightened a chameleon out of a crimson rose bush. Like some loathsome mark of evil inside an enchanted wood — the wand of thorns placed amidst the heavy, glittering vestments of royalty or the line of chalk drawn in the black clay of a hushed, magical clearing — a white streak ran down its sleek back, from flattened head to pointed tail, a sign it could not wash off, a sign that marked it forever. Then it tilted backwards and the white line catapulted out of sight to be replaced by the long, transparent belly, before it fell into the mud with an ugly flop. Clutching her arms about her and shuddering, she ran up the steps to the veranda, out of the rain.

Her aunt, sitting on a battered wicker chair with the red and black ledgers of the T.B. After-Care Sanatorium on her knees, looked up to see the girl still quaking and said, 'You can't shake off that much rain. Better go up and change quickly.'

But Amla sat down on the worn coir mat at her feet, thinking that the rain water would cleanse her of the chilling vision, thinking the rain would cool and subdue her prickling dread. Once she had her lips under control she said, 'It's so nice to feel cool once again,' and began to lift wisps of wet hair off her face, tucking them behind her ears with streaky neatness that her aunt seemed to notice and approve though she only said, 'You'll get fever that way.' She continued to scratch at her ledgers with a splintered penholder, now and then twisting aside to dip the thick, nearly splayed nib into a pot of ink on the table beside her. The dry, grating sounds of her labour were softened by the gush of rain about them and sky, cloud and water were all one, descending like one vast spirit upon house, garden, city, plain. But the sense of grace, of munificence was already gone out of it, had, perhaps, streaked away with the chameleon's streaked back, and the monsoon pouring down around them was no more than an already established season.

'When I was small,' aunt Lila said in her abrupt, dismissing voice, between a jab at the bottom of the inkwell and a scratch at her untidy ledger, 'when I was small I used to run out in the rain and stand under the gargoyles and jump up and down with excitement.'

'Yes, aunt,' said Amla in a voice so brittle it might well have broken. 'It seems to me you enjoyed all our youth and so we were born middle-aged.' She was angered at her aunt for having taken out of this rich, rushing shower all the freshness and delight she might have — and for one short moment had found — in it, in the heart of her cupped hands and on the crimson rose leaves. It seemed to her that her aunt accused her of being too old for her age, with too much covering over too little core — and she was depressed to think of the grain of truth in it. Putting her arms around her knees in a pitying, orphaned gesture, she laid her face in the wet folds of her *sari* and wondered how this abrupt, angular old creature could have a foster sister so entirely different as her mother. Mother, sitting among her azaleas and orchids on a very different veranda, watching a rain and a mist of a very different quality, a mountain quality quite beyond the scope of this city.

After a while the ledgers were banged shut, pen and inkwell shoved across the gritty tabletop, and her aunt said, in a voice cut into neat black-and-white, cut-and-dried strips, 'No matter what you feel, the fact is you are still very young and healthy and it's a shame to waste that. Come with me to the sanatorium this afternoon, why don't you?'

'No aunt, not till I need to go in myself.'

'You are a morbid lot, you young ones,' sighed Lila Chatterjee rising and searching for her slippers under the chair. 'I don't know what it is that has diseased your generation — the very freedom we fought for and gave you, perhaps?'

'Freedom, freedom!' Strange how often the old, withered woman used this word, strange how often it rang through the exhausted, crumbling house of marble and dry rot. 'Freedom came the year I was twelve years old. Even freedom is old now.' She lifted her face out of her lap but could not stand the intense, suffering look on her aunt's narrow face, looked out on the unceasing rain instead and heard her aunt click her tongue and rattle her papers in disgust.

Out of all this rattle and clatter, her sharp voice snipped through. 'Old age will come, Amla. You will regret it then,' and she trailed off, her voice floating back from a distance. 'Old age will come, disease and disappointment. Don't be impatient for it, it will come. Then there'll be nothing to do but regret all the waste. You'll see,' and her voice was sucked into the vacuum of the prematurely dark rooms beyond.

Feeling insulted and threatened, feeling she had deliberately been left alone on the veranda to watch the rain and damp, damp and rot creep up at her, Amla was sparked by that rare, life-giving spark of defiance that Nirode, too, had felt in him, again and again.

Not much of a fire, but just enough to make her get up and go stamping up the stairs to her room which had once been her cousin Rita's room. To all intents and purposes, it still was. True, Amla's slippers were stacked on the little shoe stand and the great black wardrobe that did not shut properly showed, through a crack, the swing and sway of Amla's pagan *saris* and the desk was cluttered with letters from Kalimpong, crayons and paperback novels borrowed from her colleagues at work. Propped against a brass lampstand, with a fringed shade, was a drawing of hers, done swiftly on the back of a stiff invitation card — a drawing of the house in Kalimpong, the eaves and balustrades dripping with orchids, a pear tree looming over the roof like a matriarchal blessing, the garden terraced down to the gold edge of the card, all in a scramble of pen-and-ink dahlias, pen-and-ink gladioli. Looking at it in astonishment, as though she had not expected to find anything so fresh and impetuous in her cousin Rita's room, she crossed over to the window. Someone had shut it at the start of the downpour. She swung open the clumsy wooden shutters with bubbles of varnish gluey to her touch and let the spray drift in, pleasing herself with the thought that it came from the hills, from Kalimpong, from the great soft clouds that descended from the blue hills to the river and the plains. She stood with her back defiantly turned upon Rita's great brown volumes on physics on her brown counterpane with its faded paisley design, on the ungainly black armchair that seemed to have been resurrected from some ghost-ridden *dak* bungalow in the districts and watched with absorption the rain uncoil and flow down the central channels that halved the big, loose plantain leaves at her window, all glossy and finely ribbed, of a springing, dauntless green. The garden below her window was inundated. Grass stems swayed drunkenly in the rising pool of water and small insects rose out of it to sit on the tips of the bending blades of grass, as though awaiting rescue. Rain had washed the temple trees to an even darker, richer green, their crooked, serpentine branches to coal black and the tangle of wild rose bushes to a wild, rich crimson. At the far end of the garden, a magnolia tree held out its great white blossoms to the clouds, like exploded candles, the wicks soaking in the rain, the cups filling with it.

Wishing she had brought some of these great chaste blossoms into this drab room with her. Amla turned around and changed into dry clothes, crisp fresh cotton that smelt of scorched starch. She found her mood had altered. Her blood flowed to a smoother measure. She sat down on the bed drew out an old hard-covered atlas from Rita's crowded shelves, a few sheets of clean drawing paper and began to draw, her crossed legs serving as a wobbly table. She did not today draw the modern housewife peering anticipatorily into a pressure cooker or the angular knee and the tailored trouser leg of a gentleman smoking a filter- tipped cigarette. Today she drew the insects that clung with wet feelers to blades of grass — real ants, real grasshoppers and then unreal ones with crazy legs and gigantic eyes. A caterpillar fashioning a long umbrella out of a strip of plantain leaf. Squirrels with stiff pepper-and-salt tails — more pepper than salt — struggling to light a bonfire in which to roast their nuts. A thin yellow kitten distastefully negotiating a puddle in a saucepan boat. A flowering grove of trees — and here she drew the crayons to her and painted the flowers butter-yellow and breadcrust-brown, ice-green with honey stamens — and the tiny creatures that peopled it when no one was looking. Now she touched a sketch with the soapy heads of her crayons, now she scribbled a few lines of nonsense rhyme in Bengali. While drawing a gang of ladybird footballers playing with a soft *neem* pod, it occurred to her — not with a start but with a steady rising of serenity — that she had not enjoyed herself so much since she came to Calcutta.

She was frowning in an excess of care, hesitation and mother love over this gracile, patter-footed, whisper-voiced little world that seemed to have shot down the central channel of a smooth green plantain leaf, on a stream of rainwater, to land with a splash on her windowsill, when Nirode came in. She was so intent, the rain so lulling, she did not hear him walk up the long veranda and only when he spoke to her did she sit up into an L of stiff fright and immediately, by reflex action span her hands protectively over her private vision.

'Nirode,' she said accusingly, seeing him stand there in a ragged blue shirt that was wet about the shoulders and khaki trousers spattered with mud up to the knees, his emaciated face surrounded by the customary screen of yellow smoke.

'Working?' he asked. 'Aunt assured me you were being lazy and painting your toe nails for a party when you should have been helping her at her soup kitchen.'

'Did she say that?' Amla cried, so enraged at being interrupted and smacked right back into the foully rotting grey city, that she didn't know who enraged her more — Nirode with his mocking smile and stale odour of tobacco, or her self-righteous aunt. 'I *will* paint my toe nails then, the brightest scarlet she ever saw. That'll give the nasty old thing something to think about.'

Nirode's eyes scampered about as he sat down at the foot of her bed. 'I thought you got on so well — you and that Ancient Mariner. Are you drawing, Amla? Let's see.'

'No!'

'Why so fierce today?'

Amla began to fold the big sheets, clumsy in her fury. When Nirode reached across to pull the thick packet away from her, she shouted, 'I said no! I said no!'

'But you'll smear the crayons,' he said laughing. Then seeing her temple throb with a pulse he could not remember having seen there before, he surrendered it to her. 'Is it so secret?'

'Secret, yes, secret.' She had her back to him now as she stood at her desk, thrusting the papers away into some spider-webbed pigeonhole. Her voice sounded muffled and cindery, like a bonfire smouldering in the increasing rain. 'I have to keep things secret in this horrible city you told me was so wonderful, such a challenge. If I were back in Kalimpong, I wouldn't have minded showing them to you, I should have *liked* to show them to you. But here, here,' she turned her profile sharply on the slope of her shoulders and he saw it glisten like dull copper, 'here one must hide such things, cover up their weaknesses, protect their fragility, even destroy them if one doesn't want to see them get covered with filth and blood and rot. Nothing delicate can survive *this.*'

'I'm glad to see you're not a delicate one, that you're surviving with great gusto.'

'Surviving! Yes, I'm surviving — I suppose that is just what one would call this state of existing, just breathing and eating and going around with a perpetual head-ache and stomachache.' She was banging drawers shut with excessive loudness and so did not see Nirode wince, heard only the mockery in his voice...

'Then you must admit it is challenging to be asked to survive and live in a city where it is so difficult to do so.'

'I don't have your morbid tastes.'

'I am not morbid,' his voice snapped as though a little cinder from her dampened fire had caught him and set him alight. 'Good God, I've dragged myself through every stage of morbidity in order to arrive at this state of health, but who sees that? You probably think those knobby-kneed apes on the golf course, Jit and Sonny and that bunch, you probably think them healthy — healthy bodies, healthy minds, as that Black Crusader downstairs would say. But I live in a rat hole, I live off my friends and eat their food, drink their drinks in order to get on with my own life without wasting time on inessentials and you decide I'm the morbid one. Sometimes when you open your mouth, I see mother walking out of it with a grey silk umbrella in her hand like a weapon with which to batter me.' In the excess of anger, his fingers were trembling and he laced them around his lighted cigarette, stared down into its cage and his shoulder blades rose in two such sharp ridges that Amla felt her heart slice open, felt pain enter at the sight of his emaciation, at his complete isolation gone so far beyond anyone's touch.

'I'm not the diseased one,' he spoke more calmly. 'You've already discovered the pill that keeps the bogey away — the secret pill of secretiveness. You've just told me that you've discovered that anything that is of value is vulnerable, violable and that it must be protected as fiercely and madly as you can humanly protect it. Don't you see that my whole life is a process of just that? And that that is the process of retaining one's sanity? I used to imagine that what I was fighting to keep private and untarnished was my vanity, an imbecile desire to communicate through some art — I was too damned stupid even to care which one. Well, that came to a bloody end, Monisha probably told you and at the end of it I realized that the only thing I wanted to protect, what any sane man needs to protect, is his conscience. Oh, individuality you might call it or conscience, as I do, or anything — but there must be this essence inside you, and you must keep it secret in order to keep it bearable. Mixing, diluting, muddying it — that's the disease.' His voice fell so low, she came back to the bed to sit beside him and listen, but she did not say one word for fear of stopping the words she had waited to hear him say. 'I don't envy you your inexperience, Amla,' he said, looking up at her taut face. 'I don't envy you being in the thick of all the pleasure and despair you expose yourself to so — so morbidly. What hell that used to be! You know,' he inhaled, remembering a dark, dry summer evening beside a lake, drew it into him with a mouthful of rank smoke, 'you know, I once told a friend — a friend who has become a Buddhist now, an acolyte — that life lived to be a success only follows one success after the other, but eventually has to bend with the arc and arrive at the bottom. And since I never was any good at going along with the others, I thought I would take the other direction and follow failure after failure and reach the bottom of the arc much quicker, while I was still young enough to see and feel and understand with every one of my senses. But that was the mistake.' He flung the cigarette out of the window, into the rain. 'You can't descend to such complete darkness, such complete isolation, all exposed. That's where you most need your covering, your carapace. That's where you most need to know how to hide, because not only is it unbearable to expose yourself to such agonies, it is also pointless, it wears you away and leaves you — nothing. Do you read Camus, Amla?'

'No, I don't think —'

'He wrote that "in default of inexhaustible happiness, eternal suffering would at least give us a destiny. But we do not even have that consolation and our worst agonies come to an end one day." '

He heard again the gentle David's cry of protest, saw his raised arm in its swinging white sleeve and the suburban train come wailing out of the city. Amla, too, cried out — but not in protest. Her's was a stifled cry of agitation, of utter dismay and the hand she raised was immediately halted in mid-air.

'All this fighting to carve out a destiny for oneself — it's nothing compared to the struggle it is to give up your destiny, to live without one — of either success or sorrow. But it's a greater victory, because it brings you, in the end, silence and solitude and those are the two most powerful things of all.' He watched her face as he said this and saw how the membranes of her eyes quivered like disturbed water. He shook his head slowly, as though he wondered if he had really spoken these words of his aloud or merely turned them over in his own mind. 'Will you give me tea, Amla?' he asked, getting up from the bed. 'Then we could go out together. I think it's time I took you to meet a friend of mine. His name is Dharma. He is a painter.'

Grinding through the city in a tired, bulging bus, she kept her face fiercely turned to the window, away from Nirode's blank impassiveness, away from the congealed, swaying mass of damp clothes, greased black hair and the sullen apathy of clerks and shoppers, all pressed together into this airless cube on its mournful journey through the city. The window offered scarce relief. It looked out on streets that hissed and sizzled with sooty rain, on a yellow dog nosing a rubbish bin that lay on its side, spilling its contents across the pavement. Outside a sweet shop sat a naked boy with a vacant, moronic face and flies buzzed from his slippery nose and mouth to the mounds of orange and green sweets and back again. At one bus stop, a gang of clerks armed with umbrellas attacked the bus and each other, screaming and struggling as though to be left behind by it meant certain and horrible death in the rain. Amla understood now why Nirode chose to live in a locality such as this: it could not, after all, make any difference to him whether he lived amongst men serene and reasonable and gentle or men who fought like crows over every fresh carcass. In his state of purely detached acceptance of a world not worth realizing, nothing could matter enough to trouble him. In fact, it was easier for him to live here where he could rest in such anonymity, upon the heave, swell and drift of the great black wave, a part of the crusted flotsam on its crest, allowing it to carry him, in perfect indifference and without any certitude of destiny, moving only because the tide made it move, continuing only because it continued. One day it would break on the shore and, with it, he would sink quickly, silently into the sand.

The red ammunition factory, the high walls of a jail, palm trees, aerated water stalls, peeling hoardings, factories, puppies, ditches, rickshaws — they rode through them in the swelling, bursting bus, then got out to walk down the lane that vibrated with its everyday uproar. Mud, slush, overflowing drains, all one ugly turmoil to force one's way through. By the time she came to the low white house with its single narrow entrance, she was nearly tottering with weakness, as though Nirode had injected a fatal drug into her veins and it was turning her blood grey. Nirode glanced at her, pushed the door open, pushed her through it, pushed it shut.

They stood in a still room in which the rings of the rickshaw coolie's bells seemed to dissolve, one brass bell after the other, dissolve into puffs of pollen that floated and fell softly, softly on the big symmetrical squares and oblongs of canvas that leaned against the walls. An easel stood there like a patiently waiting gallows. She stared back at it.

'He will be outside,' said Nirode, and gave her another propelling push. They crossed the room, out to the veranda which overlooked the green pond, sloping palm tree, white geese. There Dharma reclined on his mat, geometrically folding his *pan* leaves and watching his pet geese with those heavy-lidded eyes that cast shadows of darkness on to his cheek-bones, crescents shadowing crescents with a kind of sad but attentive symmetry.

When he spoke to them, inviting them to sit down and she answered and lowered herself on to the mat, she felt herself being torn, torn with excruciating slowness and without anaesthesia, from the Amla of a day, an afternoon ago. Miraculously, there was no blood, only the broken nerves hanging there, exposed to the clammy air, like cut telegraph wires glinting in moonlight.

They rested and talked, even laughed a bit and she realised gradually that she was not lying on the blood-soaked scene of a misfortune, but had been lifted and carried away to some secret shelf that jutted out of and away from the round earth and there she was at last given — by the glimmer of glowworms rising from the saturated earth to light pale grottoes in the foliage, by the white geese walking off to sleep in single file and by the infinitely careful and fastidious hands of Dharma preparing a *pan* leaf for her — an anaesthesia that transported her on to another level of awareness, one she had never inhabited or visited before. Looking at Dharma, she felt certain it was he who had held to her taut, frightened face that merciful magic mask, telling her in his cool voice to breathe deeply, to lie still, to forget the pain and fear.

Dharma's magic was immediately apparent to her, but Dharma himself did not figure very largely or substantially in that first memorable evening. She remembered just a few inconsequential things he said — 'No, my dear Nirode, there can be no phoenix in the heart of such destruction. The anarchistic genius of Calcutta is intrinsically negative. *"Cholbe na,"* that is the battle cry of all its processions and demonstrations, *"cholbe na."** It can only end in annihilation.' 'Rabindranath Tagore? Ah, only the Bengali's wish fulfilment, that was Tagore.' She remembered those very dark and hypersensitive fingers preparing a *pan* leaf, gently waving aside the rank smoke of Nirode's cigarettes, drawing a swift design in the air. Behind him, a tapestry of phantom glow-worms, the sounds of Gita Devi's *puja,* its unharmonious bells and ominous conch shell groans, all softened by the drizzle of mosquitoes.

All evening she watched his hands in a passion of curiosity and premonition. They seemed to mark her, impress themselves upon her: the frenzied pattern of lines that cut and slashed the brown palm to an impenetrable jungle. What would a palmist have made of those lines and their ramifications — those twigs, branches, vines, lianas? She knew that the touch of these wild, strange hands would be gentle and permanent. She saw Dharma was chivalrous, tender, subtle, prophetic.

All that Nirode noticed was how she snapped her answers at his many probing questions, how she bit off the ends of her sentences as though they were threads, with ugly, abrupt sounds that resembled

---

* "Won't do."

185

— so Nirode thought — her aunt's speech. Yet all her answers were positive and in the affirmative and when Dharma followed up all this questioning and testing, so unusual for him, with a request to her to sit for a portrait, her answer was immediate, abrupt and positive. Nirode's cigarette tumbled out of his mouth, the entire packet went flying over the floor, he was so thunderstruck. He could not tell what astonished him more — that Dharma should indicate a wish to paint a human figure, a female form, a portrait or that Amla's cry of, 'Yes, I will,' sounded so eager and passionate and yet as inevitable as the answer a powerful hypnotist draws out of his patient. He looked from one to the other and saw them regarding each other with perplexed, even fearful frowns.

'Who is he? What do you know of him, Nirode? Tell me, Nirode, tell me,' she pleaded and Nirode drew his knees up to his chin and groaned. But he tried to help.

'Don't be led by that air he has of a damned mystic, the shady impresario of the invisibilities of this world. He's just a painter, not even a very steady or confident one, he seems to be feeling his way still —'

'Feeling his way? Feeling his way? What else would an artist be doing, for God's sake? If an artist simply plucked steadiness and confidence out of his paint-box like a number eleven brush, where would his painting be?' She wore her hair pulled down over her ears, it gave her a martyred look. 'It seems to me there are too few painters — artists — willing to admit they have no confidence in what they are doing and that they're still feeling their way along. Doesn't one do that all one's life?'

'Do then, do. Be a good girl and go feel your way through to Dharma's mystery and leave me to do my cataloguing, will you?'

She could not leave and go away, still loaded with her frenzied thoughts of Dharma. She wanted so much to share the aching burden of them. Raising her hands on either side of he face, like two dramatic candle flames, she worried Nirode. 'And those pictures, those pictures, what do they mean, Nirode? Do you know what they mean?'

'Artistic mysteries and revelations are all beyond me, Amla. You know,

"Ghosh Mosh Chunder Bose my name,
in Radha Bazar I keep —"

'No, Nirode, no! You must tell what you know, I have to know.' Her despair stammered and stilled in the face of Nirode's disgust. She faltered, 'I-I can't go and sit for the portrait without knowing what he means to do.'

'Hell, do you think I know?' Nirode cried. He had planned to get along with the catalogue, a boring duty he had shirked too long and then to sit back against a stack of bookribs and revel again in the scrolled, illuminated *tankha* David had sent him from Sikkim, which he wished to unroll about him, through the paper dust and book shadows, like a mosaic of shining hieroglyphs that would show him the way out of it all. Then Amla came and was not willing to sit quietly and turn the pages of the books he offered her, but insisted on imposing upon him emotions she found herself unable to manage alone. Her unprotected state of nerves unsettled him, made him wary and offhand as did his mother's attentions and Monisha's silent agony behind the barred windows of her house. He gave Amla one look of annoyance, then kept his face averted because he could not bear the light of a face so devoid of the secrets that made life bearable. He had hoped he was done with such revelations, he could not undertake to involve himself in another one, and he said, 'You'll have me thrown out of this house. Amla. You imagine it's some shady den made for animals like me to hide in, but actually it's so damned respectable that even brother and sister are suspect once they're over fourteen.'

Amla, choosing not to listen to a word of his, sat down on his only chair, a backless one of canvas and put her feet up on a great pile of books, looking over her knees at him. She studied the sullen shadows under his eyes and the very thin, straight line of his mouth, then nerved herself to ask 'Is it always such a confusion and panic? Have you felt love to be like that, too, Nirode? Does the dust ever settle and the clouds break up and everything straighten and simplify itself — into love?'

'Amla,' Nirode said, after a silence filled with dry distaste, 'Amla, I fear I must disappoint you, but I'm not your school chum with whom you can gossip the afternoon away, exchanging confidences about ooh, those wiggly waggly crazy feelings one gets when one meets one's heart-throb. I suggest you go home to mother a while and grow up a bit by listening to her experiences of love.'

'What do you mean?' Amla was at first bewildered by a coldness that she saw was more than morbid, was insane, but through her bewilderment and shock, anger began to cut in with great, slow, white slashes.

'Oh, she has a vast store of them, you'd learn by that. She'll tell you about love better than an outlawed hermit crab like myself can. Ask her about the love that made her swallow father whole, like a cobra swallows a fat, petrified rat, then spews him out in one flabby yellow mess. Ask her about the love that makes her perch on her mountain top, waiting so patiently and surely for retirement and tedium and the last wormy twisting of lust to send Major Chadha-Chadha! -into her open arms.'

'Nirode, you are mad!' she cried, leaping up to stand over him but afraid to come too near this pale, bony monster who seemed to live on his venom alone. Only their shadows touched, hers shaking wildly with rage at him and fear of him. 'You are mad, utterly mad. You sit here by yourself, turning away every friend and helper who has ever come to you — fighting off their affection and their help — fighting to be alone just in order to sit here by yourself and turn into a madman. What do you know of people's feelings any longer? What do you understand by the word love? I don't believe you've ever felt it, felt anything, not even as a boy when we all imagined you were so sensitive and so devoted to mother. You know nothing of human beings. What do you know of mother? Or her relationship with father? What do you know of Major Chadha?'

Nirode held himself back from her with a cold, stiffened distaste for her emotion, her violence and Amla could not know what fear it was that sharpened his words with such astringency. 'I know of their little Monopoly and mah-jong games, she wrote herself. I can see them, the major with bushes of hair bristling in his ears, bushes of hair tickling inside his nose and his red pop eyes trying to nudge the *sari* off her shoulder. I can see her leaning across to give him a good look into her blouse, saying "Ah-ha, ah-ha, I have you now," the way she does. Don't imagine that isn't also an aspect of love of which you, you *human beings,* claim to know so much.'

'More than you, more than you. My God, Nirode, you cannot live here in this foul hole, imagining the world to be so depraved. It is you, it is you who are depraved, who makes love into something ugly and degenerate. Let me tell you something about mother and how she felt about —'

'Not in here, please, not in my house.'

'You — you can be a *rat,* Nirode, a rat,' she whispered and rushed out into the courtyard, fiercely questioning herself, wondering why she had come to Nirode, in his miserable room, to ask him about, of all people, Dharma. This seemed to her the worst defilement into which this insidious city had cheated her and in her agitation, she nearly ran into the latrine, was thrown back by the heavy fumes that came from it and, turning around, discovered that she had lost her way out of the enclosed courtyard. Its brick paving was thickly covered with fruit peels, congealed balls of rice, coconut fibres matted with the food leavings it had scraped off dirty dishes and unspeakable rags, all flung down from the balconies that surrounded it to a height of three floors. Most of the balconies were dark and seemed to be inhabited, if at all, by bats. A few of the rooms were lit by exhausted naked bulbs and one by a long strident tube of neon that proclaimed the lodger's prosperity. But no lodger was in sight that evening, most of the rooms were shut and padlocked. Whirling around, she faced an exit from this nightmare arena — the kitchen through which she had to pass before achieving the nameless lane. Here Nirode's landlady squatted, vigorously stirring a great pot redolent of asafoetida and talking venomously to herself. Nevertheless she heard Amla's flying steps, turned around and let forth a scream of alarm at the sight of a young girl in a green and white patterned *sari* and a temple flower in her hair. 'Eh, eh,' she screamed at Amla who was trying, vainly, to slip past. 'Eh you, you aren't getting away from me like this. Who are you, eh?'

Nirode was drawn out of his cell by these sounds of suspicion and battle, he explained to the landlady and hurried Amla away, swearing at people he did not quite identify. The lane outside was ill-lit and empty save for a tired rickshaw coolie who had drawn his vehicle into this backwater of the mighty Dharamtalla and slept beneath it, his feet sticking up as straight and wooden as the shafts of his idle rickshaw. They halted before this still tableau, eyes fixed upon it.

'Want me to come along to the bus stop?' Nirode asked, forcing her past it.

'Get me a taxi,' she snapped. 'No, don't come with me, I'll go to the bus stop myself — no, I want a taxi. Get me a taxi and — and get back to your beastly books.'

He shrugged, flaunting his indifference at her and strolled casually down the pavement, all littered with scarlet and milk-white pyjama strings, talking mynahs, fruit barrows, glass bangles and plastic combs. She found herself unable to push past on her own, past the glutinous bodies of the shoppers, the whines of the importunate vendors and beggars, and was forced to keep at Nirode's side till a large, grumbling taxi was finally secured. She could not speak to him for rage and he said nothing either, merely slammed the door shut so that rust flew out of its innumerable cracks and turned away. She found herself craning to see him hurry down the dark lane with the eagerness of an epicurean rabbit, hastening towards the delights of his illuminated Sikkimese scroll.

At every turn, on every road, the city thrust its ugly apathy at her like a beggar thrusting his mutilated hand through the window and laughing because he knew she must pay him her conscience money. Everywhere there was the tip-tilted rubbish bin, the nude child playing in an open drain, the vast confectioners stirring great cauldrons of milk while perspiration made their bare torsos glitter metallically. Everywhere the sullen, prophetic queues at dark doorways that bore signboards celebrating Ayurvedic Eye Specialists, Urinary and Venereal Disease Specialists, Lady Gynaecologists and World-Famous Homeopaths. Everywhere traders sat beneath their plaster idols of Ganesha and Lakshmi, fiddling about their nostrils with thoughtful enjoyment and everywhere women set out little braziers to catch stray bits of breeze and fan out into those quilts of dungcake smoke that choked and stifled the streets every evening. Amla watched, straining her eyes, watched to see what else there was besides this want of care, this want of will. She saw no glimmer, no shade, no sound of love. Did love exist here at all? Was it only a bitter farce of extortion, like the willed mutilation of his hand by the desperate, mocking beggar? Sbe shut her eyes then, making herself believe that love could be born, could exist, but only in the form of a little sweet, short anaesthesia.

Amla's love, knowing no possibility of manifestation, became one uncontrollable desire to communicate, signalling with forlorn glow-worm desperation from the still twilight of her frustration. Nirode, out of his apathy and wisdom, had shut his eyes to it, but it signalled still and made Monisha smile. She seemed to see a grotesquely comical sign placed on Amla's back, transforming her into one of those sad, incompetently painted clowns of the itinerant circus who, nevertheless, draw their laughs. Amla, who had swallowed the family pride like an iron rod that could not be dislodged, did not know how to respond to laughter directed at her when she did not want it. In her confusion, she overlooked the flaw in her own love and saw only that Monisha was as hard as she was mysterious, as unresilient as she was sensitive and as sarcastic as she was wounded. If Nirode's suffering had made him an ill-tempered hermit, then Monisha's suffering — but had she suffered? When? Why? In what horrific country, by what evil hand? — had made her not only distant, but devoid of the compassion which in Amla was so quick and unstinting.

191

She came to tea in response to Amla's note, but brought along her husband and a niece and for them Amla had not bargained. She felt insulted that Monisha should not respect her need of private confidences. Aunt Lila decided that it was only proper for her to preside over the tea and while Monisha fed the child sweets, she asked Jiban a series of uninteresting questions relating to the very dull Ministry in which he worked. Jiban was as dull as she was, but more prolix. Amla wondered if he really enjoyed himself as much as he seemed to, sitting back on the slippery leather chair, shaking and swinging the leg he had placed across one thigh, stirring his tea — which he liked excessively sweet — and droning such marvellous sentences as, 'It is a sight to sadden one's heart, these virgin forests laid low by the fell hand of man,' and 'I believe I am supported in my belief by no less a poet than William Wordsworth who addressed Nature as "The Wisdom and Spirit of the Universe! Thou Soul that art the Eternity of Thought!"' She was filled with a lust to take up an axe and chop through all this dead, soggy, termite-gnawed wood in order to get at Monisha, the lost princess of the fairy tale who sat somewhere in the deepest shadows of this forest, silent and unattainable.

Eventually, the little girl named Bun Bun was the one who freed Monisha from the magician's evil forest. She wanted Monisha to show her the garden and both sisters jumped to their feet in response to her demand and, leaving Aunt Lila to the droning Jiban together in the slowly darkening room, they went down the cracked marble stairs to stand, at last, in the tall monsoon grass, explaining to Bun Bun who the two blind marble goddesses were. Once they had answered her many questions, she ran away to pick up the temple flowers that lay in the grass, whole and perfect still and Amla at last had her sister to herself. Then she discovered she did not know how to tell her about Dharma. It had not been so difficult with Nirode who had required no preliminaries and who had seemed to sense what she had come to say.

'Have you heard from mother?' she asked finally because Monisha seemed perfectly content to stroll up and down the shadow-strangled garden in silence, listening to the mosquitoes drizzle about her ears with an expression of immutable melancholy.

'Oh yes. She writes long letters, she must be lonely. It is raining very much there.'

'I don't think I have replied to her last letter. I just can't write to her these days, I don't seem to be able —'

'Do you come home very late from the office?' Monisha asked, without the faintest curiosity, standing still to study a spider enthroned on the exact heart of its sagging, sticky web between two twigs of the magnolia tree.

'No, I get away from there as early as I can. I don't think I'm really made for a job in an advertising firm — ' she pushed and pushed at the Tibetan turquoise ring on her finger — 'it doesn't seem to be the right career at all.'

'The right career? For you?'

Amla was stung by this familiar acidity of Monisha's tongue that surfaced so seldom but then sharply, making her wince. 'For me, I don't think I should have gone straight from art school into advertising, it is too violent a let-down.'

'Oh,' said Monisha, as though only vaguely enlightened. 'Will you change then?'

'To what?'

'I don't know,' Monisha mocked. 'To art. I suppose.'

'How can I — I want to be independent too.'

'Of mother? It is easier not to be.'

'I don't think I could stand having aunt convert one of her store rooms into a studio for me and then lock me in to paint.'

'Then what will you do?'

Amla did not answer at once. The question involved so much more than her sister could imagine in her reticence and weird innocence, black-browed and with a cynical but uncertain mouth.

'I don't know,' she said again and again, all day and all night. 'It isn't really the painting or the principles that are worrying me,' she confessed. in a bid to win Monisha's curiosity and so open the way to advice and better than advice, corroboration. These words seemed spheres of cool clouds above the exhausted, outlived city.

Suddenly looking amused and shrewd, Monisha asked, 'Friends?'

'Yes —'

'Then make none.'

Amla was not so much taken aback by the advice as by the fact that Monisha should offer any at all. It struck her now that Monisha was in no position to offer advice; if she did. it was bound to be somehow weird and disturbing and unreal, like the one she had called, so clearly and abruptly, from the window of her barred home as Amla was leaving — advice that had slipped off its silver tray, slopped over and spilt, useless to the thirsty one to whom it was offered.

But Amla took it for what it was worth, simply. 'I never could avoid them,' she said miserably. 'Do you remember during the summer holidays I never was content merely to write to school friends who had gone away? I had to replace them with the gardener's children and go off to the orchard to build camps and fuss over dolls. You never needed to — nor did Nirode. That was lucky for you.'

'Lucky?' The word cracked, like the corrugated shell of a nut to fall apart and reveal the core — shrivelled and rotten. Amla flung out her hand to seize something, anything — not this useless, dead core that rattled out of the two halves of Monisha's single word. 'One must have someone who reciprocates, who responds. One must have that — reciprocation I think.'

'Must?'

'Don't you think one must?'

'If one could be offered that alone, by itself, silent, discreet, pure, untouched, *untouchable — then,* I suppose, yes.' Monisha spoke in a swift rush of almost inaudible words, slurring them over as if she were hurrying towards something, away from them. 'But what if it were offered to you all sticky with threads and strings and labels glued to it? Demands, proprietoriness, obligations, extortions, untruths, bullying? Would you take it then?'

Amla concentrated so fiercely as to be able to take in every single word, follow each thought of her sister's, always connecting them with Dharma, Dharma's painting, Dharma's request and Dharma's wife. She realised now that Monisha had been swimming alongside her, under the surface, silent, without a single tell-tale bubble to give her away, till she surfaced at last, close to her, with too brilliant an explosion of sound and motion: she had, after all, seen and sensed everything. Amla swung around, at last to talk openly and saw Monisha turn away, nod and smile at Bun Bun who had climbed the garden wall and slithered down to stand before her aunt, dismayed by a streak of green grime down the front of her pink satin frock.

'It doesn't matter, Bun Bun,' Monisha was saying. 'I'll take you home and change you before anyone sees.'

'Oh, must you go?' cried Amla.

'There's Jiban,' said Monisha, 'nodding to us to come,' and giving Bun Bun a little push, she went slowly and resignedly through the poisonous bright green of the monsoon grass, once more the lost princess of the fairy tale, under a secret spell. As they collected their belongings and said their farewells, Amla wondered how and why it was that Monisha had been married to this boring nonentity, this blind moralist, this complacent quoter of Edmund Burke and Wordsworth, Mahatma Gandhi and Tagore, this rotund, minute-minded and limited official. Why had their father chosen him from amongst other young men surely known to him, or to his friends and relations, whose names must have been proposed when word was sent around that the eldest daughter was to marry? Was it merely because Jiban was so unquestionably safe, sound and secure, so utterly predictable? Or was it because fathers did, unconsciously, spite their daughters who were unavailable to them? And why had Monisha, with that powerful silent stubbornness of hers, never rebelled? Amla tried to picture an evening of theirs — Jiban on the big fourposter, his compact silhouette like a misshapen S, shaking and swinging one leg quite mindlessly as he diligently read the *Amrita Bazar Patrika,* and

Monisha — but she could not, by any stretch of imagination, see Monisha seated beside him with her mending, or a book, discussing his day at the office or her day in the kitchen. Monisha she saw as seated upright and mute in one corner, her gaze fixed on some mysterious point as though it were a secret window opening on to darkness, gazing and gazing, with not a word to say of what she saw.

Amla was sober, reflective as she said good-bye to this sister and the beaming man who was saying, to his snivelling niece, 'I trust you have thanked your aunt and great-aunt for this most enjoyable evening spent under their auspices.' Amla stood watching them arrange themselves in the car and, as it drove away, wondered if one single word would be spoken by any of the occupants.

She turned to find her aunt standing behind her, chewing her underlip in furious reflection. They went in together, slowly.

'Aunt,' Amla asked, 'why did they marry?'

Her aunt shook her long hands at the ends of stiff wrists in an awkward gesture that denoted bafflement.

'Did you meet him before they were married?'

'Yes. Your father asked me to visit his family and report, so I did. I met Jiban and his family before your parents did.'

'And what did you report?'

'That they were a respectable, middle-class Congress family, completely unsuitable to Monisha's tastes and inclinations. So your father decided he was the right man, that it was the right family.'

'Why?' Amla exploded on the twilit veranda. 'How unfair, how criminally unfair.'

The old woman shrugged. 'I thought so too, but perhaps he thought he was being sensible — that Monisha ought not to be encouraged in her morbid inclinations and that it would be a good thing for her to be settled into such a stolid, unimaginative family as that, just sufficiently educated to accept her with tolerance. That is how your mother excused its happening.'

'Did she think that — that Monisha was morbid?'

'I can't remember her exact words any more,' the old woman said crossly, sitting down in her battered wicker chair and picking up a messy piece of embroidery on which she tortuously worked out her moods. 'How can I remember? There are more important things to keep one's mind on than other people's words and emotions and — marriages. If you want to get anything worthwhile done in this world, keep clear of those things.' Her eyes started and flashed behind the steel-rimmed spectacles in a way that always aroused Amla's concern and troubled admiration. 'Leave men to run that part of life, I always say. I used to say it to your mother, trying to get her to help me in my work, and she'd laugh — oh, all airy and flighty she always was — she'd laugh and say, "Men? But what do they know of the matters of the heart?" They know nothing of course, inadequate at that as at everything else, but they like to imagine they run everything, so women ought to just go on and let them imagine it while they get on with the work,' and, in her agitation, she snapped a silken thread in two and was obliged to thread her needle once more, with trembling clumsiness. In dismay Amla watched the misshapen butterfly on the square of green cloth grow more and more distorted and unrecognisable and wondered whether it would join her aunt's other pieces of embroidery that so tastelessly decorated the interior of this mausoleum. 'I learnt it the hard way,' she went on. 'And so did my girl Rita, for all my advice and warning. However, we must be grateful that she found her way out as quickly as she did — and now she is at last doing the work that she was made for. I often wish she could work on it here in India, where I could see her sometimes, but — ' and the unhappier she grew, the harsher was her voice — 'but it is good, it does me good to think of her in Paris, working with some of the finest physicists in the world...'

Amla sighed, folded her arms about her knees and resigned herself to listening, once again, to the trials of her cousin Rita and the valour and intelligence with which she got the better of them.

In reply to Amla's forlorn letter, her mother wrote an agitated reply:

'...If only I had been proven wrong in my light-hearted prediction, if only she had proven different, I should have found the surprise in itself appealing. But there is no appealing element in it at all, Amla, nothing joyful and unexpected and lovely. She is a nurse, she has large, rough hands. Of course, Arun writes of her "chestnut hair" (his description) and "blue eyes," her "loyalty and selflessness," but in the photograph I enclose for all of you to see, I see only her big hands, those raw, hard-worked hands. And of course she wishes to continue her work and of course Arun supports her in this. "Another three or four years, mother," he writes, but I know, I know. We shall never see Arun again. If he did return, it would be only for a visit. How could Agnes, his Agnes, his clean, efficient, blue-eyed nurse possibly put up with our laxness, our lack of formaldehyde and pinkie and starched white night clothes and balanced diets? One need only look at those hands in the photograph to know they dip themselves compulsively in a solution of dettol and wipe the white enamel dishes cleaner and cleaner. She could never live with us. Nor we with her. I wrote Arun a million sad questions — "Does she care for music? Does she play any instrument? What does she read?" But I know the answers already: "She sings well, mother and likes the old folk songs. No, she doesn't get much time to read, her working hours are long and arduous..." And for your father's sake, I have asked questions about her family, background, property etc., but it is no use. Look at those great rough hands, please look at them.

'Why did I stand down in the garden, making a pretence of inspecting my apricot trees, when I waited for the postman? What wretched mail. Arun ruins this day that has emerged washed and peerless from weeks of rain and here's your letter too, full of worries and regrets. I reproach myself for having come up to Kalimpong, to live in my lifelong ivory tower. I should have kept on your father's house in Calcutta, made a home for you children there. But when he died, I could only think of returning to the hills. I had always dreamt of Kalimpong, Amla, even in the best years. Now I know I made the decisions and changes too abruptly, without thinking clearly. Here are you, already regretting your career and situation. Here's Monisha writing such detailed rot about her impossible family — as though she had actually immersed herself in it or as though it were a theatre to her, I cannot really tell. And Nirode, mute and in exile: all I know of him is what you and Monisha write and I know you gloss things over so as not to cause me pain, for he must be living so sordid an existence, I cannot bear thinking of it. And now Arun's gone from us to his blue-eyed Nurse Agnes and they'll never come to me as son and daughter. If they come, they'll come as strangers. It is my fault, of course, for not having kept on the Calcutta house and kept you all with me, for having sold it and come to live alone in this secluded paradise which seems to have no channel of communication with your very real and rough lives in the city, away from me.

'And the day was so lovely. I could see villages in the valley below, scattered flakes of red and white in the neat tea gardens. And the sky was rinsed and sparkling like glass, the Kanchenjunga hidden by the whitest fleece of clouds. All the woods blue and misty. And my garden lifting out of the rainwater, so brilliant but it seems my instincts have all been wrong, my paradise is a fool's abode and I have lost touch with my closest ones...'

So, in the end, she went to Dharma unprepared and unfortified, feeling grotesquely unequal to the situation. Yet he himself was so gentle, so withdrawn as he studied her and drew the first fine strokes on a clean sheet of paper, that she gradually grew still and began to wonder why she had been clamouring and struggling like a rabbit in a trap, tearing herself to shreds. He himself said nothing to soothe her, indeed had very little to say. He concentrated entirely on the curve of her neck and the fall of her hair, drawing with an intentness and swiftness that was quite painless and this he continued to do for the first half a dozen sittings. Amla would emerge from the bus, reeling from the diesel fumes and odour of the exhausted home-going crowd, push open the narrow green door with an apprehension of crisis, find Dharma waiting for her, sit down upon the white divan to which he motioned her and then, as though she had unwittingly assumed a masterly yogic pose, find herself growing calmer, more definite and capable in Dharma's presence. The strokes of the charcoal stick, the rubs of a rag or his flat thumb, these eliminated, minute by minute, the unnecessary panic within her. When the time came to leave, she was able to do so without that tearing sense of having met with a dreadful accident that she so often had when away from him.

One day he raised his leathern eyelids a bit, looked from the scarred art paper at her and said, 'This is very good of you, to sit so patiently through the preliminaries. They are never very interesting for the model. But it is so many years since I have worked on a human model. I feel an incompetent student again.'

'If you let me see the sketches, it will be very interesting for me, not boring at all.'

'You may have them. I don't need to sketch any more, we can begin with the paints next time.'

She reached forward for the sketches eagerly, but when she saw her small sections helplessly scattered through many pages, scarred with harsh charcoal or dissected into even finer sections with pen and ink or pencil, she shuddered and dropped them on the divan beside her. It was too unsettling to be vivisected in this fashion. She felt again as though she were lying on a white slab in a morgue, beneath Dharma's scientific fingers, not to be anaesthetized but to be cut open and taken apart. She did not take the sketches with her when she left and Dharma took note of this with the faintest saurian flicker of an eyelid, but said nothing.

The next time she visited him, she found him seated comfortably before a low easel, working on a canvas already threaded and embroidered with a curious pattern formed of the sapless veins of dry leaves, the sagging threads of a spider's web, the capillaries of a corpse pumped clean of blood. Suspended in this hummock, her hand hung ghost-like and disembodied, holding a long stick between two fingers. Queasily, she went closer to study it, and found nothing ghost-like about it at all — it was her own living hand, brown and knuckled, eager and inept. There it hovered, caught motionless in the flux of a search, pausing in a moment of questioning, anxiety and optimism. This made Amla clutch her own left hand to her body and look at in horror, as though it were detached from her wrist by a sudden operation, the flesh and cut veins exposed to sight and touch. She stood watching Dharma paint and found that what this hand held in its fingers was no harmless stick but a fine paint-brush. No, but Dharma knew too much of her, saw her too clearly! She was startled enough to try and turn and run, but Dharma halted her with his words.

'Sit down. Amla. You need not really model today. I've been working from one of the sketches all day and the painting comes so easily now. I feel I know the entire history of your hand. It is such a pleasure to paint it.'

'I can see you do know it,' she said through dry lips.

'Talk to me Amla. Nothing will distract me today. Tell me about your hand, what it does. Tell me your history.'

She was tongue-tied and he was the one who talked, while he painted canvas after canvas, sometimes working on two at the same time. Across them various portions of her torso drifted, alive and rich-blooded. yet torn away from the whole Amla and related instead, to the strange surrealistic backgrounds of those paintings — landscapes and objects that were weird and disturbing, with a sense and proportion belonging to another sphere, not her own. Yet she felt she understood them, was related to them — perhaps because of those painted, disembodied hands and ears and lips of hers that made contact with them on canvas.

The more complex grew this unreal relationship of Amla, Dharma, canvas and paint, the more direct, simple and forthright he became, abandoning his early well-defended concentration for a gentle, sympathetic cordiality. Soon it was she who talked, answered his questions and then expanded the answers. Ease and pleasure swelled their conversations, friendship entered it and Amla relaxed at last.

'How is it,' he asked, 'that you have those high, sharp cheekbones, almost Mongolian? Have the years you spent in the hills had such an influence as to alter your very bones, Amla?' He was mixing fresh paints on his palette, with care and deliberation — nothing was left to chance in Dharma's art, his instincts always went ahead of him, leading him surely and his technique followed closely behind.

'I don't doubt in the power of the Himalayas to do that,' Amla said, smiling, drawing a finger along her cheekbones, 'but the truth is my mother is part Nepalese. She was born in the house in Kalimpong where she lives now. Her father married twice — first a Bengali woman of his own caste and chosen by his family — she was the mother of my aunt Lila and after she died, he married a Nepalese girl, my grandmother. We liked to believe he met her in a tea garden, found her plucking tea leaves as he rode by on a pony — it makes such a lovely picture, so unusual in our society, don't you think? Unfortunately, the truth is that my Nepali grandmother belonged to a very uninteresting bourgeois tradesman's family — they traded with Sikkim and Bhutan, and, I do so hope, Tibet. They owned property in Calcutta and around Kalimpong — tea gardens and things. My mother has *her* mother's high colouring and cheekbones — I think my sister and I have inherited the latter.'

Dharma was watching her over his palette, intently. 'How refreshing,' he said, 'to think of an old, caste-bound family like your father's admitting a breath of mountain air into their closed house.'

'Oh, by the time my mother was old enough to marry, her family had more property than my father's family which had by then lost most of what they had had. They were a very quarrelsome and uncooperative lot and it all dwindled away. I'm afraid the marriage must have been something of a financial settlement and — and I don't know if my father didn't regret it later.'

'Why? If he had married for financial reasons, then he did very well for himself, didn't he?'

'Yes, but he hadn't quite bargained for mother, just for her houses and tea estates. Do you know, when I was small, I thought she got the worst of the bargain — just look, even we still think of marriages as bargains! — but now he's dead and she's growing rather old and demanding, I've changed my mind a bit.' Glancing sideways at

Dharma, she noticed an alteration in his expression, from that of a passive listener to that of a prejudiced participant and wondered if he disapproved. She felt curiously pleased to think he was taking in her chatter so seriously, giving it consideration. Before she had come to Calcutta, she would not have been able to speak in this fashion and she wondered if it was the city or Nirode or knowing Dharma that had made her change. She had never before thought or spoken objectively and analytically of her parents and to speak of them in this manner was a strangely exciting novelty. She cast the same look across her childhood now and that of her sisters and brothers and talked to Dharma about them as she sat on the white divan, playing with empty tubes of paint, while the geese cackled in the saturated foliage outside and in the twilight glow-worms appeared and began to perform their mysterious ceremony of lights.

'My father always got on her nerves by simply never doing anything. I always see him lying back, indolently, like an overfed house cat against mother's embroidered Tibetan cushions, toying with a cheroot or a glass of whisky or both. One or two of his coat buttons were always undone about the middle and my sister and I used to turn our eyes away from the untidy gaps — children hate to be reminded of the flesh and blood of their parents, don't they? I remember meals for which my mother would prepare some marvellous Tibetan dish. She is a very proficient cook — that is the Bengali in her — and my father would pick up a fork, separate a noodle from a bamboo shoot, then put his fork down. His servant would come forward with his glass and he would drink that, smilingly, watching us eat. And my mother used to often arrange musical soirees of a quite professional standard in our house in Calcutta, when we came down in winter. I remember a great *shehai* player coming to one of them. He played ravishingly and all the guests — connoisseurs mostly — and my mother had their eyes closed and were swaying their heads and even we children had goose pimples prickling all over us as we sat on the carpet, right at the back. My father half-lay against a bolster and smiled his vacant feline smile and had his glass filled and refilled and as the hours wound around that long, sweet *shehai,* which was no better than a noisy pipe, a piece of plumbing to him, he fell asleep, his head drooping forward and his mouth open and wet.. My mother was sitting with her head bowed and her eyes closed in pleasure. Then she opened them and glanced at him and I saw that glance. I saw such terrible contempt and resentment in her eyes — just for a second before she closed them again and lost herself in the music. When he came up to Kalimpong and saw her wandering about her garden, touching her flowers, he never followed her. He used to lie back against his cushions, idle and contented — contented, I think, in his malice.'

'He drank very much then. Is that how he died?'

'No!' Amla exclaimed, still astonished by the truth. 'He died in an automobile accident, here in Calcutta. He had been lunching at the Bengal Club with an English friend — he couldn't, of course, be a member of that club himself and as they drove out of the gates, a passing lorry smashed their car to bits. It seems to me that was the one active, violent moment of his life, that the rest of it he spent in sleeping and drinking and idling, but perhaps I am wrong. My brother Arun says father taught him to play cricket and my brother Nirode tells me that he loved horses. Nirode thinks his own loathing of animals is the direct cause of my father's unfairness to him. He was imperiously unfair — and that is a positive, active state, too, isn't it? I've been telling you how he was always drinking and smiling his knowing, spiteful smile, yet when I think of it, there was sometimes an emotion in him that must have been very violent to show at all on his face, even so faintly.'

'Violent?'

'Yes, I remember mother crying and noise — I can't remember why, but it had something to do with what he said or did. But did he? It astonishes me now — he was very soft, really, like warm wax, hot to touch. And once, in Kalimpong, he walked up to the house, through the garden, with my sister and me and he suddenly tapped a butterfly that sat vibrating on a huge flower and he said, "Look at that. Study that. Forget yourself in that study. Then you will be fortunate — like your mother." And he smiled his diseased,

204

unpleasing smile and walked on and we trailed behind him, feeling horribly depressed.'

'Your mother does not sound to me like a person who could forget herself in study.'

'You are right, she is not. I don't know what my father meant — perhaps only that she had forgotten him, deliberately, shut her mind to him by concentrating it on flowers and music and fine food, things he shunned. I cannot say. Do you think children are ever really able to unravel the truth about their parents?'

Dharma had turned around to work on a canvas, a flagrant one that leapt and panicked like a fire about Amla's two outstretched arms. He said evenly, 'My own parents died while I was a young boy. I had a child who left me when she was fifteen. I have no way of answering your question, Amla, intriguing as it is.' His brush worked quickly in long, rich strokes of vermilion and ochre, scarlet and flesh-pink.

All at once Amla was struck by the vast difference in the pictures he used to paint and the ones he was painting now. In the new ones, she was always the model and about her his *old,* careful surrealistic world had panicked and erupted into a tumult. She felt afraid now, longed to struggle away from any responsibility that might be levelled at her. She felt afraid of the arms and flames that wound about each other with such ferocity and ardour. 'It has nothing to do with me,' she insisted, wanting her relationship with Dharma to be something quite different, something normal and everyday and gentle, not complex and disturbing and unreal as what he painted these days. She got up abruptly and went to one corner of the studio where some of his old pictures were stacked. One of them was unfinished. He had interrupted his work on that when Amla appeared and left it undone in order to start working on her portrait. She tried to fill the virgin gaps with possibilities, saw herself enter it and turn everything about her, in that calm picture, upside down, set it on fire and greet the flames with wild arms.

When she put back the canvas and turned, she found him watching her. 'You have not told me enough of your mother, she is still a mystery to me,' he said.

Amla sat down again. 'A very beautiful mystery,' she said, trying to retain the lightness of tone, but not succeeding. 'She is the most beautiful woman I know and very accomplished. None of us is like her, so polished and balanced and contained — like a well-cut jewel. I will read you her letters one day, to show you how warm-hearted she is, inspite of her self-absorption, how full of impulses and instincts she can be. Yet at the core of it all there is this cold, frosty love of power — like a concealed fluorescent bulb. I can't describe it or explain to you why I sense it, but I'm certain it is there. Perhaps I understand it because, really, I am a bit like her and so is Nirode and we share this secret inner coldness and outward impulsiveness with her. Only Monisha, amongst us all, has taken after my father. She has his silence and a touch of his malice — oh, bleached, refined, purified to just a pale shade of it, harmless to anyone but herself, but the shape, the design of it remains in her eyes and on her mouth. Dharma,' she broke off suddenly, *you* talk to me now. Tell me why you left that picture unfinished and how you might have finished it.'

He threw down his brush and began to work with a palette knife, vigorously. 'I don't care to waste time on that any more. I've other things to do now.'

'What?'

He did not reply but continued to work and Amla watched him recreate her arms, down to the palest scar at her elbow which she had long ago forgotten. There was this eeriness in Dharma that made her, as it made many others, attribute unseen and undefinable qualities to him, feeling that these must exist behind those heavy lids, in the flashes of his disconcertingly clear pupils. Surely it must be the very cause of his strange art. There was no comfort in it, no shade or rest. Each moment and each object hovered on the brink of crisis. In her more intimidated moments, it seemed to Amla that there was something theatrical about these long, probing evenings that they spent together. The very studio, crowded with finished canvases and yet contriving to seem stark, was an undressed stage where they performed. On one side of the stage was the clamorous lane, its rickshaws and metal-toned vendors and on the other the

206

stillness of the green pond, the single curving palm and the glow-worms hovering in Gita Devi's holy *tulsi* plant and bushes of white jasmine. Its only music was the one supplied by Gita Devi's prayers at the altar in her gleaming kitchen of which Amla never saw more than a flash of brass and a flicker of flame when, occasionally, the door blew open. The actors were Amla and Dharma, playing a sober, yet dangerous game of questions and answers — in which Dharma's answers were all questions to Amla and her own answers, further questions. He never allowed her to question him as she longed to and he rarely spoke of himself, his art, his family, his relationship with friends — all these he kept secret and, because he did so, he gave immense provocation to Amla's imagination which had retained its childhood vivacity and credulity and was her most vulnerable point.

All the outer vestments, the garb and casing of a fine and fulfilled passion were there: Amla grew pale enough to rouse her aunt's concern; at the office she worked so poorly that Mrs Basu was compelled to show her, in many disagreeable ways, that she had no patience with commercial artists who despised their employment; she went shopping and bought herself rich and fantastic *saris* and then was tearful with dissatisfaction; she felt limp and wasted till the day's work was over, the office shut and she could get into the turbulent bus and travel, at last, to the tacit welcome of Dharma and his studio.

In the hours she spent there, she became another Amla, a flowering Amla, translucent with joy and overflowing with a sense of love and reward. Here she could talk as, all day long, she could not talk, of things to which she scarcely gave a thought before, only because she knew Dharma would like to hear these details and their context and because Dharma would translate them into something that had both meaning and form. Here her small wildflower humour could blossom and Dharma smiled to see her cover sheets of his own art paper with her busybody parrots and lost ladybirds. It was only during these hours that she felt that life had. after all, offered her that for which she was born. While in his presence, the obstacles to receiving this gift did not exist. The studio seemed to be without walls, its interior melted into a dreamlike exterior that was boundless, in which time ran at a different pace from reality and the dimensions were altered and suited to another world — an evening world, lit by a sun already over the horizon, but still radiant, as in that short, poignant moment of perfect luminosity before night descends. This world bore resemblance to the one Dharma painted nowadays, for here too, each object was definite, sober and recognisable — here an easel, there a model, behind the door a fire glowing and beyond it, greenery waving its fingers at the window and the procession of seven white geese... But, just as in Dharma's paintings, each of these objects acquired a silent, pressing symbolism. Who were these seven white birds walking in single file with ritualistic lugubriousness across the garden that was swooning in a dense mauve mist? At night in her dreams, Amla believed that they were former models turned into white birds by Dharma, warning and scolding her in their harsh, broken voices. And the longing arch of that single palm as it stretched over the pond, never quite meeting its shimmering reflection it could so easily be a melancholy maiden, dying of unrequited love. The old, paint-smeared easel bore Amla's arms, then her silhouette, then her long hair and held them to this strange, pure, but distorting light and in their rigidity they acquired a kind of mortality that terrified the sleeping, dreaming Amla. In those lonely hours of sleep the hallucinatory quality of Dharma's painting seeped into her actual life and she would sit up in bed and watch, in horror, the reality of their meetings melt and disintegrate and then re-appear on canvas — but in fragments and as symbols. This confluence of two rivers, of waters of two colours, two depths, made itself felt all day by its silence and its power. There were moments when Amla feared to touch a paint-brush, feeling it might take wing and fly out of the window, or the ring on her finger, half expecting to see a caterpillar crawl out of the Tibetan turquoise.

She fought to over-tip this too perfect balance between reality and hallucination, the present and the future that was not to be. While she chattered about her family, her home, trees and pets she had loved, she was only trying to colour the intangible world Dharma painted around her with the brightness and solidity of a happy childhood. In his questions and in her own answers she was always seeking for something that in this precarious situation, would emerge as tangible and permanent. But these were the two things Dharma was unable to offer her and could not promise her — tangibility, permanence. Whatever it was that he felt for her, whatever it was that he gave to her, could only be translated on to his canvas in terms of a vast, silent change. The understanding between them was an interior volcano, colouring the water of his existence and splashing on to his canvas the tints of the upheaval within him.

Amla dared not, at first calm and console herself with the heady thought that she was the cause of this great change. While she sat for Dharma, no visitors ever came to disturb them — neither fellow artists nor friends nor relations — and so Amla never heard another's opinion on his new, apocalytic style and had no way of knowing exactly how powerful a revolution had taken place. But when the fetishes, the symbols and the dream images began slowly to disappear from the paintings and more and more of Amla began to appear, whole and alive and meaningful in herself, then apprehension made her very heart darken and tumble. Over the weeks she had watched the incorporate horror of his earlier surrealisms filter softly out of the whorled paints, so meticulously employed and a new and refreshing realism push its way through as though from the rubble of a post-war ruin — at first tentative, then shocking in its rawness and finally marvellous by the very virtue of its existence.

Now Dharma talked less, interrupting his work only to order her to raise her eyes or tilt her chin. She became silent and, in the painful rigidity of her pose, fell to brooding, wondering if Dharma saw in his model anything more than inspiration that had come to him so unexpectedly and opportunely, offering him rescue from the complexities of microscopically observed nature to which he had enslaved himself for so many years, as though inflicting upon himself a discipline that was to prepare him for this reincarnation. For he was truly reincarnated as an artist, first in the school of surrealism and then in a school where portraiture was vividly linked with the silent, intangible train of dreams that impress and influence the human body far more than the slashing and scarring of reality itself. The earlier dream images remained caterpillars entwined about the wings of butterflies, railway tracks gleaming across a calm, afternoon desert to abruptly disappear into the silver haze of a mirage, cloistered rocks engraved with the symbols of secret creeds — but from them emerged, with growing clarity, the creature created by these dreams.

One day Amla came in to find him painting the turquoise ring she always wore on one finger and coming closer, she saw crawling out of that veined blue stone a worm, exactly such a glaucous, fleshy worm as she had often dreamt of seeing emerging from her little ring, leaving a trail of slime across her fingers. It had crept out of her nightmare to push its insidious head out of the painted stone and arouse, in the painted Amla, that very turbulence of disgust, revulsion and fear that so often assailed the dreaming Amla. The strange thing was that she had never spoken to Dharma of this nightmare.

Her carefully assimilated composure cracked and shivered upon seeing this secret dream symbol recreated by Dharma and she could not refrain from asking him agitatedly what he meant by it, what made him know this nightmare of hers, what made him capable of reproducing such emotions of hers as she had never revealed to him.

'But you did,' he said. 'I saw them in your face the first day you came to see me, the day Nirode brought you here and you looked so utterly dismayed and fearful. I saw it again the day you went across to that unfinished canvas in the corner and examined it with such trepidation. These days I see it whenever you glance across at my work — but of course you avoid doing that as far as possible.' He smiled. 'Think back, wasn't the first time you saw the worm the evening you came to visit me, with Nirode?'

'How can you know things I never told you about?' Her whole body had weakened and she sank on to the divan.

Dharma smiled at her with such sweetness as to cancel out all the uncanniness of his revelation, then turned to his paint brushes and began industriously to clean them, spattering himself and Amla with coloured turpentine. He had done with the portrait.

'I don't think you know,' he said, 'that I began my career as a portrait painter. When I was a boy I used to sketch my master in school and the sketches were so accurate that I was expelled, giving me full time to carry on with my obsession. I did portraits of my family and their friends and began to receive commissions. Very dreadful they were — I think photographs could have shown more imagination than those pedantic, heavy-handed reproductions I used to do in the dark oils so beloved of the Bengali school. I soon turned to more inspiring subjects, but it was in portraiture that I took my training. I learnt quite early those insidious tricks of looking at the model when she is well occupied with something, at making her tell me little stories and secrets, at making her confide in me just a little bit more than she would to anyone else. You see, I am really a bad listener, I cannot respond in anyway but this one, with my paint-brush. My paintings are my only response to your charming confidences. Terribly inadequate, aren't they?'

'Even so, they are just a little bit more than I can take,' Amla said with an unexpected tartness that made Dharma glance at her in brief surprise.

'One day, when you have time, I might show you some of the old portraits. I haven't kept many of them, but I think my wife still has a few I did of her and our family. Then you could compare them with this one I have just completed of you and you will think they are done by two different painters. I myself cannot tell you the reason for that. Probably there are many reasons. Technical improvement is one, naturally. But amongst them is the fact that in you I see the inner being closer, closer to the surface than in that of any other woman I have painted. The women I have painted are the women of *my* family and *my* wife's family: they are all covered with many thick, slack layers of prejudice, convention, ignorance and reticence. You are such an entirely different creature, even your physiognomy is different. When you came, with Nirode, that first time, I thought that if I looked closely enough I would actually see through the skin and flesh to the network of veins and arteries within, that I could note the very alterations in the colour and quality of the blood that ran in you. Of course I did not want to, it was not your physiology that startled me. I was interested in that green shadow, there in the cradle of the clavicle, just beneath your chin, cast by that same pear tree you talk so much about to me. And that very small and innocent ear in which I see the quiver of reflected water, mountain water. In your curled fingers I can see all the playthings of your childhood, pebbles and crayons and the small furry bodies of your pets. When you look at yourself in the mirror, while you are turning the coil of your heavy hair on top of your head, what do you see? Amla doing her hair or an entire life-time, the memories of it, the marks of it? When I look at you it is as though a map of human life is stirring, assuming vivid colours, moving and growing. However often I paint you, I shall never be able to cover all those forms and colours you assume when you pose for me. It is like painting a fascinating landscape, one that not just one but an entire school of painters is willing to paint over and over again and when they leave the site, they leave with the sense that something more could have been done with it.'

'And have you reached that point now?' Amla asked in a hoarse voice. 'Of leaving the site?'

'A portrait painter is more fortunate than a landscape painter in that,' Dharma said, holding up a cleaned brush and admiring the gloss of its thick black bristles. 'His model is not one that has to be deserted and left behind. It is living, moving and it speaks and dreams.'

In the still old garden new trees of balsam sprouted bright flowers of cherry-red, white and pink. Sitting at her window, overlooking these unexpected blossoms, Amla wrote a long delayed letter to her mother, wrote in a free and sweeping hand. 'Now one feels winter close by, the city has turned sweeter, so much sweeter and fresher and younger, mother, one can breathe again.'

She even went to see Nirode again, in a spirit of ungrudging forgiveness and also some forgetfulness, drew him out of his dark cell, sat with him in a fly-ridden tea stall drinking black and acrid tea and declared it was very good. At a book stall where Nirode showed inclination to linger, she ripped stained and tattered volumes from his hands, tossed them down and bullied him towards a bus stop, unintimidated by the long grumbling queue. 'A long bus ride,' she said. 'It's months since I felt I should really enjoy a long bus ride.'

'What makes you go on so many then?' Nirode asked sourly. He hated queues, never stood in one, but today Amla made him.

'You'll see,' she said, smiling.

'There's no surprise in that, I've known Dharma for years.'

She did not mind. She was, in fact, grateful for direct attention being paid to a relationship so pallid that no one else had tried to give it the strength of recognition. 'You haven't seen his new pictures,' she said.

Queuing up was getting on Nirode's nerves. 'I find them all too damned frustrating,' he grumbled. 'No wonder they never were a success. Who wants to be taken for a worm and given a grub's eye view of rank wild life? It's an insult to the intellect. In any case, I loathe nature.'

'Wait, just wait,' Amla said, as jubilant as a well-rewarded explorer and the bus arrived. That evening at Dharma's ranked always, for Amla, as the peak of her season of love — that tautly strung moment when all flowers are in bloom and all fruit is ripe, when bees are contented, the nights are gentle with sleep and the days rounded, fulfilled and memorable. This was the perfection that every lover strains to make the criterion and in it lay all the joy and the sense of being the right person in the right place that love should have made diffuse and scattered gently through the season. It had not done so, it could not, but that one evening it offered itself to her as the perfect, unscarred globe of a newly ripe pear. In Dharma's measured talk and serene appearance, in Nirode's appreciation of the change she had wrought in Dharma's art, Amla was content. She gave no thought to the worm embedded in the fruit.

She laughed with pleasure when Nirode, sullen so far, started with surprise at the sight of the finished portrait on the easel, even took the cigarette out of his mouth and held it, burning between his fingers, while Dharma brought him more to see. She exchanged looks with Dharma as Nirode went through them, confusion softening the skeletal rigidity of his cautious face.

He said at last, 'Am I looking at them in the right order?' 'The right order,' said Dharma. Today he was not painting, he was comfortably seated on a mat, rolling himself an exquisite *pan* leaf.

'Then I am looking upon the history of a revolution — the Dharmic revolution!' Nirode turned to congratulate the painter and Amla was relieved to see in him those strains of enthusiasm and appreciation she thought had died in him long ago. 'I'm glad,' he said. 'Dharma, thank God you've crawled away from your eternal little spiders and their terrible great webs. They were such a strain on my eyes.'

Dharma laughed. He nodded across at the old canvases lined up against the walls and asked 'Are those quite worthless then?' .

'Compared with these, yes. Never show one to me again. I feel suffocated in those half-lit burrows, all choked with unidentifiable weeds. Here there's space and thought and challenge.' He looked again at a painting in which bright birds swam in a goldfish bowl and Amla's ringed hands fed them with fire. 'One can look at them and think and expand. I think that is what you must have done — painted and painted till, your world began to spread and expand — '

'Towards human beings again. I should not have thought my old friend the recluse would congratulate me for doing something so foolhardy.'

'Foolhardy if you move towards them unarmed,' Nirode snapped and struck a match violently. He went and flung himself down on the divan and Amla grew uneasy as she saw his face darken. 'Not if you make your own terms and get them to accept those. That's what I think you *have* done, that's why these pictures appeal to me.' He stared at Dharma with some hostility but also curiosity. 'You understand perfectly well what I'm talking about, don't you? That's what those long, long railway tracks you repeat again and again really mean — the offering of new terms of your own. Then you discard them. And,' he gestured towards the easel, 'here's Amla. I think I understand why.'

214

'Perhaps you over-simplify a much more involved process. Nirode? Perhaps you colour it with your own experience and your stand in the world, not so very like mine after all?'

'Perhaps.' Nirode leant against the wall, inhaling smoke, looking more tired and careless again. 'How can I help it? That's the only way I can grasp this surprise you've sprung on me. Amla spoke of it but — you never hinted at so much, Amla.' She smiled to see him relax, said nothing.

'I don't think she realised exactly how great a change it was,' Dharma said in his slow, even voice. 'She seems unaware of it still. She is the one person who dived under that wily, powerful city of yours and stumbled upon my lost underworld. She made contact with my silent, secret dream-creatures and they directed her on to me. I never thought I should so much enjoy meeting a human being again in my green world where I never allowed so much as a footprint. But I did, I did,' and he looked, not at Amla, but at her luminous portrait on the easel. 'I enjoyed it so much, I feel quite prepared to return to the world she came from on her delightful visit,' and now he turned to look at her and she accepted that moment as the only one of fulfilment she was to know. Then he said to Nirode, 'Of course, on my own terms.'

They laughed. 'What?' said Nirode. 'Return to Calcutta?' and the gaiety began, in which the men spoke of old friends, listened to Amla's animatedly expressed impressions of them, tumbled them together like clowns and laughed. They were lighthearted as they had never before been, in each other's demanding company. No one spoke of tomorrow. But avoiding all mention of it so scrupulously involved a strain. That strain made the perfection of the moment, of the delicate peak, shiver and crack. When they left, late that evening, Amla and Nirode were quiet — through exhaustion or the apprehension of the inevitable decline, neither cared to think.

All the same she hurried next day to Dharma. When she entered the studio, she found it an altered place. Her portrait was no longer on the easel. It stood amongst some of the earlier surrealisms, on the floor, against the wall. Dharma sat before a lowered easel, doing a charcoal sketch on a sheet of paper pinned to a board. His model who sat on the divan, Amla's divan, was a young man. Amla was to discover, in the course of that stifling, stilted evening, that he was the collegiate son of an artist friend of Dharma's, a boy with pretensions towards the literary life, but neither aptitude nor even ambition. So much one could make out from his face, delicate and effeminate, with the typically Bengali combination of intense romanticism and ineffectual discontent, making him look consumptively attractive beneath the dark locks of well-oiled hair. With his new insight into the dream world of his models, Dharma was drawing. into that face terrifying vistas of failure, irresponsibility and moribundity. The work required great concentration and he did not say much to Amla.

She revisited him several weeks later with Nirode. They saw he had been hard at work on a series of harshly impressive portraits, at once delicate in technique and powerful in inference. He drew his models from amongst his old friends, their uncertain, unguided offspring, passers-by in the busy lane outside, vendors, cadgers, housewives and children. He seemed to be working desperately hard. He said he was preparing for an exhibition.

Darkness fell on the city. It fell so quietly, naturally and with such ineluctability, that Amla accepted at last that this was the true colour of Calcutta and that the luminous island she had visited, where goose feathers shone like white china and each fold of a rolled *pan* leaf was sharp in clarity, was only a portion of a dream world, real only by reflection. It had not been illuminated by the cheerful sun of her childhood but by the supernatural vision of those who live always underground, in the dark. Now she awoke to reality and the curiously lustrous and isolated world of Dharma retreated to a bitter latitude.

She could not rid herself of the sense that, however intangible, she belonged to it still, that she existed in the real world of the city only as an observer, that she could never truly inhabit it. So, when she heard Jit's invitations over the telephone, she always replied,

'Thank you so much, but I'm afraid — ' and went home, instead, to brood alone in her room or in the still garden, while her aunt paced the veranda like a grounded bat.

One day, as Amla came trailing up the marble stairs, her aunt could no longer restrain herself and burst out, 'I don't like to say anything, I can see you're in no mood for talking but, Amla, it's wrong.'

Amla started like a ghost disturbed in its prowling and frowned. 'What is?' she asked, so flatly as to make it quite clear that the answer was of no consequence to her.

'To waste — ' her aunt's large, bony hands shook and scattered the grey stillness in her effort to be coherent and to impress. 'To waste — all this spirit and youth and intelligence in yourself — please don't go away, stay with me.'

'No.'

'But listen, child, listen. Your mother is away on her mountain top, too busy looking after her orchids to give a thought to what you are going through — '

'Do you know what I am going through?'

'Yes, I know,' her aunt pleaded, rough and intense. 'I saw my daughter suffer through it, Amla, don't forget. She wasted years of her own spirit and independence in those few weeks of her marriage. You must have heard how it ended, with that other woman — '

'Yes, aunt, but I haven't such problems, not being married.'

'What is the difference?' she cried. 'Women place themselves in bondage to men, whether in marriage or out. All their joy and ambition is channelled that way, while they go parched themselves. My Rita broke away, I made her and I'm not sorry. Read her letters and you will see how she has grown young again, how her life has expanded.'

'Yes, yes, and what do you think I should do?' Amla cried in irritation, shaking the chair that she had held on to while she stood listening.

'Give it up. Break it off.'

'What?'

'This, this man, Amla. Don't be annoyed with me for knowing.'

Amla looked up at her face that was lined with intensity and saw neither busy philandering there nor idle curiosity. She looked down at the two rows of her knuckles laid on the chair-back and said flatly, but gently, 'What if he is worth it all, aunt? Not just another third-rate fraud like Rita's husband was, but a — a very fine artist, a very great man who saw something in me that — that directly inspired his work — '

'But don't you see then?' her aunt interrupted harshly. 'He uses you, something in you that he needs. But the rest — what does he care for that?'

'I don't know.'

'Yet you want to hang on and wait to find out?'

'Yes, I think that is what I am doing.'

The old woman leapt out of her chair, her very bones jarring with rage. 'What is the good of it all?' she said desperately. 'What is the good of our growing old and suffering and working in order to show you what we've learnt by our experience? Every generation is as foolish as the last and yours is surely the most foolish one of all, the most selfish and — frivolous. We at least were dedicated to a very great movement outside our own immediate wants and whims and we won you your freedom, but what do you do with it? Give it back to the old, dying generation to hold and look after while you carry on with your petty affairs, too timid and hopeless to concern yourself with anything bigger.'

'I'm only a girl, aunt, I'm only one person, not a whole nation you have to bully and prod into health and prosperity,' Amla shouted and went up the stairs to her room in cold anger. Her aunt followed her to apologize, but then found herself too proud, too thoughtful and too tired to do so after all.

Watching her, Nirode grew steadily more depressed. It unsettled him to think that a matter of so little inherent consequence as the change in Dharma's style had caused him so much astonishment and pleasure. He had imagined he could observe all change, for better or worse, with unshakable equanimity and he disapproved of the delight he had felt in looking at those pictures. Similarly. he was disturbed to find that Amla's sick, gaunt looks did more than offend him, actually involved him and made him realize that she suffered. He had imagined that he had climbed into a superior latitude where such things, the affairs of his and other people's hearts and bodies did not matter and was now dismayed to find that such things could indeed still distract him and pierce his cool, painless insularity. It was necessary to repair this breach, to seal it up and reinforce it with his cynicism and his philosophy. In order to do this, he had to be rid of the cause of his unhealthy distraction and it was for this reason, rather than to help Amla, that he went to Dharma determined to make him settle the matter.

He was perfectly aware of the ludicrousness of the situation and it made him skittish. He was relieved to find Dharma as busy as a fowl feathering its nest, with new canvases and when Nirode saluted him by asking, 'No more young models in thrall, Dharma? Did Amla frighten you off?' he barely noticed.

After a while, however, he put away his brushes and took Nirode for a stroll around the pond and said, 'Ask her to come and see me, Nirode, I should enjoy that. All this madness of work, these hundreds of new paintings, this art, that is destroying me with its power and its demands — all this is the young woman's doing. Or is it? Since she came to model for me, I have not had the time to sit down here in my garden and think about it, as it deserves to be thought about. When the exhibition opens, all my old friends and my enemies, the critics, they will all wonder and ask, "What made him change? How did this come about?" There are many answers I could give them and the easiest and simplest would be: "A young girl sat for me, a young girl more transparent than the finest leaves and the gauziest webs I have painted in all these dusty years. Every dream of hers, dreamt since childhood, has moulded and coloured that loveliness of hers. She made me see what the subconscious does to an impressionable creature, how much more power it has on them

219

than sun and circumstances put together. And this is the revelation that made me clean my paint-brushes, freshen my palette, choose a clean canvas and begin on a new era, the one you have come to see." Do you think that would satisfy them, Nirode? Does it satisfy you? Or does it not seem the whole truth after all? There must be more to it, of course there must and perhaps the change would have come even if I had not met her, probably other forces would have operated to make me stop at my old game and begin the new one...'

'It's not only your painting that has changed, Dharma,' Nirode said. a trifle drily, finding something unpalatable in this discourse of Dharma's. It seemed to him that a new self-centredness was eclipsing Dharma's once brilliantly clear and detached vision. 'You've suddenly taken to talking.'

Dharma laughed. 'That's my old age, Nirode, that's only an old man's senile garrulousness. I wouldn't ascribe anything so boring to your young sister. She's all candour and grace and balance. Ask her to come and see me.'

'Will you paint her again?'

'Oh no, no. Not just now, I have quite enough for my new exhibition and at the moment it is the working classes that interest me. I had not thought that they dream at all, but I was wrong, quite wrong.' He placed his hands behind his back and paced with calm stateliness, seeming to be no longer aware of Nirode who glanced at him sideways — a discretion that had not formerly been necessary.

'All this portraiture is making a more sociable man of you, isn't it?' Nirode asked at last, bluntly.

Dharma paused at the edge of the still pond and began to smile as he saw his white geese swim silently across it, their rounded breasts parting the pond's ceiling of paludial flat weeds and leaving a wake of disturbed glassiness behind them. He watched them waddle up the bank, fussily shaking the muck from their waxed feathers, before he spoke. 'So it has, Nirode. Like you, I find myself inexorably drawn away from my island, back to the mainland again. Tell me, did you feel a certain small but quite definite relief at going back to the amenities, the relaxations that society provides?'

'Amenities?'

'The not having to think solely about one's own state of mind, the dealing with problems not too close to one's own heart, but at a more comfortable distance?'

Stiffly, Nirode replied, ' I haven't crossed any such margin nor do I plan to,' and he refused an invitation to dinner with Dharma and two fellow artists who were expected to arrive soon. When he slammed the green door shut behind him and walked down the lane, he felt too offended to be able to think but, rattling home in the bus, he felt oddly disconsolate and smoked one half of a cigarette after the other, throwing them out of the window with distaste. He wondered if man did not lose something of himself in this quarrel with his instincts and if, in being a victor, there was not also a part of him — a part that had been remote, curious and unique — that was vanquished. And if it was not better therefore to be — to be what? What can a man be if he is not a freak? If he journeys, his body and mind will suffer expense and perhaps the moral of it all is not to avoid the expense, but merely to make the journey worth the expense.

One evening when Bose dropped in and was boring him with interminable tales of disinterested, ill-mannered, commercial-minded publishers, he was struck by inspiration and jumping off a pile of old books, he bundled Bose out of the room, into a bus and so to his aunt's house. The suggestion he put to Bose and Amla out on the veranda there was received by Bose with incoherent but total optimism, but Amla was sullen and refused to bring out her drawings. All they could persuade her to do was read the manuscript Bose hopefully left behind. It kept her awake half the night with its sweet, jumping delight that had somehow escaped from the tedious old man's brain, like children long locked up and now set free in a glorious garden of mud-puddles, burrows and low-hanging trees. Almost without conscious effort, her crayons raced and tumbled in an effort to match the marvellous frolic of these little creatures that had jumped out of the restrictive jingles of the *Panchatantra* into a complex, brightly-coloured prose of which no one had imagined that Bose could be the creator.

She was surprised next morning, to find herself still excited about them and eager to show them to the writer of this so unexpectedly wonderful manuscript. In the noisy coffee house where she met him during the lunch break, she readily agreed to a partnership.

Borne on the high tide of this novel activity, she even went to visit Dharma once again. On her journey to that island house, she felt her very life blur and dim into the creeping swamp of farewell. She prepared to meet the flurry of activity of which Nirode had warned her — the waxing stream of visitors, admirers, agents, promoters, buyers and models. This made her proud and irritable all the way in the bus, but when she entered the studio, she found this facade not, after all, necessary.

'You've come at the right time — this is the lull before the storm. Your instincts are as mysteriously accurate as a butterfly's,' Dharma told her. 'How does a butterfly, sitting on a leaf, know when a nasty boy creeps up with his fingers flexed to grasp its wings? Somehow it knows and flies laughingly away the split second before the fingers close over it. You have the insect's instincts yourself, you know when you must fly, when you can rest, where you are going and how to return.'

Amla found the smile on her face turned into an independent creature, aching with the effort to remain where it was and conscious of the pain and the rigidity this involved. 'To be called an insect — that is praise from one who has loved and painted them so often in the past.'

'I still do,' he said, waving his hand at the new canvases, still glazed with wet paint and on some of them worms contorted, butterflies burnt and snails raised their tentative antennae. 'Of course there is a change in the manner in which I paint them.'

'Yes. In the old pictures you seemed to love them for themselves — their quaintness and complexity — but here they are symbols of other matters, not all of them loved. How much your style has

222

changed,' she said, biting on the words and finding them tart, cold to her teeth.

'So has yours. I find you changed in these weeks I have not seen you,' he said, more reflectively. 'Come, let us go out and sit on the veranda. I shall make you the best *pan* you can find in Calcutta and I'll tell you how you are changed.'

There followed a long pause in which they moved and settled, admired the winter mists rising about the pond, the white flowers starring the shrubbery and the dull silver glints of flitting moths. Dharma opened his silver box and became engrossed in a ritual in which he showed a sensuous absorption. When he spoke again, he kept his eyelids lowered and said something that astounded her. 'You are now grown very much like my daughter during the last days she spent in my house and you arouse in me the same feelings that she did at that time.'

'What were they?' 'Impotence. Helplessness. I never wanted her to change, I wanted her the same, always the same, beside me. But, like her, you too are slipping out of the chrysalis — what a marvellous, soft, sleepy state of being that is, neither of you realised. I see you also turning into a bright insect, attracting trouble wherever it flies, throughout its brief days. What can I do to prevent the change?' His voice was even but heavy, as though it dragged upon the earth. 'I hate to see that change.'

'But she was ill — how could she help it?'

'She was not ill! Who told you that?' He raised his lids now and the china-white pupils flashed. He stabbed a silver pin through a green cone held between his fingers — with savagery, she thought.

'I don't remember, but I've heard it said she died of cholera.'

He stared at her, but Amla knew instinctively it was not her face he was studying, but the collective face of society, the weak, amorphous, irresponsible face he hated so much. 'Poor girl,' he said softly, at last. 'Mrinalini-Shonalini. That is her fate then. To be dismissed as dead while she still lives.'

'Still lives?'

He shrugged and dropped his eyes, assuming the rhetorician's discursive manner once more. 'So I assume. But perhaps I am wrong and you are right. You probably know as much of the recent years of her life as I do or as little. When she left me, it was a final parting in every sense. Her mother still cries for her, keeps her old clothes locked in a box under her bed, but I do not. When she left the house, I told her she could not return.'

'Why?'

'Because she left at the age of fifteen, because she left together with her first cousin, my sister's son, a boy whom I had brought up as her brother, a weak, brainless and conceited boy of sixteen. Do you think I could forgive her that disgrace?'

Amla feared she was going to giggle, out of sheer hysteria. Was this revelation tragic? Or ludicrous? Did it prove Dharma a single-minded and saintly ascetic who had avoided the slightest touch of taint? Or a self-righteous, blind, unfeeling zealot? What was it in society that he truly hated — the rules and restrictions that he verbally opposed or their transgression that he secretly feared and loathed? How much that she had seen in the man remained true still, how much had turned false and uncertain? Before her eyes he became one of the models of his own paintings — the mandarin eyes shadowed with secrets, the mouth tightly closed to danger, the outlines blurring into a landscape that was at once recognisable and unreal, a nightmare that had obsessed her in her sleep but became formless and nondescript in waking. She stared and stared but the wavering lines would not fix and settle again and their constant movement made her feel sick.

'Then that is why you left the city and began to paint those queer underworld paintings,' she said at last.

He smiled a strangely caustic smile. 'Young people of the scientific era like to reduce things to pat solutions — x plus y equals z — don't they? But they scarcely ever fit. As it happens, I was prepared to continue working and living exactly as I had always done — indeed, I thought it a matter of principle to do so. It was my wife who could not bear the house where my daughter was born and lived, with her cousin, for those fifteen years. She begged me to leave the house and city, but since I could not bear to go very far from Calcutta, we came to this suburb. I believe this move rescued her sanity and I am glad I made it. She is afraid to meet anyone, her family or old friends who knew our daughter. I no longer am — nothing that concerns my daughter concerns me. But I have promised her I will deal alone with any people this new exhibition of mine may bring to our house, she need never meet anyone she fears or do anything that causes her strain.'

Almost in response to his pious declaration, Gita Devi's brass bell began to ring, her conch to moan and from the window incense curled in loops of sweetly cloying blue. The ominous noises of the call to prayer came to an end and the recitation began, low and urgent. Out on the veranda where the damp from the garden made visible coils of its own, soft and serpentine, Amla and Dharma listened dumbly to prayers that were meaningless to them.

'I don't know if this exhibition pleases her. The paintings she has never even looked at.'

'Not even the old ones?'

'No. Nothing ever distracted her attention from our daughter and it still does not.'

'Does she — does she sympathise with you or with the girl?' Amla whispered the question, half-ashamed. It was their solitariness on this soft, green island that had made such a question possible.

Another glint of his pupils, like the insides of orange peels, fresh and moist. Amusement in that strange twist of the lips. 'Our relationship is not all so straightforward and pat, married relationships never are. There is the matter of loyalty, habit, complicity — things I couldn't talk to you about till you married and knew for yourself.'

Amla shrank against the wall. If Dharma locked her out, it was her fault for having tried to enter — but she had not thought him capable of such a rejection, not gentle Dharma with his broad, sensitive fingertips and always low voice. It was time now certainly

225

to rise and leave, but she could not do it. She could not go, leaving Dharma on the other side of the margin, drawing the curtains on his privacy with his wife with whom he had committed the terrible sin of casting out a young daughter and who, unlike his wife who was repenting in the bubbling prayer of a sinner in despair, would not retract. He was solid and immovable against the blue and mauve and grey of the evening. For a few moments she had been revolted by the immobility, the permanence of his dark and unkind position. During those moments she felt herself to be the daughter, the outcast. But seeing his hands stroke the silver floriate design of the box at his knee, she was no longer his by blood, she was the lover again, quivering from one blow yet unable to forgo the next.

'And why do you compare me with your daughter as she was during the time of your estrangement?' she asked, smiling — the smile had become a nervous symptom, living an uncontrolled life of its own.

'Because you came here today as rebellious as she and, like her, with the same expectation of parting.'

Those broad-tipped fingers, in following the intricate pattern of the filigree, had followed the intricate convolutions of the heart again, as they had often done in the days when she posed for him. Here, once more, was that uncanniness, that eeriness about him that set him apart from the humdrum and invested him with all the glamour of mystery, the glamour that lured young girls to his studio, then turned them into white geese forever paddling on his secret pond...

Like the enchanted maiden of lore. she had willingly let herself be lured. She had revelled in the enchantment, been grateful for its joy. What was it now that made her jump to her feet, hurry to say the farewell he had predicted, rush through the door to the wild and well-known world again? Perhaps a scarlet surge of family blood, always as bright and quick and responsive in her as in her brother and sister. Or the realisation that the chalk line of division had been drawn between her and Dharma and to defy and cross it would mean, as in some half-understood ritual of black magic, destruction.

Or the newly imposed sense of Gita Devi on the other side of the wall, saying her prayers in her kitchen-temple of polished brass and incense, braziers and hibiscus, to whom Dharma was bound, by his inhuman act of rejecting their joint child, to shield and protect from further distress and possible insanity. Gita Devi appeared now to Amla as the base of all Dharma's actions, the spread lotus that bore the weight of the god absorbed in his meditation and the spinning out of his *karma*. A combination of all these revelations and inspirations filled her, expanded her, made her rise and float and on its drift she left the house, feeling as emptied out, frangible and exhausted as if a high fever had drained her.

The opening day of Dharma's exhibition was heralded by posters in dramatic ash-grey and scarlet, pasted on walls that were daubed with spittle and reeked of urine. Amla, who had torn up her invitation to this event, went instead to the races, with Jit. While earnest young men in shabby white jostled each other for a view of the startling canvases and the painter smiling stilly in the centre, Amla jostled too — against her will she jostled as Jit led her to the marquee, out of the marquee, into the stalls, out of them, to the betting booths and away from them, always in the thick of over-dressed and over-excited crowds, crying, sometimes, 'But the horses, where are the horses?'

'They'll come, they'll come,' he smiled, meaning that they were incidental, but took her, all the same, to the stables. Here the crowds were composed of emotionally involved gamblers to whom the nervous quivers of a horse's knobby knees meant portents of an earthquake, the set of their fly-troubled ears the position of the world to come. Too many heads, black and glistening with sweet oil. Too many stains of perspiration on the backs of men struggling towards the booths or up a tree and in the arm-pits of silk-swathed women whose eyes were tigresses prowling behind their dark glasses. Too much strain and hostility, too much noise.

Fighting through it, they made their way to the stairs and stumbled past aisles of affronted knees before Jit could find her a seat of her own where she could sit with her arms wrapped tightly about her as though to hold herself safe, as one would hold a child out of a mob. But here, in the members' enclosure, the mob was discreet, the gentlemen took fond care of their fine suits and raw silk ties and the ladies of *saris* especially worn to flower in the sun, for clusters of tropical blossoms unwound from hem to hem, brilliantly coloured

Here there was leisure in which to mark one's little programme, to smile at the fanciful names of the horses, to look out across the trim and measured, green and red whorls of the race-course to the tufted trees at the edge of the Maidan, the squat dome of the Victoria Memorial, the solitary ominous finger of the Ochterlony Monument and the grey mass of the city beyond, working and pleasing itself to a quick death. These Amla scanned with narrowed eyes, looking, she said, for horses.

It was the birds that caused the quick movement of her eyes to halt and had Jit looked closely, he would have seen, reflected in the deep brown of her irises, those great-bodied rain trees at the edge of the course, alive and tossing uneasily with the excited stirring of huge flocks of birds. So restless and impatient was their movement that the stillness of the reflecting eyes was broken and rippled into many silent quivers of apprehension.

'How strange,' she said, to herself.

'What?' asked Jit smiling, satisfied, indulgent.

'Those birds. They stay in the trees inspite of all those crowds around them, all that shouting and jumping and pushing. They won't give up their trees. They're not afraid. Isn't that strange?'

'Observant brown eyes,' said Jit, a fond, middle-aged lecher. 'You should make me a good partner. Come, help me choose a winner.'

Another time Amla would have dealt him a nicely pointed rejoinder, but now she was anxious and in a great hurry to turn her mind to something else. She did not trust it at all today, not at all. 'Yes, let's see, let's see,' she said and, chewing a pencil, she read the names from the booklet Jit gave her. 'Ranjit — Dixieland — April Shower — Jhansi-ki-Rani — Tara — Hi Jinks — Nature Boy,' she recited them in a chanting, ritualistic tone that was lost in the roaring of the gambling crowd. She chanted like a child left in the dark trying to frighten away a vision of disaster, symbolised by the stirring of the birds who were not afraid, who waited. These were city birds, belonging to death's city, where funerals were processions that celebrated the city's chief deity, Kali, that fed her fires with its quickly rotting offerings draped with garlands of marigold and tuberose. These were birds that knew such processions, associated them with the burning *ghats,* that were not afraid of the sweet-fleshed corpses burning there, for they fed on them. Amla feared them today. She chanted 'Toofan — Chanchal — Zulfiqar — Rio Rita...'

From this massed impatience and lust of the mob, the horses burst forth like glorious streaks of freedom — the free instincts, bodied in shining chestnut and glossy black, liquid-eyed and with their tails and manes flying. They streaked over the trim course, flashed past neat white fences as though released from the very hearts of these men who watched. Amla had laid no bet, but she found herself on her feet, taut with longing, her hands clenched. She wished these horses to flee — oh not to turn each fenced corner, not to keep to the channel of brown dirt between the mown green — but to fly straight on, over the heads of the lusting mob, clean over their heads, over the city and up into the clear, pale sky where lust did not exist and there was only space, wind and space. She urged them to be free with every throb of blood in her body. Aghast, she watched them pile into a conglomeration of black and chestnut at one corner, almost cried aloud, 'Don't stop! Straight, straight ahead!' The horses themselves seemed to have stumbled upon this obstacle of conflicting instincts to turn? To fly? What? — for they tangled and the speedy fluidity of their race clogged suddenly. One horse tripped on this invisible web of conflict, slid, fell and rolled. Another hesitated, dipped, stopped short. The others reared, whinnied, pranced on delicate hooves in their frenzied confusion and then urged by their screaming jockeys, resumed the race, flew on. The crowd, roaring for continuity, for action, fell back into an attitude of prayer.

But the horse that fell, it lay at the corner in a kicking fury. Amla saw its nervous legs thrashing. Then it was hidden by a thick dark screen. Amla saw what this screen was — it was the descent of the birds who had risen, crying in triumph, from the trees, risen like a fine-woven net against the opalescent sky and, net-like, descended on the flailing horse, poured and swarmed about it, with beating wings and tearing claws, to jab and tear, jab and tear at the feast for which they had waited. All within seconds, this happened. Within seconds a white van marked by a blue cross was speeding towards it. Its neat body of white paint and bright metal obscured the terrible sight from Amla. If there was a gun shot, it was silenced before it spoke, buried under the din of gambling and when the van moved away, leaving nothing on the track but some dark patches in the disturbed dust, the horses had flown up into sight again.

Cheering, the crowds were cheering. Leaping up and down and apart, they cheered and cheered. Why? Because one of these fleeing, ecaping creatures had been caught and sacrificed? Because its blood and torn flesh lay in the dust for the birds to feed on? No, no. They cheered, they cheered — the favourite, the favourite had won! The horse that had died was only an outsider.

'Come on, Amla, come on!' Jit was yelling. 'Let's collect our little bit — won't be much but, dammit, it's a win!'

Amla sat down in her chair. She refused to move.

Mother

From the discord of traffic below, some long-drawn notes separated, then repeated and, finally, distinguished themselves as notes of music, and as the traffic hesitated — curiously, hopefully — the harmonium began to play and the drum to throb. A harsh but generous and vibrant voice burst out singing, flinging from a painfully distended throat, copper-tinted and wine-red notes to the windows and balconies above the narrow street.

At that hour there were no children in the house to clamour for entertainment, to be held over the balcony rails so that they could study and read romance into the strolling musicians. It was an hour when the women, relaxing after the strenuous exercise of the midday meal, had not yet plunged into the fire and steam of preparations for dinner. As they lounged about in the first-floor hall, some massaging oil into their heads or combing their hair or cracking betel nuts between broad-bladed scissors, they were receptive to the prospect of a little entertainment. They lifted their heads and smiled at each other with surprised and tentative delight, and when an older aunt rose, twitching the edge of her *sari* over her head and went to the long window with its wooden lacework at the rims, the younger ones felt free to follow her, her curiosity their permission. When they glanced, in passing at Monisha, she obediently put down her book — fortunately for her, its title, *Cities of the Plain,* meant nothing to them — and went to look.

The figures of the musicians were so ragged and dun that she did not immediately locate them amidst all the litter and rubble of the choked street, its *pan*-spattered newspaper scraps, its discarded cigarette packets and the many bare, scarred and scabbed legs all merging into one dreary and restless channel of squalor. She saw that the knot of onlookers was collecting outside a pinman's room where dirty laundry was piled from floor to ceiling and small children tumbled in its multi-coloured masses while the tired washerman, with one rag tied about his forehead and another about his hips, lifted and manoeuvred a heavy coal iron with evident fatigue. Just outside his room was a big poster, flaunting in red, the lurid head lines of a sensation-loving weekly. Below it squatted the drummer. The harmonium player, who was also the singer, circled the ring that the onlookers had formed around her, with one arm flaying the battered old instrument strung from her steeply sloping shoulders and with the other flinging large, beseeching gestures at the audience, illustrating the pathos of her song.

Once distinguished from the rest of the ill-dressed, undernourished crowd. these two figures were indeed striking. There was something hunted and furtive in the manner in which the drummer squatted but, in the upthrust of his chin and the sombre glitter of his eyes beneath the dishevelled fall of hair, there was something defiant and gallant that was grandiosely contradictory arousing the speculative and the romantic in his onlookers. Monisha found herself wondering if he was the husband of the singer who had to sing in order to buy him his liquor or whether he was the woman's brother-in-law who had run away with her, thus disgracing them both in their village and caste and having to earn so precarious a living in this unrelenting city. Or whether she was a witch and had bewitched him. Or ...an infinity of possibility in those wild eyes of his, as proud and as defeated as a caged animal's. Less in the woman — too rugged a creature to play the part of a paramour, her poverty had destroyed her sex, cancelling out the characteristics of lover and mother, giving her something of the brusqueness, the uncompromising harshness of the professional hermaphrodite. Her pounding arms, the great prominent ridge of her collar-bone beneath the glistening skin, the flat and untimid way her large feet walked the circle on the pavement, these were brazenly masculine. Beneath the swaddling rags neither breasts nor crotch made a single gentle, cradling curve. But the face, the face was that of the Eternal Mother, the Earth Mother, a face ravaged by the most unbearable emotions of woman, darkened and flayed and scarred by them, giving that large mouth a tortured and pitiful down thrust and the terrible black eyes an eternally unfulfilled promise of vision, of understanding, of boundless love. Those eyes swept upwards at the corners, through the net of wrinkles and scars, almost to the line of her loose, multi-coloured hair partly oily black, partly dyed dull orange with *mehndi* leaves and partly a sad and shrivelled grey. They rolled up at the overhanging balconies and windows and Monisha, shrinking away, felt certain that a glance of those enormous and brilliant black eyes would dissolve and disintegrate her into a meaningless shadow.

As she looked down upon that powerful and arresting face, she fought mentally to construct a barrier before her, as one might hold a chair in front of one if a tigress were to approach. She feared that woman's emotions that had spread through her eyes like dark lakes, that had given her voice that cruel, biting edge as of a dull, persistent knife. On what ground did those emotions rain their fire? On her parents betraying and murdering each other in madness? On her building the funeral pyres of her own children? On her worship of the goddess Kali? This woman had slit throats and drained blood into her cupped hands. She had bathed and soaked in the sweat of lust. Her black eyes were depthless, rimmed with shadowing purple. And as she circled the little ring, pacing with the restlessness and eloquence of a caged animal, she sang those songs that touched, in every line, on love, on wine, on roses and on death. Her spectators shook their heads in an excess of understanding and, every now and then, uttered a cry of appreciation, of agreement. Even some young loiterers who had strolled up in expectation of hearing something bawdy, seeing something lewdly suggestive, stayed on as though the woman's long fingers had grasped them by the roots of their hair, seized fistfuls of their veins and arteries and almost mystically communicated to them the primaeval truth that underlay the banalities of her verses about the dying rose, the empty wine-glass.

235

Not one line of her song, not one word was original. But she illustrated it is not the original that lies so close to the heart.

Even the women in the quiet hall upstairs who would never have dared destroy their safe ideal of a life of subdued emotion by admitting that such things as love and betrayal were, even they leant low on their elbows pressed their soft, full arms on to the pointed woodwork with pleasure in the pain it gave them and softly clucked their tongues and shook their heads, sighing. It seemed as if even they dreamt dreams, though reality had never lent them the faintest encouragement by corroboration.

Monisha alone was untouched. More than ever before, she felt the power of fear over her. To begin with she persuaded herself that what she feared was this fountain of raw passion these strolling musicians had sent up in their spectators' hearts. Slowly she began to realise that in her heart no fountain had spouted and that what she feared was the great empty white distance set between her and this moist, crimson flowering of emotion in the street below. Reaching out to touch it, to beg it to communicate with her, her finger touched only the cool dry skin stretched tautly over her cheekbones and chin. All about her heads swayed and drooped, heavy with melancholy. All about her low, saturated sighs rose and sank. Everyone in that afternoon audience seemed intensely capable of responding to passion with passion, to sorrow with sorrow. Monisha alone stood apart, unnaturally cool, too perfectly aloof, too inviolably whole and alone and apart.

Pressed into a corner of the deep window frame, she stood erect as though measuring her spine against the sun-warmed plaster of the wall. She drew her arms about her, thinking, 'All the others understand this woman and her song. I do not. I do not know what she is singing about. What is a dying rose to me but a collection of petals drooping, growing limp and brown and giving off an odour more putrid than sweet? What does it mean to me if a wine-glass is drained and stands empty? What marvel, what miracle lies in one small measure of liquid that this woman and her audience should feel so bereft when it is gone? Is there really anyone who lies awake all night waiting for love, for a lover? Do they really not feel disgusted, hopeless, exhausted? I don't know, I know nothing. Wine is nothing to me nor a dead flower nor a girl left waiting on her balcony at night. But it seems I am ignorant and these are symbols of an essential wisdom that has eluded me. And it has been my own fault because I gave up the quest for it too soon, never seriously believed in it, abandoned it before it truly began, thinking it not worth my while to search a treasure that would cost me endless devastation. I chose to stand aside and allow it to pass by and now when it returns to terrify me with its wisdom, I do not recognize anything in it but the terror. These people know and feel something I do not, they are all nodding in agreement with the singer, they understand what she is singing to them. If I won a war over the mind, then they lost a war to their instincts and it seems my victory has less value than their loss.

'Yet, did I not once possess it — this essential instinct of theirs? Why am I so sad? Why am I so afraid? Do I recall a time — oh, an epoch — when I understood as well as they? Then I feel bereft because I have forgotten, I have lost touch. No, it is not sadness that makes me ache in every limb. I am standing here, pressing myself against the wall so as not to feel senior aunt's flesh bump into me. I could not bear to have her touch me while she is sighing and humming and swaying to this loud music. I could not bear to touch, however vicariously, this appalling exhibition of a passion that ravages the soul and body and being. If I did, I should be a traitor and a liar. I have never been touched by it nor ravaged. I bear no scar on my body. I am different from them all. They put me away in a steel container, a thick glass cubicle and I have lived in it all my life, without a touch of love or hate or warmth on me. I am locked apart from all of them, they cannot touch me, they can only lip-read and misinterpret. Similarly, I cannot really hear them, I cannot understand what they say. I have never touched anyone, never left the imprint of my fingers on anyone's shoulders, of my tongue on anyone's damp palate.

'What a waste, what a waste it has been, this life enclosed in a locked container, merely as an observer and so imperfect, so handicapped an observer at that. Why do I stand here, watching and listening, unable to understand a single word or gesture, each one of which moves my companions nearly to tears? If they wanted me, if they cried out that they were drowning or burning or dying of disease, I would not hear them. If they reached out for my hand, I could never receive their fingers, hold their palms: there would be this sheet of glass, of metal between us. I have not given birth, I have not attended death. All the intervening drama has gone by, unwound itself like a silent, blurred film that has neither entertained nor horrified me. It has unwound itself and now there is nothing. Oh yes, there is this street, there are many people, one of whom is singing. But if a great fog were to roll across the scene or a terrible cyclone to snatch it all away and scatter it upon the sea like so much flotsam, it would be all the same to me. I should remain alone, apart and enclosed within myself, beyond their touch...'

Had any of that household turned to glance at her, they would have seen her pallor alter within that moment, seen her flush dramatically, her eyes start and her hands begin to quiver. None looked at her, they were hanging over the windowsill to fling down their copper coins and beg the woman for one more song. Beside them, Monisha was on fire to experience desire, to experience feeling. She turned away from them, her movements jerky and only half in control and began this panicked search for feeling. It did not exist in this stale room, filled with the sounds of other people's emotions. She hurried out of it. She ran along the empty corridor, turning one corner, then another. Her eye flickered briefly over the wooden railing, but met with the eternal washerwoman at work in the courtyard below and flinched away from a sight so common, so accustomed. She ran on. The door to the kitchen stood open. A low fire palpitated untended and threw no heat on her as she hesitated, half-giddy, at the door. But metal containers of steel and tin gleamed in a variety of tones, some muted and negligible in unclean corners and on high shelves, some brilliantly commanding in the glare of the now descendant sun. One caught her eye for it was painted red and its mouth was topped by a funnel that drained the sunshine from the window into its wide cup and down its slender neck.

Rushing to it, she caught it up with one hand, then supported its weight, greater than she had expected, with the other. She staggered out to the still corridor. Stopped. Turned back. Placed the tin on the floor and caught a box of matches off the shelf with one clean swoop of her shaking hand. Crushing the box to the handle of the tin, she lugged it out. It bumped against her legs as she ran, but her legs seemed to need this dull whipping in order to make them move. The door to her room was shut, she herself had drawn the two sagging leaves together when she left it, over an hour ago. With her foot, she opened it and one leaf crashed against the wall, swung back against her as she stumbled through, cracking against her bent knee. She did not shut it this time. She was in a hurry, a great hurry.

This room, too, was full of the lifeless appurtenances of a past spent inside this barred enclosure. She ran through it, clutching the red tin container with its large funnel jiggling loosely and complaining against the sharp rim of the opening. The bathroom door stood open, silently but preparedly inviting. She went in and put down the container. The floor had been recently wiped and was dry, the tap was not leaking anymore: perhaps the water supply had been cut again, as it so often was in the afternoon. Giving the tap her attention for only a second, she whirled around to shut the door. The two leaves would not interlock. She jerked them apart and hurled them together with stunning accuracy. Now that action had seized her in its maniac grip, she seemed to have seized the very secrets of action itself and her grip was so powerful she could not have loosened it if she had thought to do so. She shot the big bolt into the two metal rings that waited for it. She turned to the small window, above the bathing enclosure. It was shut, as always, against the slyly snooping windows of the neighbouring house. She dropped to the floor with sudden gracelessness, as though the strings of co-ordination were cut, making her collapse heavily. She pulled out the funnel irritably, threw it against a wall. It did not roll but lay dead, silent, the big tin eye watching her, unblinking. She returned its glare, then lifted the tin by its bottom rim. She lifted it as high as she could, with some effort for it was heavy, more than half full. On lifting it, the liquid contents hiccupped, hesitated, then came out readily and unstintingly as a natural phenomenon. Her body was braced against its fire, but it was barely warm and soothing, a bath of oil that a baby might relax in — if it were not for the harsh, pungent odour of kerosene. When her blouse and *sari* were soaked, she lowered the tin. Her arms relaxed a moment, recollecting their strength. They needed that in order that she might keep the matchbox steady, in order to strike the match. To her astonishment, the very first match struck fire, and its clear flame was as straight and golden as a promise kept. She brought it close to her face so close that she flinched and dropped it in her lap. The oil soaking her garments responded with a leap of recognition. Two elements had met and in their embrace she was caught. Warmth, heat, terrible heat, a bright glare, smoke, an unbearably loud noise, bubbling, hissing, a gigantic cracking and whipping in her ears — heat seared her eyeballs — a great fog enveloped her, not the white one of dreams but black, acrid, thick — and God, the pain! Here it was on her eyes, her face, here it came — there, all over — with her arms she wrestled with it, she fought it, it was not what she wanted — she screamed 'No! No! No!' Screamed, screamed. Fell unconscious. Very quickly fell unconscious.

No ashes of that fire drifted out over the city, no wind carried the smoke away to inform others of the cloistered tragedy. Later, neither Nirode nor Amla could say that they had smelt, felt death in the air that lustrous winter afternoon when they sat in the garden, smiling at Professor Bose's jubilation over the first printed copy of the book he and Amla had brought out together. They admired the large fresh print and the clear blue and elegant greens and brick-russets of Amla's pictures that splashed about the margins. They ran their fingers over the handsome navy blue binding and complimented the printers who had done the work cheaply and well. They called to Aunt Lila to bring the tea out on the lawn and, over its orange-scented steam, no one wondered why Monisha had grown so still or when they had last met — was it a week, a fortnight ago? — or why their meetings were so indefinite and insubstantial, or whether she would have enjoyed being with them while they discussed their new venture — the monthly children's magazine that Bose was to write and Amla to illustrate. No one thought of her that honeyed afternoon, yet when Nikhil blundered out of the house towards them, like a scorched, half-charred moth, his eyes red and wet, they looked at the black ash of death on his hands and knew instantly it was Monisha's.

What followed was so clumsy, halting and stagy, that it had the quality of a nightmare in which delay, misunderstanding and misinterpretation play the demons. Who was this messenger? Nirode had not seen him before and Amla, in her shock, could not recognise him as the eager boy who had smiled at and confided in her. He is not that boy, she told herself in silent dread, he is some madman escaped from a charnel. Then what relation had he to Monisha whose name he spoke repeatedly, with intense horror, as though he saw her before him, trailing her fingerless hands? 'Monisha *di*,' he kept repeating with parched urgency and her relations stood about him with their faces wiped clean of blood and understanding, as though the familiar name had assumed a monstrous proportion they could not equate with it. Then the old aunt came to them, staggering, for she was the only one who recognised the messenger of death, who had met him before. There was a strange scene where she tugged at the sooty hands of the boy crying, 'Tell us, tell us,' and he pulled away, shocked that she should touch the ashes on his hands. For a long while, an utterly wasted while, they stood pulling each other this way, that way. Saying words that, stark and unaccompanied, did not convey the details without which this thing — this dark burnt bat that had flown out of the night to find it still day — could not be accepted.

It was Professor Bose who gave them the impetus to break away from this farce, by squealing suddenly, 'I must catch my bus,' and scuttling agitatedly away, flapping and jerking down the drive, his umbrella flying behind him. With him the farcical element was gone, they realised something of the truth and began to run towards the car.

Then Amla realised she was barefoot. Should she run back for her slippers? She hesitated. Nirode clutched her arm. She was lifted into the car beside him. She wondered how she could think of her

241

slippers now when Monisha lay dead. Her aunt was crying, trying to cover up the sight and sound of it with her slack grey *sari* and only contriving to make the sound more animal and grotesque. Nirode clutched her arm, clutched it till it hurt.

Delay dogged them all the way. Aunt Lila's driver did not know the way to Monisha's house. Nikhil had to direct him but kept forgetting to do so, then suddenly screaming in rage at yet another wrong turning and the driver would have to brake sharply and reverse against the traffic, snarling it up fiercely. The Anglo-Indian driver of a violet Hudson shook his fist at them, bawling, 'No bloody shame at all, no bloody shame!' They stared at the vomit-coloured hair on the brown brow and the great red fist, taking in his words reflectively — shame, they repeated to themselves, shame, shame. Then the lanes of the old city narrowed, barrows and playing children obstructed them. As they drew closer to Monisha's house, smoke began to creep up and spread — not billows of light smoke that might lift up into the sky and float, but smoke like masses of dirty wool, too heavy to rise, profuse and exhausted upon the earth, a dreary smoke that rose daily from the small smouldering fires that housewives placed in the doorways to catch the eddies of breeze. It might have been the smoke from Monisha's private fire, so still was it, so resigned.

Through this smoke they saw the hazy figures of the curious who had gathered outside the house waiting for sooty whiffs of scandal and sensation to seep out to them. Nikhil gulped something unintelligible and the car stopped. The crowd fell back but looked at them with veiled, yet bumptious curiosity. That Monisha should attract their attention seemed unbearably cruel to them and they hurried past into the house.

At the end of that long drive, with all its pauses in which they might have prepared themselves and made their acceptances, the body was still a shock. None of them had actually expected to see Monisha lying there dead. For this they had been unable to prepare themselves. They had allowed themselves to be led past the shrouded members of the family, up the stairs to the small barred room and then jerked back against each other turning their heads away in sudden horror. Amla's eyes closed the split second she realised that the soft mould of the white sheet on the bed was Monisha. Nirode was not so quick — he saw Monisha's face what was left of it. He saw that all Monisha's abundant hair was burnt away, he saw that her very features were burnt off the skull, that neither eyes nor lips nor nose existed any more in that mass of black torment. He saw a fingerless hand upon the sheet, mutilated and charred. He saw that much before he could turn and put his face down on his arm.

The family pressed about them at the door, closing them in, waiting to see them touch Monisha weep a bit. They clustered close to them, shutting off all routes of escape and Nirode, Amla and their aunt stood against the wall like condemned prisoners, with a similar instinct to mask their fear and conceal themselves behind an unfelt stoicism.

At last someone gently drew the sheet up over the face and hand. Then they could look up and see that it was Jiban who did it. For the first time since they knew him, he had done a thing which they could understand. Then he was led up to them by one of his sisters. For a long time they avoided looking at each other. Then he said, rustily linking one word with the other, 'If this terrible thing is the fault of anyone — it is mine. Forgive me,' and immediately, when he had said this, their brief sympathy with him was abruptly eclipsed, they forgot him, they left him to make his own terms with it all. His sister led him away to make him drink some tea.

They were there, it seemed, till very late at night. People came and went. Already they were all in white. In the courtyard and hall there was wailing. There was also talk — explanations, details, but always about Monisha's death itself, not its long preparation of which her own family thought as they stayed close to her room where it was quieter and people neither moved nor spoke much, but seemed to be in the spell of Monisha's own silence, her now unimpeachable silence.

Later, a voice explained to them, 'At that time there was no one in the house. We were all away. Only the women were there, in the hall. They did not even notice when she left the room — she had been sitting with them, reading a book. Then they heard her scream and saw smoke coming out into the corridors and they ran. She had bolted the door from the inside. It is a very heavy door, you can see for yourself. And being only women, they could not break it down. They brought many kinds of implements from the kitchen but were unable to break it. Only when the neighbours came did somebody climb up and break the glass of the ventilator. It is a very small ventilator, but Nikhil had also arrived and he climbed in. By then she had been silent for a long time. There was no water supply. We had to fetch it from the storage bins in the kitchen. By then it was much too late...'

At that moment Nirode's silence broke and fell away. In a brief flash of comprehension he realised what he must do. He must take Monisha away. They were shocked. How could this be done? It was her husband's house. He would do it. Impossible. At dawn the funeral must leave from here. It would leave from her aunt's house. She must be taken away, unaccompanied by them, in peace.

This was not done. Their own mother would understand this if she were here. She was not going to be allowed to come before the cremation was over. She would understand.

How could such a thing be done in the middle of the night? The neighbours would be doubly suspicious. That was no concern of theirs. Their car stood outside and it would take Monisha away. As people fell aside, making way for the light stringbed on which Monisha lay, hidden and apologetic, as she was carried precariously down the stairs, all sympathy fell aside too. Now there was only an air of outrage and injury and by the time they reached the hall, the silence that had settled made it clear that Jiban's family washed its hands of these rude strangers who refused to honour ceremony even in so grave an event.

But they took Monisha away and for a few hours before morning, she could lie in the quiet house in undisturbed solitude. It seemed a cruel thing to drag Monisha out of one fire, the one of her own making, only to consign her to another, next morning. Of this they would not think. They wanted only to give her, before the total annihilation, a little respite, a little solitude and so they remained outside the room where she lay. Out on the veranda it was dark and only behind the silhouettes of the trees and the neighbouring houses was the sky tinted a livid, alarming pink by the sleepless lights of the city.

Below them, in the park garden, frogs croaked conspiratorially, quark-quark-quark, now and then sending a leaf into sudden, bounding motion.

Like these invisible frogs, Amla's thoughts also lay still for long periods, then leapt about, panic-stricken in the night. She noted that her feet were still bare, that she had gone into the city in bare feet. She remembered how Professor Bose's absurd little figure in its short brown coat and long white *dhoti* had gone flapping frightenedly down the lane, like a creature from one of her own drawings. She contemplated her own drawings. Then Dharma... And all the while, at the back of a mind that could not grapple directly with the powerful thing at hand, she knew that Monisha's death had pointed the way for her and would never allow her to lose herself. She knew she would go through life with her feet primly shod, involving herself with her drawings and safe people like Bose, precisely because Monisha had given her a glimpse of what lay on the other side of this stark, uncompromising margin. Yet she was unable, that night, to think of the path or the jungle of compromise or isolation and watched bleakly, mindlessly, the white curtain in the doorway slowly blowing into the still room, then slowly drifting out again.

At intervals Nirode said, 'Go to sleep, Amla, go to sleep, I'll stay,' and to his aunt he would say, 'Go to bed, aunt, you must have some rest.' He seemed unable to remain still or silent, he was filled with an immense care of the world that made him reach out, again and again, to touch Amla's cold hand when he saw it shake or embrace the old woman in the battered wicker chair when he saw her weep.

He pressed them to him with hunger and joy, as if he rejoiced in this sensation of touching other flesh, others' pains, longed to make them mingle with his own, which till now had been agonisingly neglected. There was so much he wanted to tell them — to reassure them that no outrage had been committed, that Monisha had died from an excess of caring, in a fire of care and conscience and that they too must accept, with a like intensity, the vigilance of heart and conscience, allowing no deed of indifference or incomprehension to drift by, but to seize each moment, each person, each fragment of the world and reverence it with that acute care that had driven Monisha to her splendid death. He could not, tonight, find words for his joy and certainty and despair, and said only, 'Sleep, rest. Aunt, Amla.' He felt excited as a religious fanatic is excited by the death or the celebration of the death of a saint. He felt himself elevated to an unimaginably high vantage point from where he could see the whole fantastic design of life and death, of incarnation followed by reincarnation, of unconsciousness turning into consciousness, of sleep followed by waking. It was a landscape like that of the worlds, the planets and he was able to see the rising of the sun, followed by the rising of the moon, the dimming and flaring of stars in the firmament and everything was explained, everything was lucid, reasonable, marvellous. This lucidity made him transparent, allowing night and sorrow to merge with his own ecstasy till everything became one, became unified and understandable. It seemed to him that he had listened to silence till out of silence silent music had sprung, spiralling upwards, so sweetly consummate, that it made the long silence worthwhile. Or that he had been staring so long into the darkness that now at last his eyes had grown accustomed to it and been able to distinguish shapes, shadows, faint lights in it that were beautiful and full of promise and, more strangely still, were gently familiar.

'Sleep, sleep,' he urged the restless women, still too agitated to share his calm vision. When Amla's head fell heavily against the balcony rail, he drew his fingers down the cold curve of her cheek tenderly. He loved her, loved all women who slept with tears cold on their cheeks at night. He would have liked to cradle her in his arms, carry her into this divine world of which he had been permitted, at last, a vision. But she was sleeping now, he would not disturb her. He turned instead to the old woman and embraced her, concerned about her age and frailty. 'Mother will come tomorrow,' he said, softly. 'She'll understand, aunt. Don't worry. Don't cry. Sleep a little.' She seemed comforted by his touch, slept fitfully, noisily, while he protected her with his with new tenderness and sympathy for all her long, dreary experience. Finding her hands cold, he went into her room to fetch a shawl but could not find one. In nervous haste he drew a tablecloth off her bed table, a bright green one with the white cross-stitch covering its coarse weave, and this he draped about her with anxious care. In her sleep she clutched it as a child clutches at a soft cloth, holding it close to her face for comfort. Then he knelt beside Amla, drew her *sari* about her bare shoulders. She awoke and sighed, 'If I had taken her away, taken her home — '

'No, no,' he interrupted and, smoothing down her hair, tried in ardent silence, to impress upon her the full value of Monisha's death, too great a value to forgo out of distress or guilt or deceit, but the very key of all grace, all design in life, the very essence of it, exquisite and irreducible. Smoothing down her hair, holding her head against his shoulder, he alone waited wide awake outside the door, assuring Monisha of these few hours of rest and, at last, understanding.

When Nirode found himself pressing his chest against an iron rail, scanning the clear white sky with eyes that burned from sleeplessness, his too-quickly flowering ecstasy began to acquire the brown edge of anguish. The thought had, occasionally, visited him that now his mother would come, now he would meet her and talk to her and the knowledge had given him relief, a harsh thunderstorm relief. But in the hours between Monisha's cremation and the arrival of the plane bearing his mother, the relief slowly altered to a terrified apprehension — not only of this dramatic end to the long estrangement between him and his mother, but of the feeling that never again would he know that alleviation of the torment of conscience, that drugged, dull sleep in which he had rocked obliviously for so many years, successful in his deceit, scornful of his success, stagnant and dehydrated of all ambition, communion, relationship, joy and responsibility. Monisha's death had brought them all flooding into him with the onrush of a great stormy wave and he had opened his heart to it with gratitude. But now already he was beginning to feel the torture that accompanied such grace and he knew he would never again be able to avoid it, turn his back on it. Here he stood in the crowd at the airport, waiting to accept it, praying to be able to do so with something of Monisha's unconscious philosophy. The whine of the approaching plane grew urgent, menacing and he cowered, bowing his head to the vision of the silver bird plunging out of the sky, diving towards him with shrill accusation.

When he looked up, it had rolled to a halt, people were stepping down the ladder and straggling across the airstrip. His moist palms slipped on the rail and he did not think to light a cigarette as he distinguished and watched the stately and precise figure of his mother parade out of the brief shade of the stretched, glinting wings of the aeroplane, walk past the irrelevantly sketched line of palms that fringed the airfield, then turn towards the gates where a little group of people stood seized by impatience. She looked straight at Nirode.

He had not prepared his reception of her. He held out an arm, dropped it and did not know what to say. But he could not take his eyes off her. He watched her petrified, as she came up with her exact and measured walk, straight towards him. She is still beautiful, he thought with fear, a fear that contracted and expanded inside him like a membranous shield that covered and constricted his heart. She is still beautiful, he repeated and her beauty compelled him to embrace her. He embraced her slender, upright body in its folds of white silk, touched the hands that had sketched designs in the air of glorious futures for her sons and daughters and now were devoid of rings. In his numbness, he prolonged the embrace and then felt her draw away, push him away with a cool, dispassionate movement so that she might stand alone and free. He fell away and felt himself drained of blood and passion: he realised she did not want him any more. It was so simple, this rejection, this gesture he had thought

248

would free him forever, give him the liberty that belongs only to those without heritage. He had waited for this gesture and now it had come and left him — free. He stood and watched her move away, walk on, indifferent to his following her or not. She crossed the yard with the other passengers, went into the lounge and he still stood by the rail, contemplating this unanticipated and desolate liberty that her small gesture had so silently and irrevocably maneouvred.

He did, of course, follow her. They even spoke while waiting for her luggage to be brought to her. But she did not look at him once and he knew it was not out of cold vengeance but out of sheer disinterest. She no longer needed him nor her other children. She was a woman fulfilled — by the great tragedy of her daughter's suicide — and it was, he saw, what she had always needed to fulfil her: Tragedy. Her life so far had been a dazzling sketch, executed with skilful flourishes, a matter of fine, dashing lines, of hints of vibrant colour — mahogany and gold and fascination. But incomplete, without a background, for oh, the background provided by a slack, sprawling drunkard, absurd in his too tight silk coat and a flimsy glass of liquor trembling in his hand, it had never fitted, she had preferred to do without it. Now Monisha's death had brought the shades and depth of the most appropriate possible background flooding in — a mass of darkness, abundant with shadows and hints of distant light, which gave this brief sketch of herself a breadth, a philosophic dimension and a lovely, whispering mysteriousness filled with the murmurs of subsiding tragedy: its great weeping, its long preparation, its awesome climax. She was no longer a woman thwarted, but a magnificent portrait, a figure, calm and pale, in a great tragedy.

She moved more precisely, more regally than Nirode had remembered and he felt it was a new grandeur in her, as if she felt herself to be carrying a marble vessel containing the holy oils of disaster and she had to move with care in order to contain them, keep them seemly and restrained. She did not allow Nirode's panic to jog her elbow, she would never allow the pleas and demands and needs of anyone, not her children, not her lovers or admirers, to

249

displace one drop in this majestic vessel that she held like a goddess. As she walked, she cut a swath of silence through the crowd and Nirode, following her with her bags, vividly recalled how he, as a small boy, had fawned at her feet, almost grovelling over her long white toes, while she fastened her ear-rings and glanced with the same smile of pride from his little bowed back to her reflection in the mirror. Now he found himself trailing her again, collecting the furtive glances of the audience in order to present her with their awe. Yet he did not offer them to her, he knew she did not need them, for now there was this silent austerity about her that had peeled the large rings from her fingers, impressed the hollows beneath her eyes with the purple imprints of sleepless nights and made her keep her hands quietly to herself in a manner which stated, quite emphatically, that she would never stretch them out again towards anyone, she was concerned only with holding this vessel of sorrow and death. She was by no means revelling in this part she played of high priestess at a ritual sacrifice, she was obsessed by her part as only a great actress can be, to the point of merging completely with the role, leaving no division whatsoever. If people stopped talking to look at her, it was as much on account of an instinctive recognition of this rare quality in her, as of her beauty. From these groups of flaccid women crossly managing their tired and whining children and tourists with painful sunburns and powerful cameras, she stood out as a work of art in a crowded, stuffy gallery.

Nirode imagined that on that day twilight fell early in order that the city might darken itself and not intrude upon her grief. As they drove through it, he saw lights flower out of the dirt and shadows, as if people lit *diyas* in honour of her. She was their goddess, unseen, but instinctively acknowledged by dwellers of huts and tenements along the great streets of Calcutta. He imagined he heard drums throbbing beneath the cacophony of traffic and the wailing and chanting of hymns dedicated to her exalted presence. Lights swam through the smoke and night like proferred garlands. Loftily, she paid no attention at all.

She asked him when Monisha had been cremated. He stuttered a reply. She asked him where the ashes were. Fighting an impulse to throw himself across her lap and sob, he told her, somehow, that they waited for her in an urn in her room. She fell silent and contemplated the dark for the rest of the journey.

Amla waited on the steps of the still house, agitated as a moth. Formulating replies to her mother's most likely questions, she asked herself, again and again, why she had submerged herself in the aqueous swaying underworld of Dharma's art when, on the surface, Monisha had fought her battle alone, how it was that she had done nothing about the uneasiness and suspicions she felt whenever she met Monisha, why she had not taken her away from such blatant oppression and destruction, home to Kalimpong. Kalimpong, Kalimpong, the name rang in her ears like the bells that Tibetan monks clashed and clanged cheerfully amidst swirls of blue incense and chequers of sunshine and geranium, above which was seated the supreme deity, her mother, with downcast eyes and exquisite lips. . . Now coming out of the car, now coming up the steps, as serene and inscrutable as Amla had pictured her, yet as disturbing as a vision of that consummate wisdom besides which all others were incomplete, aborted beings.

She flew up to meet her, crying so hard that she did not at once notice that her mother barely glanced at her and was, in fact, about to walk past her. Through her sobs, she felt the coolness with which her mother suffered her damp embrace and at last fell back, frightened, to look anxiously at Nirode who wore the expression of a sleepwalker. They stood together In the doorway, utterly baffled and forlorn, watching the frigid little gesture of recognition their mother made towards her half-sister, Lila.

There was little speech between them. Their mother asked them a few questions about themselves, but with such apathy in her expression, that they only murmured their replies, incomprehensibly and turned the lifeless conversation to unrealistic enquiries about her journey, and to the cable that had arrived from Arun about his plans to return immediately.

'I have cabled him not to come,' she said in an even voice. 'But, who knows, he might leave before the cable reaches him. He may come, he may not...'

She retired to her room almost immediately after this little farcical scene of reunion, with great finality in her parting. The moment she had disappeared up the stairs, the old aunt, who had been fidgeting about in a kind of harsh fury, suddenly shattered the cool, formal image of this eerie evening by jerking herself out of her black box-chair crying hoarsely, 'Yes, yes, we all fill up our lives fast enough again. Does anyone still really miss the one who is gone?' and she stalked off to her room, a comfortless and battered creature whom no one tried to follow or console nor did she expect them to.

Amla could not leave the evening so empty, so wretched and forced herself to go up the stairs, secretly, to her mother's room — the room where Monisha had spent one night, where white curtains hung in the doorway, sucked inwards by the breeze and then slowly released and drawn out again, like the breath of a sleeping woman. Amla had expected the room to be dark, to find her mother on the bed, if not weeping and willing, at last, to gather Amla to her breast. But the lights were on, glinting off the metal urn on the large desk and too late Amla discovered her mother occupied in unpacking her suitcase. She glanced quickly up at her daughter and the swiftness with which she looked away reiterated her rejection.

'Yes?' she enquired with such asperity that Amla felt weak and breathless, murmured, 'I only came to say good-night,' and fled down the stairs.

Nirode looked up to see her come stumbling down and he paused in his restless pacing of the floor. 'Amla,' he said, 'come out, come out with me. I can't stand it here. Let's go for a walk.'

'She is Kali,' he cried, 'Amla, I know her now. She is Kali, the goddess and the demon are one. When I was driving through the city with her and I saw the sky darken, and people put on lights in her honour and heard them wail and chant and I knew at once then, that she is Kali. She has watched the sacrifice and she is satisfied. Don't you see, Amla, the satisfaction on her lips? See how still and controlled her lips and hands are because she has at last seized and mastered death, she has become Kali — '

'She's mother, Nirode,' Amla interrupted, fiercely trying to regain the old order of her life. Her slippers made frightened sounds in the dust and dry leaves of the dark lane where they walked and the gas lamps shielded slim stamens of blue flame, too dim to throw any light upon their quick, hurrying figures. 'She is mother, mother,' Amla repeated.

'Mother, mother — Kali is the mother of Bengal, she is the mother of us all. Don't you see, Amla, how once she has given birth to us, she must also deal us our deaths? Oh, I see so clearly now. I feel my skin is stripped away and my interior has melted into the exterior, I know it so well. I see now that she is everything we have been fighting against, you and Monisha and I. And she is also everything we have fought for. She is our consciousness *and* our unconsciousness, she is all that is manifest — and all that is unmanifest...'

'Mother,' Amla groaned. 'Nirode, that is all.'

'No, Amla. no — there is no all in what you see — it spreads and spreads far beyond, it compasses not just this one earth but all the planets, all the centuries, night and day, light and dark. She is not merely good, she is not merely evil — she is good and she is evil. She is our knowledge and our ignorance. She is everything to which we are attached, she is everything from which we will always be detached. She is reality and illusion, she is the world and she is *maya*. Don't you see, in her face, in her beauty, Amla, don't you see the amalgamation of death and life? Isn't it perfect and inevitable that she should pour blood into our veins when we are born and drain it from us when we die? Oh, I have such a vision, I don't know if I can bear it — and survive. Monisha's death — Monisha dead. I am sentenced to death, too, now. I am prepared and waiting for it. I have heard her approach — death, Kali. She watches me all the time now, Amla and while she watches I grow more and more vividly alive by the minute and also closer and closer to my death. I am so *stretched,* so open to this vision. I can feel it seep into me, like night, like night turning my blood black.'

'You are alive, Nirode. You'll stay alive.'

'Ah yes. but only as long as she pleases to see me breathe and live. I know why I'm living, at last, I know now where I'm going — towards her, towards her. She is waiting, can't you see.'

They halted and stood, trembling, listening to the sounds of a procession that wound through the city at that very hour, chanting the goddess's name and beating on drums. Close about them fell silence and they turned to look back at the big house behind the shrubs. It was unlit, it seemed uninhabited, one sleeping mass against the soft, misty sky that was tinted a livid pink by the lights of the city burning beneath it. Then they saw a white figure step out on to the upper veranda, stand silently at the rail and watch them.

❑❑❑

Across the Black Waters

Mulk Raj Anand

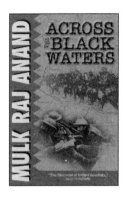

'... is probably (Anand's) best novel since Untouchable, for it exactly communicates the claustrophobic tension of man in the front line, the imminence of death, and the pervading sense of inevitability which is the source of Anand's anger, and at the same time, is at the root of so much Indian fiction. We never lose awareness that his is an Indian novel...'

— *Alastair Niven, British Literary Critic*

Also in Orient Paperbacks
- ❏ Lajwanti & Other Stories
- ❏ Things Have A Way of Working Out & Other Stories
- ❏ A Pair of Mustachios & Other Stories
- ❏ Lost Child & Other Stories

Cry, The Peacock

Anita Desai

Cry, the Peacock is the story of a
young girl, Maya, obsessed by a
childhood prophecy of disaster. The
author builds up an atmosphere of tension as torried and
oppressive as a stiffling Indian summer, both in the
crowded, colouful cities and the strangely beautiful
countryside.

' Anita Desai creates a stained glass landscape with details
of images, colours and odours...*Cry, The Peacock* is the
product of a mellowed craftswoman.'

— *Statesman*

Available at all bookshops or by V.P.P.

**Orient
Paperbacks**

5A/8 Ansari Road, New Delhi-110 002